Two little words would change their lives forever . . .

In *Fancy Free*, **Catherine Anderson** introduces a tempestuous pair in a tale of revenge. But will the best-laid plans of the wild-hearted couple backfire before the wedding night?

He was "mad." But there was still one unconventional young woman who would marry the earl. **Loretta Chase** tells her surprising story in *The Mad Earl's Bride*.

In **Samantha James**'s emotional romance, a young woman's reckless scheme to defy her father's ultimatum leads to a hasty union and unexpected passion, and she is truly *Scandal's Bride*.

More Dazzling Romance from

Catherine Anderson
CHERISH

Lorretta Chase
DON'T TEMPT ME

Samantha James
SINS OF THE VISCOUNT SUTHERLAND

Three Times A Bride

Catherine ANDERSON

Loretta CHASE

Samantha JAMES

AVON

An Imprint of HarperCollinsPublishers

This is a work of fiction. Names, characters, places, and incidents are drawn from the author's imagination or are used fictitiously and are not to be construed as real. Any resemblance to actual events, locales, organizations, or persons, living or dead, is entirely coincidental.

AVON BOOKS
An Imprint of HarperCollins*Publishers*
10 East 53rd Street
New York, New York 10022-5299

First Avon Books paperback printing: May 2010

Avon Trademark Reg. U.S. Pat. Off. and in Other Countries, Marca Registrada, Hecho en U.S.A.
HarperCollins® is a registered trademark of HarperCollins Publishers.

Printed in the U.S.A.

10 9 8 7 6 5 4 3 2 1

Contents

Three Times
A Bride

Fancy Free

Catherine Anderson

Prologue

Clint Rafferty strode across the worn boardwalk in front of the Golden Goose Saloon and shoved open the bat-wing doors. It was hot and noisy inside, reminding him of the bowels of hell that Preacher Wells thundered about on Sunday. As he'd expected, the place was full, a usual occurrence at half past ten Saturday night, and the hazy, lantern-lit interior reeked of tobacco smoke, unwashed bodies, and cheap perfume.

A girl in a blue gown stood nearby, as though placed there to greet patrons. As soon as she spied Clint, her painted mouth curved into a smile and her glittering blue eyes narrowed. "Looking for company, cowboy?" she asked, sidling his way.

Clint inclined his head politely, his mother's teachings still strong in him even at the age of twenty-seven. "No, ma'am," he drawled. "I'm lookin' for my brother."

"Is that a fact?"

Clint reined in his impatience. Though he had no quarrel with how this soiled dove or any other made her living, he'd never felt the need to pay for a woman's attention—especially

3

when he was tired and hungry and had a good two hours of chores awaiting him at home. "That is a fact."

He glanced past her toward the bar. Sure enough, there stood Matthew leaning against the polished top as if for support, his thick ebony hair lying in sweat-damp waves over his high forehead. From the looks of the kid, he was already sloppy drunk.

Clint muttered an oath under his breath.

"Are you two twins or something?" she asked, glancing back and forth between the two Rafferty men.

Folks had claimed for years that he and Matt were dead ringers for each other, and Clint guessed there were similarities. They shared the same square chin, high cheekbones, smoky eyes and black hair. But there the similarities ended. When Clint smiled, which wasn't often, no one seemed to care. But when Matt flashed that lopsided, lazy grin of his, the whole world seemed to smile with him, especially the female half, many of whom tended to go weak at the knees as well. Even now there was a woman hanging on Matt's opposite arm—a cute little redhead with big green eyes. She went by the name of Dora Faye, if Clint recollected right.

"I've got seven years on him," he explained to the soiled dove, a fact that seemed to surprise her. No sense adding that he'd spent those seven years trying to be both mother and father to Matthew and all his other brothers.

"Then this is your lucky night, sugar," she muttered, "because I just happen to be extra partial to older men."

"Thanks for the offer, but I've got hungry horses to feed and a ledger to balance yet tonight," Clint cut in before she could suggest he buy them both a drink.

She gave him a look of disappointment before shrugging one bare white shoulder. "The offer's always open. Just ask for Maydeen."

"I just might do that sometime."

Picking his way through the milling bodies, Clint headed

in Matthew's direction. Here lately, Matt's drinking sprees had become a weekly occurrence. Damn the kid's hide. He knew about the Rafferty weakness for alcohol. Hadn't he stood at Clint's side when they'd lowered their pa into his grave five years past? The old man had drunk himself to death, for Christ's sake, not to mention that his drinking had left his sons penniless. Unable to make the mortgage payments, they had lost the old home place back in Ohio and wouldn't have had a roof over their heads if not for their moving west to find land they could homestead. By the sweat of all their brows, they were finally starting to get ahead, no thanks to their father, and now here was Matt following in the old man's footsteps.

Clint's first impulse was to grab his brother by the collar and shake him. Instead he elbowed his way in beside him and propped a heel on the boot rail. "Matt, the cattlemen's meetin' is over. I reckon it's about time we thought about headin' home."

Matt turned slowly, his gray blue eyes slightly out of focus, his usually firm mouth lax at the corners. "Clint?" he asked, his tone indicating that he was none too sure.

"Who else?" Clint couldn't stifle a smile as he slowly waved a hand in front of his brother's nose. "You in there, Matthew?"

"Last time I checked, I was." Matt hiccupped, then grinned down at the woman on his other side. "This here pretty lady has been kind enough to buy me a drink, haven't you, darlin'?"

Dora Faye darted a look at Clint's face. "Evenin', Mr. Rafferty," she said in a surprisingly subdued tone. "I didn't realize that you were in town, too."

"Old Clint here, he came in for a meeting with the other big boys," Matt joked, his voice slurring. "Ain't that right, Brother?"

"Right."

Matt licked his lips, then frowned. "I di'n't think you frequented places like this."

"I don't usually. That doesn't mean I never do." Clint glanced at the glass of whiskey in front of his brother. Not a jigger but a tumbler, for Christ's sake, and half full at that. The last thing Matt needed was more liquor.

Moving quickly so his brother wouldn't anticipate what he meant to do, he reached for the glass. "You don't mind sharin', do you? The old whistle's a little dry."

As Clint curled his hand around the tumbler, Dora Faye caught hold of his wrist. "Say, there, Mr. Rafferty." She inclined her head at the whiskey jug. "Let me pour you your own drink. We've got plenty, and more where this came from."

Wasn't that just the problem? Casting a jaundiced eye at the whiskey jug, Clint saw that the container was three-quarters empty. Little wonder Matt was drunk.

"I don't mind drinking after my brother," he informed the soiled dove, forcing a grin. "Besides, it looks to me like he's had about enough."

For just an instant, her grip seemed to tighten on his wrist. Then, with a nervous smile and a flash of her green eyes, she released him, muttering something under her breath that he couldn't quite catch. Tipping the glass to her in a mock toast, Clint tossed down the liquor, then clenched his teeth at the burn. "Not bad."

Grabbing the bottle, Matt poured another measure of whiskey, some of which sloshed over the edge of the glass onto the bar. "Go ahead, Clint. Enjoy. Like Dora Faye says, there's always more where this came from."

Though Clint could have done without another drink, he didn't want his brother to consume what remained in the bottle, either. Making no objection, he drained the glass a second time and said nothing when Matt filled it with liquor yet again. Unfortunately, as he set the tumbler down for the third time, Matt signaled the bartender for a new jug.

"Forget it, Matt—you've had enough," Clint suggested softly. "Let's just call it a night, pard, and head on home."

"Don't go tryin' to play mama, big brother. I'm a little old for coddlin'."

"Coddlin' is the last thing on my mind." Clint clamped a hand over his brother's shoulder and gave him a jostle. "It's late, and we've both had a full day. It's best we go home now, okay? Build us a fire, brew us some coffee. It'll be nice for a change."

"You go ahead." Matt slipped an arm around Dora Faye's waist. "As the old sayin' goes, the night is still young." The slightly built barmaid caught him from stumbling as he shifted his weight toward her and released his hold on the bar. "I'll be home in the mornin', Clint. Bright 'n' early, and none the worse for wear, I promise."

Clint knew better. After a few more drinks, Matt would pass out and sleep until late tomorrow, whereupon he would awaken sick to his stomach and with a terrible headache.

"I guess I was just hopin' to have some company on the ride home," Clint tried. "We hardly ever get any time together when we're not working anymore."

"Maybe next time," Matt suggested. With that, he bent to nuzzle Dora Faye's ear. To keep them both from falling, she leaned into him with all her weight. "Hey, honeybee," he said. "How's about we go upstairs?"

Clint drew his hand from his brother's shoulder. "Well, I guess I'll be moseyin'."

Matt, who had abandoned Dora Faye's ear to nibble on her neck, didn't bother to respond. Heavy of heart, Clint stood there, reluctant to leave, yet knowing Matt was old enough to make his own choices. He finally turned away when he saw his brother signal the barkeep for another jug. For better or worse, Matt was on his own.

Pushing the bat-wing doors open with one shoulder, Clint spilled out onto the boardwalk and took a bracing breath. Instead of clearing, however, his head seemed to fog over even more, a result of the whiskey he rarely consumed, he decided sourly.

Letting the doors swing shut behind him, he turned left along the boardwalk, his heels tapping out a hollow-sounding tattoo on the weathered wood. From between the buildings, stripes of silvery moonlight spilled across the walkway, marking his progress.

Glancing up Main, he saw lights at only a few windows. It was almost midnight. Most families had settled in for the night. The thought made him feel sad and hollow inside. Not long ago, all the Raffertys would have been home in bed as well.

Not long ago? He squeezed his eyes closed, remembering what it had been like when his folks were alive. Wonderful, home-cooked meals. Lace curtains at the windows. The sound of laughter. Six years had passed since his ma's death, five since his da had joined her. In actuality, it wasn't so very long a time, yet to Clint, who'd shouldered the responsibility for his younger brothers, it seemed an eternity.

Pausing in front of the mercantile, he gazed with an ache of yearning at the window display, illuminated by the moon. Bess Harrison, the proprietor's wife, who was very talented with her hands, had fashioned a miniature kitchen on the opposite side of the glass. The cheery scene made him think of the drab, austere atmosphere awaiting him at home. No cheery kitchen, no place settings, no flowers, no lace curtains. It took a woman's touch to make a house cozy, and that the Raffertys sorely lacked.

Not for the first time, Clint found himself wondering if he shouldn't get married. Maybe Matt wouldn't find it necessary to stay in town so much if his home were more pleasant. Since moving to Shady Corners, Clint had accomplished a lot, but most of the improvements he'd made were on the land. The house needed fixing, and six-year-old Cody needed a mother. Even Daniel, next youngest at fourteen, was showing signs of growing up uncivilized, a result, Clint figured, of his own inadequate parenting skills.

But damn! He was a rancher, not a nursemaid. He knew cows and horses, and on occasion, how to prod his lazy brothers into pulling their own weight. But Cody and Daniel still had bad dreams about their parents' deaths that Clint didn't know how to soothe and temper tantrums he didn't understand. Worst of all were the nights Cody cried himself to sleep from sheer misery because Clint didn't know how to comfort him.

That was one of the main reasons Clint had written to his great-aunt Hester a few months back. She was a kindly woman who'd never been blessed with children of her own. Now that she was widowed, he was hoping she'd be interested in leaving Ohio and starting a new life with them here in Oregon. So far, though, she hadn't answered his letter, and now so much time had gone by that he was beginning to doubt she ever would. Which led him right back to his original thought, that maybe he should get married.

Resuming his pace along the boardwalk, he tried to imagine what it would be like to have a female in the house again. Better, he guessed. Probably a lot better. It would definitely be nice to come in of an evening to a hot, home-cooked meal, and it sure couldn't hurt to have someone around to keep up with the laundry. With eight people contributing, the pile of unwashed clothes seemed mountainous. Yep. No question about it; having a woman around the house would be a big improvement.

The way his luck had been running lately, however, none of the pretty, sought-after young ladies hereabouts would be interested in taking on such a large, ready-made, and admittedly rowdy family of males, and he'd be forced to settle for some homely girl no one else wanted.

It was a singularly unappealing thought.

One

Heart pounding in her throat, Rachel Constantine stared at her intended victim as he drew abreast of her on the opposite boardwalk. She would have been pleased to see him stagger just a little, anything to assure her he had indeed been drugged. As it was, it was difficult to tell he'd even had anything to drink.

With a sigh, she plucked her wire-framed spectacles from her nose and stashed them in her skirt pocket. From here on, she would have to settle for looking at Rafferty through a blur. Better that than risk being seen wearing eyeglasses. Most men didn't find ladies with poor eyesight attractive, and for tonight, at least, it was vitally important that Rachel be a femme fatale. *Drat!* Why did he look so sober? Had something gone wrong inside the saloon? Maybe he wasn't drugged, after all. Just the thought made her pulse race even faster and her knees go weak.

Biting her lip, she cast a glance at the saloon. To her relief, she saw Dora Faye standing inside the doors, signaling just as they had planned, to let her know everything had gone smoothly. Unless Matt Rafferty had the constitution of an ox, he would be unconscious in a few minutes. Rachel smiled into the darkness. From her hiding place in the shadows, it would do no good to wave back at her friend, so she made a mental note to stop by the saloon tomorrow to thank Dora Faye profusely. None of this would have been possible without her help.

As Rafferty moved past the mercantile, he slowed to a stop, standing in silhouette against the moon-washed glass. Rachel squinted to see him better, then wished she hadn't. He seemed taller than she remembered, maybe a little broader across the chest and shoulders as well. *Just a trick of moonlight and shadow*, she assured herself. *Don't go letting your nerves get the best of you.*

Unfortunately, it wasn't that simple. Matt Rafferty was walking, talking trouble, definitely not the type a decent young woman approached without some measure of trepidation. Nevertheless, the man couldn't be allowed to go around humiliating young girls and breaking their hearts. At the very least, he deserved to be taken to task. Because her fourteen-year-old sister Molly was his latest victim, Rachel felt that it was her job to do just that. Hence, the plan she'd concocted with Dora Faye's assistance.

As surefooted as a prospector's mule, Rafferty stepped off the boardwalk to cross the street. Watching him come toward her, Rachel felt her mouth go dry. This was it. Going down the list of dos and don'ts Dora Faye had given her, she stepped out from the shadow of the general store. "Well, hello, Mr. Rafferty!" she called, trying for a flirtatious twitter. "What a pleasant surprise!"

Evidently taken off guard, he broke stride and came to a slow stop. Without her eyeglasses, Rachel knew she tended to look a bit owlish, so she tried not to open her eyes too wide. As she closed the distance between them, his blurry edges took on better definition. No doubt about it, the man was bigger than she cared to admit.

"Rachel Constantine? Rachel Constantine, the marshal's daughter?"

Giving a throaty laugh, just as Dora Faye had taught her, she said, "How many Rachel Constantines do you think there are in Shady Corners, a baker's dozen?"

He seemed baffled by the question. Clearly, his thought processes were muddled, a sign the valerian Dora Faye had put in his whiskey was taking effect.

She drew up a few feet shy of him and struck a seductive pose. It was hard to remember all that Dora Faye had taught her—how to move, stand, and smile.

"Trust me, sir," she informed him in a twittery little voice, "there is only *one* Rachel Constantine. My pa says that after me, they broke the mold."

She immediately wanted to call back the words. Irresistible temptresses did *not* talk about their fathers. Even she knew that.

Though the eight Rafferty brothers had been living in the area for nearly a year now, her eyesight was such that she'd never gotten close enough to get a good look at any of them. It seemed to her that tongues had been buzzing forever about how handsome they all were. She was absolutely dying to see what all the fuss was about.

Not that she was personally interested. Goodness, no. She had her eye on Lawson Wells, the minister's son. Tall, painfully thin, and nearly as blind as she, he was about as far from handsome as a body could get. Consequently, he was sweet and thoughtful and caring, all the things Matt Rafferty obviously wasn't, no doubt because he was so handsome he felt he had no need to be. A pox on handsome men: that was Rachel's motto.

Even so, she was curious. At the risk of appearing myopic, she leaned closer so she could see his face more clearly and judge his looks for herself. No question about it, he *was* handsome. A bit older looking than expected, but she imagined working outdoors and drinking heavily would make anyone look older than he actually was.

Even shaded by his hat, his smoky blue eyes glistened in the moonlight like raindrops shot through with lightning. Thick waves of ebony hair fell lazily across his forehead, and whether it was a trick of light or an actual cast to his skin, he looked to be deeply tanned. Oh, yes, he was handsome, but not in the usual way. There was something about him, a lethal edge, that made her wary. *Dangerous.* Matt Rafferty wasn't merely dreamy, as rumor painted him, but dangerous. Little wonder poor Molly had come away lacerated and heartsick.

Rachel didn't like the way he studied her—a lazy appraisal, his eyes glinting as if at some private joke. It seemed at odds with the stories she'd heard, namely that he was a charmer. Instead, he was making her feel awkward and more than a little frightened, which seemed more in keeping with the stories she had heard about his older brother, Clint. Now *there* was a man to avoid, always serious, never smiling. His gray-blue eyes could sear right through a woman, according to her friends.

After completing the slow appraisal of her person, Matt flicked his gaze to hers and said in a deep, silken voice, "That must've been quite some mold, sweetheart."

Mentally, Rachel stumbled about, trying to make sense of his comment. In her bewilderment, she forgot all about looking owlish. Lands, he was attractive. No wonder poor little Molly had gotten a crush on him. "Pardon?"

A smile flickered across his firm mouth. "The mold that got broke after they made you? Judging by the results, it must've been quite some mold."

"Oh!" Rachel gave a horrified little laugh. "*That* mold. So much time passed that—well, I totally forgot—" She realized she was babbling and waving her hands like a lunatic. She punctuated the inanity with another shrill laugh.

"What are you doing out at this time of night? Good little girls like you should be home in bed with the covers tucked up to their chins."

Coming from any other man, the appellation "little girl" would have infuriated her. At eighteen, she was still new enough to womanhood to be easily offended if someone insinuated she wasn't yet an adult. Not so with Matt Rafferty. Compared to him, she'd be a child at ninety. In the silvery gloom, his features, sharp, uncompromising, and blatantly male, looked as if they had been carved from polished mahogany, giving his face a hardness that made her pulse skitter.

"Maybe I'm not the good little girl you think I am."

Touching a fingertip to the edge of his hat, he nudged back the brim and arched one black eyebrow. "Is that so?"

Shoving her hand into her skirt pocket, she curled her fingers around her spectacles and raised her chin a notch. Swamped with old resentments, she glared at him through the gloom, remembering another man who had laughed at her.

"It's been my observation that good little girls don't have very much fun."

"True," he agreed with a slow grin, "but, then, most good little girls don't realize what they're missing."

"Well, I do."

Judging by the way one corner of his mouth twitched, that proclamation amused him. "Oh, really? And who was the lucky fellow?"

Rachel couldn't see how any one fellow played into it. "Pardon?"

He chuckled, the sound a low murmur from deep in his chest.

"Is it a private joke, Mr. Rafferty, or will you share it with me?"

"It's nothing, really. Just that you answered my question."

"What question?"

"As to whether or not you realize what you're missing. I have a hunch you don't."

Rachel's chin went up another notch. "If not, why would I be here?"

"Good point. Care to enlighten me?"

"Because I'm tired of living a dull existence, that's why."

His full but firm mouth tipped up at one corner again. The grin had scarcely left his lips when he yawned. He pinched the bridge of his nose and shook his head. When he looked at her again, his eyes were a little unfocused. "So you're tired of a dull existence, are you? Why do I have this feelin' you're hopin' I'll remedy that?"

"Possibly because I am." Rachel affected a sultry smile and tried not to think about the seconds that were racing by. "Who better than you when a girl's lookin' for an exciting experience? I hear tell you're a carefree fellow and always game."

"You must have me confused with someone else, darlin'. Carefree isn't in my vocabulary, especially not when it comes to you. I have an aversion to bein' locked up, you see. A man'd have to be crazy to mess with Big Jim Constantine's daughter."

"Don't tell me you're scared of my pa?"

"Damned straight." His mouth tipped into another teasing grin that flashed perfectly straight white teeth. "And scared I'll stay as long as he's wearin' that badge."

"But, Mr. Rafferty, my pa's never gonna know about this. You have my word."

"He ain't gonna know because there ain't gonna be a *this*," he said with a laugh.

Driven to brazenness by sheer desperation, Rachel stepped closer to him. Recalling Dora's instructions, she hooked a finger under the front placket of his shirt. She couldn't help but notice how iron hard his flat belly felt against her knuckles.

Trying to remember all that her friend had told her to say, she crooned, "I know this is going to sound terribly forward, but I can't help myself, Mr. Rafferty. I want you."

His smile deepened. "Say what?"

Rachel wiggled closer, not at all sure she liked the tingling sensation in her nipples as she grazed his shirt with her bodice. "I want you." She paused, trying to remember the other things Dora had suggested she say. "I'll do whatever I have to. Deep and slow, or hard and fast, however suits you, I'm yours for the taking."

He gave another low laugh. "All right. I'll bite. Why?"

His response was so unexpected that Rachel's heart leaped. "What?"

Stressing each word as if she were an imbecile, he said, "Why do you want me?"

Of all the questions she and Dora had anticipated he might ask, this wasn't one of them. The truth was, Rachel didn't have a clue why any female would be attracted to him. Oh, he was handsome, she'd give him that, but he was also a little terrifying.

"Because you fascinate me," she blurted, which was the unvarnished truth. She *was* fascinated by him—in a morbid sort of way.

"Why are you fascinated?"

"Because you're exciting."

Even in the moonlight, she saw his eyes twinkling. He chucked her under the chin. "More exciting than you can handle. Go home, honey. If you want to cut your teeth on some poor fellow, go gnaw on your little friend Lowry, the minister's son. He won't bite back. I just might."

"Lawson, his name is Lawson. And he's not the one I'm interested in."

He touched the brim of his hat. "G'night, sweet cheeks. I appreciate the offer. It's mighty generous and about as sweet a proposition as I've ever had. But, unfortunately, I'm going to have to pass."

With that, he started to walk away. Rachel saw him sway slightly before he caught himself. Filled with a sense of urgency, knowing that this chance would be forever lost unless she acted fast, she grabbed his arm. "Please, don't go! Please?"

He swung back around. In a tone that was suddenly serious, he said, "Rachel, I told you to go home." He paused for a moment as if to let that sink in. "If you're smart, you'll run, not walk. From the way I'm startin' to feel, I'd say I've had a little too much to drink, and you're too tempting by half. My head isn't real clear. When a man can't think straight, he doesn't have as much willpower as he ought. Keep on, and I'm liable to accept your offer. We'll both regret it come morning, you more so than me."

Rachel had news for him: he would be the one with regrets. "What can I do to make you change your mind?" She pressed her body against his. "I've already thrown myself at your feet. Don't humiliate me more by walking away."

"*Christ!*" Teeth clenched, jaw muscle twitching, he squeezed his eyes shut.

Rachel rubbed herself against him more insistently. "Please?"

"Damn it, girl," he said in a gravelly voice, "go home. Play with fire and you're bound to get burned."

"Oh, yes, if you're the fire, I *want* to be burned. Please, I wan—"

He vised an arm around her waist and settled his mouth over hers. For an instant, she wasn't sure what had happened. Slowly, measure by measure, her stunned mind began to register sensations: his mouth, hot and silken, pressed firmly against hers; his arm cinched around her waist; his hand splayed over her back; his fingertips curled over her side; his steely thighs bracing hers. Fire didn't describe Matt Rafferty. A blazing inferno, more like. She felt as though she were being consumed.

Just last week, she'd finally permitted Lawson to kiss her. The techniques of the two men were about as much alike as warm milk and jalapeño juice. In Lawson's arms, Rachel had felt safe and faintly bored. In Matt's, she felt as if she were dangling from a cliff, he her only anchor. His kiss was hard and demanding. There was no shyness in him, no hesitation, only steely determination. Beneath her hands, which she'd instinctively brought up to push him away, his chest was roped with muscle that lay rigid under a layer of firm yet resilient male flesh. His torso was like an unyielding wall of granite, crushing her breasts, making her intensely aware that her body was far more sensitive and vulnerable than his.

When he finally drew back, Rachel gasped for breath, her gaze startled. "Are you still sure you want to be burned?" he demanded gruffly. "I'm warnin' you—think carefully before you answer. There comes a point where there is no turnin' back, you know, and I've about reached it."

It occurred to Rachel in that moment that he had deliberately kissed her roughly to frighten her away and that now he expected her to bolt. Well, she didn't scare quite that easily. He burned hot, all right, but thanks to some whiskey laced with valerian, his flame would soon flicker out. The most he could do in the time he had left was singe her edges a bit.

"Oh, yes," she whispered, "I still want to be burned."

For just an instant, he hesitated, his gaze delving deeply into hers as if he searched for answers. Then, as if he'd found them, he bent his head and settled his mouth over hers again, more gently this time, but with even more devastating impact.

Two

Wet silk. Cool fire. Icy flames licked Rachel's skin, making her burn and shiver.

"Part your lips, sweetheart," Matt Rafferty whispered urgently against her mouth.

Afraid to deny him for fear he'd guess that her seductive act was all a ruse, she did as he told her. The next thing she knew, his tongue slipped past her teeth. Shock snapped her body taut. She made fists on his shirt front. As if he sensed her startlement, he drew back to nibble lightly at her lower lip. "It's all right. Just trust me."

Rachel would have sooner trusted a snake, but deep within her, everything that was feminine responded to the husky timber of his voice. When he kissed her again, she parted her lips, allowing him to taste her mouth. He plundered the sensitive flesh, tickling the roof of her mouth and drawing sharply on her tongue, forcing it to dance with his in a rhythmic thrust that made her belly tighten and tingle in a strange way.

The unfamiliar sensation frightened her, but when she tried to end the kiss, she discovered that he'd curled a hand over the back of her head. She remembered his warning, that after a certain point, there was no turning back. Fighting down panic, she reminded herself he'd lose consciousness soon. But somehow that wasn't very reassuring. A flash fire could cover a lot of ground in a few short minutes.

His breathing was uneven with need, and when she writhed to disengage herself from his embrace, he moaned, the sound catching and quivering at the base of his throat. Another wave of panic surged within her when he slid his hand from her back to her side, his fingertips searching out the shape of her breast and homing in on its peak. She jerked at the contact and managed, finally, to draw her mouth from under his.

"Christ," he whispered against her cheek, each huff of his breath as hot and moist against her skin as the steam from coffee. Through the layers of her clothing, he staked claim to the hardened tip of her nipple, tugging and rolling the sensitive flesh. Rachel was so stunned by the feelings that rocked her, she couldn't breathe, let alone protest. "Ah, sweetheart," he rasped against her temple. "I want that in my mouth."

Given the location of his hand, there was little doubt in Rachel's mind what part of her anatomy he referred to. The very thought appalled her.

"I bet you're as sweet there as sun-warmed honey."

The picture that had begun to form in Rachel's mind was so indecent she nearly kicked him. How dare he even suggest—well, no woman, lady or otherwise, would engage in such outrageous conduct. She jerked his hand from her breast. Because she didn't dare reveal what was actually on her mind, she settled for saying, "Mr. Rafferty, we are standing in the middle of the street where anyone might see us."

"Then let's find someplace private," he murmured near her ear. "It's not every day I have Rachel Constantine beggin' me to make love to her."

He had that much correct, at least. With careful maneuvering, she managed to get some space between their bodies.

Cheeks afire, she found it difficult to meet his gaze, so instead she focused on his nose. Even in the dim light, she noticed that there was a knot along its bridge. She wondered if he'd broken it in a fight. Given his reputation as a scrapper, he probably had.

"How about if we go to the church?" she suggested shakily.

"Where?"

By his shocked tone, she guessed he had understood her perfectly. "The church," she repeated. "It's as private a place as we're likely to find."

"The church?" He gave a sharp laugh. "I'm not usually what you'd call a finicky man, but that's not exactly my idea of a suitable spot, darlin'."

"Of course it's suitable. One might even say perfect! Just think. Who ever goes there at this hour on a Saturday night? Even Preacher Wells is home in bed."

"That's true, but—"

"Just think of all those pews, those lovely pews, empty and waiting. It'll be dark in there. We can have hours and hours of uninterrupted privacy." On that last word, Rachel squeezed her eyes closed for a second and sent up a quick, frantic prayer that he wasn't going to be difficult. "It'll be wonderful, just wait and see."

He traced the shape of her ear with the tip of his tongue. "It just doesn't seem right somehow, fornicating in a holy place."

Of all the things she had planned on, Matt Rafferty having scruples wasn't one of them. Thinking quickly, she said, "Oh, pshaw. Paint and wood, that's all. It's the folks gathering inside the building that makes it holy, not the structure itself. A barn would be just as sacred if people gathered there to worship."

"A barn?"

"Or any other building. Trust me, if we use the church, God won't mind a bit."

He laughed again, more mellowly. "Why do I have this feelin' you're bent on doin' it on a church pew?"

Rachel assumed an impish smile and leaned back. "It's a wonderfully wicked idea, isn't it? And, oh, I do so want to be wicked. Deliciously wicked . . . with you."

It seemed to her that he was beginning to lean his weight more heavily against her. "Then let's go," he said. "Oh, and by the way, hard and fast."

"What?"

"Hard and fast," he repeated, bringing his face closer to hers as he spoke. "You gave me a choice, remember? Deep and slow or hard and fast. I'll take hard and fast."

Rachel shoved against his shoulders, but it was like trying to hold back a mountain. "Um . . . Mr. Rafferty?" She twisted her face to one side so that his hot, silken lips landed harmlessly on her ear again. Or maybe not so harmlessly. He caught her lobe between his teeth and— Rachel gulped. Oh, dear God. He was *sucking* on her earlobe. "Mr. Rafferty?" she tried again, fighting off panic. "Not out here. We have to go to the church, remember?"

"Oh, yeah . . ."

He straightened so abruptly that he staggered, carrying her along with him. She hugged his waist and struggled to regain her balance, terrified he might fall. If he landed on top of her—well, she'd be in a pickle, and no mistake. He was well over six feet tall, and probably outweighed her by close to a hundred pounds.

"Lead the way, ma'am." He stepped aside and swept his hat from his head in an unsteady bow. "Believe me, makin' love to such a pretty lady will be my pleasure."

Rachel grabbed his arm, helped him get his hat back on, and then struck off for the church, an endeavor she quickly learned was going to take far longer than she had estimated. For every step Matt Rafferty took forward, he executed anywhere from two to a dozen in either direction sideways, dragging Rachel with him.

The possibility that he might collapse in the street became more of a threat with each passing moment. If that happened, she could still steal his trousers and leave him where he lay to sleep it off, but it wouldn't be nearly as satisfying as having him wake up in church. After his public rejection of Molly, he deserved to be repaid with the ultimate humiliation. On that thought, Rachel felt him sway again. She was a little amazed at how suddenly the sedative seemed to be hitting him now.

He draped his arm over her shoulders for support. "I think I'm drunk. Not just a little, but real drunk."

"Really?" she asked, feigning incredulity.

"My senti—sendimun—well, shit. I can't even talk straight."

"Sentiments?" she supplied.

He snapped his fingers, nearly taking off the end of her nose in the process, and then started to laugh. "Sent—uh—ments. My sent—uh—ments exack-ly. Only now I can't remember what I was sent-uh-mentin' about."

Looking up at him, Rachel smiled in spite of herself. For a low-down, dangerous, heartless scoundrel, he had a way about him. She decided it was partly that lopsided grin of his, so boyishly disarming in contrast to his harshly planed features. Then, of course, there were his eyes, which always seemed to be twinkling.

"You were just making the observation you might be drunk," she reminded him.

"Boy, howdy." He snapped his fingers again. "On three measly drinks."

"You must have lost count and had more than that."

"Nope. Never have more'n that."

That came as a surprise. Unless the stories she'd heard were totally false, Matt Rafferty frequented the Golden Goose every Saturday night and drank all evening, playing cards and cavorting shamelessly. A man of moderation, he definitely wasn't.

"Oh, come on, you can tell me. You drink the well dry, right?"

He shook his head. "Nope. I don't cotton much to drinkin'."

"Since when?" she asked, curious in spite of herself.

"Since forever. Outa respe—respect for my ma. She didn't cotton to drunkenness, not in her boys. Claimed liquor 'n' Irish was a bad mix. I reckon she was right, 'cause whiskey killed my da."

"Then why drink at all?"

He started to laugh. "Now there's a plan."

She couldn't see what he found so humorous. "I take it you've considered that."

He held up a finger. "But, as you can see, plans have a way of not always working out." He reeled to a sudden stop, focused blearily on something ahead of them in the darkness, and said, "I can't hold the damned things still long enough to get a good count, but they look like too many."

She realized they had reached the church and that he was referring to the front steps. Like him, she had to squint to see them, albeit for different reasons. "Too many for what?"

"To climb." As if he found that hysterically funny, he began to laugh again. Then, with no warning, he leaned down, thumping his forehead sharply against hers. "Jesus . . ." He exhaled in a great rush. "I don't know, honey. I hate to disappoint a lady, but this is one time my good friend Henry may fail to rise to the occasion."

Thinking that he might have made arrangements to meet with his friend Henry after leaving the saloon, Rachel glanced worriedly over her shoulder. "Who's that?"

"Who's what?"

"Henry. Who is he?"

"Henry is—" He broke off and started to laugh again.

When he caught his breath, he said, "Dear God, you are sweet. Honest to goodness, pure as an angel, genuine sweet. It's been so long, I'd forgotten girls like you exist."

Rachel couldn't see what her disposition had to do with anything. "Thank you," she said distractedly. "But you didn't answer my question. Who is Henry? You didn't mention that he was going to come."

His shoulders jerked with mirth again. "He isn't. That's the whole damned problem. Ain't that a hell of a note?"

Growing impatient with his nonsensical responses, Rachel steered him toward the steps. "We shall do quite well without him, I assure you."

"Lord, help me."

A chance for revenge beckoning sweetly, she endeavored to help him up the flight of steps. So what if Matt Rafferty seemed kind of nice? She knew he wasn't, that he couldn't possibly be. If he were, he wouldn't have done something so reprehensible to her sister. Why should she show him any mercy when he'd shown Molly none?

All of a sudden, Matt reeled backward. Taken off guard, Rachel tumbled with him. Luckily, they had scaled only a few levels. Dust mushrooming around them, they landed in an ungainly heap at the bottom of the steps, Rachel's skirts and petticoats around her waist, Matt's long legs crisscrossing hers.

"Damn." After taking one look at her, he sat up and brushed at her clothing. "I apologize. There seems to be a slight hitch in my get along. Are you all right?"

With her skirts tossed up as they were, Rachel was too flustered to feel any pain, if indeed she was injured somewhere. He flashed one of those disarming grins at her. "Lucky for you, no one but me is here to see."

She shoved at his shoulder. "I'd prefer that no one see, you included."

"I'm gonna see more'n that before all is said and done."

He attempted to get up, but only made it as far as his knees before losing his balance again. He waved away another plume of dust. "Well, hell."

Rachel read the defeat in his expression and was determined to have none of it. She would get him inside that church, she vowed, even if she had to carry him every inch of the way. "You can do it," she said in an encouraging voice.

"It doesn't look like it to me."

"Yes, well, you're drunk and therefore no judge." She pushed to her feet, grabbed him under the arms, and strained to lift him. "Get up, Mr. Rafferty."

"I'm tryin'."

"Try harder!" Her throat burning from the dirt particles she had inhaled, Rachel groaned with frustration when, after utilizing nearly all her strength, he still hadn't gained his feet. "You have to make it. After getting you this far, I can't quit now."

He jerked his arms from her grasp. "Stop strainin' to lift me," he ordered gruffly. "You're gonna keep on until you hurt yourself."

After making that assessment, he just sat there. Rachel bent over him, hands braced on her knees. "Well, then? Are you going to try or not?"

He smiled blearily up at her. "You know, darlin', I don't believe I've ever run across such an eager little swatch of calico."

Rachel felt like jerking him up by his ears. "Please, Mr. Rafferty, at least try."

"Mr. Rafferty? If we're gonna get cozy"—he rose to his knees again—"then you oughta at least call me by my first name." With a great heave, he stood and started up the steps again, this time with no assistance, calling back over his shoulder, "You better get your little fanny up here and make hay while the sun's shinin'. I feel a little sick."

Rachel hurried after him. Once at the landing, she caught

his arm so he wouldn't fall again. Drawing him toward the doors, she said, "Just a few more steps."

"I hate to tell you this, but gettin' there may prove to be the easy part." He chuckled as though he'd said something hysterically funny.

She wrenched one of the double doors open and entered the church rump first, his hands clasped in hers so she could tug him along after her. When the door swung shut, an intense blackness swooped over them. The smell of varnish and beeswax assailed her nostrils. Groping blindly, she located the last row of seats and maneuvered Matt around until she could prop him up against the back of the pew.

Now all she had to do was wait for him to pass out.

That thought no sooner crossed Rachel's mind than his hands settled at her waist. With a gentle strength that, given his condition, surprised her, he drew her toward him. Even in the darkness, she had no difficulty determining that he'd parted his booted feet to pull her between his legs. No more than a black outline, he seemed to loom over her, a threatening wall of masculinity. The brim of his Stetson bumped her forehead. The next instant, his hot, oh-so-soft mouth had taken command of hers and his hands were busily unfastening her bodice.

Rachel tried to scream, but her breath was stolen by his kisses and any sound she might have made was muffled by his mouth. Grabbing his wrists, she arched away from him. Panic welled within her when she felt cool air touch her breasts. Just that quickly, he had opened her bodice. Now only the thin cloth of her chemise shielded her nipples from his searching fingers. His hard palms cupped her fullness, the contact snatching the oxygen from her lungs in a whining rush. A heartbeat later, he firmly captured the peaks of her nipples between thumb and forefinger. Rivulets of fire ran through Rachel, warming her deep within, making her pulse escalate, kindling a need for something indefinable that soon grew to an ache.

Dimly she realized she had completely lost control, that Matt had taken over. He knew his way around a woman's body, that much was clear, and he was pummeling her senses with an onslaught of feelings she'd never dreamed existed.

Struggling to clear her head, Rachel knew she had to get away from him. For some reason, he hadn't passed out on schedule, and now it was anybody's guess when he might. Even so, she had no intention of abandoning her plan, not after having gone through so much to get him here.

Before she left, she had to get his trousers off him.

Trying not to feel what he was doing to her breasts—and failing—she fumbled with his gun belt. When the buckle finally came loose, one holster swung free and the butt of the revolver smacked the pew. She winced and bent at the knees to lower the weapons to the floor before turning her attention to his trouser belt. Luckily, it was easier to unfasten. She groped for the brass buttons of his fly. At her touch in so private a place, he stiffened and sucked in his breath.

"Jesus . . ." he whispered raggedly. "Slow down, sweetheart; you're gettin' ahead of me here."

There was no way that Rachel intended to slow down. She jerked frenziedly at his trousers, her face beading with sweat, her heart thudding wildly, her breasts electrified with unfamiliar sensations where his masterful fingers toyed with her.

To her relief, he finally abandoned her breasts. A heartbeat later, however, she felt his hands at the fastenings of her skirt. She jerked more urgently at his pants, determined to see this through. Once she got away from him, she could refasten her own clothing. He was so sozzled, he wouldn't remember anything that was happening. It would be her guilty secret that he'd touched her so intimately.

Suddenly he leaned forward to press his forehead against

her shoulder. "Whoa," he said in a slurred, rather faint voice. "I don't feel so good."

Still intent on getting his trousers down, Rachel strained to bear his weight.

"Oh, Christ," he whispered raggedly.

With that, he slumped toward her. Before Rachel could react, the breadth of his shoulders struck her squarely, the full force of his considerable weight knocking her backward. She screamed, the sound echoing in the darkness as she fell. Pain exploded at the base of her skull, and a brilliant white light flashed inside her head. Then, as though severed by a sharp knife, all sensation stopped and she spun away into nothingness.

Three

Beeswax and varnish. Sun-dried cotton and leather.
As she came awake, Rachel only vaguely registered the scents.
When she started to stretch and yawn, however, she realized
something was wrong. A massive weight was pressing upon
her body. Not only was she unable to move, but she found it
difficult to breathe.

Confused and disoriented, she fluttered her lashes, becoming more aware with each passing second that her head ached.
Not just a teeny-weeny ache, but a giant, skull-crushing pain
that radiated up from the back of her neck.

"For shame!" a woman whispered from somewhere close
by. The unexpected sound made Rachel jerk. Before she could
move or get her eyes open, another feminine voice said, "I'm
telling you, Clara, the young people today have no respect."

Still trapped in a sleepy fog, Rachel frowned in total bewilderment. She didn't recognize the voices as belonging to
her sister Molly or to Mrs. Radcliff, the housekeeper. What
on earth were strange people doing in her bedroom?

She passed a hand over her face. A blur of multicolored
light swam before her eyes. Without her spectacles, she was

pretty much accustomed to everything beyond the end of her nose being indistinct, but for some reason, this morning it seemed worse than usual. Determined to clear away the cobwebs, she blinked, but her brain refused to cooperate. Objects around her went in and out of focus, rushing at her as they took on clarity, then receding a bit. Gleaming oak pews? People's faces and stained glass windows? She wasn't in her bedroom at home, that was a certainty.

"This is an abomination," some other woman cried.

"A sin against all that is holy, that's what it is!" another exclaimed.

All that was holy? Rachel had already determined she must be in the church. The question was, what was she doing there? She squeezed her eyes closed again to keep from being sick. Her head . . . Oh, God, her head felt as if it had been split by a sledge. Had she been stricken with a sudden illness? Maybe she had fainted. That would explain the oppressive weight that seemed to be holding her down. Olivia Harrington, a local matron, claimed that a lady's limbs felt heavy and useless immediately after she regained consciousness from a swoon.

Forcing her eyes back open, Rachel tried to ignore the pain and concentrate on her surroundings. Yes, she was definitely inside the church. A vague sense of alarm coursed through her. She remembered something about the church— something important—but for the life of her, she couldn't think what. She only knew she had an awful feeling that something was dreadfully wrong.

The weight that held her anchored to the floor shifted suddenly. The movement was followed by a moan, unmistakably that of a man. The sound, deep and raspy, vibrated through her torso, transforming her sense of alarm into full-blown panic. Someone was lying on her? A male someone? Oh, God. Now that she was coming more awake, she could feel his hand, large and warm, cupped over her breast. It felt as if there was next to nothing by way of clothing between his fingers and her skin.

Forgetting the pain in her head, Rachel gave a thin cry and pushed at the man's shoulders. Despite all her shoving, he didn't so much as budge. Tucking in her chin, she glimpsed wavy black hair and darkly bronzed skin. In a twinkling, her memory of the previous night came rushing back to her.

Matt Rafferty! She threw a horrified look at the sunlight streaming through the stained glass windows.

So close to her ear that his voice seemed a part of her thoughts, he whispered, "What the hell am I doing here?"

That was Rachel's question. "Off," she croaked. "Get *off* me!"

Not nearly as fast as she would have liked, he rose on one elbow. "What the—" When he glanced around them, his body snapped taut. "Oh, Christ!"

She followed his gaze and saw that a crowd of people had entered the church. She had planned for this to happen—for him to awaken, surrounded by onlookers, and feel so humiliated he wanted to die. Only she wasn't supposed to be here with him!

So many people . . . Without her spectacles, she couldn't see their faces very clearly, but even so, she couldn't shake the feeling that they were all staring at her. A prickly sensation crawled over her skin. Like vultures waiting to feed on carrion, they pressed in around her, the different shades of their clothing a kaleidoscopic blur of color beneath the pale ovals of their faces. Filled with a mounting sense of dread, she touched a tremulous hand to her throat. Her *bare* throat?

Startled, she looked down. To her dismay, she saw that the only thing covering her breasts was the thin cotton of her chemise. She gasped and brought up both hands to hide herself.

When Matt noticed the state of her clothing, he glanced down at himself. Judging by the look that crossed his face when he saw that his gun belt was gone and that his trousers had been unfastened, he remembered little of what had happened.

In a voice gone gravelly with sleep, he said, "What the hell?" As he scrambled off her, he began buttoning his blue jeans. "How did I—when did we—?"

Before he could finish, one of the church doors swung open and struck the interior wall. The bang was almost deafening. "Where is she? Rachel Marie!" Clothing rustled and shoe leather creaked as the crowd moved aside to clear a path. "Get back, folks. Out of my way!"

Even in a nearsighted blur, Rachel recognized the buckskin vest, white shirt, and shiny star that were her father's trademarks. His voice, pitched to a loud roar, was unmistakable as well. It didn't take a genius to determine that someone had gone to fetch him when she and Matt were found inside the church.

She rushed to finish fastening the buttons of her bodice before he saw her. She was only about halfway done when Big Jim Constantine finally managed to fight his way to the front of the crowd. He took one look at her and said, "Oh, Rachel . . ."

"It's not the way it looks, Daddy. Truly! Just give me a chance to explain!"

Rachel had every reason to believe her father would do exactly that. He was an easygoing and fair-minded man who always asked plenty of questions and listened to the answers before he passed judgement.

She reached up a hand. Instead of helping her up, though, her father took one look at her partially unbuttoned shirt-waist and lunged at Matt Rafferty. "You low-down miserable son of a—!"

"Daddy!" Rachel shrieked. "What are you—oh, my God! Stop it!"

Rachel may as well have saved her breath, for her father

seemed not to hear her. A tall individual of considerable breadth and girth, he landed on the younger man like a diver doing a belly flop. Matt, evidently still feeling the effects of the valerian, fell back under the onslaught, his breath rushing from his lungs in a loud *whoosh*. Before he could even start to defend himself, Big Jim wrapped both hands around his throat.

"You miserable little worm! You conscienceless son of a bitch! I'll kill you for this. I'll kill you with my bare hands!"

From that point on, everything took on a nightmarish quality for Rachel. She had the oddest feeling she was hovering somewhere above herself, that she watched everything through a plate of breath-fogged glass.

"Daddy, stop this!" She clung futilely to her father's arm. "You have to stop this. He's been drugged and can't defend himself. Oh, dear God, you'll kill him!"

Her father tried to shake her off. "Let go, girl. Dammit, let go!"

Nothing could have induced Rachel to do that. This was her fault. All her fault. Nearsighted though she was, she could tell Matt's face was turning crimson. As bitter as her feelings toward him had been last night, she didn't want him dead.

"Daddy, for heaven's sake! Look what you're doing!"

Rachel nearly wept with relief when three men rushed forward to assist her. After several attempts, the trio managed to drag Big Jim off. Judging by the way Matt choked and gasped for air afterward, he hadn't been released a second too soon.

The instant the three men turned her father loose, Rachel flung herself against him. "Daddy, you have to listen to me. This isn't his fault. I swear it. Please, you have to give me a chance to explain."

His chest heaving with exertion, her father shrugged to straighten his shirt. "All right, so explain."

Before Rachel could speak, the church doors banged open again, indicating that yet another person had entered. Bodies shuffled. The next instant, Rachel heard a horrified gasp. There was no mistaking Molly's voice, even when the noises she made were inarticulate. Rachel's heart caught. She had meant to avenge her sister, not force her to endure yet more heartbreak.

"Rachel?" Molly whispered, clearly aghast. "Oh, lands, what've you gone and done?"

Rachel thought the answer to that was fairly obvious. She'd brought Matt Rafferty down a few notches, never mind the fact that she was going down with him.

"Oh, Molly." Rachel bit her lip, wishing with all her might that her sister hadn't come into the church.

Molly shook her head. "Oh, Rachel! You did this for me. I know you did!" She pressed her hands over her cheeks. "Oh, this is awful! You got the wrong one!"

Rachel couldn't imagine what Molly meant by that, and before she had time to think about it, her father interrupted with a sharp command to explain herself. As briefly as she could, Rachel recounted the events that had led to this moment, trying her best to leave nothing out, no matter how bad it made her look. The only concession she made to that was by neglecting to mention Dora Faye. Her father could assume whatever he wished, that she had bribed one of the saloon's regular patrons to drug Matt Rafferty's whiskey or that one of the upstairs girls had done it as a favor to Rachel. It really didn't matter as long as Dora Faye didn't get into trouble.

As Rachel wound down, she watched Big Jim closely, trying without success to read his expression. "So, you see, Daddy, it really wasn't his fault. I tricked Mr. Rafferty into coming here. I would have been long gone this morning if I hadn't fallen and hit my head."

Molly wailed forlornly, which prompted Big Jim to cast

her a glare. "Enough out of you, young lady! If not for your theatrics, your sister wouldn't be in this pickle."

Rachel, always Molly's champion, leaped to her defense. "Now, Daddy, that isn't fair. Molly can't be blamed—"

"You be quiet!" Big Jim cried, cutting her off short. He pinched the bridge of his nose and squeezed his eyes closed for an instant. "All right, Rachel Marie, run all of that by me again. A little slower this time."

Resisting the urge to remind him he'd just ordered her to be quiet, Rachel cautiously asked, "Which part?"

"All of it!" her father ground out.

"All of it? Daddy, didn't you—"

Her father cut her off again, this time with a sharp jab of his finger. "All of it! And don't give me any of your sass, dammit. I'm in no mood for it!"

Rachel could see that he was perilously close to losing his temper. Forcing herself to speak more slowly this time, she once again explained how she'd come to be in the church this morning with Matt Rafferty. When she had given her father a full explanation for the second time and he still looked confused, she raised her hands in helpless bewilderment. "Which part aren't you clear on, Daddy? He callously broke Molly's heart, and I wanted to get even. With that end in mind, I had him drugged and lured him to the church, my plan being that he'd wake up this morning wearing no trousers in a packed church." When her father still looked befuddled, Rachel cried, "He humiliated my sister!" At that, Molly wailed again, more loudly this time. To be heard over the din, Rachel increased her own volume. "Is it so difficult to understand why I wanted to give him a taste of his own medicine? That's it, end of story."

"Rachel, if, as you say, all of this is about Molly and that silly crush she got on Matt Rafferty, then what the hell"—he pointed a finger at the man on the floor—"is *he* doing here?"

"I told you, I—" An awful prickly feeling crawled over

Rachel's skin. She glanced uneasily toward Molly, who was still moaning and wailing, and then at the man sprawled near her feet. "Oh, God. This isn't Matt Rafferty?" It wasn't really a question. Rachel knew by Molly's behavior and the tone of her father's voice that she had guessed correctly. "Oh, dear," she whispered. "Oh, dear . . . oh, dear."

"Oh, dear?" her father repeated. "Is that all you can say for yourself, Rachel Marie? Oh, dear?" With each word he spoke, his voice seemed to go up another octave. "You've shang-haied the wrong man, and all you can say is 'oh, dear'?"

As the ramifications of what she'd done began to sink in, Rachel threw another look at her victim. "If not Matt Rafferty, then who is he?" she asked in a quavery voice.

"Who is he? I almost kill the man, and you're standin' there, askin' me who he is? I'm tellin' you, girl, this is one time I could wear the hide off your behind with my razor strop and never feel a second's regret."

"Big Jim, let's try to stay calm," the man on the floor inserted. Though his voice still sounded a little groggy, Rachel could tell by the way he spoke that he was fast coming awake.

"Calm? I haven't known a moment's calm since the day she was born, I swear to God. I'm sorry about this, Rafferty. I truly am."

Rachel couldn't tear her gaze from the man she had believed to be Matt Rafferty until only a few seconds ago. Without her spectacles, which she never wore in public, he was little more than a blur to her. Rafferty, her father had called him. That had to mean he was one of Matt's brothers. Long, denim-clad legs, ebony hair, gray-blue eyes. Given her poor eyesight, she supposed she could have made a mistake. All the Rafferty brothers were tall, raven-haired and dark-skinned.

Recalling the nonsensical observation that Molly had made earlier, Rachel nearly cringed. *You got the wrong one!* her sister had cried. A few minutes ago that had made no sense. Now Rachel understood all too clearly.

"If you're not Matt, then which brother are you?" she asked her victim shakily.

"Clint."

For an awful moment, Rachel felt as if her heart stopped beating. Since Clint Rafferty, the eldest of the brothers, seldom even came to town, let alone patronized the saloon, she thought she must have misunderstood him. "Pardon?"

"Clint!" he repeated a little more loudly, his voice still slightly hoarse with sleep.

Four

Clint Rafferty? Feeling suddenly faint, Rachel pressed a hand to her waist. Of all the Rafferty brothers she might have chosen to cross, Clint had to be the most intimidating. Even the other men in town gave him a wide berth.

"Clint . . . ?" she said inanely. "But you never go to the Golden Goose. There must be some mistake!"

"Oh, there was a mistake made, all right," he agreed in the same hoarse voice. "It just wasn't me who made it."

A thought suddenly occurred to Rachel. "Wait a minute! You have to be Matt Rafferty. Otherwise, why did Dora Faye—" Catching herself at the last possible second, Rachel stood there, mentally swinging her arms to keep from falling in. The last thing she wanted was to get her friend in trouble.

Clint flashed her a slow, knowing smile. "Dora Faye did try to keep me from drinking the drugged whiskey, if that was your question. At the time, I wondered why. Now I know." With that, he rolled to one knee and reached for his hat. "The only mystery, as far as I'm concerned, is why she didn't step to the saloon doors and signal to you that she'd drugged the wrong man. It would've saved us both a lot of trouble."

In Rachel's mind's eye, she saw Dora Faye as she'd been last night, blurry and indistinct, standing just inside the saloon and waving her arms. Without benefit of her spectacles, Rachel had believed her friend was signaling that all was well. Instead, she'd been signaling that nothing had gone according to plan? That Rachel should retreat? If it hadn't been so awful, it might have been funny.

Gaining his feet, Rafferty said, "I hope you folks'll forgive me, but I think I'll be moseyin' along. As entertainin' as all of this has been, I've got a little brother at home to take care of and a ranch to run."

Rachel certainly had no objection to his leaving. The sooner the better, as far as she was concerned. But her father seemed to have other ideas. "Hold up there just one minute, son."

Clint dusted his hat on his pant leg. "Hold up? Don't tell me you're arrestin' me. If so, what for? Bein' in the wrong place at the right time?"

Considering the fact that her father had almost choked him to death, Rachel couldn't blame Clint Rafferty for feeling a little less than charitable.

"I wouldn't go so far as to arrest you," Big Jim said, "but there is one small wrinkle we need to iron out."

"Wrinkle?"

Big Jim inclined his head toward Rachel. "My little girl spent the night here with you unchaperoned. It don't look good. Don't look good at all."

Rachel's heart caught. "Daddy?"

Big Jim seemed not to hear her. "The way I see it—"

"Daddy!"

"Shut up, Rachel Marie," her father said with a wave of his hand, his gaze fixed on Clint. "The way I see it, Rafferty, my little girl's good name has been ruined. Plumb ruined. And only you can set things right."

"Right?" Rachel echoed. "Whatever do you mean?"

"Yeah, what exactly do you mean?" Clint asked.

Rachel didn't need to see Rafferty's face all that clearly to know he was fast regaining his senses. Unless she missed her guess, he was only inches away from losing his temper. The heels of his boots hit the floor in a sharp stacatto as he stepped over to retrieve his Colt revolvers. She watched in horrified silence as he strapped the crisscrossed gun belt around his hips and tied the holsters down to his lean, muscular thighs. In that moment, it began to occur to her that it might end up being her father, not Clint Rafferty, who was in danger of losing his life during this confrontation. The younger man had the devil's own reputation as being fast with those guns.

Without consciously making the decision to do so, Rachel inched closer to her sire. "Daddy, this entire situation should be simple enough to resolve. I mean, as I've just explained, none of this was Mr. Rafferty's fault. The way I see it, we should all just go home and forget it happened."

"Be quiet, Rachel."

Afraid for her father, Rachel turned an imploring gaze on Clint. "Don't you agree? That we should just forget any of this happened, I mean?" With a nervous little laugh, she added, "Big uh-oh, end of story. Right?"

"Rachel Marie," her father said with exaggerated patience, "this is a far sight more serious than that. Your reputation is destroyed. Mr. Rafferty understands the implications, even if you don't."

Rachel understood far more than her father gave her credit for, and she, for one, had an awful feeling this situation was getting out of control. Gesturing toward the church members, she said, "But, Daddy, everyone here heard my explanation. They all know now that nothing untoward happened."

"It's not that simple, Rachel. When a young lady spends the night with a man unchaperoned, there's only one thing that can save her good name, and that's marriage. It don't matter if anything actually happened or not. All that counts is how it looks."

"Marriage?" Molly cried. "You can't mean it!"

"Marriage?" Rachel echoed weakly. "Did you say marriage?"

"Marriage," Big Jim affirmed.

With that proclamation still ringing in the air, Big Jim caught both Clint and Rachel by the arms and, ignoring Rachel's shrill protests, hauled them to the front of the church. Once there, he immediately began hollering for the preacher. Meanwhile, Rachel tried to talk sense to him, a task that proved impossible. Her father wasn't just big and tall; he was mule-headed. When he got it into his head to do something, no one, not even his daughters were going to stop him.

Reverend Wells, a tall, rawboned man with thinning gray hair, kindly brown eyes, and a beak nose, fought his way free of the throng and rushed to his pulpit, prayer book in hand. "Big Jim, this is highly irregular. We haven't even posted any banns."

"To hell with banns: just get them married."

The minister gave an eloquent shrug. "I was just making an observation."

"Daddy, have you lost your mind? I can't marry this man!" Rachel turned on Clint. "Don't just stand there! Do something!"

Apparently unperturbed, he shrugged a muscular shoulder. "Like what? Shoot him? Sorry, darlin', but I'm not that adverse to the idea of gettin' married."

"Not adverse? How can you say that? We're talking about marriage here!"

"The way I see it, I was thinkin' along these lines, anyway."

She couldn't believe he was being so cavalier. "You're as crazy as my father is."

Big Jim motioned to the minister. "Forget all the fancy stuff, Reverend. All we care about is that it's legal."

Rachel caught her father's arm. "Daddy, stop this! It's absolute madness! Whatever are you thinking?"

"This is all my fault!" Molly cried somewhere behind them. "All my fault."

The preacher chose that moment to say in a booming voice, "Dearly beloved, we are gathered here today . . ."

Shaking his arm free, Big Jim grasped the chancel rail and leaned toward the pulpit. "Dammit, William, I said to skip all the folderol. Just get to the important parts."

Wells coughed and cleared his throat. "As I already pointed out, this is all highly out of the ordinary."

"Just do it," Big Jim shot back. "If I want ordinary, I'll ask for ordinary."

The flustered minister ran a finger down the page to relocate his place. "All right, fine. But, mark my words, it will probably take me longer to locate the important sections than it would to simply recite the entire—"

"Good grief!" Big Jim interrupted. "Are you tellin' me you don't know the words by heart?" He threw up his hands. "You've been marrying people for the last twenty years, for God's sake! How can you not know the words, William?"

Taking advantage of her father's distraction, Rachel turned to Clint. Leaning close so she might clearly see his face, she whispered, "You can't honestly intend to just stand there and do nothing to stop this."

"Who says?"

"I say!"

He stood with his hands clasped behind him, gaze fixed on the minister, expression deadpan. At the corner of his mouth, she thought she glimpsed a smile and wanted to give him a good kick for not putting a halt to the proceedings. Before she carried through on the idea, she thought better of it. Last night he'd been charming, but he'd been silly with drink and mellow from the valerian. This morning, all boyishness had been wiped from his face. If asked to describe him, she would have said he looked stern and more than a little intimidating, not at all the kind to provoke.

She jerked her gaze away and scanned the church, dismayed to see that the crowd at the back had dispersed to take their usual places in the pews, not for Sunday services as usual, but to witness a wedding. Her wedding.

That thought drove Rachel to desperate measures. Straightening her shoulders and lifting her chin to a stubborn angle, she faced her father. "Daddy, I cannot marry this man," she said, slowly and distinctly. "I absolutely can't. Nothing you can say or do will convince me otherwise."

"Of course you can," her father replied and, without so much as a pause, he drew his Colt revolver from its holster and pressed the barrel to Clint Rafferty's temple. "It's the only thing you can do, honey. Whether he meant to or not, Mr. Rafferty here ruined my little girl. Honor demands that I kill him if he don't marry you. It's the way things are, sort of an unspoken code among men. Ain't that right, Mr. Rafferty?"

"Christ," Rafferty said hoarsely.

Rachel watched her father with mounting horror, an emotion she made every effort to conceal by smiling and folding her arms. "Right. You're just going to shoot him in cold blood. After a lifetime of upholding the law? Come on, Daddy. I realize I'm a little gullible, but that's just plain silly."

With slow deliberateness, her father drew back the hammer of his gun. "You think I'm bluffin'? Think again, Rachel Marie. His fault or not, he has ruined any chance you have of making a decent marriage."

"That isn't so!" Rachel scanned the church and spotted Reverend Wells's son, Lawson, who had been courting her these last three years. "Tell him, Lawson! Tell him it doesn't matter, that you love me and won't hesitate to marry me anyway!"

Looking as though his necktie was choking him, Lawson sprang up from his seat, swallowed spasmodically, and then just stood there looking bug-eyed.

"Well?" Rachel implored him. "Speak now, Lawson, or forever hold your peace!"

To her dismay, Lawson said nothing. She sent him a scathing glare, barely resisting the urge to call him a bad egg, plug ugly, and a bootlicker, just for starters. She settled for whispering the insults under her breath.

"I guess that proves my case," her father said, gesturing toward Lawson. "Not even your own beau will step forward."

Feeling a little less certain of herself, Rachel let her arms fall to her sides. "That still doesn't mean you'll shoot Mr. Rafferty. You're only trying to frighten me into minding what you say."

"Oh, I'll shoot him," her father assured her. "Before I let him walk off scot-free, I'll blow his brains clear into next week."

She winced at the picture his threat brought to mind. "You don't mean it, Daddy. What about being marshal? You'd have to give up your badge if you shot somebody."

"That's why. Don't you see? An upstandin' man don't let another man ruin his daughter and not do something about it. If you won't marry him, Rachel Marie, I have to shoot the poor fellow. It's just that simple."

Preacher Wells chimed in with, "Do you, Clint Rafferty, take this woman, Rachel Marie Constantine, to be your lawfully wedded wife?"

Beads of sweat had sprung up on Clint's dark face. His Adam's apple bobbed as he tried to swallow. "I do," he said without a second's hesitation. Then, to Rachel, "If it's all the same to you, argue with your father later. He's got a gun held to my head, in case you haven't noticed."

"Don't worry. He won't really shoot you," Rachel assured him.

"Wanna bet?" Big Jim grinned broadly and curled his finger over the trigger.

Clint squeezed his eyes closed. "Jesus Christ! Do what he tells you, Rachel!"

Rachel's stomach plummeted. "Daddy, this has ceased to be entertaining. What do you think you're doing, threatening an innocent man's life like this?"

"Innocent," Clint inserted, "there's the key word."

The preacher cut in once more. "And, do you, Rachel Marie Constantine, take this man to be your lawfully wedded husband, to love, honor and obey until death do you part?"

Rachel rolled her eyes and smiled sweetly at the minister. "Mr. Rafferty may be quaking in his boots, but I certainly am not. Blizzards will fly in August before any of you hear *me* say 'I do.'"

Big Jim smiled at the preacher. "You heard her. She just said 'I do,' clear as you please."

"I did not!" Rachel said with a scandalized gasp.

"You did so!" Big Jim argued.

Glancing apologetically at Rachel, the preacher said, "I heard her, Big Jim, but I'm not entirely certain she meant—"

"Keep your opinions to yourself and just finish the ceremony," Big Jim instructed.

"By the authority vested in me . . ." the preacher began.

Clint overrode him in a louder voice. "Marshal, would you mind pointing that gun somewhere else besides at my head?"

"Such tactics will never hold up in a court of law," Rachel cried. "These are the nineties, I'll have you know. You men can't marry us women off against our wills anymore. We have legal recourse!"

As though to punctuate that pronouncement, the preacher said, "I now pronounce you man and wife!" and slapped his prayer book closed.

A sudden silence descended over the church. A silence so

thick that Rachel felt as if she were drowning in it. She stared at her father, scarcely able to believe he'd betrayed her like this. Her father, who had always loved her so well. Ever since the death of her mother, he had been the only person she could trust.

With a sad smile, he finally drew the gun barrel from Clint's temple. As he slowly let the hammer back down, he said, "Well, honey, for better or worse, you got yourself a husband."

Five

Less than an hour later, Rachel found herself a mile outside of town, alone with a complete stranger who also happened to be her lawful husband. To complicate matters further, he'd chosen not to rent a wagon for the return trip to his ranch, which meant that she was ensconced on the saddle in front of him and forced to endure the intimacy of his touch for the duration of the ride. Her valise and satchel, joined together at the handles by a length of rope, were draped over the horse's rump behind him like an ungainly pair of saddlebags.

Convinced he must be furious—she couldn't imagine his being anything else, despite his denials inside the church—Rachel racked her brain for a way to defuse his anger before they reached his ranch and he did something they both might regret.

"Mr. Rafferty?"

At the sound of his name, he stiffened slightly, his hand on her midriff shifting position, the proximity of his fingertips to her breast a subtle reminder that she was now his wife and therefore his possession. "You can call me Clint now,

Rachel. It's more or less an accepted thing, the use of first names between husbands and wives."

"Yes, of course, Clint." The lump of anxiety in Rachel's throat felt the size of a goose egg. "I, um . . ." She tried desperately to swallow. Tears of frustration filled her eyes, making the surrounding woods seem even more blurry. In the distance, she could see the craggy peaks of the Cascades, which, without her spectacles, looked like gigantic, indistinct lumps, their snow-swept slopes glistening brilliantly in the July morning sun. "I was just—well, I know you must be angry. Possibly even livid. I certainly can't blame you for that, and I want you to know that I'll do whatever I possibly can to resolve matters."

"Really?" He hunched his broad shoulders around her and tipped his hat back so he might watch her face. "And tell me, Rachel, just how do you plan to resolve matters?" His smoky blue eyes twinkled warmly into hers. "Correct me if I'm wrong, but I thought things were already pretty much settled."

"Settled? We're married, Mr. Rafferty! Don't you realize what that means? I can't believe you've agreed to this."

He smiled slightly, his ebony lashes drifting low over his eyes to partially conceal his expression. "I guess maybe the situation is a little more frightening for you than it is for me."

"Frightening? Why should I feel frightened?" she asked. "I think it would be more accurate to say I feel uneasy."

The creases that bracketed his mouth became deep slashes as his firm lips drew into a smile. "All right, you probably feel more *uneasy* than I do, then. And I can't blame you for that. You barely know me, and now I suddenly have control over your life. That has to be unsettling."

Rachel could have gone all day without hearing him put it into words like that. Control over her life? Oh, God . . . She blinked and averted her face, uncomfortable with the silence that fell over them but uncertain how to break it. With nervous fingers, she plucked at the folds of her skirt, wishing she were anywhere but there.

"If it's any comfort at all," he finally added, "I'm not a mean-natured man. You don't need to feel afrai—" He broke off and fell silent. "Uneasy, you don't need to feel uneasy."

Looking up at him, she felt breathless. To her frightened mind, he seemed taller and broader across the shoulders than he had earlier, a muscular wall of power that might at any moment be targeted at her. *Control over her life*? Oh, it was far more than that, she thought dismally. Far, far more.

Clint heaved a weary sigh and shifted his weight in the saddle. For just a moment his thoughts turned toward home, where his brothers, completely unsuspecting that they had a new sister-in-law, awaited his arrival. Because of them he hadn't protested the marriage to Rachel, and for the life of him, he couldn't regret that decision now. The Raffertys, Clint included, needed a woman in the house, and left to his own devices, Clint wasn't at all sure he could have found one who compared to Rachel Constantine. She wasn't just beautiful, which was a definite plus as far as he was concerned, but she had nice manners and was well-spoken. She'd be a good influence on his brothers, a real good influence. He pictured her in a bib apron with a streak of flour on her cheek. His stomach growled just at the thought. Lord, he couldn't remember when he'd had a good home-cooked meal.

No, he couldn't muster up any regret about marrying Rachel Constantine. The words "manna from heaven" kept popping into his mind. To him, that was what she was, a miracle that had accidentally dropped in his lap. Besides, it wasn't as if this was his fault. He hadn't set out to entrap her or anything. Far from it. And he wasn't the only one benefitting. His own selfish reasons aside, Rachel would have been crucified by the so-called righteous citizens of Shady Corners if he hadn't made an honest woman of her. This marriage was the best thing for her.

Glancing down at her, Clint saw that the bewildered, worried expression was still in her beautiful blue eyes. If they knew each other better, he might be able to guess what she was thinking. How did a young woman feel when she'd just married a man against her will? And a stranger, at that? Clint didn't suppose she felt like whooping for joy.

For just a moment, he toyed with the idea of waiting until he exercised his conjugal rights. Just as swiftly, he discarded the idea. From the instant he'd said "I do," he'd been determined to make the best of this marriage. With that aim in mind, he had no intention of sharing a bed with Rachel and refraining from touching her. Just the thought set his nerves on edge.

He already had enough on his plate without having to deal with sexual frustration. The way he saw it, intimacy between him and Rachel would only make it easier for them to forge a friendship. Some people might say he was going at things ass-backward, but so what. He was new to this marriage business and was making up the rules as he went along.

Though his recollections of last night were a little muddled, some parts were picture clear. He recalled how she had felt in his embrace, how unbelievably sweet she had been, as if God had made her especially for him. Her kiss, as he remembered, had been awkward and shy, definitely not that of an experienced woman, but even so, he knew there was passion within her to kindle. That had been apparent in the way she'd opened her mouth to him and molded her body to his. His main problem would be to get her back into his arms again. Once he had her there, he didn't doubt his ability to arouse her. At the thought, a searing heat formed low in his belly.

Becoming more mindful by the moment that it was still

morning and, therefore, a long while till nightfall, Clint forced his thoughts away from lovemaking. "About your sister Molly," he said softly. "If Matt truly did humiliate her in front of her friends and make her cry, I'm really sorry."

"He didn't just make her cry," she corrected. "He broke her heart." Her large blue eyes flashed to his. "Just because she's only fourteen, that doesn't mean she's too young to fall in love, you know."

"Of course not," he agreed. "If anything, she's probably capable of loving even more intensely because of her age. It's my experience that we tend to guard our feelings a little more closely as we get older."

She looked mildly surprised to hear him say that. "You aren't going to say it's all nonsense then? About Matt breaking her heart, I mean?"

Gazing down at her, Clint had an almost irresistible urge to kiss the little frown wrinkles from her brow. Why, he couldn't say. True, he'd cast an admiring eye in Rachel Constantine's direction more than once since moving to this area. But being a young and healthy bachelor, he'd cast an admiring eye in lots of girls' directions. Maybe that was his trouble. He and his friend Henry hadn't had the pleasure of a lady's company in a good long while, and pent-up need was playing heck with his self-control. "No," he said hoarsely, "I don't think it's nonsense. That isn't to say I believe Matt meant to hurt her, or that he even knows he did."

"How could he not know?"

Clint sighed. "Rachel, my brother has probably broken a dozen hearts, and I doubt he ever realized it. He's a very handsome fellow with a charming way about him. More than one—"

For the first time that day, she smiled. Only slightly and very fleetingly, but it was a smile just the same. The brilliance of it cut him short and left him with absolutely no recollection of what he'd been about to say. "Handsome and charming, is he? Do you realize how much you two look alike?"

For a second, Clint couldn't think how to reply. Then he decided to fall back on plain old honesty, which had never failed him yet. "Matt and I are like two identical chunks of agate, one polished and the other not. I have all the same surface, darlin', but I'm missin' the shine."

Her large blue eyes moved slowly over his face. After looking her fill, she smiled again, still only slightly, but with devastating impact. Looking down at her, Clint decided he could probably become a millionaire if he could figure out a way to bottle that sweetness of hers. "I've never seen your brother, so I can't say for sure, but I find it difficult to believe he outshines you by much."

Uncertain how to accept the compliment graciously, Clint decided to ignore it. "What've you been doin', girl? Walkin' around town with your eyes shut?"

"Pardon?"

"How else could you miss seein' my brother?"

Her cheeks turned an embarrassed pink. "I misspoke. Of course I've seen him, just never from up close."

Clint found it rather incredible that Matt, who was attracted to pretty women like bees to honey, had never homed in on Rachel. She was one pretty little gal, make no mistake. "Well, trust me, honey, he doesn't just outshine me. If women's reactions to him are any indication, we're talkin' a total eclipse. Just you make sure you don't fall for any of his blarney. Mistake or no, you're married to me, not to him."

He clicked his tongue to the horse and nudged it to a faster pace. At just that moment, a jackrabbit bounded out from a clump of brush onto the road. The unexpected flash of movement spooked Clint's roan, and before he could react, the stallion reared to strike the air with its front hooves. Rachel had no stirrups with which to balance her weight, and the only thing anchoring her to the saddle was Clint's hold on her. Fearful that she might get hurt, he tightened his arm around her waist as he struggled to regain control of the horse.

When the huge animal had finally quieted, Clint realized that in the confusion, he had moved his palm upward on Rachel's ribs to partially cup her breast. She clearly didn't appreciate the familiarity. Either that, or the stupid horse had scared her half to death. As near as he could tell, she had all but stopped breathing.

"Rachel?"

Very carefully, he slid his hand back down to its former resting place, then leaned slightly forward so he might see her face. His heart caught at her expression, her eyes squeezed tightly closed, her sweet mouth aquiver as she waged an obvious battle not to cry out.

"Rachel . . ." he said more softly. "It's all right."

"Did we smash it?"

The question took him totally off guard, and he slowly circled it, not entirely sure what she was talking about. "Did we smash what?"

"The poor bunny," she asked thinly.

The poor bunny? Clint stared down at her pale face, still not convinced he was reading this correctly. True, the girl had been born and raised in town, but surely that hadn't entirely insulated her from the realities of life, rabbit stew ranking high on the list. "No, we didn't smash the rabbit," he replied in a voice that had gone oddly tight. "He made it across without even getting his fur ruffled."

Her breath rushed from her chest and her eyes fluttered open. Splaying a small hand over her throat, she swallowed audibly and gave a weak smile. "Oh, thank goodness. They're such sweet little things, don't you think? I particularly love the way they wiggle their noses."

After studying her for a moment, Clint gave himself a hard mental shake. There was no point in thinking the worst.

Just because the girl was worried about one wild bunny, that didn't mean she would be squeamish about cooking up the occasional rabbit stew.

Surely not.

Six

The Rafferty ranch was nestled among a stand of tall pines in a grassy valley completely surrounded by forested mountains. As soon as she got close enough to see it clearly, Rachel found it breathtaking.

As Clint steered his stallion down to the house, she couldn't shake the feeling of rightness that came over her. It was as if she'd been waiting all her life for this moment, and possibly for this man. Crazy, so crazy. She was making absolutely no sense. This marriage was a mockery and doomed to be dissolved. To entertain the notion that it might be otherwise was absolute madness.

As Clint drew the horse up at the edge of the porch, she saw a blur of white next to an odd-looking stump. Peering more intently, she realized she was seeing a chopping block, with chicken feathers strewn at the base. Instantly queasy, she jerked her gaze to the house itself. Anything to keep from imagining the blood and gore that must have accompanied the recent slaughter.

The house was simplicity itself, a sprawling structure of rough-hewn logs and a cedar shake roof. It wasn't pretty by any stretch of the imagination, though it could have been charming if any attempt at all had been made to pretty it up.

To say that hadn't happened struck her as a gross understatement. In fact, by the looks of things, just the opposite had occurred. Even without her glasses, she could make out a rusted old washtub on one side of the front porch with a weathered scrub board standing on end inside it and a pair of dirt-encrusted gray socks draped over its rim. Next to the tub lay a discarded flour sack, out of which had spilled some flour gone wet and gooey in the rain, then turned rock hard in the sun. Behind the flour sack, a partially used sack of spuds had been propped against the house within easy reach of the front door. All in all, the place looked as if a band of none-too-tidy squatters had taken up residence.

"Things could use some cleanin' up," Clint said apologetically.

"Oh, it's lovely. Really. I like log houses. Don't you?" In actuality, Rachel preferred clapboard, but she would never risk hurting his feelings by saying so.

Glancing back at him over her shoulder, her gaze caught on his firm mouth. She couldn't help but recall how it had felt to be in his arms last night, how dizzily she had succumbed to his kisses. Thinking back on it, she wondered how it might feel to be kissed by him again. In the light of day, would she find his embrace boring and unexciting, as she had Lawson's? Or as had happened last night, would the first touch of his lips on hers steal her breath away? It would probably be just as well if she never found out, she decided. Her sister Molly wasn't the only young girl who'd ever gotten her heart broken. Rachel had as well, and if she'd learned anything from the experience, it was that handsome men didn't find women like her attractive.

As he shifted forward to drape the horse's reins over the saddle and get a grip on the saddle horn, she felt the powerful play of muscles in his chest and arms. A shiver of awareness went down her spine as he swung from the saddle and reached up to lift her down.

"I can manage by myself," she said.

The protest came too late. Before she could so much as blink, he seized hold of her waist. Placing her hands on his shoulders, she kept her gaze locked with his as he lifted her easily from the saddle.

"I don't want you managing by yourself," he said huskily. "Not with eight of us here to help you. Just you remember that."

She was glad to note that his solemn, almost stern expression was belied by a slight smile flirting at the corners of his mouth. She wondered if he was smiling because he'd somehow sensed she'd been wondering how it might feel if he kissed her again. At the thought, a flush began creeping up her neck.

He was standing with his back to the sun, and his Stetson cast a shadow over his burnished features. Even with the lack of light, however, his smoky eyes had a lustrous glow. As he drew his gaze over her, she felt powerless to move and wasn't certain she wanted to. As she'd noted last night, there was something about Clint that captivated her. What or why was a true puzzle, but the moment he looked at her with those warm, gray-blue eyes of his, she felt sort of, well, boneless. But that was just plain silly.

Grasping her elbow in a large, capable hand, he helped her step up onto the porch. "We would've cleaned up if we'd've known company was comin'." As though to emphasize the point, he gave the flour sack a kick. "With the ranch demandin' so much of our time, things here at the house get sort of neglected." He led her to the door, then leaned around her to boot it open. "Not that I'm sayin' you should think of yourself as company, Rachel. Consider this to be your home."

With that, he swung the door open on a kitchen so cluttered and disorganized it defied description. An unusually long plank table, the surface of which was buried under piles of mercifully blurred clutter, dominated the center of the room. If it hadn't been for the occasional dirty dish mixed in, Rachel wouldn't have believed anyone actually used the table for eating. "Oh, my . . ."

Clint's hand tightened on her arm. "The boys and I will help you get things cleaned up," he assured her. "And on down the road, maybe I can put up some planed wooden walls. I know ladies are fond of hangin' wallpaper and pictures and such."

Rachel squinted to see. The interior of the house seemed unusually dim, probably because the log walls had darkened with age. The kitchen, one half of which was partitioned off from the back of the house by a wall, opened into a parlor area at the unpartitioned end, creating an L-shaped living area over which a large loft loomed.

If Clint's brothers were going to help her clean up, Rachel hoped they came bearing broad-blade shovels. On second thought, even shovels might not do it. In every corner, as far back into the house as she could see, there were piles of junk. Old newspapers, empty food tins, dirty laundry, school books, slates . . . It looked as if someone had tossed all the contents of the house onto the floor, given them a stir, and then kicked the mixture out of the way to create traffic paths. Never, not in all her born days, had she seen such a horrendous mess.

From out of the rubble, an ebony-haired little boy suddenly appeared. Rubbing one eye with his fist, he surveyed Rachel from his other.

"Who're you?"

As he drew close enough for her to see him clearly, Rachel thought she'd never clapped eyes on a cuter little fellow. She guessed him to be about six, and he looked exactly how she imagined Clint must have at that age, compact and wiry, with burnished skin and an unruly shock of pitch-black hair.

"Well, hello," she said, crouching to greet him at his eye level. "My name's Rachel. What's yours?"

"Cody." When he drew his fist from his eye, he had to blink to get his sooty eyelashes untangled. She noticed that a streak of dirt angled across one of his cheeks. He regarded her for several moments, his expression more serious than a child's his age should have been. With a pronounced lisp that distorted all his S's, he added, "I'm almost seven."

"Not for nine more months," Clint corrected. "And what are you doin', sleepin' in the parlor, tyke? Not to mention it's nigh onto noon."

"Nobody woke me to go upstairs last night." Cody dragged a suspender strap up over his shoulder. "And don't call me 'tyke,' Clint. I'm too old for little kid names."

Rachel couldn't suppress a smile. "I thought you were at least eight," she fibbed. "You must be very tall for your age."

Cody rewarded her with a pleased grin that revealed large gaps where he was missing front teeth. "Clint says I'm only knee high."

"Yes, well, considering how high his knees are, that's rather tall for someone your age," Rachel observed diplomatically. "I think lofty stature runs in your family." She glanced up at Clint. "You didn't mention having a brother so—" She nearly said "little" but stopped herself.

"Grown up?" he inserted quickly.

Rachel smiled and pushed to her feet. "Exactly."

He flashed her a meaningful look. "Like I said, I have my reasons for wantin' a wife."

Now that Rachel had met Cody, she could understand Clint's willingness to do nearly anything to ensure the little boy's happiness, even playing groom to her bride in a shotgun wedding. The problem was, his feelings were bound to change, if not when he learned she was half blind, then when he saw her in spectacles. Given the severity of her eye problem, her glasses had unusually thick lenses that would have detracted from her looks even if she'd been the most beautiful woman in the world. Rachel had learned the hard way that handsome men wanted to be with equally handsome women, which she definitely was not when she had spectacles perched on the end of her nose.

Before Rachel could stand back up, an older boy came tearing down the loft ladder into the kitchen. In the process of buttoning his blue jeans, he froze when he spotted Rachel. "Well, dammit, Clint!" The youth hurried to get his pants fastened. "You could've hollered out that we had us some company."

"Meet Daniel," Clint said by way of introduction, glancing first at Rachel, then inclining his head at the boy. "Fourteen, goin' on eighty. Excuse his language, but I ran low on soap."

Since soap was clearly a commodity in short supply, Rachel had no difficulty believing that. Daniel's undershirt, which had once been gray, was now more of a brown. Still hunkered in front of Cody, she bestowed a friendly smile on him. "Hello, Daniel. I'm pleased to meet you."

He inclined his head. "Same here."

Good manners, it seemed, were another area Clint had neglected. She stood and surveyed the kitchen, feeling overwhelmed. Clint had gone along with marrying her because he needed a woman around the house; he'd made no secret of that. He was, in short, offering her a life here in exchange for her skills as a housekeeper and cook. It was just that simple.

Most women, Rachel knew, would be insulted. They wanted a man to be attracted to them for their looks, to love them for their personalities, to marry them for reasons of the heart. But Rachel had learned long ago not to expect any of those things. She wasn't insulted by Clint's offer. To the contrary, she was titillated, not to mention sorely tempted to take him up on it.

There was just one problem. A rather big problem. Since

the death of Rachel's mother when Rachel was four, Mrs. Radcliff, the housekeeper her father had hired, had seen to the running of the Constantine household. A woman who resented any interference whatsoever, she had not encouraged Rachel or Molly to assist her with any of the chores. Consequently, Rachel's knowledge of homemaking was limited. By closely following a recipe, she could cook simple dishes, and she figured common sense would see her through most of the housecleaning chores. But laundry? She'd rinsed out her ribbed cotton hose a few times, but other than that she'd never washed, starched, or ironed a single garment. As tempting as she found Clint's proposition, she wasn't at all sure she was equal to the challenge.

On the other hand, this was her chance—probably her one and only chance—to have the thing other girls took for granted, namely a handsome young husband who made her pulse race and her skin tingle. For so long now, Rachel had been resigned to settling for second or third best. Marrying Lawson. Playing the role of a minister's wife. Pretending she didn't want or need any excitement in her life. Now, through a quirk of fate, she had a chance for more. So much more. Every time she remembered the kiss she and Clint had shared, she fairly shivered with anticipation.

Madness! She should know better than to get her hopes up like this. Hadn't she learned anything the last time she'd gotten her heart broken? Was she really so foolish that she was willing to risk that kind of pain again? It wasn't as if she could keep her poor eyesight a secret from Clint and all his brothers permanently or even for any length of time at all. Sooner or later, one of them would catch her wearing her spectacles, and Clint would discover the truth—that she was half blind and, to rectify the problem, had to wear horribly ugly glasses. Once that happened, there'd be no more spine-tingling kisses. He would probably make up any excuse he could think of to get rid of her.

Unless . . . maybe . . . Oh, God, it was crazy to even consider it. But she'd heard tell of other marriages that had started shaky and ended up just fine. Why, even her own father had admitted once that her mother hadn't been all that crazy about marrying him at first.

Of course, Mama hadn't been blind as a bat, either. Still— what if she could keep her eyeglasses a secret? The only time she absolutely had to wear them was to read, and she could try to avoid doing that in front of anyone. If she was careful, really careful, it might be months before Clint learned the truth, and maybe by then he would like her so much for herself he'd no longer care if she wore spectacles.

As crazy a plan as it was, one glance at Clint cemented it in Rachel's heart. He was, without question, one of the handsomest men she'd ever met. To a girl like her, who'd long since given up on dreaming, his offer was irresistible. She had to take a chance. If she got her heart broken again, so be it. At least she wouldn't go to her grave wanting to kick herself for never trying at all.

Her decision made, Rachel quickly assessed the mess that surrounded her. Everywhere she looked, there seemed to be stacks of dirty dishes. She had an awful feeling that her ability to balance a book on her head while climbing a flight of stairs might not come in very handy around the Rafferty place.

"I, um, don't know quite where to start . . ." She turned to look at Clint. "Did you say you had chores to do?"

"Only a few," he assured her eagerly. "This bein' Sunday, we set aside most of the day for indoor chores. As soon as I finish, I'll come back inside and help."

"Have you any bread baked?" Rachel prayed so, for she'd never turned out a loaf of bread in her life.

"No. We usually make up enough on Sundays to last us the whole week. Like I said, Sunday's our indoor day."

Rachel's stomach tightened. "I hope you have a cookbook. I don't know the ingredients for bread by heart."

"No cookbook, exactly. But we do have a collection of recipes my grandma and ma wrote down over the years. Nothin' fancy, just loose sheets of paper in a wood recipe box my pa made."

"Do you have one for bread?"

"Sure do. Otherwise, I'd be lost. I don't know the ingredients by heart, either."

Rachel relaxed slightly. She'd be successful enough at culinary endeavors so long as she had recipes to follow. The cleaning would be a simple matter of following her nose. The main problem she would have was with the laundry. Then she would definitely need help. Maybe if she did passably well at all the other things, Clint wouldn't mind that too much, though.

So unexpectedly that it startled her, Clint yelled, "Everybody hit the deck up there! It's nigh onto noon! Time to get to work!"

From the loft came the sounds of mattress ropes creaking and feet hitting the planked floor. In less than a minute, one dark head appeared at the top of the loft ladder. Then another. Before she knew it, four indistinct young men were standing above her. Taking turns, they came down to join ranks with Daniel and Cody.

With the arrival of each one, Clint called off his name and age. "Cole, seventeen. Jeremiah, twenty-four. Joshua, nineteen. Zack, twenty-two."

As each young man was introduced to her, Rachel smiled and inclined her head. When Clint wound down, she said, "I'm pleased to meet all of you."

"Not all," Cody corrected her. "Matt ain't here. He's twenty."

"Oh, yes, Matt," Rachel said cautiously. "How could I have forgotten?"

Cody wrinkled his nose and regarded Clint speculatively. "You didn't say how old you are," he reminded his eldest brother.

To Rachel's surprise, Clint stepped up beside her and draped an arm over her shoulders. "I'm twenty-seven, scamp, which makes me plenty old enough to settle down, and that's just what I've decided to do. This morning, Rachel and I got married."

"You what?" "Why didn't you tell us?" "I thought I was gonna be your best man!" "Jumpin' Jehoshaphat! You've gone and done what?" "I thought Lawson Wells was her beau."

"I beat Lawson to the draw and asked her first," Clint said. "Let it be a lesson to you. Don't leave a pretty girl footloose and fancy free for too long a time, or the first thing you know, she may marry some other fellow."

"I didn't even know you knew Rachel that well," Zach said.

"Why didn't you tell us you were thinkin' about marryin' her?" Joshua demanded.

"Oh, wow!" Cody cried excitedly. "You mean she's gonna stay here?"

Clint held up a hand. "Yes, she's gonna stay," he assured Cody. Then to the older boys, "As for all your questions, we just decided to get married, that's all. I'm countin' on all of you to make Rachel feel welcome."

"You're sure enough welcome!" Cody assured her. "Especially if'n you can bake cookies like the kind Clint brought home from the church social last year."

Rachel blinked. Cookies? "Of course I can bake cookies," she assured him. "As long as there's a recipe included in those loose papers Clint mentioned."

Marginally less enthusiastic, but warmly all the same, the older Raffertys expressed welcome, Jeremiah, the next oldest to Clint, finishing with, "We'll be proud to call you sister, Rachel. Welcome to your new home."

Sister. Hearing the word brought a stinging sensation to Rachel's eyes that felt suspiciously like tears. She blinked a little frantically, convinced they would all think her crazy if she got weepy-eyed and sentimental over something so silly. It was just that she'd always wished for a brother, and now she had seven of them, four of them older than she. It was almost as though Clint had known how fiercely she'd wanted an older brother to look out for her.

"And I'll be pleased to call all of you brother," she said in an oddly tight voice.

The courtesies thus observed, Clint drew his arm from around Rachel and systematically began naming off his expectations.

"Rachel's gonna be cleanin' this place up," he started. "I want each of you to help her in any way you can. Understand? Jer, you hightail it out to the porch and bring Rachel's grips into the bedroom. Joshua, you haul her up some buckets of water to heat on the stove. No point in her havin' to wear herself out at the pump. Zach, you gather up all the things she'll need: a broom and mop, clean rags, and whatever else she wants. Cole, while they're doin' that, you and Daniel and Cody get busy pickin' things up and puttin' them away. In their proper places, mind you, not just any old place. And, Cody! Nothin' under the bed, you understand?"

Rachel's head was swimming by the time Clint stopped issuing orders. He drew to a close with, "Now all of you, listen up. From here on out, Rachel's word is law inside this house. I'm sure she'll be makin' up some new rules around here, and I expect each of you to mind what she says, just like it was me. Got that? No sassin' her, or I'll kick your butts."

Zach, who was standing close enough that Rachel could clearly see his face, turned a solemn regard on her. After a long moment, he smiled slightly and winked irreverently. He obviously wasn't intimidated by his older brother.

Clint rubbed his hands together and turned to arch a questioning brow at her. "Did I leave out anything you'd like said?"

"Only thank you." Rachel smiled. "For making me feel so welcome."

Joshua piped up with, "Welcome? Rachel, it's a wonder we ain't on our knees in gratitude. It's been so long since we had a decent meal around here, we've forgotten what good food tastes like."

Rachel could only hope she didn't disappoint them. First things first, though. Before she could try her hand at cooking, she had to muck out the kitchen. Luckily, she had plenty of helpers.

Seven

Two hours later, Rachel had the kitchen cleaned up enough to start mixing bread dough. After enlisting Cody's help in locating the recipe box Clint had mentioned, she announced to all the older boys that it was time for them to take a much-deserved rest, preferably some place other than in the kitchen.

When they solicitously offered to help her with the cooking, Rachel waved them off, saying, "No, no! I'm funny that way, I guess. I like an empty kitchen when I cook. Too many cooks makes for oversalted porridge, you know."

"I never heard that sayin'," Joshua commented.

Neither had Rachel, but it served her purpose, which was to evacuate the kitchen so she could slip on her spectacles undetected to read the bread recipe.

As the last Rafferty trailed off, Rachel dived her hand into her pocket for her spectacles. Something sharp pricked her fingertip. "Ouch!" She jerked her hand back out, saw a bead of blood, and frowned in bewilderment. "What in heaven's name?"

More gingerly this time, she reached into her pocket. As

her fingers curled over the wire frames, her heart felt as though it dropped, not just to the region of her knees, which is how it usually felt when something awful happened, but clear to the floor. Her spectacles! The frames were hopelessly mangled, and as she lifted them from her pocket, she saw that both lenses were absent from their holes. Fishing more deeply in her pocket, she soon learned why. Each lens was shattered. It had been one of the jagged pieces of glass that pricked her finger.

Stunned, Rachel could only stand there for a moment, staring blankly down at her ruined spectacles. How had this happened? She no sooner asked herself that than she remembered falling in the church last night. Evidently her spectacles had been broken then.

As the first wave of shock subsided, she turned her gaze toward the recipe box. Panic rose within her. She quickly tamped it down. Reading without her spectacles was nearly impossible but not absolutely so. If she held the written material right in front of her nose, she could usually make out the letters. It would be tedious, but beggars couldn't be choosers.

"Oh, lands!" she whispered under her breath. "Why my glasses? Why not an arm or leg? I could better do without either."

Returning her ruined spectacles to her pocket, she advanced determinedly on the recipe box, her chin raised high. It took some searching, but she finally located the bread recipe. Peering intently at every ingredient until she could bring the letters and amounts into focus, she managed to mix a triple batch of yeast bread. After letting the three bowls of dough rise once on the cookstove, which still held banked coals from the supper fire the boys had built last night, she punched it down and shaped six loaves. As she recalled, Mrs. Radcliff had always rubbed her loaves with melted lard, covered them with a towel, and left them on the slightly warm stove to double in size. After finding three clean linen towels—no easy feat—Rachel followed the housekeeper's example. When she could finally step back to admire the fruits of her labor, she felt as proud as if she'd given birth to six babies.

Returning to the recipe box, she applied herself to the task of finding something to fix for supper. Since she hated to eat meat, knowing that the practice caused some poor animal to suffer, she settled on venison stew—minus the venison, of course. Oh, yes. This was going to work famously, she assured herself as she began peeling vegetables. Delicious hot bread and stew for supper would make a good first impression on all the Rafferty men, young or old.

"Jesus Christ!"

Clint couldn't quite believe his eyes when he entered the kitchen. His cookstove had been transformed into a huge, misshapen mushroom! At least, that was how it looked at first glance. At second glance, he saw that the mushroomy cap was actually some sort of dough. Mountains of the stuff oozed over the sides of the stove and dripped in gooey rivers toward the floor. Useless, the family's scruffy, mixed-breed excuse for a cattle dog, was pulling off strips of the stuff and eating it.

"Rachel?"

Clint glanced around the kitchen, which had undergone a more favorable transformation than the stove, thank goodness. Even the window over the dry sink now sparkled. Sitting almost regally in the center of the otherwise bare table was a pot of peeled and quartered vegetables covered with water. The makings for a stew or soup, he guessed, and saw that he was right when he spotted the open recipe box. The uppermost recipe was for his ma's venison stew.

Following the sound of voices, Clint went in search of his bride. He found her in the loft with his brothers. The only one of the Raffertys missing, Clint realized, was Matthew, who was still in town, more than likely nursing a hangover. Rachel sat in the center of Zach's bed, her slender back to the log wall, her skirts tucked modestly around her criss-crossed legs. The six boys—no matter how old some of his brothers grew, Clint still thought of them all as boys—were gathered around her, four sitting Indian-style on the bed, two kneeling on the floor with their elbows on the mattress. At the center of their circle was an array of playing cards.

"Here they come, folks, down and dirty," Cole said.

"Down and what?" Rachel asked with a giggle. To Jeremiah she queried, "Are you sure there's such a thing as beginner's luck? I'll never manage to pay all this back to you fellows."

The mess downstairs momentarily forgotten, Clint leaned a shoulder against the partition, one of two half walls that divided the loft into three proportional sleeping areas for his brothers. For a moment, he allowed his gaze to linger warmly on Rachel, then he glanced around at the boys. Apparently they were teaching her how to play poker and were fleecing her in the process. Normally he might have scolded, but it had been so long since he'd seen the six of them interacting this way and having a good time that he didn't have the heart. Even though he didn't hold much with gambling, Clint was a firm believer in having fun, and all of them seemed to be doing that.

"Pair of deuces showin'," Cole said as he dealt a last, face-up card to Zach. "Holy Moly, look at that king. Possible straight!" he cried as he doled out cards to Cody. "And the lady draws a lady! Look at that pair of queens showin'," he yelled as he slapped down Rachel's last card. "Did I hear you askin' if there's such a thing as beginner's luck? Darlin', just look at that. Unless somebody's got somethin' really impressive hidin' in the hole, you're our biggest winner so far."

Rachel touched a hand to her bodice, her big-eyed innocence too genuine to be feigned. "Truly?" She leaned forward to squint at a pile of rocks that lay on the bed. "How much will I win?"

Cody bounced forward to take a quick count. "Fifty dollars!" he said breathlessly. "Wow! If only it was real money, you'd be rich."

Clint relaxed slightly. At least they weren't gambling for actual money. He should be thankful for small blessings, he guessed. At just that moment, Rachel caught sight of him. "Clint? Is that you?"

He chuckled. "Damn, girl, are you stone blind? Of course it's me."

A faint flush touched her hollowed cheeks. "Your hat was shadowing your face," she explained. "I couldn't see you clearly. Besides"—she waved a hand at all his brothers—"just look at all of you. I've never seen so many people look so much alike."

Thus reminded of his manners, Clint swept his hat from his head. "I hate to interrupt the game, but we have a hell of a mess downstairs. What is that stuff that's all over the top of the stove?"

Her eyes went even wider, if that was possible. Tossing down her cards, she scrambled off the bed, elbowing boys out of the way en route. "My bread!"

"Bread? That's bread?" Clint guffawed. "How much yeast did you use?"

Rachel raced by him. Clint caught her arm before she reached the ladder. "Whoa, there. Just slow it down. No point in takin' a tumble."

Setting her back a step, he went down the ladder first so he could ensure her safe descent. "Careful," he cautioned, his gaze fixed anxiously on her small feet. "The rungs are tricky until you get used to them."

After gaining the kitchen, she stood in frozen silence,

staring at the stove. "Oh no! My beautiful babies! What on earth happened to them?"

Useless, whose hunger was apparently satisfied for the first time in his misbegotten life, licked his mottled chops, plopped down beside the stove, and whined. It suddenly occurred to Clint that perhaps he shouldn't have allowed the dog to continue eating the dough.

"Christ," he said under his breath, eyeing Useless's belly, "I hope he doesn't get sick."

Rachel huffed indignantly. "Are you saying my bread may make him sick?"

"I was thinking of the yeast, that maybe it isn't good for dogs." Clint dragged his gaze from the canine. "It looks to me like maybe you put too much in."

"Only what the recipe called for, one cup per batch."

"A cup?" Clint whistled. "No wonder you have dough everywhere, honey. You must have misread the ingredients. My ma's recipe calls for one quarter cup yeast per batch."

At that moment, all the boys came spilling down the ladder. When they saw the mess on the stove, their eyes widened in amazement. "Wow!" Cody cried. "Will we cook all of it?"

"No, Cody, I don't think it'll be edible once we get it scraped up," Clint replied. "Useless is the only one who gets bread tonight."

"Oh, darn!" Cody said. "I've had my mouth set for hot bread all day."

Rachel looked so upset that Clint hastened to say, "It's not that bad, Rachel. We can have biscuits tonight, and you can make bread tomorrow."

With that, he rolled back his shirt sleeves and set himself to the task of cleaning up the mess. Ten minutes later he had revised his earlier opinion that it wasn't that bad. He'd never seen so much bread dough. Worse, damn near all of it had stuck to the warm cast iron, creating a mess that was nearly impossible to clean. In the end, he resorted to scraping the goo up with his knife.

"Are you sure you only put in a cup of yeast per batch?" he asked Rachel. "I gotta tell you, I've never seen fifteen cups of flour go so far in my life."

"Nine," she corrected. "The recipe called for three cups of flour per batch, nine if it was tripled."

Clint paused in his scraping to regard her thoughtfully. "No, honey, the recipe calls for five cups of flour per batch, so a tripled amount would be fifteen. You misread more than just the amount of yeast, evidently. Do you have poor eyesight or something?"

At the suggestion, her cheeks flushed a pretty pink and her eyes took on a shimmer of indignation. "Lands, no, I don't have poor eyesight!"

Judging by her expression, Clint could see that he'd made a mistake asking. Females were sensitive about things like that, he guessed. Thinking quickly, he endeavored to mend his fences, making mental note not to call her eyesight into question again. "You're right. It was silly of me to suggest such a thing. No small wonder you misread the writing. Threes and fives look a lot alike, and I've used that recipe so many times, I've probably smeared ingredients all over the numbers, making them hard to see."

Looking relieved to be let off the hook, she nodded decisively. "Yes, I'm sure that's it. The recipe did have lots of smears on it." She wrung out the rag she was using. "I'm so sorry about the mess, Clint. Truly, I am. You really don't have to help me clean up. I can do it by myself."

She looked so adorable standing there that Clint wouldn't have left her to finish by herself for anything in the world. He would have to go out to the barn to do the milking later, but otherwise he was staying inside for the remainder of the day. There was no reason he could think of that he should be separated from his bride. The way he saw it, they had little enough time left before nightfall to get to know one another. If he hoped to make love to the girl before their marriage saw its first sunrise, he had his work cut out for him.

When Clint sat down to supper that night, he nearly broke a tooth on one of Rachel's biscuits, and then he almost went blind looking for the meat in her stew. After taking several bites of the concoction, which was way too salty for his taste, he decided there must not be any meat in it. Regarding his wife the length of the long table, he smiled slightly. She was eating away, clearly oblivious to the fact that there was anything missing.

"Rachel, from now on when you need some meat, just ask the boys and one of them will go fetch you some. We have beef and venison aplenty in the smokehouse."

"Meat?" She fastened startled eyes on him, her spoon suspended partway to her lips. "Whatever would I need meat for?"

Clint deepened his smile. "To cook?"

She returned her spoon to her bowl. "Oh, no, I couldn't."

"Couldn't what?"

"Cook meat."

Her response effectively brought to a halt every spoon at the table. Clint glanced around to see that all his brothers—excluding Matthew, who'd not yet come home—were staring at his bride, their expressions curiously blank. Not that he blamed them. He wasn't sure he'd heard her right himself.

"Did I understand you to say you can't cook meat?" he asked, hoping to clarify matters.

She daintily wiped each corner of her mouth with a fingertip, clearly at a loss without a proper napkin. "That's right. I don't eat meat."

Clint barely managed to suppress a hoot of laughter. "Why ever not?"

Her already wide eyes seemed to grow even larger. "Well,

because! It's so cruel!" She looked around at his brothers. "I can't believe a single one of you would be so mean as to actually go out into the woods and shoot an innocent deer just so you could have venison in your stew." She smiled brilliantly. "Not when it tastes perfectly fine without it."

Clint was convinced she was teasing. "Rachel, honey, everyone eats meat."

"Not everyone. I certainly don't. And if I'm to be the cook in this house, none of you shall, either."

Stunned silence. Clint gave each of his brothers a meaningful look. Clearing his throat, he said, "Maybe we should discuss this later."

"There's nothing to discuss," she said sweetly. "Unless, of course, someone else is volunteering to cook." She looked around the table. "You all don't mind, do you? Eating meatless meals, I mean?"

Clint could scarcely believe his eyes and ears when every last one of his brothers shook their heads and said, "No, we don't mind!" almost simultaneously. He scowled his displeasure at each of them. "All of you know very well that you like meat. How can you sit there and say you won't mind doing without it?"

Josh said, "Well, maybe a couple of times a week, one of us can cook, and on those nights, we can have meat."

"Do we get to eat eggs?" Cody asked glumly.

"Yes, of course," Rachel assured him. "And there's no meat in cake or cookies."

Cody brightened at that news. "We don't gotta have meat, Clint. Not if it makes Rachel sad to cook it."

Jeremiah looked as if he were about to bust with laughter. "We wouldn't want to be cruel to animals. I guess eating them qualifies."

Clint didn't see the humor. "Might I remind you that we're operating a cattle ranch here? We raise and sell beef."

Rachel looked appalled. "Oh, my, I never thought about it

like that. I suppose the cows are killed once they're sold, aren't they?"

"That's how folks who live in town get their hands on steak, Rachel. They buy cows raised on cattle ranches and butcher them." Clint set his teeth at the distress he read in her expression. Then, before he could stop himself, he added, "A lot of cows aren't butchered, though." He groped for another lie, anything to make her feel better about what he did for a living. "Dairies, for instance. Lots and lots of cows are sold to dairies."

"And a bunch are sold for breeding purposes!" Cole inserted.

"That's right," Daniel agreed. "Without plenty of bulls and cows left to reproduce, we'd have no newborn calves each spring."

Cody beamed a smile. "And they're used to make shoes and boots, too! So, see, Rachel? Not all of 'em get sold for steak."

Rachel touched a hand to her throat. "Oh, my . . . You know, I never stopped to think about it, but my opera pumps and high-button shoes are made out of leather."

Afraid she might try to convince them they should all go barefoot next, Clint broke in with, "This really is good stew, Rachel. What's that spice I taste?"

"Salt," Jeremiah supplied.

Clint reached for his glass of water to wash down the taste. "Mmm-mmm."

Eight

Shortly after the supper dishes were washed, Clint hustled the boys off to bed and maneuvered Rachel into the downstairs bedroom, which adjoined the parlor. With no lamp lit and only a few feeble moonbeams streaming through the double-hung window, he figured it was dark enough to undress without embarrassing her.

Rachel said nothing when he took off his shirt. But as he removed his gun belt and reached for his belt buckle, she let out a shrill squeak. "What're you doing?"

Clint froze. "Undressing?"

"Why?"

He circled that carefully, not at all sure he knew how to reply. "Well . . ." He sent a loaded look at the bed. "I usually do before I go to sleep." Not that he had any intention of sleeping. "Don't you?"

"But where is your nightshirt?"

"My what?"

"Your nightshirt. Surely you don't—" She broke off and swallowed. Even in the dimness, he saw her throat convulse. "Surely you don't sleep in your altogether."

Clint rubbed a hand over his face. It didn't take a genius to realize she was as nervous as a long-tailed cat in a roomful of rockers. He abandoned his intention to undress and stepped slowly across the room to her, taking care not to make any sudden moves. Judging by her pallor, which made her look sort of luminous in the moonlight, she was already scared half to death.

"I don't have a nightshirt," he informed her cautiously.

She looked scandalized to hear that. "You don't? Well . . . until you can purchase one, I suppose you'll have to sleep in your . . . in your unmentionables."

"My what?"

"Your"—she lowered her voice—"your underwear."

In the summer, Clint wore knee-length cotton underdrawers. Somehow he didn't think that was what she had in mind. "Rachel, honey, I'm not going to hurt you." He smoothed a tendril of dark hair away from her cheek. "In fact, I'm hopin' to make you feel real nice."

Her gaze skittered from his. "That's fine. I mean—well, I know about—well, you know." She airily waved one hand and then leaned slightly toward him, gave a little laugh, and whispered conspiratorially, "It's just that I'd rather not do it naked."

An ache of tenderness swelled in Clint's chest. He traced the hollow of her jaw with his thumb. "How are we going to manage, then?"

"With a minimum of fuss?"

He nearly chuckled. But gazing into her eyes, he read her fear and realized it wasn't all that funny. With a minimum of fuss? He had a feeling the slower he went and the fussier he was, the better it would be for her. Of course, she didn't know that.

She toyed nervously with the top button of her shirtwaist. "I also absolutely must insist that you buy a nightshirt, post-haste."

Clint imagined how his brothers would tease him if they saw him wearing one.

"We'll see. For now . . ." He caught her chin on the edge of his hand and tipped her face up for his kiss, confident that he could stir her to passion if only she would relax. Instead, she went as stiff as a twice-starched collar.

"Rachel," he scolded huskily, "don't be afraid."

"I'm not." She whispered the denial against his lips.

Settling a hand at her waist, Clint knew the instant he touched her that she was lying. Her body was rigid. Pressed close to her as he was, he could feel the rapidity of her breathing and imagined he could hear her heart pounding. He only hoped he could make her forget her girlish fears by kissing her.

He was about to try when a thump came from somewhere beyond the bedroom door. The next instant, an eerie wail echoed throughout the house. Then someone yelled, "Clint! Hurry! Somethin's wrong with Useless!"

By the time Rachel and Clint arrived in the kitchen, the dog had worked himself up to a full-fledged cacophony, his howls resounding. Instantly aware that the canine's belly was abnormally distended, Clint dropped to his knees.

"Oh, shit! The yeast dough! The poor bugger ate too much, and it wasn't done rising."

Cody gasped. "Is he gonna die?" he asked in a quavery voice.

"No," Clint assured him. "But I bet he's got one heck of a bellyache."

He glanced over his shoulder at Rachel, wishing he could return with her to the bedroom and finish what he'd started. One look into her wary blue eyes told him that it was probably a good thing he couldn't. It was too soon for a consummation of their marriage. She needed time to get to know him first, and it was his responsibility as her husband to see she got it. He might even have to give her as much as a month, perish the thought.

"It looks like I have to stay up and play nurse to Useless. Care to join me?"

She smiled, plainly grateful to be given a reprieve. "Sure."

So it was that the two of them prepared to spend their wedding night fully clothed, playing nursemaid to a sick dog. A little after midnight, Matt finally wandered home. After Clint informed him of his marriage to Rachel, Matt joined them in their vigil, taking a spot beside the dog on the floor. Initially things were tense: Rachel openly hostile, Matt sullen. Clint decided then and there that the two of them had to discuss the bad feelings between them, all of which seemed to revolve around Rachel's little sister Molly.

When encouraged to air her grievances against Matt, Rachel started off by accusing, "You deliberately led my sister on and then heartlessly humiliated her!"

Matt cried, "I did not!"

From there, the fight was on, with Clint playing referee. After the two combatants had vented their spleens, he was able to maneuver them into a more productive exchange, during which it was discovered that Molly had failed to tell Rachel the entire story.

"When she walked up to me on the boardwalk that afternoon, she had cotton stuffed into her dress," Matt explained.

"Cotton?" Rachel repeated blankly.

"Yeah." Matt gestured vaguely at his chest. "You know . . . to make herself look older."

Rachel's eyes went round with astonishment. "She didn't!"

Matt nodded grimly. "Some of the cotton was poking out, only she didn't know it," he elaborated. "Above her neckline. Everyone saw it. A couple of the younger boys started laughing. When Molly looked down and saw what was amusing them so much, she started to cry." In his earnestness, Matt stopped petting Useless and leaned forward to look her directly in the eye. "I did tell her to go home, Rachel, just like she says I did. But I didn't do it to be mean, and I didn't intend it to hurt her feelings. It was just—well, she was so embarrassed, I don't think she'd have had the presence of mind to move otherwise."

Clearly mortified, Rachel cupped a hand over her eyes. "Oh, dear . . . Cotton? Why would she do something so silly?" She shook her head. "No wonder she came home sobbing. She must have been humiliated to death. Why didn't she just tell me the truth? I would've understood. Instead, I've been blaming you."

"She was probably ashamed to tell you." Matt smiled slightly. "When we're that age, all of us do crazy things in the name of love. I even serenaded a girl under her bedroom window once."

"That isn't crazy, it's sweet."

Matt laughed. "You haven't heard me sing!" He glanced at Clint. "Your turn to share, brother. What crazy stunt did you pull?"

Clint chuckled. "Leave me out of this."

Rachel sighed and nibbled her lower lip. "I guess I owe you an apology, Matthew. I'm sorry my sister made such a pest of herself. It sounds as though she dogged your heels constantly."

"Oh, she wasn't that bad," Matt said. "Not for the most part, anyhow. Except for when she followed me into the bathing house. Three men smoking cigars dived under the water when they saw her, and I had to buy them all new smokes. I could've wrung her neck that time."

"The bathhouse? She followed you into the bathhouse? Oh, just you wait until my father hears. She won't be able to sit down for a week."

Matt began to look worried. "Maybe you shouldn't tell on her," he suggested. "I don't want her getting into trouble. She's just a kid. Kids do dumb things."

Matt's attempt to intervene on Molly's behalf completely won Rachel over. Her eyes took on a suspicious shine. "Maybe you're right. Being embarrassed in front of her friends was probably punishment enough." She glanced at Clint, then averted her face. "I feel really bad. After everything that's happened, and now I learn that Molly brought all her heartache on herself."

"All's well that ends well," Clint assured her.

"Ends well? You've suffered dearly for her antics. Here you are, married to me."

Clint smiled. "Like I said, all's well that ends well."

By morning, Useless was much improved, if not completely recovered. Still a little worried, Clint allowed the dog to remain in the house while he and Jeremiah went out to milk the cows and gather the eggs.

When the two older brothers exited the house, Cole and Daniel were already out in the yard getting that day's stove wood chopped and moved onto the porch. "What's Rachel fixin' for breakfast?" Cole called out as Clint passed by him en route to the barn.

"Biscuits!" Clint called back, hoping even as he spoke that Rachel's second attempt proved more edible than her first. "Since she was up all night, I said we could make do with hot biscuits and sorghum."

Cole made a face, but he took the disappointment in stride, accustomed as he was to eating whatever he could scrounge.

A few minutes later, as Clint made his way back to the house, Cole yelled, "Shouldn't've left Useless inside! He reared up on Rachel and knocked the gallon of sorghum out of her hands."

"It went all over everywhere," Daniel elaborated. "Rachel, the floor, the table. Talk about a mess. To top it all off, she got sidetracked tryin' to clean up the syrup and burned the biscuits."

Clint groaned. He entered the kitchen to find Rachel still on her hands and knees. By the looks of her face, he guessed she'd been crying. He knelt to help her, and within a few minutes, the majority of the sorghum was mopped up. Unfortunately, the stickiness had seeped into the unvarnished planks, and their shoes stuck to the floor when they walked across that spot.

"Well, this day is off to a wonderful start," Rachel said morosely. Then, out of the blue, she started to giggle.

Clint couldn't see what was so funny. Nothing had gone right since her arrival, after all. Then he realized that was exactly why she was laughing: because they were off to such a bad start. Leave it to Rachel to find some humor in that.

With a weary chuckle, he sank down on a bench. "Well, I guess if we make it through this, we can make it through anything."

Red in the face and holding her sides, she gave a breathless nod and then managed to squeak, "Oh, Clint! The bench. That's where I spilled more sorghum, and it wasn't wiped up yet!"

He reached back to feel and swore under his breath. "Well, hell." This time it was his turn to dissolve into laughter. He laughed until he ached. Until tears rolled down his cheeks. Until he was weak.

"Things have to get better," he finally managed to say. "They can't get worse."

Rachel could have told Clint that, around her, things could always get worse. Bad luck was to her what miracles had been to Jesus, and over the next few days, it seemed that fate was out to prove it. One morning as she walked from the chicken coop back to the house, she didn't see a piece of firewood one of the boys had dropped on the steps. When she tripped over the wood, she smashed every one of the eggs she'd just collected for breakfast. Since eggs were one of the few things she seemed able to cook without disastrous consequence, it was no small matter.

Her cooking . . . It wasn't just bad, it was awful. Since she still hadn't worked up the courage to tell anyone how blind she was, Rachel had no idea what Clint must think. That she was the stupidest creature ever born, she supposed. And she couldn't much blame him. One time she misread the labels on the storage barrels and accidentally used salt instead of sugar in an apple pie. Another time, she used three times the soda called for in a cookie recipe. It got so bad that Rachel wanted to duck every time anyone took a normal-sized bite of anything she cooked. Unless she remembered to taste things herself as she went along, she could never be sure she hadn't misread a recipe or mistaken one ingredient for another.

Unfortunately, her failures didn't occur only in the kitchen. In addition to being unable to follow a simple recipe accurately without her spectacles, Rachel soon discovered another flaw in her character: extreme absentmindedness. No matter how important the chore, if she allowed herself to be distracted midway, it was a sure bet she would forget whatever she had been doing, oftentimes with catastrophic results. On one such occasion, she had put a laundry tub full of white clothes on to boil over a fire out in the yard. As she stood there, stirring away and gazing off into a blur of nothingness, she heard Cody crying and abandoned her post to go find him. He was horribly upset, and she soon discovered why. Clint's birthday was coming on July sixteenth, and Cody had nothing to give him as a present.

Unable to bear seeing the six-year-old cry, Rachel applied herself to the task of cheering him up. Since they had an oversupply of old newspapers and plenty of flour, she suggested they make Clint a gift from papier-mâché. They had decided that a bowl to hold his pocket change would be an ideal gift, and Rachel was just mopping up Cody's last tears when a shout came from out in the yard. In a twinkling, she remembered her laundry. But by then it was too late. To say that it had gotten scorched was an understatement. Incinerated, more like.

Failure . . . It might not have been so hard to take if only she hadn't come to care so deeply, not just about Clint, with whom she strongly suspected she was falling in love, but about Cody and Matt and all the others. Each of Clint's brothers had become special to her in some way: Cody because he so desperately needed a mother, Matt because of his tendency to drink, and Cole because he needed help with his spelling, something Rachel was able to assist him with by having him spell out loud. The list went on and on. For the first time in her life, Rachel felt needed, truly needed. She wanted so badly to stay with the Raffertys, to feel as though she belonged with them, to know she wasn't just a temporary fixture. Instead, because of her continual bungling, she half expected Clint to send her packing. She certainly wouldn't have blamed him if he had.

To ensure that he didn't, Rachel made plans to bake him a special cake for his birthday—chocolate with fudge frosting—according to Cody, his absolute favorite. On the big day, everything went perfectly. The cake came out of the oven looking divine. Her frosting was flawless, exactly the right consistency. When everyone gathered around the table to eat, Rachel was so proud of herself she had tears in her eyes.

Then Clint took his first bite of cake. Though he was far too polite to let on, Rachel knew something was wrong by the way his eyes darkened.

"What?" she cried.

He waved a hand and tried to smile. "It's nothing," he managed. "Really, Rachel."

She didn't believe that for a second. She took a bite to see for herself. Salt. The frosting was delicious, but the cake itself tasted awful. Rachel nearly gagged. She couldn't imagine how Clint managed to sit there, pretending it wasn't so bad.

Suddenly, it was all just too much. In a twinkling, she remembered every disastrous mistake she'd made since coming there. Now, to add insult to injury, she had ruined Clint's birthday. Even Cody looked at her with accusing eyes.

"I'm sorry," she whispered to no one in particular. "I'm so—sorry."

The final blow occurred when Rachel turned to flee the house. Useless was lying on the floor behind her, and with tears blurring her already poor vision, she mistook him for a rug, tripped over him, and sprawled face first on the floor. Matt reached her first. He was the one to help her stand, the one to check her hands for scrapes and brush her off. The others hovered around, all of them making sympathetic noises, none of them saying what she needed to hear. What that might have been, Rachel didn't know. She just knew she was humiliated to the marrow of her bones.

Looking up at Matt through her tears, she remembered his saying that he'd once advised Molly to run along home, not because he wished to hurt her, but because she needed the prompting. For different reasons, Rachel wished he'd given her the same advice. Anything to have avoided this.

With agonized movements, she retreated toward the door. With each step she took, all their faces became less distinct. Except for Clint's, of course. His, she decided, had been carved in her heart, never to be forgotten, never to blur, no matter how far away she was from him.

With a low sob she couldn't stifle, she jerked open the door and fled. She couldn't go on like this. It wasn't just she who was suffering; all of them were.

Nine

For at least a full minute after Rachel fled from the house, no one spoke. Then everyone tried to say something at once. Clint held up his hands.

"I'll go get her."

Cody ran up to hug his leg. "Tell her it don't matter. We can make another cake."

"Sure we can!" Daniel agreed.

"She just needs more practice cooking," Jeremiah insisted.

Glancing around at all their faces, Clint realized that his brothers were as hopelessly in love with Rachel as he was, albeit in a different way. He ruffled Cody's hair. "I'll bring her back, tyke. Don't you worry." Glancing at Jeremiah, he added, "This could take a spell. While you guys are waiting, why don't you whip up another cake real fast?" He glanced meaningfully at Cody. "A birthday party just isn't a birthday party without cake."

Jeremiah nodded. "Sure, Clint. Just don't expect much. My cake may not taste much better than Rachel's."

Clint nearly said that *anybody's* cake would taste better

89

than Rachel's, but he bit back the words. The less said, the better, he decided.

He found Rachel hiding in the barn loft. She was weeping copiously, her sobs deep and tearing. Just listening to her was enough to break Clint's heart. Swinging a leg over the top ladder rung, he stepped off into the loose hay and made his way toward her. Where bales were missing, there was no bottom to the softness, and he lurched. Dust particles seared his nostrils.

The instant Rachel sensed his presence, she held her breath to stop crying. Crossing his ankles, he dropped to a sitting position beside her, propping his elbows on his knees. After a long moment, he said, "You know, Rachel, none of us care if you can cook."

With a catch in her voice, she cried, "What do you mean, you don't care? That's why you brought me here! To cook and clean and make the house nice."

"And you've done that." He recited a list of things she'd done. "Seeing Cody all cleaned up for supper every night, havin' flowers on the table and the place all shiny clean, those are the things that matter. You bein' a great cook doesn't."

"You're just saying that!" she said shakily.

Clint turned his hands to gaze at his palms. As he listened to her stifled sobs, he curled his fingers into tight fists. "Rachel, I'm not just saying it. You've no idea what it was like around here for the boys before you came. Daniel and Cody used to have terrible dreams almost every night about our folks dyin' and the hard times we went through after. Now they hardly ever wake up crying." He waited for a moment to let that sink in. "Your bein' here has given them a sense of security, that everything is okay in their world. And—" His throat went tight. "And, all that aside, I think I'm falling in love with you."

She went instantly silent and turned to look at him. Clint met her gaze steadily.

"You'll stop thinking so the minute you hear the truth," she informed him in a tremulous voice. "I'm not just a bungler, like you think. I can't see."

"Can't see what?"

"Anything! I'm nearly blind. To see, I have to wear spectacles over a half inch thick."

"I thought you said you didn't have poor eyesight."

She cast him a look that spoke volumes. "That wasn't a lie. My eyesight isn't poor, it's downright awful."

Clint regarded her for several long seconds, remembering all the times she'd looked up at him just as she was doing now. Before, he'd always believed she was enthralled and hanging on his every word. Now he realized she looked at him with that wide-eyed intentness because she was trying to *see* him.

"My God . . ." he whispered. There had been so many signs. Now that she'd told him the truth, he couldn't believe he'd been so blind. "Why haven't you been wearing your glasses then, sweetheart?"

"They got broken. I always carry them hidden in my skirt pocket and only sneak them out when I have to. When I fell in the church, they got shattered. At home I have extra pairs, but here I don't."

"You should've told me! I would have gone to town and gotten your spare spectacles, honey. I can't believe you've gone around all this time unable to see." He sighed. "As soon as I can get away—let me see—Saturday, I reckon. That's only four days. I'll take you into town and we'll get your spare spectacles. Can you wait that long?"

Her chin started to quiver, and her beautiful eyes filled with sparkling tears. "You wouldn't mind?"

"Mind what?"

"My wear—" Her voice broke. "The spectacles? How ugly they make me look? You wouldn't care?"

It hit Clint then, like a fist in his guts. This girl that he was coming to love so much had been badly hurt, and he had a nasty feeling it had been by a man. He caught her small chin in his hand. "Rachel, you couldn't look ugly if you tried."

"Yes," she squeaked.

That single word imparted a wealth of pain. Clint bent to kiss the tears from her cheeks. "Not in spectacles a half inch thick or even an inch thick. You're the most beautiful girl I've ever seen, Rachel, and I'd like to kill the bastard who told you otherwise. Who was he?"

"Nobody. Nobody important, anyhow. He left town after I told him about my eyes. He sort of eloped without me."

Word by word, Clint dragged the story out of her and then pieced it all together. It sounded to him as though Rachel had come perilously close to being seduced by an opportunistic scoundrel. She'd been fifteen, only a year older than her sister Molly. The man, a Bible salesman who peddled tonics on the side, had reneged on his promise to marry her when he realized she had poor eyesight. The way Clint saw it, that had probably been Rachel's lucky night. A man like that would have used her, then abandoned her along the wayside somewhere.

"No wonder you went after Matt with such vengeance when you thought he'd deliberately hurt Molly." Clint drew her into his arms. "You were getting revenge for yourself as well." He ran a hand up her back. "Ah, Rachel. So many wasted tears. Don't cry any more, sweetheart. I'll think you gorgeous in spectacles, I promise."

"You will?"

"Absolutely."

She sniffed. "I won't wear them except for when I have to. Like when I'm cooking and stuff." She drew back slightly. "I'm really not a bungler that often when I can see what I'm doing."

Clint smiled slightly. "You can wear your eyeglasses all

you want. I'll be so busy thinking about other things when I look at you, I probably won't notice."

"What other things?"

"Let me show you." It was all the opening Clint needed. Bending his head, he settled his mouth over hers. "Oh, yes, Rachel, girl," he whispered against her lips. "Let me show you."

Rachel . . . As their kiss deepened, her name was like a song in Clint's mind. He peeled off his shirt and spread it over the hay to protect her from the scratchiness. Then, so sweetly he could scarcely credit it, she surrendered to him. Over the years, Clint had heard lovemaking described in every possible way, but this was the first time he had ever thought of it as sacred.

That was how it seemed with Rachel, sacred. She was like an angel in his arms. A silken, wonderfully warm little angel who made all his dreams come true. Never had he seen anyone so beautiful. Ivory skin. Full, perfectly shaped breasts with rosy tips that tasted like nectar. A slender waist, just perfect for his hands. Gently flared hips. Long, shapely legs. Clint went over every inch of her and decided there wasn't a single thing about her he would change. Including her eyes . . .

He made love to her carefully, taking his time, lingering over her body to make certain she was as aroused as he was before he took her. It was the most incredible joining he had ever experienced, and judging by Rachel's cries of elation, she felt the same way.

Contentment . . . Utter fulfillment. Afterward, Clint held her in his arms, wishing they could stay right where they were and make love again and again. Instead he would have to pluck the hay from her hair and take her back to the house for his birthday party. Wasn't that a fine kettle of fish? The only present he really wanted was to make love to his wife again, which he probably wouldn't be able to do until everyone in the family went to bed that night.

Ah, but then, what a birthday celebration he would have. Clint sighed and pressed his lips against Rachel's temple, promising himself he would make love to her all night, that dawn would find her still whimpering with pleasure in his arms.

The sun was just peeking over the horizon when Rachel opened her eyes the next morning. As usual, Clint's side of the bed was empty. Running her hand caressingly over the sheet, she found it still warm from the heat of his long, lean body. Even as the memory of last night's coupling ran through her, the familiar sound of the rustling husks under her fingers made her smile. While making love to her, Clint had cursed the husks for the noise they made and suggested they get a feather-tick mattress as soon as possible. When she had pointed out how many chickens would have to die to fill a mattress with feathers, he'd nearly laughed until he cried. Then he'd settled back down to making love to her again. Sweet, wonderful love.

Finally, after a month of tension and nervous, sidelong glances, he'd decided to make love to her. And make love he had, taking her higher and higher until she was drenched in the purest bliss.

Even though her experience was admittedly limited, she was sure now that no wanton could have responded more totally. And, oh, how glorious it had felt to surrender to the man she loved.

She was well and truly a woman now. A woman desperately, totally, and forever in love with her husband. Her smile took on soft edges, and she let her eyes drift closed. Deep inside, where the sweetest of sensations still throbbed ever so gently, she felt different. Changed. And yes, beautiful.

All because Clint had touched her where she'd never been

touched before. And kissed her. And fused his hard, strong body with hers until she'd nearly exploded with the pleasure and joy of it.

She'd expected pain, and he'd given her ecstasy. She'd be prepared for disappointment and found herself soaring. She'd feared a maidenly embarrassment, and instead had found herself entranced. Desire rose in her again like a river of warm honey, and, suddenly restless, she stretched out her legs. Beneath the faded quilt, her skin tingled, eager to feel again the slow stroking touch of Clint's big hand.

Lifting drowsy lids, she looked toward the window where a blur of pink and gold promised a glorious sunrise and an even more glorious day. A good day for outside chores, she thought, pleased that she was beginning to think like a rancher's wife.

After all, a rancher's wife was just as involved with the successful functioning of the place as any hired hand. More so, she thought, thinking of the mountains of clean clothing required by eight men, not to mention the victuals they needed to fuel those active Rafferty bodies. Clint and Jeremiah had more fence wire to string today, and Zach needed to finish patching the roof on the chicken house. She herself had a mound of ironing to tackle right after breakfast, and she really should get to the mending today. And then there was bread to make, and while Cody was busy helping Daniel muck out the stable, she would try once more to bake him that mess of cookies he wanted so desperately.

An annulment? Not on her life. She threw off the quilt with a newfound confidence. So what if she wasn't the greatest cook in the county and the kitchen floor always seemed to need sweeping? Clint smiled a lot more often than he frowned these days, and Cody was thriving. She'd even heard Josh whistling in the bathtub Saturday night, and Matt hadn't spent a Sunday nursing a hangover for more than three weeks running. As for Daniel, that boy was going to break hearts someday.

All because there was a woman in the house. A married woman, she thought, reaching for her bloomers. A wife and mother.

A mother? Dear God, it was possible now. More than possible. Holding her breath, she reverently placed a hand over the slight swell of her belly. Oh, it would be so wonderful to know that a baby was already growing inside her. Clint's baby.

Tears came to her eyes at the thought of giving him a child of his own, perhaps a dark-haired little girl with the lopsided Rafferty grin she adored. A sweet-smelling, pink-cheeked daughter, maybe even a whole passel of pigtailed little girls to spoil him rotten. After all he'd sacrificed for his brothers, all the backbreaking hours of labor he'd put in to keep them fed and clothed and safe, he deserved to be pampered a little.

As she dressed hurriedly, she envisioned this same house with cheery wallpaper covering the rough-hewn logs and the happy laughter of children mingling with the deeper chuckles of adoring uncles. At Christmastime, Clint would play Santa Claus. And on Easter Sunday, after they'd all trooped home from church, Cody and Daniel would hide the colored eggs while she prepared perfectly brewed coffee and feather-light biscuits. And then, they would watch as the little ones searched for the eggs, one huge, happy family of Raffertys. Later, when everyone was bedded down, she and Clint would come together in this same bed. Their marriage bed.

Still smiling, she tied her hair away from her face with a plaid taffeta ribbon as bright as her mood and headed for the kitchen. Her family needed her.

Ten

"Oh, no!"

Rachel raced across the kitchen, waving away smoke as she went. Using her apron as a pot holder, she jerked open the oven door and snatched the cookie sheet from the rack. She'd failed again. In place of the deliciously browned gingerbread men she'd envisioned as she'd mixed and rolled and formed the batter, she had contorted lumps of burned, foul-smelling dough.

After starting the day so positively, Rachel could scarcely believe things had gone sour so quickly. A ranch wife, was she? Sick with disappointment, she carried the ruined cookies to the open window and tossed them onto the dirt. At the same time, she saw Clint heading with long, impatient strides toward the porch. "Dammit, Rachel, are you trying to burn the house down?" he called teasingly when he caught sight of her at the window.

"It isn't funny, Clint Rafferty!" she shouted back. "I swear I did everything right this time, and they just up and burned. I even had Cody read the recipe to me three times so I'd be sure not to make a mistake. I think it's the dad-blamed stove, that's what I think. I hate the darned old thing!"

97

"Now, darlin'," Clint began as he entered the kitchen, only to stop dead when she whirled toward him, her eyes huge and wisps of soft brown hair curling against her neck where it had escaped the ribbon.

"It *is* the stove," she declared, waving her hand toward the smoke that billowed from the oven. "Not even God himself could produce a decent meal on that . . . monster."

Clint only just managed to keep from grinning. "Guess it is a mite old at that, but Sam Butts at the mercantile swore it was in good working order when he sold it to me."

"Old," she insisted, her slightly narrowed eyes darting blue daggers, first toward the stove and then toward him. "That contraption was *old* when Methuselah was still a boy."

"Did you test the temperature by sprinkling flour on the bottom of the oven?"

"Of course I did! It's the stove, I tell you."

"And when you checked the flour to see how brown it was, could you see it clearly?"

She gestured vaguely with a hand. "Sort of."

The smoke had cleared enough now that Clint could see her cheeks, and he couldn't help but admire the lovely pink they were suddenly turning. And with each agitated breath she took, her breasts pushed against the thin material of her pretty blue shirtwaist.

He advanced slowly, careful to keep his expression sober. But Lord save his sorry hide, she was pretty when she got upset. And almost as pretty when she wasn't, come to think of it. He could have done a lot worse for himself. Hell, he still couldn't believe his luck.

"Well, if you're right, I guess we'll just have to add a new stove to our list," he offered in as sincere a tone as he could manage. "Right after I buy a new pair of spectacles for my nearsighted little wife." When she shot him another glare, he held up a staying hand. "Just on the off chance it's your eyes that's the problem and not the stove. If you can't see to do a proper sprinkle test, honey, it's a little hard to get the oven temperature just right. Not saying that's the case."

Her soft mouth firmed, and her chin hiked a little higher. "But I was so careful!"

Clint's heart caught at the pain in her eyes. To him it was just a sheet of burned gingerbread, but to Rachel it obviously meant a lot more. "It isn't your fault. Once we go to town and get your spare spectacles, stuff like this won't happen anymore."

"I promised Cody gingerbread and milk when he finished his chores."

Her lips quivered ever so slightly before she turned away. In the past, Clint had had a busy man's impatience with displays of emotion. Not only were they nonproductive and time-consuming, but he'd always considered them to be a surefire sign of weakness. With Rachel, however, he couldn't quite manage to feel impatient. He guessed he should thank the good Lord he'd never had sisters. They would have all been spoiled rotten.

"Cody'll understand," he said, turning her toward him again. His breath caught when he saw tears dulling the vibrance of those out-of-focus blue eyes.

"No, he won't, and I don't blame him," she murmured, lowering her gaze to the level of his chest. "A promise is a promise."

Unable to resist, Clint slid his arms around her waist and pulled her closer, remembering as he did how soft and warm her skin felt against his palms. And how eagerly she'd welcomed him into the moist cradle of her thighs.

"Then we'll make more," he found himself promising, and in a voice so husky it sounded alien. "I'll help you."

She smiled a little at that before shaking her head. "There's no more flour," she murmured, bringing one hand up to rest against his midriff. "At least none I'd want to use."

Cupping her face, he nudged her chin higher, waiting

until her gaze found his before he gently asked, "What happened?"

She shook her head, and he found himself wanting to kiss her so badly he was all knotted up inside. All morning long he'd been looking for an excuse to ride back to the house. And her. Not so much to kiss her again, though that was on his mind, but more to make sure he hadn't imagined the look of pure happiness he'd seen in her eyes over breakfast. It wasn't every day a man found himself in danger of busting his buttons out of sheer male pride, but damn, he felt good. Just knowing he'd been the first to see that creamy skin in lamplight put a lump the size of an egg in his throat.

Damn, he loved her. Not that he was anywheres near ready to say that out loud. Last night he'd gone so far as to tell her he *thought* he was falling in love with her, but that was a far cry from admitting he was already a goner. A man had to consider the consequences before he gave up that much of himself, especially to a woman who'd been so reluctant to share his name—and so nervous about sharing his bed.

"Tell me what happened to the flour," he urged, more to hear the music of her voice than from any burning curiosity.

"You'll think I'm hopeless."

Using his thumb, he brushed away a smudge of flour from her chin and felt her tremble. Her skin was supple and warm, her milk-white flesh rose-petal soft. Beneath the plain blue skirt that hid all but the toes of her shoes, her thighs were sleek and delectably plump, her calves perfectly formed, her ankles trim. Tonight, when the lamp was turned low and the door locked, he would lap every inch of her with his tongue, and she would make that little growling sound in her throat again.

His body swelled against the fly of his jeans. "I think you're adorable."

"No, I'm not. I'm clumsy and nearsighted and I can't sew a straight seam."

"You just need your glasses and a little practice, that's all."

Rachel felt a little flutter in the vicinity of her heart. Though it hurt to admit it, even to herself, she craved Clint's approval. Almost as much as she craved his love.

Even so, she forced herself to be honest. Despite the fact that their marriage had been precipitated by trickery, or perhaps because it had, she desperately wanted their life together to be based on mutual trust. Still, it took her three gulping deep breaths before she was able to blurt out, "I tripped over the train you carved for Cody and, uh . . . dropped the flour crock."

"It broke?"

She nodded and said, "It took me an hour to get the flour swept out of the floor cracks. And while I was busy doing that, Useless stole the chicken Daniel plucked for tonight's dinner."

"You let Daniel kill a chicken?"

"Oh, no. The poor thing died of old age. That's why it's so awful that Useless stole it. I mean, it's probably not very often that a chicken just up and dies like that."

"Probably more often than you think. Every spring we buy batches of chicks, all at the same time, so when they get old and start keelin' over, they tend to go one right after another. I wouldn't be surprised if another one isn't breathin' its last right this minute. We might have chicken for supper yet."

"Only if I don't let Useless steal the meat!"

"Heaven help us," Clint drawled, his eyes taking on a sudden twinkle within the frame of his sin-black lashes.

"That's just it, Clint. I'm beginning to think that not even Gabriel and all his archangels can make me into the kind of wife you deserve."

His firm mouth twitched at the corners. Then it curved slowly into a lopsided, boyish grin. The look in his eyes, however, was hot enough to heat her blood.

"Far as I'm concerned you can burn gingerbread from now till doomsday, Rachel, and I'll not offer one word of complaint," he said in that gravelly voice she had come to love. "Not so long as you keep snugglin' that nice little fanny of yours up against me of a night."

He skimmed a hand up her side to her breast. His fingers were hard, his touch gentle as he cupped her flesh. "As for the damned flour, it isn't your fault Cody left his train layin' out."

Though two layers of clothing prevented skin from caressing skin, she began to burn where his hand pressed. "Mmm," was all she could manage as a response.

"As for the stolen chicken, I guess I could shoot Useless," he offered.

Unable to restrain herself, Rachel arched toward him and at the same time encircled his strong brown neck with her arms. "Just kiss me," she whispered, drawing him down to her.

His groan shuddered against her parted lips a split second before his mouth closed over hers. His lips were hot, his breath moist, his tongue arrogantly demanding.

Rachel felt her heart begin to race and a dull roaring filled her ears, as eagerly, desperately, she arched against him, her body responding as though driven by a will of its own. She exulted in the harsh rasp of his breathing.

When his hands tugged her shirtwaist free, she gasped. When his fingertips sought her breast again, she moaned. Between hard, eager kisses, she tore at the buttons of the chambray shirt he'd plucked straight from the ironing basket that morning.

Just as her shirtwaist fell open, she heard a sound. A voice, calling Clint's name. A woman's voice. He jerked free, his hands instinctively drawing her against the protection of his big chest, even as he turned toward the sound.

Heart thundering, and lungs starved for air, Clint fought to clear his head. He knew that voice. . . .

"Clinton? Is that you?"

"Aunt Hester?" he said in stunned disbelief, a split second before his aunt's rotund form filled the doorway.

Like a plump blackbird spreading its wings, his aunt, dressed head to toe in mourning, held her arms out at her sides. "I got your letter, and here I am, come to keep your house and help raise those dear great-nephews of mine!"

Eleven

Rachel poked her fork forlornly at the stewed turnips remaining on her plate, unable to force another bite past the bitter lump lodged in her throat. To her right, Cody was busily gnawing the last few shreds of meat from his second chicken leg. To her left, Matt was shoveling down his third piece of sour lemon pie. Rachel had to admit that prior to Aunt Hester's arrival two days ago, the boys had never eaten so heartily nor praised the food more fulsomely. Even Clint had taken to coming to the table with an eager glint in his eyes.

Oh, he never came right out and said he preferred Aunt Hester's cooking to the pathetic offerings *she'd* put on the table, but the signs of his newfound contentment were so obvious that even she, blind as she was without her spectacles, could see them.

Take this morning, for example, she thought, stabbing her fork at another perfectly cooked turnip slice. Why, the man had actually waxed poetic over his portly aunt's buttermilk biscuits. His brothers had been too busy to comment in kind, engaged as they had been, slathering on strawberry jam that

Hester had brought with her from Ohio. The mound of biscuits had disappeared from the basket in a trice—unlike *her* biscuits, which generally lasted a good three days.

"There's more pie, boys," Aunt Hester sung out from her place to Clint's right.

"I'll have another piece," Cole said eagerly, shoving his plate forward.

"Me, too, Aunt Hester," Cody shouted. "I ain't never tasted anything so good."

Aunt Hester beamed as she slid huge slabs of pie onto each of their plates. "Clint? There's one last piece of pie here with your name on it."

"No, thanks, Aunt Hester." Clint put down his fork and leaned back. "But like Cody said, that's about as good as pie gets."

"Why thank you, Nephew. That's just about the nicest compliment a lady can get from a gentleman."

At that, Matt leaned close to Rachel's ear to whisper, "Remind me to use that line on Dora Faye next time I'm in the Golden Goose."

Rachel gave his booted foot a good kick, which only served to widen his wicked grin. "Careful, Sis," he whispered, offering her a broad wink. "That there's the foot I use to prop up the bar of a Saturday night."

Seeing his brother cozying up to Rachel like a stallion sniffing heat would normally put Clint into a foul mood, but with his belly full of his aunt's good cooking he was too mellow to do more than scowl a warning in Matt's direction.

For some reason he couldn't fathom, Rachel seemed different since Aunt Hester's sudden arrival. Though he wasn't partial to analyzing emotions—his or anyone else's—he couldn't help noticing how quiet she'd turned, like an unshielded lamp suddenly extinguished by an unexpected gust of wind.

Rubbing a hand across his belly, he thought back to the

scolding Aunt Hester had given him her first night on the place. "Why, the poor girl is plumb worn to a nub," she'd chastized. "Trying to handle a house full of rowdy men and deal with all their trappings is more than a new bride should have to do."

Maybe Aunt Hester was right, Clint thought, staring the length of the table at his wife's bowed head. Unlike other nights when she'd been slaving over steaming pots, her shiny brown hair was neatly tied back by a plain black ribbon, and her white shirtwaist was crisp with fresh starch and neatly tucked. Damned if she didn't look as young and innocent as a school girl, he thought, covertly eyeing the swell of her breasts under the modest attire.

Guilt stabbed him hard, reminding him of all that he and his brothers had demanded of her these past weeks. Hell, he'd brought her home to a pigsty and all but insisted she turn it into a home. And without much help, if truth were told. At least, not much from him.

But that was about to change. Now that Aunt Hester had a good hold on the running of the house, Rachel would have more time for fun. In a day or two, the branding would be done and he'd be able to take some time off. If he got a decent price for the beef this year, he might be able to treat Rachel to a few days in San Francisco. He'd heard tell of some right fancy hotels, with beds soft enough even for her delicate skin.

Just thinking about the two of them stealing off alone had his blood heating. Aunt Hester's arrival had put a crimp in his lovemaking, no doubt about it. This winter, he would build on another bedroom for himself and Rachel that would afford them a little more privacy, but for now he couldn't help worrying about making noise. The boys had all moved into two of the sleeping areas upstairs, leaving the third empty for Aunt Hester. But that didn't put the woman far enough away to suit Clint. Those damned corn husks! They crinkled every time a man so much as wiggled a toe.

Which was why Clint looked forward to a stay in San Francisco like a parched man did drink. Lord, but Rachel'd be a pretty sight with her hair spread out on one of those lacy hotel pillows.

"Aunt Hester's promised to make me cookies after the dishes are done," Cody piped up between bites. His announcement jerked Clint from his mental meanderings back to the present. "Didn't you, Aunt Hester?"

"I recollect I did," Hester acknowledged with a nod of her graying head.

"I'll help," Rachel volunteered, rising quickly to take up her still half-filled plate.

"No!" chorused Cody and Daniel before exchanging sheepish looks.

"Uh, that is, you're lookin' kind of tired tonight," Daniel amended quickly. "Ain't that right, Clint?"

Still clutching her plate, Rachel squinted the length of the table at the blur she knew to be her husband.

"Actually, I was just thinkin' she looked particularly tidy tonight," Clint drawled.

Tidy? Rachel glanced down at the plain black skirt more suited for a matron of advanced years than a bride. She'd worn it because the wide sash reduced her waist to a mere wisp, something she'd heard men found irresistible. Instead, Clint thought she looked *tidy*. Lord, he might as well stand up in church and declare her a miserable failure as a wife *and* lover.

The lump in her throat took on sharp edges. Just when she had finally begun to feel at home, the family she'd grown to love was letting her know how little they valued her. "I suppose I should really attend to the mending—"

"Bless your heart for offering, but there's no need," Aunt

Hester interrupted in her hearty midwestern twang. "Since I had a few spare minutes, I managed to finish the last of it before supper."

Rachel blinked, seeing the overloaded mending basket in her mind's eye. It had always seemed like an unscalable mountain. "All of it? The socks, too?"

Though she couldn't see Aunt Hester's face, she could hear her answering chuckle. "Why, child, it wasn't such a chore, not when a body knows what she's doing."

Which I don't, Rachel thought, turning away from the table.

Just a few minutes before noon the following day, Clint came in from the fields in hopes of stealing Rachel away on a nice long ride for a picnic. For dessert, he planned to make wild and noisy love to her. As he entered the kitchen, he slapped the dust from his hat and tossed it onto the table. Aunt Hester was outside boiling linen, and the house seemed strangely quiet. Too quiet, come to think of it.

"Rachel? Where are you, girl?" Hearing no answer, he strode impatiently toward the master bedroom, his boot heels thudding noisily on the freshly waxed planks. "Rachel?"

The door stood open. Inside, where the knotty pine bedstead gleamed under a fresh coat of polish, the rag rugs were almost bright as new and the windows actually sparkled. Aunt Hester had worked her magic once more, and Clint allowed himself a rare moment of self-congratulation. Despite temporary inconveniences because of inadequate sleeping arrangements, writing to Aunt Hester had been a stroke of genius, sure enough. Finally, he had the smoothly running home he'd craved. Once he got a master bedroom built onto the existing house, everything would be perfect.

As Clint moved into the immaculate bedroom, he thought it seemed too empty. Even the dresser that had held Rachel's female doodads looked a little too naked for his peace of mind. Alarm snaked through him, settling its coils around his gut and squeezing hard. Heart tripping, he strode to the armoire and tore open the door. Rachel's side was empty. There wasn't a fussy shirtwaist or leg-of-mutton sleeve or long skirt in sight. Even the jumble of small shoes in the bottom had disappeared.

"Shit!"

Leaving the armoire door open, he turned to the chiffonier and jerked open the drawers one by one. All empty, save for the last which held his long johns and socks. Damn the woman's hide; she had a wagon load of explaining to do.

Seconds later Clint strode furiously across the yard toward his aunt. "Have you seen my wife?" he demanded, planting his feet wide and jamming hard fists on his hips.

Aunt Hester finished pinning one of Cody's shirts to the line before turning her gaze in his direction. "Last I seen, she was riding out of here on a bay mare with all her belongings strapped on the rump," she declared, her mouth tugged down by the weight of her glum mood. "Riding astride, I might add, with her petticoats hiked clear to her knees and her bloomers displayed for the whole county to see."

Clint snapped a fast look at the rutted trail heading toward town. Whatever dust Rachel had raised had long since settled, and the only thing moving between him and the distant horizon were swaying pine trees.

"Why?" he muttered, forgetting for a moment he wasn't alone.

"Don't know the why of it myself. I asked, mind. But all she gave me was a damned fool answer."

"Which was?"

"That she kept up her end of the bargain, but now that I'm here, she don't have to anymore." Hester fastened worried eyes on him. "Nephew, never mistake it. I'd rather leave than cause trouble between you and your missus. I guess, in my eagerness to make myself needed, I might've started off a little strong. Maybe she felt like I was pushing her out."

"That's ridiculous," Clint bit out. And he truly believed it was. "You've been nothin' but sweet and kind since you've been here, Aunt Hester. If Rachel felt shoved out, it was because she wanted to feel that way."

His aunt didn't look reassured. "Sometimes we women see things a little different than you men." She sighed, snapping the wrinkles from a shirt. "She said to tell you to pick up the mare at the livery, by the way, rather than at her house."

That news only added more fuel to Clint's mounting rage. So, she didn't wish to see him, did she? Not even for the few short minutes it would take for him to pick up the horse? Well, fine. That was just fine.

He raked a hand through his hair, his temper aboil and his gut tight. Damn it to hell, no woman was worth this kind of aggravation, especially when he'd been as patient as a man could be.

"I expect you're aiming to go after her," Aunt Hester said.

Damn straight he was going after her, Clint thought, clenching his teeth so hard something popped alongside his jaw. She was his wife, wasn't she? She belonged here with him. In his bed—

Shit! Maybe his lovemakin' wasn't as great as he liked to think. Could be he hadn't been patient enough with her that first time. Or skilled enough, for that matter. Given his limited experience with women, he'd tried his best to do right by her. But maybe his best hadn't been good enough. Especially not after those first nights, what with Aunt Hester listening in, and all.

Clint stared off into the distance, his throat stinging so sharply with unshed tears, he felt about as old as Cody. Was that the reason Rachel'd hightailed it back to her da at the first opportunity? Because he had disappointed her? Shame scalded his insides, burning deeper and deeper until he damn near doubled over. If a man couldn't satisfy his woman in bed, he didn't *deserve* to keep her.

"No, I'm not aimin' to go after her," he said in belated answer to his aunt's question.

"But, Nephew, that's just plain—"

"No buts, Aunt Hester. I'm not goin' after her. I have better things to do."

Squaring his shoulders, he turned away and headed for the barn. He was a Rafferty, damn it. Rafferty men had pride. Rafferty men didn't beg any woman to stay if she really wanted to leave. But, damn, it hurt.

Clint shoved open the bat-wing doors and headed into the Golden Goose. The monthly cattlemen's meeting had lasted longer than usual, and remembering how he'd met Rachel after the last meeting a little over two months ago, he'd been so tense all evening, his throat was raw with thirst. Squinting in the smoke and lamp oil haze, he cast a look-see toward the bar, half expecting to spot Matt or one of his other brothers bending an elbow. This time he saw only Dora Faye. Judging by her scowl, she wasn't planning to lay out any welcome.

"You got your nerve comin' here tonight, Clint Rafferty," she said when he drew up next to her.

"How so?" he asked before signaling the barkeep to bring him a bottle. "Rye," he amplified. "The kind you keep on hand for bankers and politicians." He flicked Dora Faye a glance. "And two glasses."

"One," she corrected in a trice. "I'm particular about who I drink with."

Clint shoved back his hat. "Meaning you ain't interested in drinkin' with me?"

She turned her back to the bar and rested her elbows on the polished surface. Another time Clint might have enjoyed the snowy expanse of female bosom above the gaudy lace of her cheap green dress. Tonight, however, he had one thing on his mind, and one thing only—pouring enough whiskey down his throat to take away the empty feeling in his belly. Now he knew how his da must have felt after losing his ma. Hollow clear to his marrow. Not really caring if he lived or died. Rachel had been gone a month now, and every second had been an agony for him.

"Suit yourself," he said to Dora Faye as he tipped the bottle over the glass. A second later, he slugged down the liquor. Five drinks later, some of the knots in his mood had come untangled, but not all.

"For someone claimin' she's not eager for my company, you sure are hangin' fast to my shirttails," he told the soiled dove sourly.

"Only so's I can tell you what an ass I think you are. You broke Rachel's heart, you bastard."

Clint bit down hard. "The hell I did," he retorted. This time when he poured, his hand wasn't as steady as it should have been. And when he downed the triple shot, the whiskey had suddenly acquired a foul bite. Or was it loneliness he was tasting?

"She's lost weight since she come home. Big Jim's at his wit's end."

Clint tapped the bottle with a forefinger. "Sure you won't have a drink?" he offered, trying to ignore what she said. "There's plenty left." A good half jug, by his reckoning. Too much to waste.

"Last time I saw her at the mercantile, her eyes were all red from crying."

Clint poured faster this time, slopping the equivalent of a shot on the bar. Shrugging, he swiped his forearm across the spill, then downed the whiskey that *had* ended up in the jigger. No good. He could still see Rachel's face on the pillow, her thick brown hair spread like a dark angel cap on the slightly singed linen.

"Nobody told her to go," he muttered, his voice whiskey thick.

"Maybe not in so many words," Dora Faye exclaimed in a low hissing whisper. "But a woman as sensitive as Rachel can read between the lines."

"What the devil are you talkin' about?" Clint demanded, his head beginning to swim ever so slightly.

"You jackass! I'm talkin' about that bully of an aunt you imported."

Clint drew his head back and squinted down his nose at his red-headed accuser. It took a full second to get her face in good focus, and then he realized he liked it better when he couldn't see the green sparks shooting out of her eyes. Was this the way Rachel felt without her glasses? he wondered. Like the whole world was on the opposite side of fogged glass?

"Bully? Aunt H—Hester?" Damned if the whiskey hadn't numbed his tongue instead of his head. "Is that what Ra— Rachel told you?"

"Not in so many words, but I could tell she was hurting." She poked a finger at his chest. "Rachel gave everything she had to that ungrateful family of yours, and what did she get back? Not so much as a 'thank you, ma'am' or a 'don't let the door hit you where the good Lord split you.'"

"Where the good Lord what? Now wait just a minute—"

She jabbed a finger at his nose this time. "So she can't cook as good as a woman who's been doing it for thirty years or more? She tried her best, didn't she? And maybe she did singe a few underdrawers, but that don't mean you boys didn't have clean clothes when you needed 'em, along with a smile and a cheery word when you come home tired and hungry."

"I never said—"

"That's just it, you fool cowboy. You never *said* nothing she needed to hear, like how much you appreciated her tryin' so hard. Or how nice it was that she was there when you come home, or how pretty she looked, or how sweet it was at night to pull her close." She paused to haul in a breath. "Instead, you washed your hands of her the minute you didn't need her any more. Even in the bedroom, behind closed doors, you worthless toad."

Recalling the nights after his aunt's arrival when he'd felt too self-conscious to make proper love to his wife, Clint felt heat sear his cheeks. "What occurs between a man and his wife behind closed doors is no concern of yours," he muttered, staring at the amber liquid in the bottom of his glass.

"Pathetically little happened for you to keep secret, from what I heard! Crinkling corn husks, my hiney."

Clint stared at her in amazement. "Is *that* why she left? Because I was worried about makin' noise and wasn't very—well, you know?"

"That and other things. Like maybe because you never told her you loved her. Don't deny it. If you had, she never would of left, not in a million years."

Clint bristled at that. "I did so! Plain as can be! I told her several times."

"Not according to Rachel. She says you told her you *thought* maybe you did."

Clint had no answer for that. Thinking back on it, he recalled now that he had skirted the issue, telling Rachel he thought he loved her, but never saying he knew it for certain. "That still didn't give her any call to leave," he said under his breath.

Dora Faye, who glared at him nearly nose to nose, caught the words. "Oh, really? And what would have convinced her to stay, you stubborn mule? You married her for her talents as a housekeeper. As I understand it, you never made any bones about it, not from the very first, and Rachel feels like she failed you at every turn." When Clint tried to protest, she waved him to silence. "Her words, not mine. After good old Aunt Hester showed up, she didn't feel needed anymore.

In fact, she felt like she'd done such a miserable job that you were all hoping she'd leave."

"That is *not* so."

A pulse throbbed in Dora Faye's temple. "She thinks you wish you'd never married her in the first place."

"That's silly."

"Is it? I don't think so. And after you think about it, I don't think you will, either." She fixed him with those fiery green eyes of hers for a long moment. "She's leavin' on Monday, you know. Goin' back east to stay with some relatives and go to some kind of school. And why wouldn't she? Now that you've tossed her back, she has no hope for making a life here in Shady Corners."

Twelve

The church seemed to be unusually crowded for early services. Rachel stood just outside the doors with her father and sister, held back by the press of people trying to move en masse into the church. Molly kept standing on tiptoe, craning her neck to see. "I wonder what's happening?" she asked for at least the dozenth time.

"I have no idea," Rachel replied.

"Well, I'm going to find out!" her father vowed.

He began shoving his way through the crowd, cutting a path for Rachel and Molly in his wake. They fell in after him like farmers behind a plow. Just inside the church doors, Rachel realized the interior of the building seemed oddly quiet. Once people got inside, they usually visited right up until the preacher stepped to his pulpit. She strained to see over the shoulders of men, wondering why the crowd seemed to have gathered at the back of the church.

When at last her father had worked his way through the throng, Rachel felt sure she would discover what was holding everyone back from finding their seats. But at first glance around the church, she saw nothing unusual.

"Hells bells, there she is. Took you long enough, darlin'. We were about to give up on you."

Rachel's heart leaped. She would have recognized Clint's voice anywhere. She homed in on the sound and finally made out his blurry outline. He was sitting on the floor, almost precisely where the two of them had been discovered together that other ill-fated morning over two months ago. His back was supported by the rear church pew, one knee raised so he might rest his arm. Beside him sat a jug of liquor.

"Folks, may I present to you my wife?"

Her only thought to get out of there, Rachel pivoted to leave. But the crowd had closed ranks behind her, and there was no way out.

"You can't run from me, Rachel. Hightail it, and I swear I'll come after you."

She turned back to find that he had pushed to his feet. "Why are you doing this?" she asked thinly.

"The way I hear it, you're planning to leave town. I thought maybe I should clear up a few things before you take off."

"What things?" she asked expressionlessly.

"Like the fact that I love you." He took a step toward her." And that I think you're beautiful and sweet and absolutely wonderful. And that's not to mention that I can't live without you."

Rachel felt her skin pinken, and she lowered her gaze to the floor. "Oh, Clint, don't."

"Oh, Clint, don't? Why not? Do you think I want to lose you? Dammit, Rachel, you had no business runnin' off without talkin' to me. Do you think I care that much if Aunt Hester makes good pies? Hell, no. I like pie as much as the next man, but I can live without it, and so can my brothers. What we can't do without is the heart of our family. The love and the laughter. Havin' someone around who'll leave the laundry tub to boil dry if we need her. Someone to tell stories. Hell, even Useless misses you."

She squeezed her eyes closed. "You don't need me. None of you do!"

"Matt's drinkin' again!" he bit out. "And last night I joined him. Cody's got the nightmares again, too. To top that all off, there's beef and venison hangin' in the smokehouse again, and I gotta tell you that neither the buck or the steer died of old age. And there's chickens gettin' their heads chopped off right and left. You gotta come back, Rachel. That's all there is to it. To save the poor animals, if for no other reason."

"You'll just have to save them yourself."

"The place is goin' to rack and ruin without you."

"Not with Aunt Hester there! I'm sure she has everything under control. She's a paragon."

"She's someone to help you with the work, and nothin' more. Someone to make life a little easier so you can have more fun with your family. When the babies start comin', she'll be an even bigger help. But the bottom line is, she's just a side dish, Rachel, not our main meal. We need you, honey." He broke off and swallowed hard. "*I* need you."

Rachel gave a start when his scuffed boots suddenly came into view. The next instant, his large warm hand curled under her chin, and he forced her to look up at him. Rachel discovered that she was standing so close to him that she could see the sooty lashes that lined his eyes, the stormy gray-blue of his irises, the burnished tone of his skin. Her heart kicked hard against her ribs. He looked good enough to eat. He surely did.

"You have to come home," he said huskily. "There aren't any flowers on the table, and I love you so much, I can't live without you."

With no warning, he bent and began fishing in her skirt pocket. When he came up with nothing, he dived his hand into her other pocket as well. A satisfied gleam entered his eyes. The next thing Rachel knew, he was settling her spectacles on her nose. Bending slightly at the knees, he made a great show of looking her over. Then he flashed her a devastating grin.

"I knew it. You look adorable in spectacles." He glanced around, as if to draw comment from others present.

Someone nearby said, "I didn't know you wore spectacles, Rachel."

Clint replied, "She darn sure does. She just doesn't wear them in public because she has the fool notion they don't look good on her. I disagree. I think she looks beautiful in them."

Rachel cried, "Clint, stop it. You're embarrassing me!"

"Then come home with me," he demanded in an oddly gruff voice, "so I can tell you in private how beautiful I think you are."

Tears filled Rachel's eyes, and her spectacles began to fog over. Clint took hold of her hand.

"Please, Rachel. Come back home where you belong. Every hour I spend apart from you, I die a little more inside. Please . . ." When she didn't immediately speak, he hastened to add, "I'm sorry you felt cast aside after Aunt Hester came. Lookin' back, I can see how it must have seemed to you, me all of a sudden backin' off and usin' the corn husks as an excuse. But I swear it wasn't that way. I truly was worried about her hearin' us."

Rachel shot a horrified look around. "Be quiet! Do you want everyone to hear!"

"See?" he said with a devilish grin. "It's a private affair, isn't it?"

She narrowed her eyes, but it was all she could do not to smile. "You've made your point."

"Then come home," he said huskily. "Where we can talk in private."

"Oh, Clint. Are you certain you really want—"

He cut her off with a kiss that answered her question far more eloquently than words. A sweet, wonderful kiss that sent tingles down her spine and made her toes curl. Exactly the kind of kiss Rachel had always dreamed of and had never received. Until she met Clint Rafferty, of course.

"I love you," he whispered against her cheek. "Please believe that, Rachel. I'll love you forever."

The throbbing timber of his voice, so packed with emotion, would have convinced Rachel. The way his hands shook when he touched her was added proof that he was sincere. Joy welled in her chest, nearly cutting off her breath, and she threw herself into his arms.

His arms . . . His wonderful strong arms. The instant they closed around her, Rachel knew she was where she belonged and where she would remain.

For the rest of her life.

CATHERINE ANDERSON, the award-winning author of both contemporary and historical fiction, lives with her husband and three canine friends—a mixed spaniel named Kibbles and two Rottweilers named Sam and Sassy, who seem to think they are teacup poodles and that obedience training is for people.

The Mad Earl's Bride

Loretta Chase

Prologue

Devon, England
June, 1820

The Devil was partial to Dartmoor.

In 1638, he rode a storm into Widdecombe, tore off the church roof with a lightning bolt, and carried off a boy who'd been dozing during the service.

This was merely one of several personal appearances. More often, though, Satan appeared in disguise as an enormous black hound or a ghostly stallion galloping across the moors.

His attachment to the area surprised no one, for Dartmoor could not have been better fashioned to suit satanic natures.

Storms lashed the rocky uplands, which loomed stubbornly in the path of Atlantic gales. Heavy damps swirled into the valleys, blanketing villages in impenetrable mists, shutting off communication and travel for days.

Then there were the bogs, filling the hollows and crevices of the highlands, shrinking and swelling with changing weather and season.

Narrow tracks of firm ground coiled through this unwelcoming terrain, yet even the paths could be perilous. At night, or in a mist or storm, it was easy enough for the unwary traveler to lose his way and—if he were especially unlucky—slip into a pulsing morass from which he would never emerge.

Some believed Dartmoor's mires were the Devil's own traps, devised to suck their victims straight down to Hell, Aminta Camoys told her son.

It was twenty-year-old Dorian Camoys's first visit to Dartmoor and the first time he'd seen his mother since Christmas.

"Most considerate of the Archfiend," he replied as he walked with her to the edge of the narrow track. "After slow suffocation by quicksand, the unfortunate sinner will find Hell's torments less shocking to his sensibilities."

She pointed to a suspiciously verdant patch in the bleak wastes below. "Some are bright green like that. There's a larger one half a mile ahead, but it's gray—much better camouflage."

The afternoon had been bright and warm when they'd first ridden out, but a chill wind whirled about them now, and gray clouds swept in, driving out their wispy white predecessors and blanketing the moorland in shadows.

"Thank you for the directions, Mother," Dorian said. "But I do believe I can find my own route to Hell."

"I collect you've found it." She glanced at him and laughed. "Like mother, like son."

He was like her, in more ways than many would suspect.

Although at six feet tall he was by far the larger, the physical resemblance was inescapable. While fully masculine—and puffy and pale at present, thanks to months of dissipation pursued as diligently as his studies—his was the same exotically sculpted countenance.

At the moment, one would never suspect that she, too, was addicted to sins of the flesh. He was the only one, apart from her lovers, who did know. Dorian was her sole confidante.

My mother, the adultress, he thought, as he gazed at her.

Like him, she detested hats, resenting even that small concession to propriety. She'd taken off her bonnet as soon as they'd ridden out of sight of the house. Thick raven hair like his, though much longer, whipped about her face and neck in the sharpening wind. And when she turned to him, the same unblinking yellow stare met his.

Because of those odd-colored eyes and their disconcerting stare—and because he kept to himself and hissed at anyone who came too close—the boys at Eton had nicknamed him Cat. The nickname had followed him to Oxford.

"You'd better take care," she said. "If your grandfather finds out something besides studying is to blame for your pallor, you'll see all your carefully laid plans swept into the maelstrom of his righteous wrath."

"I've exercised considerable ingenuity to make certain he doesn't find out," Dorian said. "You may be sure I shall make a deceptively healthy appearance at Christmas for the annual lecture intended to guide me through the new year. After which I shall watch him scrutinize—for doubtless the hundredth time—every penstroke of the academic reports, looking for an excuse to yank me out of university. But he won't find his excuse, no matter how hard he looks. I'll have my degree—with honors—at the end of next Easter term, and he'll be obliged to reward me with a year's trip abroad, as he's done for the others."

"And you won't return," she said. She moved away, her gaze turning to the surrounding moors.

"I'll never be free of him if I do. If I don't find work abroad, I'll be tied to his purse strings until the day he dies."

That prospect was intolerable.

His grandfather, the Earl of Rawnsley, was a despot.

Dorian's father, Edward, was the youngest of the earl's four sons, all of whom, with their spouses and offspring, lived at Rawnsley Hall in Gloucestershire, where His Lordship could control their every waking moment. The adults might go away on short visits and spend time in London during the Season, and the boys eventually went away to school; but Rawnsley Hall was their home—or prison—and its master ruled them absolutely. Always, wherever they were, they must behave and think as he told them to.

They did it because they had no choice. Not only did he control all the Camoys money, but he was utterly ruthless. The smallest hint of rebellion was promptly crushed—and the earl had no scruples about how he did it.

When, for instance, whippings, lectures, and threats of eternal damnation proved ineffective with Dorian, Lord Rawnsley turned his vexation upon the incorrigible boy's parents. That had worked. Dorian could not stand by and watch his parents punished and humiliated for his faults.

Consequently, though he'd been born quick-tempered and rebellious, Dorian had learned very young to keep his feelings and opinions to himself.

His outward behavior strictly regulated, all he had to call his own was his mind—and it was an exceptionally good one. That, too, he'd inherited from his mother, the Camoys not being renowned for intellectual acuity.

Since Dorian had performed brilliantly at Eton, his grandfather had been obliged to send him on to Oxford. In another year, Lord Rawnsley would be obliged, likewise, to finance the year abroad.

Dorian would have one year on the Continent to look for work. He was sure he'd survive, and he wasn't concerned about living in poverty at first. He would move up in the world eventually. All he had to do was concentrate as he did with his studies . . . and keep his sensual weaknesses under stricter control.

The thought of his weaknesses drew his mind and his gaze back to his mother. She had taken off her gloves and was playing with her rings.

Gad, but she loved trinkets—and fashionable gowns, and Society . . . and her romantic intrigues.

He wondered why she'd come to Dartmoor. She'd been born and reared here, yet it hardly suited her nature. She was meant for the gaiety of Society, for parties and gossip and admiring men swarming about her.

He'd expected to find her bored frantic. Instead, she seemed quieter than he could remember her ever being. He supposed her recent illness accounted for the apparent tranquillity. All the same, he couldn't help wondering why, when the doctor proposed a change of air, she'd asked to come here, of all places. She'd been quite adamant about it, Father said.

He approached her. "I wish you would think about coming to stay with me on the Continent," he said.

"Don't be absurd," she said. "I cannot live in a garret. And don't pretend you'll miss me," she added irritably. "I never was the least use to you. I had all I could do to look out for myself. It isn't easy, as you well know. Lud, I'm so tired of it. You've no idea the relief it is to be here, away from temptation and the everlasting thinking and planning and lying. And pretending, always pretending. No wonder my head still aches. It's so in the habit of laboring, it doesn't know how to stop. When there's nothing to think about, it makes something."

She thrust her hair back from her face—a habit of his, too, and one that had always irritated his grandfather. "That's the trouble with secrets," she said. "You can never be rid of them. They haunt you . . . like ghosts."

He smiled. "Your sins are not so grave, Mother. Bertie Trent's grandmother* goes through lovers as she goes through bonnets, they say."

Her brooding gaze upon the bleak wastes beyond, she did not seem to hear him. "I dreamt my sins took the shape of phantasms," she said in an odd, low voice. "They pursued

---

*See *Lord of Scoundrels* by Loretta Chase, published by Avon Books.

me, like the Furies in Greek myths. It was frightful—and so unjust. I can't help my nature. You understand."

Dorian understood all too well. He loathed the weakness in himself, but no matter what he did, he could not master it. He could not resist the scent of a woman; he could scarcely resist the mere thought of one. Time and again the need drove him—and Lord, the distances he traveled, the subterfuges he resorted to . . . for what always, afterward, left him sick with disgust.

It was not nearly so bad with her, he was aware, but then she was constantly under scrutiny, which he wasn't, and she was a female, smaller in her sensual appetites as she was in size. Still, even her little escapades had taken their toll on her health.

He ought to heed the warning, Dorian knew. She'd only recently recovered. That made it more than six months since Mr. Budge, the Camoys family physician, had diagnosed a "decline." She'd spent half that time between a chaise longue and her bed.

Dorian could not afford so long a period of debility. He would fall behind in his studies . . . and the trip abroad would be delayed . . . and his bondage to his grandfather would stretch on . . .

He shook off the grim prospect. "It's Dartmoor," he said lightly. "Every foot of ground seems to have a spook attached to it. Small wonder you dream of ghosts and demons. I should be amazed if you didn't."

She laughed and turned back to him, her melancholy mood lifting as swiftly as it had descended.

From then until the end of Dorian's two-day visit, his mother seemed to be her lively self again. She related, along with more Dartmoor legends, all the London gossip gleaned from her friends' letters, and told slightly improper anecdotes that made Father blush, yet laugh all the same. Away from Rawnsley Hall, Edward Camoys was more human and less his father's puppet, and though he still treated his wife like a wayward child, that had suited them both for years.

All seemed well when Dorian departed.

He had no idea that his father had secrets, too, and as the months passed, Edward Camoys would find them increasingly difficult to conceal.

Aminta Camoys's letter writing, like Dorian's, was erratic at best. That was why he suspected nothing, though he didn't hear from her after early September.

It wasn't until shortly before Christmas, when Uncle Hugo, the earl's eldest and heir, turned up at Oxford unexpectedly—and, as it turned out, against the earl's orders—that Dorian learned the truth.

Then, deaf to his uncle's warnings, Dorian boarded a mail coach headed north.

He discovered his mother where Hugo had said she was.

It was a private, exclusive, and very expensive lunatic asylum.

Dorian found her in a small, rank room, strapped to a chair. She wore a stained cotton gown and thick, rough stockings on her delicate feet. Her long black hair had been sheared to a dark skullcap. She didn't know who he was at first. When, finally, she recognized him, she wept.

Dorian did not weep, only cursed inwardly while he unfastened the cruel straps. That sent the attendant running out of the room, but Dorian was too distraught to care. He carried his mother to the narrow bed and laid her down and sat beside her and chafed her icy hands and listened, his gut churning, while she told him what they'd done to her.

She'd fallen ill again, she said, and in her weakness, she'd let her secrets out. The earl knew everything now, and so he'd locked her up to punish her because she was a scarlet woman. Her keepers mortified her flesh to make her repent: they starved her and dressed her in stinking rags and made her sleep on filthy linens. They thrust her into ice baths. They shaved her head. They would not let her sleep: they beat on the door and called her a whore and a Jezebel and told her the Devil was coming for her soul.

Dorian didn't know what to believe.

Though she sobbed uncontrollably, her speech was coherent. Yet Uncle Hugo had said she'd gone after Father with a knife and tried to burn down the Dartmoor manor house. She heard voices, he said, and saw things that weren't there, and screamed of ghosts and cruel talons ripping into her skull. Edward Camoys had told nobody about her condition and tried to look after her himself, with the help of the local doctor, Mr. Kneebones. But the earl had visited them in Dartmoor a month ago and, horrified at what he found, summoned physicians from London. Deciding she needed "expert care," they'd recommended Mr. Borson's private madhouse.

"Don't look at me so," she cried now. "I was ill, that was all, and the pain was dreadful, tearing at my skull so that I couldn't see straight. I couldn't think. I couldn't watch my tongue. Too many secrets, Dorian, and I was too weak to keep them in. Oh, please, darling, take me away from this wicked place."

Dorian didn't care what the truth was. He knew only that he couldn't leave her here. He looked about for something to wrap her in, to keep her warm, so that he could carry her away, but there were only the rank bedclothes.

He was tearing them from the bed when the attendant returned, with reinforcements—and Dorian's grandfather.

The instant the earl entered, Aminta turned into a she-demon. Uttering obscenities and threats in a guttural voice Dorian couldn't believe came out of her, she lunged at Lord Rawnsley. When Dorian tried to pull her away, she clawed his face. The attendants grabbed her and swiftly shackled her to the bed, where she alternated between bloodchilling curses and heartwrenching sobs.

When Dorian objected to the painful restraints, the

attendants—on the earl's orders—removed him from the room, then from the building altogether. Shut out, Dorian paced by his grandfather's carriage while his mind replayed the scene over and over.

He could not stop shuddering because he could not shake off the sickening comprehension of what his mother must feel. In the unpredictable moments of clarity—like the one he'd encountered first—she could look about her and recognize what she'd become and where she was. He could imagine her rage and grief at being treated like a mindless animal. He could imagine, all too vividly, her terror as well—when she felt her control slip and the darkness begin swamping her reason. He had no doubt she knew what was happening to her: she'd said as much, that she was weak and couldn't keep things in.

She knew her once-formidable mind was betraying her, and that was worst of all.

And that was why, when his grandfather came out, Dorian gathered his shattered composure and swallowed his pride— and begged.

"Please let me take her elsewhere," he said. "I'll help look after her. I needn't return to Oxford. I can finish later. I know Father and I can manage with the help of a servant or two. I beg you, Grandfather, let—"

"You know nothing about it," Lord Rawnsley coldly cut in. "You know nothing of her tricks and subterfuges, her madwoman's cunning. She played your father for a fool and did the same with you this day. And now Borson says there is no telling what damage you've done—taking her part against those who know better, and making promises you cannot keep. She will be agitated for days, weeks, perhaps." He pulled on his gloves. "But it was ever this way. You were always her creature, in character as well as looks. Now you mean to throw away your future—to care for one who never cared for anybody but herself."

"She's my mother," Dorian said tightly.

"And my daughter-in-law," was the grim retort. "I know my duty to my family. She will be looked after—properly— and you will return to Oxford and do your duty."

Two weeks later, in the midst of a violent fit, Aminta Camoys collapsed and died.

She died in the madhouse Dorian had been unable to rescue her from, while he was at Oxford, burying his rage and grief in his studies because he had no choice. He had no money and no power to rescue her, and his grandfather would punish anyone who dared to help him.

He told nobody what had happened, not even Bertie Trent, the only friend Dorian had.

And so no one but the Camoys family—and then it was only the immediate family—was aware that Aminta Camoys had died, a raving lunatic, in Mr. Borson's expensive hellhole of a madhouse.

Even then, she wasn't left in peace. His grandfather let the curst doctors hack into her poor, dead brain to satisfy their grisly curiosity. The brain tissue was weak, and they'd found evidence of blood seepage. A vessel had burst during the last fit—one of many that might have burst at any time, so fragile they were. Her earlier decline, the doctors decided, must have been the first outward sign of an inner deterioration that had begun long before. The headaches were further symptoms, caused by the slow leakage.

There was nothing anyone could have done for her, they claimed. Just as medical science had no way of detecting such defects early on, it had no way of curing them.

And so Borson and his associates absolved themselves of all blame—as though they had not made her last months a living hell.

And the Camoys saw to it that no blame or shame would be attached to the family, either.

She had "sunk into a fatal decline"—that was the story they gave out, because no Camoys, even one by marriage, could possibly be mad. No hint of insanity had ever appeared in the family in all the centuries since Henri de Camois had come over from Normandy with the Conqueror.

Even among themselves, they never openly referred to her insanity, as though giving the truth the cut direct could make it go away, like an unsuitable acquaintance.

That was just as well, as far as Dorian was concerned. If he had to listen to the heartless hypocrites pontificating about his mother's madness, he was bound to commit some outrage—and be destroyed, as she had been.

After the funeral, he returned to Oxford and buried his feelings, as usual, in study. It was the one thing he could do, the one thing his grandfather could not crush or twist to suit his tyrannical purposes.

Consequently, at the end of the term, Dorian not only earned his degree but did what no Camoys had ever done before: he won a first, *In Literis Humanioribus*.

The traditional celebration followed at Rawnsley Hall. It was the usual hypocrisy. Dorian had never truly been one of the Camoys and he knew his academic triumph stuck in the collective family craw. Still, they must give the appearance of family unity, and for Dorian, pretending was easier this time, with freedom so near. In a few weeks, he would be upon the Continent—and he would not return to England until his grandfather was sealed in the tomb with his saintly ancestors.

In the meantime, Dorian could play his role, as he'd done for years, and bear their pretense and hypocrisy.

Pretending, always pretending, his mother had said.

Her mind had broken down under the strain, she'd believed.

Too many secrets . . . too weak to keep them in.

He didn't know that hers were not the only secrets she'd let out.

He did not find out until twenty-four hours after the so-called celebration. And then Dorian could only stand and listen helplessly for an endless, numbing hour to the chilling speech that shattered and scattered his plans like so much dust and left him with nothing but his pride to sustain him.

Dorian was turned out of Rawnsley Hall with six pounds and some odd pence in his pocket. This was because Lord Rawnsley had expected him to hang his head and make penitent speeches and beg for forgiveness—and Dorian had decided that the earl could wait until Judgment Day.

His grandfather had called him a whoremonger, a slave to the basest of appetites, who shamelessly and recklessly pursued a path that could only lead to madness and a hideous death from the foul diseases contracted from the filth with which he consorted.

Though Dorian knew this was true, he found he must be sunk beyond shame as well because he could not find a shred of remorse in his heart, only rage. He would not, could not submit to his grandfather, ever again. He would starve and die in a filthy gutter, rather than go crawling back.

He left fully aware that he'd have to survive entirely on his own. The earl would make trouble for anyone who aided his errant grandson.

And so Dorian went to London. There he assumed a new identity and made himself one of the insignificant masses. He found lodgings—a dank room among the teeming tenements of the East End—and employment as a dockworker by day and a legal copyist at night. There was no future in either occupation, but then, he had no future, with all respectable doors shut to him. Still, even when the dock work dwindled from time to time, the lawyers kept him busy. There was little danger of their running out of documents. And when the drudgery threatened to crush his spirit, a few coins could buy him the temporary surcease of a relatively clean whore and a bottle.

The months stretched into years while his grandfather waited for the prodigal to crawl back on his hands and knees and the prodigal waited for his grandfather to die.

But the influenza epidemic that bore off Dorian's father, his Uncle Hugo, two aunts, and several cousins in 1826 left their lord and master untouched.

Then, in the summer of 1827, Dorian suddenly fell ill—and sank into a decline.

One

Dartmoor, Devon
Early May, 1828

*Dorian stood in the library of Radmore Manor, look-*ing out the window. In the distance, the moors stretched out in all their bleak beauty. They beckoned to him as strongly now as they'd called to his sickly fancy months before in London, when he'd fallen so dangerously ill, too weak even to hold his pen.

In August, Hoskins, a solicitor's clerk, had found him barely conscious, slumped over an ink-splotched document.

I'll fetch a doctor.

No. No doctors, for God's sake. Dartmoor. Take me to Dartmoor. There's money . . . saved . . . under the floorboard.

Hoskins might have absconded with the little hoard, and heaven knew he needed money, living on a clerk's pittance. Instead, he'd not only done as Dorian asked but stayed on to look after him. He'd remained even after Dorian recovered—or seemed to.

That apparent recovery had not deluded Dorian. He'd suspected, early on, that the illness, like his mother's years earlier, had simply been the beginning of the end.

In January, when the headaches began, his suspicions were confirmed. As the weeks passed, the attacks grew increasingly vicious, as hers had done.

The night before last, he'd wanted to bash his head against the wall.

. . . pain . . . tearing at my skull . . . couldn't see straight . . . couldn't think.

He understood now, fully, what his mother had meant. Even so, he would have borne the pain, would not have sent for Kneebones yesterday morning, if not for the shimmering wraith he'd seen. Then Dorian had realized something must be done—before the faint visual illusions blossomed into full-blown phantasms, as they had for his mother, and drove him to violence, as they had done her.

"I know what it is," Dorian had told the doctor when he came yesterday. "I know it's the same brain disease and incurable. But I had rather finish my time here, if it can be managed. I had rather not . . . end . . . precisely as my mother did, if it can possibly be helped."

Naturally, Kneebones must satisfy himself and arrive at his own conclusions. But there was only one possible conclusion, as Dorian well knew. His mother had died within eight months of the onset of the "visual chimera"—the "ghosts" she'd begun seeing while awake, not simply in dreams, as she'd said.

Six months was the most Kneebones could promise. He said the degeneration was progressing more rapidly in Dorian's case, thanks to "a punishingly insalubrious mode of living."

Still, Kneebones had assured him that the violent fits could be moderated with laudanum, in large doses.

"Your father was too sparing of the laudanum, fearing overdose," the doctor explained. "Then, when your grandfather came, he raged about my turning that unhappy woman into an opium addict. And then the fancy experts came, calling it 'poison' and saying it *caused* the hallucinations—when it was the only means of subduing them and quieting her."

Dorian smiled now, recalling that conversation. Opiate addiction was the least of his anxieties, and an overdose, in time, might offer a welcome release.

In time, but not yet.

Outwardly, he was healthy and strong, and in Dartmoor, he'd been free of the self-loathing that had haunted him since his last year at Eton, when temptation, in the shape of a woman, had first beckoned, and he'd found he was no match for it. Here, as his mother had said, there was no temptation. When he felt the old itch and grew restless, he rode through the moors, riding long and hard, until he was exhausted.

Here he'd found a refuge. He meant to enjoy it for as long as he could.

Hearing footsteps in the hall, Dorian turned away from the window and thrust his hair back from his face. It was unfashionably long, but fashion had ceased signifying to Dorian years ago, and it certainly wouldn't matter when he lay in his coffin.

The coffin didn't trouble him much, either, and hadn't for some time. He'd had months to get used to the idea of dying. Now, thanks to the promise of laudanum, his remaining anxiety was eased. The drug would stupefy him, sparing him full awareness of the wretched thing he would become, while those who looked after him needn't fear for their lives.

He would die in something like peace with something like dignity. That was better than the lot of scores of wretches in the cesspits of London, he told himself. It was better than what his mother had endured, certainly.

The library door opened, and Hoskins entered, bearing a letter. He set it face down on the library table so that the seal was plainly evident.

It was the Earl of Rawnsley's seal.

"Damn," Dorian said. He tore the letter open, scanned it, then handed it to Hoskins.

"Now you see why I chose to be a nobody," Dorian said.

Hoskins had learned Dorian's true identity only yesterday, at the same time he'd been informed of Dorian's medical condition—and offered the opportunity to depart, if he wished. But Hoskins had fought and been wounded at Waterloo. After the horrors he'd experienced there, looking after a mere lunatic was child's play.

Moreover, to Dorian's vast relief, Hoskins's manner remained matter-of-fact, with occasional ventures into a gallows humor that lifted Dorian's spirits.

"Is it the irascibility of age?" Hoskins asked mildly as he handed the letter back. "Or was the old gentleman always like this?"

"He's impossible," Dorian said. "Born that way, I suppose. And quite convincing. For most of my youth, I actually believed I was always the one at fault. There is no dealing with him, Hoskins. All one can do is try to ignore him. That won't be easy." He frowned at the letter.

His remaining aunt, Hugo's widow, had visited Dartmoor a short while ago and spotted Dorian on one of his gallops through the moors. She'd written the earl a highly exaggerated description of Dorian's riding garb—or lack thereof—and passed on a lot of local gossip, mostly ignorant speculation about the reclusive eccentric living at Radmore Manor.

The earl's letter ordered Dorian to appear—his hair properly shorn and his person decently attired—at a family council on the twelfth of May, and explain himself.

If they wanted him, they'd have to come and get him, Dorian silently vowed, and they would never take him away alive.

"Did you wish to dictate a reply, sir?" Hoskins asked. "Or shall we chuck it into the fire?"

"I'll write my own reply. Otherwise you'll be targeted as

an accomplice, and made to feel the weight of his righteous wrath." Dorian smiled faintly. "*Then* we'll chuck it into the fire."

On the twelfth of May 1828, the Earl of Rawnsley and most of his immediate family were gathered in Rawnsley Hall's drawing room at the moment that a section of the ancestral roof above them chose to collapse. In a matter of seconds, several tons of timber, stone, and miscellaneous decorative debris buried them and made Dorian Camoys—one of the very few family members not in attendance—the new Earl of Rawnsley.

In a small sitting room in a house in Wiltshire, Gwendolyn Adams read the weeks-old newspaper account several times before she was satisfied she had not overlooked any details.

Then she turned her attention to the other three documents on her writing desk. One was a letter written by the present earl's recently deceased aunt. According to it, her nephew had turned into a savage. His hair hung down to his knees, and he galloped half-naked through the moors on a murderous white horse named after a bloodthirsty pagan god.

The second document was a draft of a letter from the earl to his "savage" grandson. It gave Gwendolyn a very good idea why the heir had failed to attend the funeral.

The third document was the present Lord Rawnsley's reply to his grandfather's obnoxious letter, and it made Gwendolyn smile for the first time since the duc d'Abonville had arrived and made his outrageous proposal.

Abonville's mother had been a de Camois, the French tree from which the English Camoys branch had sprouted centuries earlier—and thus Rawnsley's very distant cousin. Abonville was also the fiancé of Gwendolyn's grandmother, Genevieve, the dowager Viscountess Pembury.

The pair had attended the Camoys's funeral, after which a

harassed solicitor had sought the duc's assistance as nearest male kin: papers needed signing, and any number of legal matters must be attended to, and the present Lord Rawnsley had refused to assume his responsibilities.

Accordingly, the duc and Genevieve had journeyed to Dartmoor. There, they discovered that the new earl had fallen victim to a terminal brain disease.

Gwendolyn's smile faded. Bertie Trent, her first cousin, had taken the news very hard. At present, he was hiding in the stables, sobbing over an old letter, creased and faded past legibility, from his boyhood friend Cat Camoys.

She moved the papers aside and took up the miniature Bertie had given her.

The tiny likeness allegedly represented Bertie's friend. It had been painted years earlier by a singularly inept artist, and it did not tell her much.

Still, twenty-one-year-old Gwendolyn was too levelheaded a girl to base the most momentous decision of her life upon a picture two inches in diameter.

In the first place, she knew she was no great beauty herself, with her pointy nose and chin and impossible red hair. She doubted that her green eyes, to which several suitors had composed lavish—and very silly—odes, compensated for everything.

In the second place, physical attractiveness was irrelevant. Rawnsley had not been asked to fall in love with her, nor she with him. Abonville had simply asked her to marry the earl and bear him a son to save the Camoys line from extinction.

She'd been asked to do this because she came of a phenomenally fertile family, famous for producing males. Both characteristics were critical, for the Earl of Rawnsley hadn't much time to sire an heir. His physician had given him six months to live.

Unfortunately, there were no documents offering any

insights into the brain disease itself. The little Genevieve and Abonville knew they'd learned mainly from the earl's manservant, Hoskins. His Lordship had volunteered no details, and pressing him for information would have been unkind, Genevieve had said.

Gwendolyn frowned.

Her mother entered the room at that moment and softly closed the door behind her. "Are you truly thinking it over?" she asked as she took the seat next to Gwendolyn's desk. "Or are you only making a show of hesitation for Papa's benefit?"

Though she had taken time to reflect, Gwendolyn did not feel hesitant. She knew the task she'd been asked to undertake would not be pleasant. But that did not daunt her in the least.

Unpleasantness was only to be expected. Illness, whether of the mind or the body, was disagreeable; otherwise so much labor wouldn't be dedicated to making it go away. But illness was also exceedingly interesting, and lunatics, Gwendolyn felt, were the most interesting patients of all.

Lord Rawnsley's case, combining both a mysterious neurological disease and aberrant behavior, could not have excited her more.

If the Almighty had sent her a letter, signed, witnessed, and notarized, she could not have felt more certain that He, in His infinite wisdom—about which she had entertained doubts on more than one occasion—had made her expressly for this purpose.

"I was making absolutely certain there wasn't anything to think about," Gwendolyn told her mother. "There isn't."

Mama gazed at her for a long moment. "Yes, I heard the celestial summons—as clearly as you did, I don't doubt. Papa is another matter, however."

Gwendolyn was well aware of this. Mama understood her. Papa did not. None of the males of the family did. That included Abonville. Gwendolyn was sure the marriage idea was one her grandmother had planted in his head while convincing him it was his own. Fortunately, Genevieve had an enviable talent for making men believe just about anything she wanted them to.

"We'd better let Genevieve talk him round," Gwendolyn said. "Otherwise he will create delays by raising a lot of needless obstacles, and we have no time to lose. There's no telling how long Rawnsley will retain his reason, and he must be of sound mind for the legalities."

That wasn't Gwendolyn's only anxiety. At this very moment, the Earl of Rawnsley might be taking one of his reckless rides and risking a fatal tumble into a mire.

Then she would never have a chance to do something truly worthwhile with her life.

Before she could voice this concern, her mother spoke.

"Genevieve has already begun working on your father," she said. "She knew what your answer would be, as I did. "I shall go downstairs and signal her to administer the coup de grâce." She rose.

"Thank you, Mama," Gwendolyn said.

"Never mind that," Mama said sharply. "It is not what I would have wished for you, even if you will be Countess of Rawnsley. If that young man had not been Bertie's friend, and if he had not looked after your idiot cousin all through Eton—and doubtless saved his worthless neck a hundred times—" Her eyes filled and her voice was unsteady as she went on, "Oh, Gwendolyn, I should never let you go. But we cannot leave the poor boy to die alone." She squeezed Gwendolyn's shoulder. "He needs you, and that is all that ought to matter, I know."

Dorian Camoys stood, trapped, in his own library.

Less than a fortnight had passed since the duc d'Abonville had turned up at the door.

Now the Frenchman was back—with a special license and a female he insisted Dorian marry forthwith.

Dorian could have dealt with the Frenchman and his ludicrous command easily enough. Unfortunately, along with Lady Pembury and the girl Dorian had not yet met and knew better than to consider meeting, Abonville had also brought his future grandson, Bertie Trent.

And Bertie had got it into his head that he would stand as his friend's groomsman.

When Bertie got something into his head, it was next to impossible to get it out. This was because Bertie Trent was one of the stupidest men who'd ever lived. This, Dorian had long ago recognized, was the reason Bertie was the only friend he'd ever had—and one whose childlike feelings Dorian couldn't bear to hurt.

It was impossible to rage at Abonville properly while trying not to distress Bertie, who was so thrilled about his best friend marrying his favorite female cousin.

"It's only Gwen," Bertie was saying, misconstruing the issues, as usual. "She ain't half bad, for a girl. Not like Jess—but I shouldn't wish m'sister on anybody, especially you, even though you'd be m'brother then, because I can't think of anything worse than a fellow having to listen to her the livelong day. Not but what Dain can manage her—but he's bigger than you, and even so, I daresay he's got his hands full. Still, they're already shackled, so you're safe from her, and Gwen ain't like her at all. When Abonville told us you was wanting to get married, and he was thinking Gwen would suit, I said—"

"Bertie, I wasn't wanting to get married," Dorian broke in. "It is a ridiculous mistake."

"I have made no mistake," said Abonville. He stood before the door, his distinguished countenance stern, his arms folded over his chest. "You gave your word, cousin. You said you recognized your duty, and you would marry if I could find a girl willing to have you."

"It doesn't matter what I said—if I did say it," Dorian said tightly. "I had a headache when you came, and had taken laudanum. I was not in my senses at the time."

"You were fully rational."

"I could not have been!" Dorian snapped. "I should never have agreed to such a thing if I had. I'm not a damned ox. I shan't spend my last months breeding!"

That was a mistake. Bertie's round blue eyes began to fill. "It's all right, Cat," he said. "I'll stick by you, like you always stuck by me. But you must have promised, or Abonville wouldn't have said you did, and talked to Gwen. And she'll be awful disappointed—not but what she'll get over it, not being the moping sort. But only think how we could be cousins, and if you was to make a brat, I could be godfather, you know."

Dorian bent a malignant glare upon the accursed duc. This was his doing. He'd filled Bertie's head with the kinds of ideas he was sure to set his childish heart on: standing as groomsman for his dying friend, becoming Dorian's cousin, then godfather to imaginary children.

And poor Bertie, his heart bursting with good intentions, would never understand why it was impossible. He would never comprehend why Dorian needed to die alone.

"I'll stick by you," he'd said—and Bertie would. If Dorian wouldn't wed his cousin, Bertie would stay. Either way, Dorian wouldn't stand a chance. They would never let him die in peace.

Once Dorian was no longer capable of thinking for himself, Bertie—or Abonville or the wife—would call in experts to deal with the madman.

And Dorian knew where that would lead: he would die as his mother had, caged like an animal . . . unless he killed himself first.

But he would not be hurried to his grave. He still had time, and he meant to enjoy it, to relish his sanity and strength for every precious moment they remained.

He told himself to calm down. He was not trapped. It only seemed that way, with loyal, dimwitted Bertie on one side, prating of godchildren, and Abonville on the other, blocking the door.

Dorian was not yet weak and helpless, as his mother had been. He'd find a way out of this so long as he kept a cool head.

Half an hour later, Dorian was galloping along the narrow track that led to Hagsmire. He was laughing, because the ruse had worked.

It had been easy enough to feign a sudden attack of remorse. Given years of practice with his grandfather, Dorian had no touble appearing penitent, and grateful for Abonville's efforts. And so, when Dorian requested a few minutes to compose himself before meeting his bride, the two guests had exited the library.

So had he—out the window, through the garden, then down to the stables at a run.

He knew they wouldn't pursue him to Hagsmire. Even his own groom wouldn't venture onto the tortuous path this day, with storm clouds roiling overhead.

But he and Isis had waited out Dartmoor storms before. There was plenty of time to find the cracked heap of granite where they'd sheltered so many times previously, while Dorian beat back the inner demons urging him toward the old habits, the illusory surcease of wine and women.

Even if they searched, his unwanted guests would never find him, and they would give up awaiting his return long before he gave in. He had not yielded to his private demons or to his grandfather, and he would not yield to an overbearing French nobleman obsessed with genealogy.

There would be no more submitting to Duty. The new Earl

of Rawnsley would be dead in a few months, and that would be the end of the curst Camoys line. And if Abonville didn't like it, let him uproot one of the French sprigs and plant him here, and make the poor sod marry Bertie's cousin.

Because the only way she would marry Dorian Camoys, he assured himself, would be by coming into Hagsmire with the entire bridal party and the preacher, and even then someone would have to pin the groom down with a boulder. Because he would dive into a bottomless pit of quicksand before he would take any woman into his life now and let her watch him disintegrate into a mindless animal.

Thunder rumbled faintly in the distance.

Or so Dorian thought at first, until he noticed that the rumble didn't pause, as thunder would, but went on steadily, and steadily grew louder. And the louder and nearer it came, the less it sounded like thunder and the more it sounded like . . . hoofbeats.

He glanced back, then quickly ahead again.

He told himself the recent confrontation had agitated him more than he'd suspected, and what he believed he'd just seen was a trick of his degenerating brain.

The ignorant rustics, who believed pixies dwelt all over Dartmoor, had named Hagsmire for the witches they also believed haunted the area. During mists and storms, they mounted ghostly steeds and chased their victims into the mire.

The hoofbeats grew louder.

The thing was gaining on him.

He glanced back, his heart pounding, his nerves tingling.

Though he assured himself it couldn't be there, his eyes told him it was: a demonic-looking female riding an enormous bay. A tangled mane of fiery red hair flew wildly about her face. She rode boldly astride, a pale cloak streaming out behind her, her skirts hiked up to her knees, shamelessly displaying her ghostly white limbs.

Though it was only a moment's glance, the brief distraction proved fatal, for in the next instant, Isis swerved too sharply into a turning.

Dorian reacted a heartbeat too late, and the mare skidded over the crumbling track edge and down the slippery incline—toward the quagmire waiting below.

The pale mare managed to scramble back from the edge of the murky pit, but she threw off her master in the process.

Gwendolyn leapt down from her mount, collected the rope she'd brought, and climbed down the incline to the edge of the bog.

Several feet from where she stood, the Earl of Rawnsley was thrashing in a pit of grey muck. In the few minutes it had taken her to reach the bog, he'd slid toward its heart, and his efforts to struggle for footing where there wasn't any only sucked him in deeper.

Still, the muck had climbed only as far as his hips, and an assessing glance told Gwendolyn that this patch of mire was relatively narrow in circumference.

Even while she was studying her surroundings, she was moving toward the mare, making reassuring sounds. She was aware of Rawnsley cursing furiously, in between shouting at her to go away, but she disregarded that.

"Try to keep as still as possible," she told him calmly. "We'll have you out in a minute."

"Get away from here!" he shouted. "Leave my horse alone, you bedamned witch! Run, Isis! Home!"

But Gwendolyn was stroking under the mare's mane, and the creature was quieting, despite her master's shouts and curses. She stood docilely while Gwendolyn unbuckled the stirrup strap, removed the stirrup iron, and rebuckled the strap. She looped one end of the rope through the strap and knotted it. Then she led the mare closer to the bog.

Rawnsley had stopped cursing, and he was not thrashing

about so much as before. She did not know whether he'd come to his senses or was simply exhausted. She could see, though, that he'd sunk past his waist. Swiftly she tied a loop at the free end of the rope.

"Look sharp now," she called to him. "I'm going to throw it."

"You'll fall in, you stupid—"

She flung the rope. He grabbed . . . and missed. And swore profusely.

Gwendolyn quickly drew it back and tried again.

On the fifth try, he caught it.

"Try to hold on with both hands," she said. "And don't try to help us. Pretend you're a log. Keep as still as you can."

She knew that was very difficult. It was instinctive to struggle when one was sinking. But he would sink faster if he fought the mire, and the deeper he was, the harder it would be to pull him out. Even here, where it was safe, the soggy ground was barely walkable. Her boots sank into mud up to the ankles. Isis, too, must contend with the mud, as well as her master's weight, and the powerful mire dragging him down.

Still, they would do it, Gwendolyn assured herself. She looped the reins through one hand and grasped the stirrup strap and rope with the other.

Then she turned the mare so that she'd be moving sideways from the bog, and started her on the first cautious steps of rescue. "Slowly, Isis," she murmured. "I know you want to hurry—so do I—but we cannot risk wrenching his arms from their sockets."

He collapsed as soon as he escaped the mire, but Gwendolyn had to leave him while she returned to the bridle path with Isis. Though the horse had been good and patient through the ordeal, she was restless and edgy now, and Gwendolyn was worried she might stumble into the mire if left unattended. One could not look after horse and master simultaneously.

By the time she'd settled Isis with Bertie's gelding, re-
trieved a brandy flask from the saddlebag, and hurried
back to Rawnsley, he had returned to full consciousness. To
extremely bad-tempered consciousness, by the looks and
sounds of it.

His black mane dripped ooze from the mire, and he was
cursing under his breath as he shoved it out of his face and
dragged himself up to a sitting position.

"Devil take you and roast you in Hell!" he snarled. "You
could have killed yourself—and my horse. I told you to go
away, curse you!"

A mask of grey-green slime clung to his face. Even under
the mucky coating, however, his features appeared stronger
and starker than in the miniature. This was a hard, sharply
etched face, while the painted one had been sickly looking
and puffy.

The rest of him was not sickly looking either. The earl's
bog-soaked garments clung to broad shoulders and back, a
taut, narrow waist, and long legs—and every inch of that was
solid muscle.

The reality was so unlike the picture that Gwendolyn
wondered for a moment whether someone had played a joke
on her, and this wasn't Rawnsley at all.

Then he pulled off his mud-encrusted gloves and wiped the
filth from his eyes with his fingers and looked at her . . . and
she froze, the breath stuck in her throat as her heart missed
the next scheduled beat.

Bertie called him Cat because, he said, that's what all the
fellows at school had called him. Now Gwendolyn understood why.

The Earl of Rawnsley's eyes were yellow.

Not a human brown or hazel but a feline amber gold. They
were the eyes of a jungle predator, burning bright—and dangerous.

Fortunately, Gwendolyn was not easily intimidated. The

shock passed as quickly as it had come, and she knelt down beside him and offered the flask with a steady hand.

Her voice was steady, too, as she answered. "No self-respecting witch would go away on a mere mortal's orders. She'd be drummed out of the coven in disgrace."

He took the flask from her and drank, his intent yellow gaze never leaving her face.

"You may not know that all the best witches come to Dartmoor for their familiars," she said. "A black cat is de rigueur. Since you're the only one available—"

"I'm not available, and I'm not a damned tabby, you demented little hellhound! And I know who you are. You're the curst cousin, aren't you? Only one of Bertie's kin would come galloping into a mire in that lunatic way and blunder about, risking a horse, as well as her own scrawny neck, saving a man from what she got him into. And I didn't ask to be saved, Devil confound you! It's all the same to me—I've already got one foot in the grave—or didn't they tell you?"

"Yes, they did tell me," she answered calmly. "But I did not come all this way only to turn back at the first obstacle. I am aware it is all the same to you. I realize the mire would have saved you the trouble of putting a pistol to your head or hanging yourself or whatever you had in mind. But you may just as easily do that later, after we're wed. I regret the inconvenience, my lord, but I cannot let you die before the ceremony, or I shall never get my hospital."

In the past, Gwendolyn often obtained satisfactory results from startling statements.

It worked this time, too.

He drew back slightly, and his furious expression softened into bewilderment.

"It is simple enough," she said. "I need you, and you need me—although I cannot expect you to believe that at present since you know next to nothing about me."

She glanced upward. "We are about to be inundated. We

will need to find shelter—for the horses' sake, I mean, since you won't mind dying of lung fever, either. That is not altogether inconvenient. Waiting out the storm will give us a chance for private conversation."

Two

"Oh, no, you don't," Dorian said. *The words came out* in croaks. His throat was raw from shouting the objections she'd been so stubbornly deaf to.

Ignoring her outstretched hand, he staggered to his feet. Staying upright proved even harder than getting up.

Mires, it turned out, didn't simply swallow you. His mother had failed to explain that they chewed first. They tried to suck the skin off your bones and crush your organs and muscles into jelly. Every inch of his body, inside and out, was throbbing painfully. He ignored it.

"There will be no private tête-à-têtes," he said, grasping her arm and marching her to the incline. "We have nothing to say to each other. I am taking you back to the house, and then you will go back where you came from."

"I don't think that's a good idea," she said. Her voice remained level, and she made no effort to free herself from his grasp.

He let go abruptly, wishing he hadn't grabbed her slim arm in that oafish way. She had no choice but to follow him, unless she meant to take up residence in Hagsmire.

He started up the slope alone.

After a moment, she followed. "Why did you bolt?" she asked.

"I took a lunatic fit." He trudged on.

"That often happens when one converses with Bertie for any length of time," she said. "Sometimes I have to shake him. Otherwise, he will go on and on and lose track entirely of what he's saying, and one can grow quite giddy trying to follow."

"I'm very fond of Bertie," he said coldly.

"So am I," she said. "But he is miraculously stupid, isn't he? Cousin Jessica says he was born with his foot in his mouth and has been unable to get it out since. I suppose he must have made the most harrowing vows of eternal devotion to you. He was blubbering into his handkerchief when he came out to tell me you'd bolted. So there was no getting an intelligible explanation out of him. And Abonville said only that he'd made a terrible mistake, and Genevieve must take me back to the inn."

"Obviously you heeded Abonville no more than you did me," Dorian said irritably. "The words 'go away' appear to have no meaning for you."

"If I always did what I was told, I should never accomplish anything," she said. "Fortunately, Abonville is aware that I do not blindly obey orders. And so, when I said I must go after you, and my grandmother agreed, he took Bertie back into the library, and they made direct for the brandy."

They had reached the bridle path. Dorian wanted to get on his horse and ride so he wouldn't have to listen to her, but his leg muscles were giving way.

His hair was thick with mire ooze, and the cold slime dribbled down his neck. Thanks to the slime, he stank to high heaven. He was too tired and shaken to care.

He staggered to a boulder and sat down and stared at his

sodden trousers while he waited for his respiration to slow and his brain to quiet.

"It would appear there has been a misunderstanding," she said.

He couldn't understand why she wouldn't keep her distance from him when it must be obvious to her by now that he was deranged. It was certainly obvious to him.

He pushed a hank of soggy hair from his eyes and looked up at her. Though she didn't appear as demonlike as she had before, galloping after him, she still looked like a witch. A young witch, with her sharp little nose and chin and narrow, uptilted green eyes—and the hair, the wild mass of red hair. It wasn't even a normal red but a strange maroon, glinting fire even in the gloom of the approaching storm.

All the same, strange as she was, Dorian couldn't believe he'd actually mistaken this young Englishwoman for one of Satan's handmaidens.

He should not have let himself become so overwrought, he reproached himself. If he had stayed with the two men and argued patiently and rationally . . . but he hadn't. Instead, he had run away—from temptation, yes, but they would think he'd fled a mere girl—and now they would have no doubt he was a lunatic. Abonville would probably have him examined and certified non compos mentis.

"Damn me to hell," he muttered.

"I don't mean to plague you," she said, "but I cannot work out what happened, exactly. What did they say about me that made you bolt? I have been wracking my brains, but all I could think was that Bertie—"

"I didn't know what to do with him!" he snapped. "The silly sod wants to stay with me—to the tragic bloody end—and I'll never get rid of him without resorting to violence." *Then they'll lock me away*, he added silently.

"I can make him go away," she said. "I'm one of the few

people who can actually communicate with him. Is that all?"

"All?" he echoed. "No, that isn't all. I want the lot of you gone. I don't need Bertie about, sobbing the instant my tragic condition is hinted at. I don't need Abonville telling me what's good for me and what I ought to do. I've had a lifetime of that. And most of all, I don't need a wife, damn and blast him!"

The demons in his breast cried that a wife was what he most needed, and conjured erotic images he hastily thrust away.

A pucker appeared in her brow. "That is odd. I should not have thought Abonville would misunderstand. His English is excellent. Or have you changed your mind about getting married? I do wish you would explain, my lord. It is very difficult to respond sensibly to a situation when one is so utterly in the dark."

"I did not change my mind," he said, beating back an insane urge to smooth the furrow from her young—too young—brow. "I vaguely remember Abonville's and your grandmother's visit—whenever it was—and his explaining how he and I were cousins about a thousand times removed. That's all I remember, and it's amazing I recall so much, considering I had swilled about a gallon of laudanum shortly before he arrived."

Her expression cleared. "Oh, I do see now. Some individuals become extremely docile under the influence of opiates. You must have amiably agreed with every word they said— and all the while you had no idea what they were talking about."

Thunder grumbled in the distance, and black clouds were massing above their heads. She appeared to heed the threatening weather not at all. She only watched him with quiet concentration. The steady green perusal was stirring a dangerous yearning in his breast. He beat that back, too.

"I tried to explain," he said stiffly, "but he refused to listen to me."

"I am not surprised," she said. "He was sure to think the Rawnsley he encountered the first time was relatively sane—because that Rawnsley sensibly agreed with everything Abonville said. Today, when you disagreed, he was bound to ascribe it to a temporary fit of insanity."

"The thought has crossed my mind," he muttered.

"Many people respond to seemingly irrational behavior in the same way," she said. "Instead of listening to what you said, he probably tried to drum rationality into you by repeating his point over and over, as one drums the multiplication tables into children. Even medical experts, who ought to know better, believe this is an 'enlightened' way of dealing with individuals in an agitated state."

She wrinkled her pointy nose. "It is most annoying. No wonder you lost your patience and dashed off."

"That was a mistake, all the same," he said. "I should have stayed and reasoned with him."

"Waste of breath," she said briskly. "Your mental balance is in doubt. The explanation must come from one whose sanity is not doubted. I will explain to him, and he will listen to me."

She paused, looking about her. "The storm is not rushing upon us as quickly as I expected. For once, Providence shows some consideration. I should have hated going back without having the least idea what was wrong. Not that I am altogether happy with the answer. Still, one cannot hold a man to a promise made when he was not properly in his senses."

Bertie had said she wasn't the moping sort. Even so, the faint note of resignation in her voice made Dorian feel guilty. She had saved his life. Though he wasn't at all sure he'd wanted to be saved, he could appreciate the courage and efficiency with which she'd acted. She'd also calmed him. She'd listened. She'd understood.

He looked away, wondering how much of an explanation he owed her and how much he could trust himself to utter.

A jagged branch of fire darted over a distant ridge. The heavens rumbled.

He brought his gaze back to her. "Does it not strike you as . . . morbid?" he asked. "That I should take a wife, now of all times?"

She shrugged. "I can understand how it might seem so to you. Yet it is not much different than a decrepit old man marrying a young woman, which happens often enough."

It did happen, Dorian knew. Such a marriage meant a few months, perhaps a few years, of catering to a drooling invalid. The reward of a wealthy widowhood and independence more than compensated, evidently.

He was hardly the one to revile a woman for acting out of greed. It wasn't as though he'd ever been a saint.

Moreover, he was aware that some women had remarkable powers of endurance. Was there so much difference, he wondered, between lying with a man who was as good as a corpse and lying with a drunken, lusting oaf, insatiable while the need was upon him and soddenly morose afterward?

That was the man he'd been, not so very long ago.

He shuddered—at the past and at what his future held if he yielded to his baser self and took what she offered.

"We had better start back," she said. "You are tired and wet and chilled."

She turned and moved toward her horse.

Dorian rose and followed, relieved that she sought no further explanation. Though he'd already said more than he wanted, he still wanted to tell her more, to explain. But that would mean describing the sordid life that lay behind him and the helpless imbecility that lay ahead. Better to leave it as it was, he told himself. She seemed to accept the situation.

They reached the bay gelding, and Dorian was so busy telling himself to hold his tongue before it got him into trouble that he didn't pause to think but picked her up and set her upon the saddle.

Too late, he remembered it was a man's saddle.

She swung her leg over and settled comfortably astride, naively exposing to his view several inches of feminine underthings.

Between the dirty draggle of her petticoats and the slime-encrusted boots, her muddy stocking hugged a slender, curvaceous calf.

Dorian backed away, silently cursing himself.

She didn't need his assistance. He could have mounted his own horse and started for home and let her take care of herself. He had just escaped a mire. No one would expect him to play the gallant at such a time, and she was obviously not a helpless female.

He should not have allowed his mind to wander into the past. He should not have touched her or come close enough to notice what her legs were like. Already he could feel his resistance weakening, was aware of the excuses forming in his treacherous mind—the false promises he knew better than to trust. There would be no relief for him, or release, if he yielded to this temptation. There never had been before: only a temporary oblivion and self-loathing afterward.

He hurried to Isis and hastily mounted.

Gwendolyn Adams was not the granddaughter of a famous femme fatale for nothing. Though she had not inherited Genevieve's raven hair or heart-stopping countenance or subtly seductive ways, Gwendolyn had inherited certain instincts.

She did not have much trouble interpreting the Earl of Rawnsley's expression when his exotic yellow gaze wandered to her leg.

She did not have much trouble, either, interpreting her own reaction when his gaze lingered at least two pulse beats longer than delicacy allotted. The hot spark in his eyes had seemed to leap to her limb and set a little fire to it that darted up under her petticoats and past her knee, teasing her thighs with its naughty warmth before it swirled into the pit of her belly. There it set off sensations she had heard of but never before experienced in her life.

She had never dreamed the mad Earl of Rawnsley would arouse such sensations, but then, he was nothing like what she'd expected.

She had read about quicksand and the agonizing pressure it exerted. She was sure he must feel as though he'd been run over by a herd of stampeding bulls. Yet he had picked her up as easily as he might pluck a daisy from the thin Dartmoor soil. Now she watched him swing his long, powerful body up into the saddle in one easy motion, as though he'd done nothing more tiring than pick wildflowers.

Puzzled, she followed the earl in silence down the narrow, winding track.

Rain was falling, but halfheartedly. The worst of the storm seemed to be rampaging in the southeast.

Rawnsley trotted on steadily, never once glancing back at her. If his horse had been fresh, Gwendolyn had no doubt he would have galloped out of Hagsmire in the same desperate manner he'd galloped in.

Abonville had—with the best of intentions, assuredly— thrown him into a dangerously agitated state. It was bound to happen again, and the duc was sure to make the worst possible decisions out of the best possible motives. She had seen it happen too many times: greedy physicians, eager to make heaps of money trying their ludicrous theories out on hopeless cases, and loving families blindly agreeing out of desperation.

But the medical experts were men, and with men, everything was a war of sorts. Doctors were bound to battle disease, at times, as though the victims as well as the illness were mortal foes. Then the physicians wondered why their patients turned hostile.

What Rawnsley needed was a friend. At present, though, thanks to Abonville—and poor, stupid Bertie—he viewed Gwendolyn as the enemy.

"Drat them," she muttered. "Leave it to men to make a muck of things."

She was silently reviewing her long litany of grievances against the male of the species when Rawnsley drew his mare to a halt.

Gwendolyn noticed that the track had widened. There seemed to be enough room to ride abreast.

Rawnsley was waiting for her to catch up, she realized with amazement. Her spirits rose, but only a very little bit. Experience had taught her not to leap to conclusions, especially optimistic ones.

When she came up beside him, he spoke.

"You mentioned a hospital," he said, moving on again. His voice was hoarse and unsteady. Exhaustion and inner distress were easy enough to diagnose. The distress itself was more difficult to analyze. He was not looking at her but watching the path ahead, and his long, wet hair hung in his face, concealing his expression.

"I have been trying to guess why you would come to marry a dying madman," he continued. "You said you needed me. I assume it's the money you need." He gave a short laugh. "Obviously. What other reason could there be?"

That was rather a crass way of putting it. Nevertheless, it was true enough, and Gwendolyn had determined at the outset to be honest with him.

"I do need the money, to build a hospital," she said. "I have definite ideas about how it should be constructed as well as the principles according to which it must be run. In order to achieve my goals—without negotiation or compromise—I require not only substantial funds, but influence. As Countess of Rawnsley, I should have both. As your widow, I should be able to act independently. Since you are the last of the males of your family, I should have to answer to no one."

She glanced at him. "You see, I did take all the details of your present situation into account, my lord."

He was looking straight ahead. He had pushed his sopping mane back from his face. She still couldn't read his expression, but she saw no signs of shock or anger.

"My grandfather would turn over in his grave," he said after a moment. "A woman—the Countess of Rawnsley, no less—building a hospital with the family fortune. All that money thrown away upon peasants."

"Wealthy people don't need hospitals," she said. "They can afford to keep physicians about to attend every trivial discomfort."

"And you mean to run it according to your principles," he said. "My grandfather had a very low opinion of feminine intelligence. A woman with ideas of her own, in his view, was a dangerous aberrant of Nature." He glanced at her, then quickly away. "You present me with an almost irresistible temptation."

"I hope so," she said. "There is not another man in England whose circumstances are more neatly suited to my aspirations. I grasped this almost immediately and was quite frantic to get here before you killed yourself. You see, I am much more desperate to marry you than you could possibly be to marry anybody."

"Desperate," he said with another short laugh. "I am the answer to your prayers, am I?"

The halfhearted rain was building to a steady drizzle, and lightning skittered at the edges of the moorland. Still, they were not far from the house now, and traveling on lower ground than before.

He seemed to be mulling the matter over.

Gwendolyn waited silently, resisting the urge to pray. She

did not wish to tempt Fate into more practical jokes. It had already landed him in a mire.

She contented herself with a few cautious sidelong glances at the man she'd come to marry. The rain was washing some of the muck away, and even though his face was still dirty, there was no mistaking the nobly chiseled profile.

He was terribly handsome.

She had not expected that. But then, she was used to expecting the worst. The possibility of finding him attractive had not entered her calculations. She was adjusting those calculations when he spoke again.

"I came here to finish my time in peace," he said. "I hoped that if I kept to myself in this isolated place and didn't bother anybody, no one would bother me."

"But we have come and turned everything upside down," she said. "I can understand how frustrating that is."

He turned to her. "Abonville won't leave me alone, will he?"

"I shall do my utmost to persuade him to respect your wishes," she said cautiously. She couldn't promise Abonville would keep away forever, yet she did not want to use the duc as a threat. She did not want Rawnsley to feel he must hide behind a woman's skirts. One of the most disagreeable aspects of being ill was feeling helpless and utterly dependent upon others.

"If I do as he asks and marry you, he'll probably leave me in peace, at least for a time," Rawnsley said. "The trouble is, I should have you about instead, and yet . . ." His gaze drifted to her leg, then upward. After studying her face for a brooding moment, he returned his attention to the track ahead.

"I have not had a woman in nearly a twelvemonth," he said tightly. "I had determined to put such matters behind me. Apparently, that species of saintliness is not in my nature, and a year is not nearly long enough to cultivate it. I should need decades, I suppose," he said bitterly.

Gwendolyn had not come expecting the kind of "saintliness" he referred to. She had been prepared to go to bed with him and try to make a baby regardless of what he looked like or how he behaved. If it had not seemed like cruel and unusual punishment then, it could hardly alarm or disgust her now. If a long period of celibacy—and for a man, a year must seem like eternity—and a glimpse of her leg was swaying his judgment in her favor, that was fine with her.

"If you are saying you do not find me abhorrent," she said, "I am glad."

"You have no idea what might be demanded of you," he growled. "You have no idea what kind of man I am."

"Considering what I shall eventually gain by this marriage, it would be absurd, not to mention ungrateful, of me to fret about your personal flaws," she said. "It is not as though I am perfect, either. I have made it clear that my motives are mercenary. You have seen for yourself that I am disobedient and sharp-tongued. And I know I am no great beauty. I am also obstinate. That runs in the family, especially among the females of my generation. The time may come, in fact, when you will view your loss of reason as a blessed relief."

"Miss—miss . . . Hell, I can't remember," he said. "I know it isn't Trent, but—"

"The name is Adams," she said. "Gwendolyn Adams."

He scowled. "Miss Adams, I should like to know whether you are trying to convince me to marry you or to kill myself."

"I merely wished to point out how pointless it is, in the circumstances, to quibble about our respective character flaws," she said. "And I wished to be honest with you."

A wicked part of her did not wish to be honest. She realized he was worried about his male urges clouding his judgment. The wicked part of her was not simply hoping the urges would win; it was also tempting her to encourage them with the feminine tactics other girls employed.

But that was not fair.

They had turned into the narrow drive leading to the stables. Though the rain beat harder now, Gwendolyn was aware mainly of the beating of her own heart.

She did not want to go away defeated, yet she did not want to win by unfair means.

She supposed the display of her limbs—however much her immodest mode of riding had been dictated by the need for haste and the unavailability of a sidesaddle—constituted unfair means.

Consequently, as they rode into the stable yard, she headed for the mounting block.

But Rawnsley was off his horse before she reached it, and at the gelding's side in almost the same moment.

In the next, he was reaching up and grasping her waist.

His hands were warm, his grasp firm and sure. She could feel the warmth spreading outward, suffusing her body, while she watched the muscles of his arms bunch under the wet, clinging shirtsleeves.

He lifted her up as easily as if she'd been a fairy sprite. Though she wasn't in the least anxious that he'd drop her, she grasped his powerful shoulders. It was reflex. Instinctive.

He brought her down slowly, and he did not let go even after her feet touched the ground.

He looked down at her, and his intent yellow gaze trapped her own, making her heart pound harder yet.

"The time will come when I will have no power over you," he said, his low tones making her nerve ends tingle. "When my mind crumbles, little witch, I shall be at your mercy. Believe me, I've considered that. I've asked myself what you will do with me then, what will become of me."

At that moment, one troubling question was answered.

He was aware of the danger he was in. His fears were the same as those she felt for him. His reason was still in working order.

But he continued before she could reassure him.

"I can guess what will happen, but it doesn't seem to matter, because I'm the man I always was. A death sentence has changed nothing." His hands tightened on her waist. "You should have left me in the mire," he told her, his eyes burning into her. "It was not pleasant—yet Providence does not grant all its creatures a pretty and painless demise. And I'm ready enough for mine. But you came and fished me out, and now . . ."

He let go abruptly and stepped back. "It's too late."

He was in no state to listen to reassurances, Gwendolyn saw. If he was angry with himself and didn't trust that self, he was not likely to trust anything she said. He would believe she was humoring him, as though he were a child.

And so she gave a brisk, businesslike nod. "That sounds like a yes to me," she said. "Against your better judgment, evidently, but a yes all the same."

"Yes, drat you—drat the lot of you—I'll do it," he growled.

"I am glad to hear it," she said.

"Glad, indeed. You're desperate for your hospital, and I'm the answer to your maidenly prayers." He turned away. "I'm desperate, too, it seems. After a year's celibacy, I should probably agree to marry your *grandmother*, Devil confound me."

He strode down the pathway to the house.

Three

Dorian made straight for the library, the red-haired witch close on his heels.

He flung the door open.

Abonville was pacing in front of the fireplace.

Genevieve was reading a book.

Bertie was building a house of cards.

Dorian strode in and paused a few feet from the threshold.

Abonville stopped short and stared. Genevieve laid aside her book and looked up. Bertie leapt from his chair, the cards flying about him and fluttering to the carpet.

"By Jupiter's thunderbolts!" he cried. "What's happened to you, Cat?"

"Your cousin drove me into a mire," Dorian said levelly. "Then she fished me out. Then we agreed to wed. Today. You may stand as my groomsman, Bertie."

The two elders did not so much as raise an eyebrow.

Bertie opened his mouth, then shut it. He retreated a pace, his brow furrowing.

Dorian bent his gaze upon Miss Adams, who had advanced

from the doorway to stand beside him. "Any objections, Miss Adams?" he asked. "Or second thoughts?"

"Certainly not," she said. "The ceremony may take place whenever you wish."

"I understand that everything has been prepared for speedy nuptials," he said. "If you've the preacher somewhere about, we can do it now."

He turned his stare upon the trio of relatives, bracing himself for an outburst of hysteria.

They believed he was a madman. He knew he looked like one. The rain had merely diluted his coating of mire ooze, which streamed from his sopping garments onto the carpet.

No one uttered a word.

No one moved.

Except the witch, who paid no more attention to her relatives than if they'd been the statues they were doing a splendid imitation of.

"You'll be more comfortable after you have a bath," she said. "And something to eat. And a nap. I know you are exhausted."

Every muscle in his body ached. He could scarcely stand upright. "I can be comfortable later," he said, darting another defiant glance over the mute trio. "I want to get married. Now."

"I should like to wash and change, too," she said. She stepped nearer and tugged at his soggy shirt cuff. "It will take time to send for my maid and my clothes, as well as the minister. They are all waiting at the inn, along with our solicitors. The lawyers must come, too, so that you can sign the settlements. You don't want to be waiting about for everybody in wet clothes, I'm sure."

Lawyers.

Chill panic washed through him.

They would examine him to make sure he knew what he

was doing. Very recently, the Earl of Portsmouth's fourteen-year marriage had been annulled on grounds he'd been of unsound mind when it was contracted. Miss Adams would not want to risk an annulment and lose all claim to his fortune and the title whose influence she needed.

But if they found him unsound . . . He shuddered.

"Look at you," she said sharply. "You're shivering, my lord. Bertie, do stop gaping in that fishlike way and come and make yourself useful. Take your stubborn friend upstairs before he collapses, and tell the servants to ready his bath and find him something to eat. Genevieve, you will send to the inn for what we need, won't you? Abonville, I wish to speak with you."

No one uttered a protest, not so much as a syllable.

Bertie hurried toward him, took the bemused Dorian by the arm, and steered him back through the library door.

Moments later, when they reached the stairs, Dorian saw Hoskins dart through the servants' door and hasten to the library.

He wondered whether the witch had cast a spell over the lot of them.

"Shouldn't dawdle if I was you," Bertie warned. "If Gwen catches us hanging about, she'll take a fit, which I'd rather she didn't, seeing as how she took one already and my ears are still ringing. Not but what she was right. We wasn't listening proper, was we?"

He grasped Dorian's arm and tugged. "Come along, Cat. Hot bath, Gwen said, and she got that right, too, by gad. You look like what the cat dragged in, and meaning no offense, but you smell like I don't know what."

"I told you she drove me into a mire," Dorian said. "What do you expect a man to smell like after a soak in a reeking bog?"

Unwilling to be dragged up the stairs by his overanxious

friend, Dorian shook off the helping hand and started up on his own.

Bertie followed. "Well, she wouldn't've had to chase you, would she, if you hadn't gone and bolted," he said. "Couldn't think why you'd do it. I told you she wasn't like Jess, didn't I? I told you Gwen was a good sort of girl. Did you think I'd let them shackle you to any beastly female? Ain't we friends? Don't we look out for each other? Well, I should think so, or at least I did, but then you was away a long time and never told me where you was. But you never was much for letters, and I never was much good at answering 'em anyhow, and I figured you didn't hear yet I was back from Paris."

They had reached the landing. He gave Dorian a worried look. "But it's all right now, ain't it? Mean to say, if you was looking at her over the breakfast table, you wouldn't cast up your accounts, would you?"

If he were looking at her over the breakfast table, he would probably leap on her and devour her, Dorian thought. Even now, he wondered how he'd managed to keep his hands restricted to her waist after seeing the soft, dazed expression in her eyes when he'd helped her dismount. No woman had ever gazed at him in that way. Under that look, reason, conscience, and will had simply melted away, leaving him defenseless and nigh trembling with longing. Even now, merely recalling, he could not summon up a fragment of common sense.

"I like her . . . eyes," he told Bertie. "And her voice is not disagreeable. She does not seem silly or missish. She seems a capable, sensible girl," he added, recollecting the terrifying efficiency with which she'd extricated him from the mire.

Bertie's worried expression vanished, and he broke into the amiably stupid grin that had softened Dorian's heart toward him years ago.

"There, I knew you'd see it, Cat," he said. "Sensible's the

word. Tells you what's to be done and says it plain so you always know how to go about it. And when she says she'll do it, Gwen goes and does it. Said she was going after you, and we was to stay put and keep our mouths shut tight and stay out of her way. And she did it and you come back and said you'd have her, and now we're all in order, ain't we?"

He'd had his life in order before, Dorian thought: everything in hand, his short future so carefully planned. Kneebones had promised, and he could be trusted to keep his part of the bargain: laudanum, as much as Dorian needed to keep him quiet, to let him die in peace.

Now there was no telling what would happen. He could tell his bride what he wanted, but he could not make her do it. He could exact promises, but he couldn't make her keep them. Before long, he would have no power over her.

But he could not keep his mind on the future because he could not drive out the recollection of the melting look in her green eyes. All he could think of was the night to come and the little witch in his arms . . .

Oh, Lord, and if his mind failed and he hurt her—what then?

For Bertie's sake, he manufactured a smile.

"As you say, Bertie," he answered lightly. "All in order and everyone happy."

Some hours later, Gwendolyn was sitting on a stone bench in the Earl of Rawnsley's garden, watching the blood-red sun's slow descent over a distant hill. The storm had long since swept off to ravage another part of Dartmoor, leaving the air cool and clean.

She was clean and neatly dressed in the green silk gown Genevieve had brought her from Paris, and her unruly hair had been temporarily tamed into a relatively tidy heap of curls atop her head. She hoped it would still be tidy by the time Rawnsley emerged from his meeting with the lawyers.

Gwendolyn's hair was the bane of her existence. The Powers that Be, with their usual perverse idea of a joke, had given her Papa's hair instead of Mama's.

She did not mind the color so much—at least it was interesting—but there was so much of it, a hodgepodge of twists and bends and corkscrews, each of which had a mind of its own, and all of them demented.

Her hair, which was the complete antithesis of her level, steady, and orderly personality, made it very difficult for people to take her seriously—as though being a female didn't make that hard enough already. Thanks to the crazed mass of red curls and corkscrews, every new person she met represented yet another uphill battle to prove herself.

She wished wimples would come back into fashion.

She wondered what Rawnsley's raven mane was like when it was clean and combed. She had not seen him since Bertie had taken charge of him.

She wondered why the earl kept his hair long, whether it was merely some odd masculine vanity or an act of defiance—against convention in general or, more likely, his straitlaced grandfather in particular. She could certainly understand that.

Rebellion did not explain, however, why the earl so little resembled his tiny portrait. The puffy face in the miniature had seemed to belong to a rather corpulent man. The one Gwendolyn had met hadn't an ounce of excess flesh upon his six-foot frame. His drenched shirt and trousers had clung like a second skin, not to rippling rolls of fat, but to lean, taut muscle.

Whatever was wrong with him was obviously confined to the contents of his skull.

Gwendolyn watched the light of the lowering sun spread a red stain through the deepening shadows of the moors while she searched her mental index of brain diseases. She wondered what malady corresponded to the "crumbling" he'd mentioned.

She was considering aneurisms when she heard footsteps crunch upon the gravel path.

Turning toward the sound, she beheld her betrothed advancing toward her, his face set, his right hand clutching a piece of paper.

At that moment, medical hypotheses, along with all other intellectual matters, sank into the deepest recesses of Gwendolyn's mind. When he paused before her, all she could do was stare while her heart beat an erratic rhythm that made the blood hum in her veins.

He wore a coat of fine black wool, whose snugly elegant cut hugged his powerful, athletic physique. Her glance skidded down over the equally snug trousers to the gleaming toes of his shoes, then darted up again to his face.

Cleaned of the mire's vestiges, his countenance was pale, chiseled marble. The long black hair, gleaming like silk, rippled over his broad shoulders. A burning golden gaze trapped hers.

If she had been a normal female, she would have swooned. But she was not normal, never had been.

"Good grief, you are impossibly handsome," she said breathlessly. "I vow, I have never experienced the like. For an instant, my brain stopped altogether. I must say, my lord, you do clean up well. But next time, I wish you would call out a warning before you come into view, and give me a chance to brace myself for the onslaught."

Something dark flickered in his eyes. Then a corner of his hard mouth quirked up. "Miss Adams, you have an interesting—a unique—way with a compliment."

The trace of a smile disoriented her further. "It is a unique experience," she said. "I never knew my brain to shut off before, not while I was full awake. I wonder if the phenomenon has been scientifically documented and what physiological explanation has been proposed."

Her eyes would not focus properly but wandered fuzzily downward again . . . and stopped at the piece of paper. The document snapped her back to reality. "That looks official," she said. "Legal drivel, I collect. Is it something I must sign?"

He glanced back toward the house.

When his attention returned to her, the half-smile was gone, and his expression had hardened again. "Will you walk with me?" he asked.

The backward glance gave Gwendolyn a good idea of what the trouble was. She kept her thoughts to herself, though, and stood obediently and walked with him in silence down a path bordered by roses. When they reached a planting of shrubs that shielded them from view of the house, he spoke.

"I am told that, in view of my prognosis, a guardian ought to be appointed to oversee my affairs," he said. His voice was not altogether steady. "Abonville proposes to act as guardian since he's my nearest male kin. It is a reasonable proposal, my own solicitor agrees. I've inherited a good deal of property, which must be protected when I become incapable of acting responsibly."

A stinging stream of indignation shot through her. She did not see why he must be plagued with such matters this day. All he needed to sign were the marriage settlements. He should not be asked to sign his whole life away in the bargain.

"Protected from whom?" she asked. "Grasping relatives? According to Abonville, there's no one left of the Camoys but a few dithering old ladies."

"It isn't merely the property," he said. His voice was taut, his face a rigid white mask.

She wanted to reach up and smooth the turmoil and tension away, but that would look like pity. She plucked a leaf from a rhododendron and traced its shape instead.

"The guardianship includes legal custody . . . of me," he said. "Because I cannot be responsible for myself, I must be considered a child."

He was not irresponsible yet or remotely childlike. Gwendolyn had told Abonville so. She knew her lecture had calmed the duc down, yet it was too much to hope that her speeches could fully quell his overprotectiveness. He meant well, she reminded herself. He assumed the marriage would be too great an ordeal for her and wished to share the burden.

She could hardly expect her future grandfather to fully understand her capabilities when none of the other men in her family did. None of them took her medical studies and work seriously. Her dedicated efforts remained, as far as the males were concerned, "Gwendolyn's little hobby."

"It is very difficult to think clearly," Rawnsley went on in the same ferociously controlled tones, "with a pair of lawyers and an overanxious would-be grandpapa hovering over me. And Bertie's holding his tongue was no help, when he had to stuff his handkerchief into his mouth to do it, and he still couldn't stop sniffling. I came out to clear my head, because . . . *damnation*." He dragged his hair back from his face. "The fact is, I do not feel reasonable about this. I wanted to tell them to go to the Devil. But my own solicitor agreed with them. If I object, they'll all believe I'm irrational."

And he was worried he'd end up in a madhouse, Gwendolyn understood.

That he'd come to her with his problem seemed to be a good sign. But Gwendolyn knew better than to pin her hopes on what seemed to be.

She moved to stand in front of him. He did not look down at her.

"My lord, you are aware, I hope, that the 1774 Act for Regulating Madhouses included provisions to protect sane persons from improper detention," she said. "At present, only an examining body composed of imbeciles and criminal lunatics could possibly find you non compos mentis. You need not sign every stupid paper those annoying men wave in your face in order to prove you are sane."

"I must prove it to Abonville," he said stiffly. "If he decides I'm mad, he'll take you away."

She doubted the prospect was intolerable to him. She knew he'd agreed to marry her for what he believed were the wrong reasons. She doubted he'd developed a case of desperate infatuation during the last few hours.

It was far more likely that he'd come to test her. If she failed, he would believe it was wise to let her go.

Gwendolyn had been tested before, by certified lunatics, among others, and this man was no more deranged at present than she. Nevertheless she did not make the mistake of imagining this trial would be easier—or less dangerous. She had marked him as dangerous from the first moment he had turned his smoldering yellow gaze upon her. She was sure he fully understood its compelling effect and knew how to use it.

Her suspicions were confirmed when the brooding yellow gaze lowered to hers. "What's left of my reason tells me you represent an infernal complication, Miss Adams, and I should be better off rid of you. The voice of reason, however, is not the only one I hear—and rarely the one I heed," he added darkly.

His gaze drifted down . . . lingered at her mouth . . . then slid downward to her bodice.

Beneath layers of silk and undergarments, her flesh prickled under the slow perusal, and the sensations spread outward until her fingers and toes tingled.

He was trying to make her uneasy.

He was doing a splendid job.

But he faced madness and death, she reminded herself,

next to which her own anxieties could not possibly signify.

By the time the potent golden stare returned to her face, Gwendolyn had collected at least a portion of her composure.

"I am not sure you have identified the correct voice as reason's," she said. "I am absolutely certain, though, that if Abonville tries to take me away, I shall take a fit. I went to a good deal of trouble to get ready for the wedding. My head is stuck full of pins and my maid laced my stays so tight it is a wonder my lips haven't turned blue. It took her a full hour to tie and hook me into this gown, and I shall likely be three hours trying to get out of it."

"I can get you out of that gown in a minute," he said too quietly. "And I shall be happy to relieve you of your painful stays. It would be better for you not to put such ideas into my head."

As though they weren't already there, she thought. As though he hadn't warned her: he hadn't had a woman in a year.

Though she knew he was testing her maidenly fortitude, his low voice set her nerves aquiver.

He was taller than she. And heavier. And stronger.

A part of her wanted to bolt.

But he was not on the brink of a violent lunatic fit, she scolded herself. He was feigning, to test her, and allowing him to intimidate her was no way to win his trust.

"I do not see why it would be better," she said. "I do not want you to be indifferent to me."

"It would be better for you if I were."

He had not moved an inch nearer, yet his low voice and glowing eyes exerted a suffocating pressure.

Gwendolyn reminded herself that the Almighty had been throwing obstacles in her path practically since the day she was born and had confronted her repeatedly with men determined to browbeat or frighten her.

That was sufficient practice for dealing with him.

"I know I am an infernal complication," she said. "I realize you feel put upon, and I do understand your resentment of your—your masculine urges, which incline you to act against your better judgment. But you are not looking on the bright side. A lack of such urges would indicate a failure of health and strength."

She caught the flicker of surprise in his eyes in the instant before he masked it.

"You ought to look upon your animal urges as a positive sign," she persisted. "You are not as far gone as you thought you were."

"On the contrary," he said. "I find myself in far worse case than I had imagined."

He directed his yellow stare to a point on her left shoulder where the neckline of her gown left off and her skin began . . . and instantly she became hotly conscious of every square inch of her skin.

She heard a crackling sound. Looking down, she saw the paper crumpling in his tightly clenched hand.

He looked there, too. "It hardly matters what I sign," he said. "Nothing matters that should." He crushed the document into a ball and threw it down.

Her heart was pumping double-time, speeding the blood through her veins in preparation for flight.

"Damn me," he said. He advanced.

She sucked in her breath.

He grasped her shoulders. "A pretty fellow, am I? Take a fit, will you? I'll show you a fit."

Before she could exhale, he clamped one hand on the back of her neck, pulled her head back, and brought his mouth down upon hers.

* * *

It was her fault, Dorian told himself. She should not have looked at him in that bone-melting way. She should not have stood so near and caught him in her scent, rich and heady as opium to his starved senses. She should have run, instead of staying so close and snaring him in awareness of the fine, porcelain purity of her skin.

He could not help yearning for that purity and softness, and then he could not keep from reaching for her.

He clamped his needy mouth upon her soft, trembling one, and the clean, sweet taste of her made him shiver—in pleasure or despair, he couldn't tell. For all he knew the chill was the emptiness inside him, ever-present, impossible to fill.

He should have stopped then, for his sanity's sake, if nothing else. He knew it was hopeless. This innocent could never sate him. No woman, no matter how experienced and skilled, had ever done it.

But her lips were so soft, warming and yielding to the pressure of his. He had to draw her nearer, seeking the warmth of her young body while he savored the untutored surrender of her innocent mouth.

He pressed her close, greedy for her warmth and softness. He pressed her to his famished body while he deepened the kiss, seeking desperately, as always, for more.

He felt her shudder, but he couldn't stop—not yet. He couldn't keep his tongue from searching the mysteries of her mouth . . . feminine secrets, promising everything.

Lured by scent and taste and touch, he slipped into the darkness. He stroked over her back, heard silk whisper under his fingers, and felt her shift under his touch. Then he was truly lost because she moved into his caress as though she'd done it many times before, as though she belonged in his arms, had always belonged.

Warmth . . . softness . . . sinuous curves under whispering silk, melting against him . . . woman-scent, enveloping him . . . and her skin . . .

He trailed his lips over her satiny cheek, and she sighed. The soft sound ignited the too-quick inner fuse of desire. His fingers found a fastening . . .

"If you're trying to scare me off," came her foggy voice, her breath tickling his ear, "you're going about it all wrong."

His hands stilled.

He raised his head and looked at her. Her eyes opened, and slowly her hazy green gaze sharpened into focus. His own haze instantly dissipated under that penetrating study.

"I was taking a lunatic fit," he said, aware that his thick tones told another story. He wrenched his gaze from the mesmerizing trap of hers and drew back.

Curling red tendrils had escaped their pins to tumble wildly about her flushed face and neck. Her gown was twisted askew.

He stepped back and looked at his hands, afraid to think where they'd been and what he might have done to an innocent, lusting oaf that he was.

"What is wrong with you?" he demanded. "Why didn't you make me stop? Do you have any idea what I might have done?"

She tugged her gown back into place. "I have a very good idea," she said. "I am familiar with the mechanics of human reproduction, as I told Mama. But she felt it was her maternal duty to explain it herself."

She smoothed her bodice. "I must say, she did point out a few subtleties I was unaware of. And Genevieve, as you would expect, enlightened me further. It turned out to be not quite as simple as I thought." She pushed a few pins back into her hair. "Which is not to say I haven't experienced considerable enlightenment under your tutelage, my lord," she added quickly. "It is one thing to be told about intimate kisses. Experiencing them is another matter altogether. What are you staring at?" She looked down at herself. "Have I missed something? Is anything undone?" She turned, presenting her slim back. "Do I need fastening?"

"No." *Thank God*, he added silently.

She turned back and smiled.

Her mouth was overwide. He had noticed that before . . . and felt and tasted every luscious atom of it.

He could not remember seeing her smile before. If he had, he would not have forgotten, for it was a long, sweet curve that coiled about him like an enchantment.

He did not know how to resist its warm promise. He did not know how to fight her and himself simultaneously. He did not know how to drive her away, as he must, when she made him want so desperately to hold her.

It seemed he did not know how to do anything.

The document he'd been asked to sign, the reasons they'd given him for signing, had made him face what he'd tried to ignore. He'd come, intending to scare her off for her own safety—and his peace of mind. Yet he, once capable of making hardened whores tremble, could not stir the smallest anxiety in her, any more than he could rouse his feeble conscience.

Once capable.

Past tense.

Before the headaches. Before the disease had begun its insidious work.

The answer came then, chilling him: the tenuous link between will and action, mind and body, was breaking down already. He was healthy and strong, she'd claimed, but that was only outwardly. His degenerating mind was already sapping his will.

He turned away, lest she read his despair in his countenance. He would master it. He needed but a moment. It had caught him unawares, that was all.

"Rawnsley."

He felt her hand upon his sleeve.

He wanted to shake it off, but he couldn't, any more than he could shake off his awareness of her. The taste of her lingered in his mouth, and her drugging scent wafted about him. He recalled the soft look in her beautiful eyes and the smile . . . warm promises. And he was cold, chilled to his soul.

And too selfish, too weak, he thought with bitter resignation, to let her go.

He brought his hand up and covered hers. "I do not want to go back into that curst library and listen to their solemn speeches and read their bloody documents," he said levelly. "I signed the settlements. You'll get your hospital. That is enough. I want to be wed. Now."

She squeezed his arm. "I'm ready," she said. "I've been ready for hours."

He looked down at her. She smiled up at him.

Warm promises.

He drew her arm through his and led her back to the house. It wanted all his will not to run. The sun was setting, evening closing in with its blessed darkness. Soon, this night, they'd be wed. Soon, they would go up to his room, to the bed. And then . . . God help them both.

He took her through the door and hurried her down the hall. He saw the library door standing open, the light streaming into the gloomy corridor.

He turned to speak to her—then he caught it, faint but unmistakable, at the periphery of his vision.

Tiny zigzags of light.

He blinked, but they would not wash away. They hovered, sparkling evilly, at the edges of his vision.

He shut his eyes, but he saw them still, winking their deadly warning.

He opened his eyes and they were there, inescapable, inexorable.

No, not yet. Not so soon. He tried to brush them away, though he knew it was futile.

They only signaled back, glittering, remorseless: *soon, very soon.*

Four

"*This is your doing,*" *Mr. Kneebones raged at Hoskins.* "I told you my patient's fragile health could not withstand *any* strain. I told you he must be insulated from all sources of nervous agitation. No newspapers. No visitors. You saw what the news about his family did to him: three attacks in one week. Yet you let strangers descend upon him at a time when he was most vulnerable. And now—"

"A man becomes a peer of the realm, he ought to know about it," Hoskins said. "And attacks or no attacks, it was a relief to him to learn the old gentleman couldn't trouble him anymore. And as to letting in strangers, I reckon I can tell the difference between a friend and an enemy. Even if I couldn't, I'd like to see you shut the door in Lady Pembury's face—and her the grandmother of the only friend my master ever had. Maybe it wasn't my place to tell her what was wrong with him, but I judged it best to warn her beforehand that he wasn't as strong as he looked, and his nerves weren't what they used to be."

"Which means they should not have been subjected to *any* source of agitation," Kneebones snapped.

"With all due respect, sir, you never clapped eyes on him until a few weeks ago," Hoskins said. "You may be qualified to judge his medical condition, but you don't know his character or his wishes. I've had more than nine months to learn, and I promise you, the last thing he wishes is to be treated like a vaporish female." He glanced at Gwendolyn. "Meaning no offense, my lady."

"None taken," she said. "I've never succumbed to vapors in my life."

The middle-aged veteran smiled.

Kneebones glared at her.

He'd been glowering at her ever since she'd summoned him into the drawing room, after he'd visited his patient. They had not spoken together ten minutes before hostilities broke out. Hoskins, waiting outside in the hall, had hurried in and leapt to her defense, unaware she didn't need defending.

Still, that had not been unproductive. The manservant's skirmish with the doctor had clarified several matters, and heaven knew Gwendolyn needed as much enlightenment as she could get.

Rawnsley seemed determined to keep her completely in the dark about his illness.

She had noticed something was wrong within minutes of their returning to the house, after the episode in the garden. During the following hours, while Gwendolyn was marshalling everyone into order, she had watched the earl change. By the time of the ceremony, his voice had settled into a monotone . . . while his movements became painfully slow and careful, as though he were made of glass and might shatter at any moment.

The fingers slipping the wedding ring onto hers had been deathly cold, the nails chalk white.

Only after it was done, though, and they had signed their names as husband and wife, had Rawnsley told her he had a headache and was going to bed.

She'd sent her relatives away, as he'd asked, saying the earl needed absolute quiet.

He had spent his wedding night in bed with his laudanum bottle. He had locked his bedroom door, refusing to let even Hoskins in.

This morning, Gwendolyn had taken up the earl's breakfast herself. When she tapped at the door and called softly to him, he told her to stop the infernal row and leave him alone.

Since the servants hadn't seemed unduly alarmed by his behavior, she'd waited patiently until late afternoon before sending for Kneebones.

After the doctor left the room, the patient's door had been locked again—and Kneebones refused to discuss his condition with her.

Gwendolyn regarded the physician composedly, ignoring his threatening expression. Medical men had been glowering and glaring and fuming at her for years. "I should like to know what dosage of laudanum you have prescribed," she said. "I cannot get into my husband's room to determine for myself, and I am most uneasy. It is all too easy for a patient in extreme pain to lose track of how much he's taken and when he last took it. Laudanum intoxication rarely improves either calculating abilities or memory."

"I'll thank you not to tell me my business, madam," Kneebones said stiffly. "I have discussed the benefits and risks with my patient—for all the good that does him now, after what he's been subjected to. One shock after another— capped by a hurry-up wedding to a female he doesn't know from Adam. It was as good as killing him outright. You might as well have taken a hammer to his skull."

"I have discerned no symptoms of shock," Gwendolyn said. "What I have observed—"

"Ah, yes, during *your* lengthy acquaintance with His Lordship," Kneebones said with a cold glance at Hoskins. "My lady has known him all of what—thirty-six hours, if that?"

Gwendolyn suppressed a sigh. She would get nowhere with him. He was like virtually every other physician—with the blessed exception of Mr. Eversham—she'd ever encountered. How they resented being questioned! And how they loved to be mysterious and all-knowing. Very well. She could play that game, too.

"I noticed that the hallucinations were of very brief duration," she said.

Kneebones started. He recovered in an instant, his expression wary.

She could have told him she'd been trained to observe, but she said nothing of her background or of the conclusions she'd drawn after noticing the way Rawnsley had angrily blinked, and brushed at the air near his face, as though trying to clear cobwebs. If Kneebones chose to keep her in the dark, he must expect the same treatment.

She gave him the faintest of smiles. "Did His Lordship not tell you, sir? I am a witch. But I must not waste your valuable time. You have other sickbeds to attend, I know—and I must set my cauldron aboil . . . and look about for a fresh batch of eye of newt."

Kneebones's mouth set in a grim line, and without another word, he stalked out.

Gwendolyn met Hoskins's quiet gaze.

"I don't know the dosage," he said. "All I know is what the bottle looks like—and there's more than one."

Dorian awoke from a restless, nightmare-plagued sleep to nightmarish pain.

His head pounded relentlessly. His insides churned, raw with bile.

Slowly, carefully, he inched up to a sitting position and reached for the bottle on the nightstand. He put it to his lips.

Empty.

Already? he wondered dully. Had he finished it off in a

single night? Or had several nights passed in the oppressive haze of pain and opiates?

It didn't matter.

He had seen the silvery wraiths again. Today, they'd slowly closed in from the peripheries and shimmered everywhere he looked. He had watched the wedding preparations through sparkling ripples undulating in the air like waves in a ghostly sea.

Then, finally, the silver shards had vanished from his vision and sliced into his skull like white-hot blades.

Now he understood why his mother had claimed the "ghosts" had vicious talons, and why she'd screamed and torn at her hair. She had been trying to rip the wicked claws away.

Even he had trouble reminding himself there were neither ghosts nor claws, that it was all a sick fancy.

He wondered how much longer he would be able to distinguish between sick fancy and reality, how long before he began confusing those about him with ghosts and demons—and attacked them in mindless rage.

But he would not, he told himself. Kneebones had promised that the laudanum would quiet him, quelling the delusions along with the pain.

Dorian edged closer to the nightstand and opened the door. He reached in and found the porcelain cylinder.

He took it onto his lap and pried off the lid.

The narrow bottle, nestled in a woolen cloth, lay within.

The elixir of peace . . . perhaps eternal.

He took it out and with trembling hands set the cylinder upon the nightstand.

Then he hesitated, but it was not the prospect of eternity that gave him pause. No, he was too shallow and base for that. It was the witch he thought of, and her soft mouth and slimly curved body. And that image was enough to set his mind to fabricating noble reasons for avoiding laudanum's risks: if he died before the marriage was consummated, it might be annulled, and she would not get her hospital . . . and it was his duty, besides, to get an heir.

But her hospital and the end of the Camoys would not matter to him when he was dead, Dorian reminded himself. Nor would she. He would be gone, and good riddance, and God forbid he should leave a child behind. With his luck, his offspring would inherit the same defective brain and live—briefly—and die in the same mortifying way.

He unstopped the bottle.

"I should be careful, if I were you," came a quiet, familiar voice out of the darkness. "You are married to a witch. What if I've turned it into a love potion?"

The room was black as Hades. He couldn't see her—couldn't focus past the throbbing anyhow—but he could smell her. The oddly exotic scent stole through the thundering sea of pain like ghostly fingers and lifted him up to consciousness.

"It might even be a potion to turn you into a cat," she said.

He could not hear her approach past the relentless hammering in his head, but he could smell it, the faint scent growing richer, more potent. Jasmine?

Slim, warm fingers closed over his icy ones.

He tried to speak. He moved his lips, but no sound came out. Pain slammed his skull. His stomach lurched. The bottle slipped from his hands.

"Sick," he gasped. "Christ, I—"

He broke off as something else, cold and round and smooth, pressed into his hands. A basin.

His body shuddered violently. Then all he could do was hold on to the basin, his head bowed, and give himself up to spasm after spasm after spasm, uncontrollable.

Retching. Endlessly. Helplessly.

All the while, he felt her warm hands upon him, holding him. He heard her soft murmurs above him.

"Yes, that's right. It can't be helped. It's a sick headache,

I know. Beastly thing, isn't it? Hours and hours. Then it won't go quietly, will it? Instead, it must rip out of you and take your insides with it. I don't doubt it seems that way, but you shall feel better in a moment. There. You're done."

It was not a moment, but an eternity, and Dorian didn't know whether he was done or dead. His body had stopped the spasmodic heaving, but he couldn't lift his head.

She caught him before he could sink into the revolting mess in the basin. She raised his head and put a cup to his lips. He smelled mint—and something else. He didn't know what it was.

"Rinse your mouth," she commanded quietly.

Too weak to fight, he obeyed. The tangy draught cleansed the foul taste from his mouth.

When he was done, she gently guided him back onto the pillows.

He lay there, exhausted, aware of movement. The basin disappeared, and its stench with it.

In a little while, a cool, wet cloth touched his face. Gentle, quick, efficient—cleansing and cooling him. He knew he should protest—he wasn't a babe. He couldn't summon the strength.

Then she was gone again, an everlasting time, and the pain rolled in during her absence. Though it was not so ferocious as before, it was there still, pounding at him.

This time, when the scent returned, light came with it, a single candle. He watched her shadowy form approach. He winced at the light. She moved away toward the fireplace and set the candle on the mantel.

She returned to the bed. "You are still in discomfort, it seems," she said very softly. "I don't know whether that's the original headache or the aftereffects of laudanum."

He remembered, then, the bottle she'd stolen from him. "Laudanum," he choked out. "Give me the bottle, witch."

"Maybe later," she said. "At present, I have to work a spell.

Do you think you can climb into the cauldron unaided, or shall I summon Hoskins to help?"

The witch's "cauldron" was alleged to be a steaming bath, and the spell appeared to involve her holding an ice bag on his head while she boiled the rest of him.

That, at least, was the sense Dorian made of her explanation.

He had no trouble deciding that the last thing on earth he wanted to do was climb out of his bed and stagger down to the ground-floor bath chamber.

He changed his mind when he learned his servants were prepared to carry him. He couldn't bear to be carried by anyone, anywhere.

"Your extremities are icy cold," she said as she handed him a dressing gown. She looked away while he angrily struggled into it. "Above the neck, you are much too hot. Your system is unbalanced, you see. We must correct it."

Dorian didn't care if he was unbalanced. On the other hand, he could not bear her seeing him lying helpless and trembling like an infant.

And so he dragged himself from the bed and stumbled across the room and through the door. Rejecting her helping hand, he made his way out of the room and down the stairs.

He found the small, tiled room filled with lavender-scented steam. Candles flickered in the narrow wall niches.

The scented mist, the warmth, the gentle light enveloped him and drew him in. Entranced, he walked to the edge of the sunken bath. Towels had been laid on the bottom and draped over the sides.

His impotent rage dissipated in the sweet warmth and quiet.

He flung off his dressing gown and climbed in, groaning as he slid into the steaming water and the heat stole into his aching muscles.

A moment later, a small pillow slid behind his neck. His eyes flew open.

Mesmerized by the delicious warmth, the inviting water, he had forgotten about the witch . . . and he was stark, screaming naked.

"All you need to do is soak," she said. "Lean back on the cushion. I'll do the rest."

He couldn't remember what the rest was and winced when the soft, icy bag settled onto his head.

"I'll hold it in place," she said. "You needn't worry about it slipping off."

The ice bag was the least of his concerns.

He looked down into the water. The sunken tub was not the deepest one in the world. He could see his masculine possessions all too distinctly.

Though it was too late for modesty, he drew a bit of towel over the place and set his hand over it to keep it from floating up.

He heard a faint sound, suspiciously like a giggle. He refused to look up.

"It's nothing I haven't seen before," the witch said. "Admittedly, the others were live babies or adult corpses, but the equipment is essentially the same in all males."

Something stirred in his sluggish mind. He laid his head back and closed his eyes, trying to collect the elusive bits and pieces. The hospital . . . definite ideas and . . . principles. Her relatives' puzzling obedience. Her lack of fear. The basin in his hands the instant he needed it . . . the quiet efficiency.

He began to understand, but not altogether. Many women had nursing experience, and yet . . .

He returned to the last piece of news. He could understand about the babies. Plenty of women saw infants naked—but adult male . . . corpses?

"How many deathbeds have you attended, Miss Adams?" He kept his eyes closed. It was easier to think without trying to see at the same time. His eyes still hurt. Though the pain was easing, it was still there.

"I am not Miss Adams any longer," she said. "We are wed now. Don't tell me you've forgotten."

"Ah, yes. It slipped my mind for a moment. Because of the . . . dead bodies. I am vastly interested in your corpses, Lady Rawnsley."

"So was I," she said. "But you will not believe the difficulties I encountered. Admittedly, fresh corpses are not so easy to come by. Still, that is no excuse for medical men to be so selfish about them. How is one to learn, I ask you, if one is not permitted even to witness a dissection?"

"I haven't the least idea."

"It is ridiculous," she said. "I finally had to resort to challenging one of Mr. Knightly's students. The condescending coxcomb claimed I would lose my breakfast and swoon and fall on the stone floor and get a severe concussion. I bet him ten pounds I wouldn't." She paused. "As it turned out, he was the one who went to pieces." Her voice held a quiet note of triumph. "After I'd dragged his unconscious body out of the way—I did not wish to step on him by accident—I continued the dissection myself. It was most enlightening. You cannot learn a fraction as much from a living person. You can't see anything."

"How frustrating," he murmured.

"It is. You'd think that proving myself once would be sufficient, but no. It was the one and only time I had the instruments in my hand and a corpse all to myself. All I won was permission to observe, and that must remain a dark secret, lest my family get wind of it. Even with the patients—the living ones—it was no good proving my competence to anybody. As long as Mr. Knightly was in charge, I might only assist, discreetly. He must rule absolutely, and mere females must obey orders, even when they are based upon the most antiquated theories."

Behind his closed eyes, Dorian saw the answer now, with stunning clarity.

A day earlier, the insight would have had him leaping from the bath and running hell for leather for the nearest available mire.

At present, a part of his mind suggested that fleeing was not an altogether bad idea.

But he was so comfortable, his muscles relaxing in the steaming water, his tormented head pleasantly cool.

And so he said, very mildly, "Small wonder, then, that you should leap at the chance to have a patient of your very own."

And before very long, a corpse of her very own, he added inwardly. Not that it mattered. If she wished to dissect his remains, he would hardly be in a position to object.

She did not respond immediately. Dorian kept his eyes closed, savoring the scented mist drifting about him. Her scent was there as well, rich and deep, coiling with the lavender. He did not know whether it was the scent or his ailment that made him feel so lightheaded.

"I was not implying that all members of the medical profession are imbeciles," she said at last. "But I could not trust Abonville to distinguish among them. Bertie would be worse. He'd be sure to send for experts from London and Edinburgh, and he has such a knack for blundering."

"I understand," he said. "You came to . . . save me."

"From medical bedlam," she said hastily. "I am not a miracle worker, and I know precious few brain diseases are curable. Not that I know much about yours," she added with a trace of irritation. "Mr. Kneebones is as obstinately close-mouthed as Mr. Knightly was. I knew it was a waste of breath to argue with him. Words are rarely of any use. I shall have to prove myself, as usual."

Dorian recalled her brisk, unruffled mode of freeing him

from the mire. He recalled the cool steadiness with which she'd met his attempt to frighten her away. He recalled her calm, efficient ministrations of a little while ago, when he'd been so disgustingly sick.

He considered his present comfortable state. He had not felt so tranquil in months. He couldn't remember, in fact, when he'd last felt so much at peace. Had he ever?

He couldn't recall a time when he hadn't been angry with himself for his weaknesses and seething with resentment of his grandfather, who, like the doctors she spoke of, insisted on ruling absolutely.

He opened his eyes and slowly turned his head to look up at her. She kept the ice bag in place while her cool green gaze shifted to meet his.

He wondered whether the cool detachment came naturally, or if she'd had to train herself to suppress emotion, in order to survive in a world that didn't trust or want her. He knew what that was like, and what the training cost.

"The damp does strange things to your hair," he said gruffly. "All the little curls and corkscrews sprout up every which way, making a fuzzy red cloud. Even in dry air, it seems alive, trying to do whatever it is bent on doing. 'What on earth is her hair doing?' the medical men must ask themselves. One can't be surprised at their failing to attend closely to what you say."

"They should not allow themselves to be distracted," she said. "It is unprofessional."

"As a group, men are not very intelligent," he said. "Not in a steady way, at least. We have our moments of lucidity, but we are easily distracted."

He was—oh, so easily.

The room's steamy fog had settled upon her. A fine dew glistened on her porcelain skin. Damp curls clustered about her ears. He thought of pushing the curls away and tracing the delicate shape with his tongue. He thought of where his mouth and tongue would go if he let them . . . along the moist flesh of her neck to the hollow of her throat.

His gaze skimmed down to her neckline, then lower, to where the damp fabric clung to the curve of her breasts.

Mine, he thought. And then he could not think about the future. He could scarcely think at all.

"Some men can be distracting," she said. "At times. You, especially."

If he had not been so keenly, yearningly aware of her, he would not have caught the faint, unsteady thread in her voice.

"Ah, well, I'm mad." What he felt might as well be madness. Beneath the concealing corner of the towel, the part of him that never heeded reason stirred from its slumbers.

"This treatment is supposed to have a soporific effect," she said, frowning as she studied his face.

She did not appear anxious but puzzled, which would have amused him if he had been capable of detached observation. That was impossible.

She sat near his shoulder, at the edge of the sunken tub, her legs curled up under her gown, and his base mind was fixed upon what lay beneath. He brought his hand up out of the water and rested it on the tub's curved rim, inches from the hem of her gown.

"Treatment?" he said. "I thought this was supposed to be a spell."

"Yes, well, I must not have added enough eye of newt. It is supposed to induce a pleasant drowsiness."

"My brain is becoming somnolent." His fingers touched the ruffled muslin . . . and closed upon it.

Her frowning attention shifted to his hand. "You have a headache," she said.

He toyed with the ruffle. "That does not seem terribly important at the moment."

Though the pain lingered, it no longer mattered. What

mattered was his treacherous recollection of what lay under the muslin. He drew it back.

Soft kid slippers . . . a few inches of prettily turned ankle . . . and no stockings. "No stockings," he said, his voice as foggy as his mind. "Where are your stockings, Lady Rawnsley?"

"I took them off before," she said. "They were frightfully expensive—from Paris—and I hated to risk catching them on a splinter when I climbed in your window."

He grasped her ankle. "You climbed in the window." He did not look up from the imprisoned limb.

"To get into your room. I was worried you would take too much laudanum. Not an idle anxiety, as it turns out. The solution in that bottle of yours had not been properly diluted."

She had said she couldn't let him die before the ceremony, he recalled. Apparently, she dared not let him die before the marriage was consummated, either.

And he didn't want to die before then, either, rot his black soul.

"You had to save me," he said.

"I had to do something. I know nothing about picking locks, and breaking down the door would have made a ghastly row, so I took the window route. Isn't your hand growing cold again, my lord?"

"No." He stroked her ankle. "Does it feel cold to you?"

"I couldn't tell whether it was me or you." She swallowed. "I am quite . . . warm."

He pushed the gown up higher and slid his hand over the perfectly curved limb he'd exposed. She wanted her hospital, he told himself, and she was prepared to pay the price.

And he wanted to trail his mouth over her wickedly lovely legs . . . up, all the way up to . . . His gaze shot to her hair, the wild red curls. His mind conjured a picture of what he'd find at the end of the journey, at the juncture of her thighs.

Then his gaze locked with hers, meltingly soft.

Then he was lost, rising from the water and reaching for her, lashing his arm round her narrow waist, drawing her toward him. He felt the air, cool against his back after the water's warmth, but it was her warmth he wanted.

"You will take a chill," she gasped. "Let me get you a dry towel."

"No, come to me," he said thickly.

He did not wait for her to come but swept her up in his dripping arms and held her tightly for a long, mad moment. Then he sank down with her into the scented cauldron, and as the water closed over them, his mouth found hers, and he sank deeper then, beyond saving . . . drowning in a sea of warm promises.

This was most unprofessional, Gwendolyn scolded herself as she flung her arms round her husband's neck.

It was well known that excitement of the passions exacerbated sick headaches.

Unfortunately, nowhere in the medical literature had she encountered a remedy for cases in which the physician's passions were excited. She did not know what antidote to apply when the patient's lightest touch triggered severe palpitations of the heart and a shockingly swift rise in temperature to fever point. She did not know what palliative could alleviate the coaxing pressure of a wickedly sensual mouth upon hers, or what elixir could counteract the devil's brew she tasted when her patient's tongue stole in to coil with hers.

She was aware of water lapping at her shoulders and her gown billowing up to the surface in the most brazen manner, but she could not retrieve sufficient clinical objectivity to do anything about it.

She was preoccupied with every slippery, naked inch of him, hard and warm under her hands, and she couldn't keep her hands from moving over his powerful shoulders and the taut, smooth planes of his broad chest. It wasn't quite enough. She could not resist the need to taste the smooth, water-slick skin. She eased away from his enslaving mouth and traced his wet jaw and neck with her lips while her hands continued to explore his splendid anatomy.

"Oh, the deltoid muscle . . . and pectoralis major," she murmured dizzily. "So . . . beautifully . . . developed."

She was aware of the increased urgency and boldness of his touch, and she knew her brazen behavior incited him. But his caresses were inciting her.

She felt the weight of his hands upon her breasts, a warm pressure that made her ache and push into his hand, seeking more. The sensuous mouth upon her neck simmered kisses whose heat bubbled under her skin and made her quiver with impatience. His wicked tongue teased her ear . . . maddening.

Above the water's plashing, she heard the low animal sound he made when she shivered uncontrollably and burrowed into him, as though she could crawl into his skin. She wanted to.

She could not get close enough. The water . . . her clothes . . . everything between them . . . obstacles.

"Do something," she gasped, fumbling with her gown. She tugged at the bodice, but the soaked fabric wouldn't tear. "Get it off," she told him. "I can't bear it."

She felt his fingers struggling at her back with the tapes. "They're too wet," she said feverishly. "You can't untie them. Rip it."

"Wait. Calm down." His voice was thick.

She dragged her hand down to his belly.

He sucked in his breath. "Gwendolyn, for God's sake—"

"Hurry."

"Wait." He closed his mouth over hers and swept her lunatic rage away in an endless, soul-draining kiss.

She clung to him, her mouth locked with his while he

swung her into his arms and up, out of the bath and onto the damp towels.

When he broke the drugging kiss at last, she opened her eyes to a burning gold gaze. He knelt over her, straddling her hips. His skin was slick, shimmering in the candlelight. Water streamed from his long, night-black hair.

While she watched, spellbound, he brought his hand to the neckline of her soaked gown. With one easy yank, he tore it to the waist. "Happy now, witch?" he whispered.

"*Yes.*" She reached for him and drew him down, frantic to feel his skin against hers.

Hot, hasty kisses . . . over her brow, her nose, cheeks, chin . . . and more, down over her throat to sizzle over her breasts. The scorching kisses burned the spell away, and the madness returned.

She caught her fingers in his hair to keep him there. She needed more, though she hardly knew what the more was. She felt his mouth close over the taut bud of her breast, and the first light tug shot threads of tingling electricity under her skin, into . . . somewhere . . . a world inside her she hadn't realized was there.

It was wild and dark, a pulsing jungle of sensation. He took her into the darkness, drawing her deeper with his hands, his mouth, his low, ragged voice.

The remnants of her garments fell away, along with the last vestiges of her reason. She was lost in his scent, so potently masculine, and in the sinful taste of him, and in the stunning power of muscle under taut, smooth flesh.

She wanted him to crawl inside her, under her skin. She wanted him to be part of her. Even when his hand settled between her legs, upon the most private of places, it wasn't enough, and she arched up to his touch for more.

He caressed her in secret ways that made her moan and squirm under his hand, but it was not enough. The tantalizing strokes slipped deeper, inside her. Spasms racked her, hot, delicious . . . but not enough.

She trembled on a precipice, caught between wild pleasure and an unreasoning, inescapable craving for more, for something else.

"Dear God," she gasped, writhing like one demented, which she was. "Do it. Please."

"Soon." A rough whisper. "You're not ready. It's your first—"

"Hurry." She could feel his shaft pulsing against her thigh. She dug her nails into his arms. "*Hurry.*"

Cursing, he pulled her fingers away. She could not keep away. She dragged her hands down over his belly, to the place where instinct led her. She found the thick, hot shaft. Immense. Her hand could not close about it. "Oh, my goodness," she whispered.

"Stop it. Christ, Gwen, don't rush me. It'll hurt and you—"

"Oh, Lord. It feels . . . so strong . . . and alive." She hardly knew what she was saying. She stroked the velvety flesh, lost in heated wonder.

She heard a strange, strangled sound above her.

Then he was caressing her intimately again, dragging her back into the frustrating madness. Her hand fell away from him as the furious pleasure swept her to the precipice.

Then it came, one swift thrust—and a stinging sensation that jerked her back to reality.

She gulped in air and blinked. "Good heavens."

He was enormous. She was not comfortable.

Yet she was not exactly uncomfortable, either. Not altogether.

"I told you it would hurt."

She heard the ache in his voice. Her fault, she reproached herself. Everyone knew it hurt the first time. She should not have let herself be taken unawares. Now he probably thought he'd done her a permanent injury.

"Only at first," she said shakily. "That is normal. You mustn't stop on my account."

"It's not going to get much better."

She looked into his glowing eyes, saw the shadows lurking there. "Then kiss me," she whispered. "I'll concentrate on that and ignore the rest."

She reached up, slid her fingers into his thick, wet mane, and drew him down.

He kissed her fiercely. The hot need she tasted ignited hers. She simmered in the devil's brew, and the pain and tightness bubbled away into nothingness.

He began to move inside her, slow strokes at first, but soon quickening. She moved with him, her body answering instinctively, gladly. In the intimate beat of desire, passion returned, hotter than before. She was joined with him, and this was what she'd needed: to be one, to take him with her to the edge of the abyss . . . and beyond . . . into the last, searing burst of rapture . . . and then she sank with him, into the sweet darkness of release.

Five

Some time later, enveloped in her husband's dress-ing gown, Gwendolyn sat tailor-fashion near the foot of his bed.

She had piled a heap of pillows at his back, and he sat with his legs stretched out in front of him—under the bed-clothes because she had insisted he keep his feet warm.

The debauch in the bathing room had left them famished. They had raided the larder and sneaked up to his bedroom with a tray of thick sandwiches, which they'd made short work of.

Though the bath, the lovemaking, and the meal had radi-cally improved his mood, he was not altogether tranquil.

Gwendolyn was aware of the glances he stole at her from under his black lashes when he thought she wasn't looking. She wished she knew what those troubled glances signified. At present, only one aspect of his character was truly clear to her.

Though facing a horrendous death in quicksand, he'd tried to drive her off—because he was afraid she'd fall in.

He had been willing to risk medical bedlam and eventual

incarceration in a madhouse, rather than subject her to marrying him.

Though informed of the deadly risks of unsupervised laudanum consumption, he had locked himself alone in his room—to spare her witnessing his miseries.

The Earl of Rawnsley, in short, had a protective streak a mile long and three miles deep.

Gwendolyn didn't think she was overestimating him. She'd had enough experience with her father, brothers, uncles, and cousins to recognize this particular ailment.

The awareness was doing nothing to restore her clinical detachment, which was in dangerous disrepair already.

Just looking at him paralyzed her intellect. When she recalled what that sensuous mouth, those strong, graceful hands, and that long muscled body had done to her, her entire brain, along with her heart and every other organ and muscle she possessed, turned to jelly.

His low voice broke into her bewildered thoughts.

"I don't think you ought to stay in here," he said gently.

She looked up from her folded hands. His carefully polite expression made her heart sink.

She could guess why he wanted her out of his sight. He'd probably spent most of the time since they'd left the bathing room devising a courteous way of telling her he'd rather not repeat the experience.

But she'd been rejected countless times before, Gwendolyn reminded herself, and it hadn't killed her yet.

"I understand," she said, her voice cool, her face hot. "I know I behaved shockingly. I scarcely know what to think of myself. I have never, *ever*, in all my life, reacted that way—to anybody."

A muscle worked in his jaw.

"Not that I've had so many beaux," she hurriedly added. "I am not a flirt, and even if I was, I hadn't much time for suitors. I didn't want to make time," she babbled on as his expression grew tauter. "But girls are obliged to make an appearance in Society, and then of course the men think one is like the others, and one feels obliged to pretend that's true. And I must admit that I was curious about what it was like to be courted and kissed. But it wasn't like anything, and not half so interesting as, say, Mr. Culpeper's *Herbal*. If it had been that way with you, I'm sure I should have behaved much more decorously downstairs. I should have fastened my mind on a medical treatise and not made a spectacle of myself. But I could not behave properly. I am truly sorry. The last thing I wanted was to make myself disagreeable to you."

With a sigh, she started to crawl from the bed.

"Gwendolyn." His voice was choked.

She paused and met his gaze.

"You are not disagreeable to me," he said tightly. "Not at all. Word of honor."

She remained where she was, kneeling near the edge of the mattress, trying to read his expression.

"How could you think I was displeased?" he demanded. "I all but ravished you."

Good grief, how could she be so stupid? He was upset with himself, not her. Because of the mile-long protective streak.

She tried to remember what Genevieve had told her about men—and the first time—but her mind was a jumble. "Oh, no, it was not like that at all," she assured him. "You were so very gentle—and I did appreciate that, truly I did. I know I should not have acted like a general: 'Do this,' 'Do that.' 'Hurry.' But I could not help myself. Something"—she gestured helplessly—"came over me."

"The something was your lusting spouse," he said grimly. "Which I should not have allowed myself to become."

"But we are wed," she argued. "It was your right, and it was a pleasure for me and—" Her face burning, she boldly added, "I am glad you lusted, my lord. I should have been very disappointed if you did not because I have wanted you to make me yours since . . ." She frowned. "Well, I'm not sure when exactly it began, but I know I wanted it after you kissed me." She crept toward him. "I wish you would not fret about me."

"This was supposed to be a business arrangement," he said. Shadows darkened his eyes. "No one would have known if the marriage had not been consummated. Your position was secure enough. I should not have touched you. You have no experience. You do not know how to protect your feelings. Your heart is too soft."

She sank back on her heels. "I see. You are alarmed that my feelings will become engaged."

"They *are* engaged," he said. "You have just told me as much. Not that I couldn't see it for myself. I wish you could see the way you look at me."

Good heavens. Was she so obvious?

But of course she was. She was not like Genevieve or Cousin Jessica. She had no subtlety, Gwendolyn was aware. But she did possess both a sense of humor and common sense, and these came to her rescue.

"Like a lovesick schoolgirl, you mean?" she asked.

"Yes."

"Well, what do you expect? You are shockingly handsome."

He leaned forward, his eyes narrowed. "I have a *brain disease*. My mind is crumbling to pieces. And in a few months I shall be a rotting corpse!"

"I know that," she said. "But you are not mad yet, and when you become so, you will not be my first lunatic—any more than you'll be my first corpse."

"You didn't marry the others! You didn't bed them! Damnation." He flung back the bedclothes and stalked, splendidly naked, to the window. "I didn't even want to be your patient," he said as he gazed out into the darkness. "And now I am your lover. And you are besotted. It is macabre."

He would not think it macabre if he could see himself as she saw him, standing so tall and strong and beautiful in the candlelight.

"You said yourself that Providence does not grant all its creatures a pretty demise," she said. "It does not give each of us exactly what we want. It did not make me a man, so that I could become a doctor."

She left the bed and went to him. "But now I am not at all sorry I'm a woman," she told him. "You've made me very glad of it, and I am practical and selfish enough to want to enjoy the gladness for as long as I can."

He swung round, his countenance bleak. "Oh, Gwen."

She understood then that she would not have long. The stark expression, the despair in his voice, told her matters were worse than they appeared.

But that was the future, she told herself.

She laid her hand on his chest. "We have tonight," she said softly.

He'd made her glad she was a woman.

We have tonight, she'd said.

Saint Peter himself, backed by a host of martyrs and angels, could not have withstood her. He would have let the heavenly gates slam shut behind him and taken her into his arms and devoted body and soul—eternally damned though it might be—to making her happy.

And so Dorian scooped up his foolishly besotted wife in his arms and carried her to the bed and made love to her again. And he tasted, again, the rapture of being made love to, of being desired and trusted. And later, as he held his sleeping countess in his arms, he lay awake wondering whether he was dead or alive because he could not remember when his heart had felt so sweetly at peace.

Not until the first feeble light of daybreak stole into the room did something like an explanation occur to him.

Never, in all his life, had he ever done anything that was any good to anybody. He'd done no more than fantasize about rescuing his mother from a world where she didn't belong and taking her to the Continent, where she would no longer have to lie and pretend. When he'd finally got around to visiting her here, he'd missed all the hints she dropped, and gone on his merry way. If he had paid attention instead, and stayed, and helped his father care for her, they might have forestalled his grandfather and the "experts." Even at the madhouse, when it had seemed too late, it needn't have been, if Dorian had used the clever brain he'd inherited. He should have played on his grandfather's overweening pride and sense of duty, and worked him round by degrees. Mother had pulled the wool over the old tyrant's eyes for years. Dorian could have done it, should have done it.

And he should have done it later, when the ax fell, instead of storming out of Rawnsley Hall in a childish tantrum. Then he might have accomplished something. He might have used the earl's money and influence to good purpose, in scholarly pursuits, for instance, to further knowledge, or perhaps in a political endeavor.

Everyone died, some early, some late. It was nothing to whimper about. But dying with nothing but regret and if onlys was pathetic.

That, Dorian realized, was what had kept him so unsettled for these last months.

Now, though, his soul was quiet.

Because of her.

He nuzzled his wife's wayward hair. He had made her happy. He had made her forgive the Almighty for making her a woman. He smiled. He knew that was no small achievement.

She wanted to be a doctor. Equally important, she would use the Earl of Rawnsley's money and influence to good purpose.

Very well, he told her silently. *I cannot give you a medical degree, but I will give you what I can.*

And that must have been the right conclusion, because his busy mind quieted, and in a little while, he fell asleep.

After breakfast, Dorian took her out to the moors, to the place where his mother had brought him eight years earlier.

He helped Gwendolyn from her horse—treating himself to but one brief kiss in the process—then led her to a boulder at the track's edge. He took off his coat and laid it on the cold stone and asked her to sit, which she did with a bemused smile.

"Last night you said I was not your first lunatic," he began.

"Oh, not at all," she eagerly assured him. "Mr. Eversham, who took over Mr. Knightly's practice, was particularly interested in neurological maladies, and he let me assist him in several cases. Not all the patients were irrational, certainly. But Miss Ware had six different personalities at last count, and Mr. Bowes was prone to violent dementia, and Mrs. Peebles—may her troubled soul rest in peace—"

"You can tell me the details later," Dorian interrupted. "I only wanted to make sure I had heard correctly last night. I was not fully attending, I'm sorry to say. I have not listened properly since you came."

"How can you say such a thing?" she exclaimed. "You are the only man except Mr. Eversham who's ever taken me seriously. You did not laugh at my hospital idea, and you were not horrified about the dissections." She hesitated briefly. "You are rather overprotective, true, but that is your

nature, and I know it is a very gentlemanly and noble inclination."

"Overprotective," he repeated. "Is that how you see it,
Gwen?"

She nodded. "You want to shield me from unpleasantness.
On the one hand, it is rather lovely to be coddled. Still, on
the other, it is just the tiniest bit frustrating."

He understood how he'd frustrated her. She didn't like being kept in the dark about his illness. He had treated her like
a silly female, as other men had done.

"I have surmised as much." He clasped his hands behind
his back to keep from gathering her up and "overprotecting"
her in his arms, as he very much wished to do. "Yours is a
medical mind. You do not see matters as we laymen do. Illness is a subject of study to you, and sick people represent a
source of knowledge. Their ailments make you no more
queasy than a volume of Cicero's works does me." He paused,
his face heating. "I fancied myself a scholar once, you see.
Classics."

"I know." Her green gaze was soft with admiration. "You
took a first, Bertie says."

"Yes, I am not merely a pretty fellow," he said with a
short laugh. "I have—*had*—a brain." Embarrassed, he looked
away, toward the moors. "I also had plans once, as you do.
But they were not . . . well thought out, and it all ended in . . .
rather a mess."

His throat tightened.

He told himself it was ridiculous to feel uneasy. He had
prepared himself to tell her everything. He knew it was
right. She needed to learn the facts—all of them—in order
to make intelligent decisions about her future. At present,
her attachment to him was probably little more than a new
bride's infatuation, a response to the physical passion they'd
shared. If, after he enlightened her about his past and what
the future held in store, she chose to leave, she'd swiftly re-

cover her equilibrium. If she chose to remain, she would do it with her eyes open at least, prepared for the worst. To show respect for her mind and character, as well as belief in her goals, he must give her the choice, and accept her decision, and live—and die—with the consequences.

"Dorian?"

He closed his eyes. How sweetly his name fell from her lips. He would remember that, too, no matter what happened—or he would remember, at least, for as long as his brain functioned.

He turned back to her, smiling as he shoved his windblown hair from his face.

"I know you want to hear all the fascinating details of my illness," he said. "I was only trying to decide where to begin."

She sat up straighter and her soft, adoring expression transformed into the steady green regard that had so intrigued him when they first met. "Thank you, my dear," she said, her tone thoroughly professional now. "If you don't mind, I should like you to begin with your mother."

After dinner that evening, Gwendolyn sat at a table in the library, making a list of medical texts to be sent from home. Dorian sat by the fire, perusing a volume of poetry.

She knew it had not been easy for him to talk about his past, but she was sure it had done him good. He kept too much bottled up inside him, Gwendolyn thought as her gaze strayed back to him. When people did that, matters tended to get exaggerated out of proportion, and his ignorance of medical science only made it worse.

The visual chimera he'd described, for instance, were physiological phenomena common to a number of neurological ailments, not ghastly aberrations, as he thought. Furthermore, Dorian had not quite comprehended his mother's case or the difficulties of managing lunatics. Nor had he realized that the doctors often had no way of knowing for certain until after death that the brain was physically damaged. Still, she was not sure Mr. Borson had handled the case altogether wisely.

Dorian looked up and caught her staring at him.

"You're wearing your medical frown," he said. "Am I foaming at the mouth, by any chance, without realizing?"

"I was thinking about your mother," she said. "Her hair, for instance. I'm not sure cutting it was the only option."

His face stiffened, but only for a moment. "I'm not sure what else they could have done," he said slowly. "She was tearing it out in bloody clumps, according to my father and uncle. She did not realize it was her own hair, I think. She must have believed it was the talons. The imaginary claws of the imaginary Furies."

Gwendolyn left her chair and went to him and stroked his hair back from his face.

He smiled up at her. "I give you leave to cut my hair, Gwen. I should have done it weeks ago—or at least for my wedding."

"But that is the point," she said. "I don't want to cut your hair."

"I don't wear it this way because of some mad whim you must indulge," he said. "I had practical reasons, which are no longer relevant."

"I thought you did it to spite your grandfather," she said. "If he had been my grandfather, I am sure I would have done something to vex him." She considered briefly. "Trousers. I should have worn trousers."

He laughed. "Ah, no, I was not so bold as that. When I went to London, I was concerned that someone might recognize me and tell him where I was. Then he would punish my landlady and my employers for giving aid and comfort—such as it was—to the enemy."

He'd told her about his time in London, slaving night and day. Working on the docks explained his muscles, which had puzzled her very much. One rarely saw that sort of upper body development among the nobility, though it was common enough among laborers and pugilists.

"Looking like an eccentric—and possibly dangerous—recluse keeps the curious at bay," he went on. "It discourages them from prying into one's personal affairs. Such concerns obviously applied here in Dartmoor, at least while my grandfather was alive."

"Well, I'm glad you were impractical and didn't cut your hair for the wedding," she said. "It suits your exotic features. You don't look very English. Not in the ordinary way, at any rate." She paused, struck by an idea.

She stood back to consider him . . . and grinned.

He grasped her hand and drew her toward him, and tumbled her onto his lap.

"You had better not be laughing at me, Doctor Gwendolyn," he said sternly. "We madmen don't take kindly to that."

"I was thinking of Cousin Jessica and her husband," Gwendolyn said. "Dain is not ordinary-looking either. She and I seem to have similar taste in men."

"Indeed. She likes monsters and you like lunatics."

"I like you," she said, snuggling against him.

"How can you help liking me?" he said. "I spent hours yesterday talking of little but medical symptoms and insane asylums. And you listened as though it were poetry and all but swooned at my feet. It is too bad I haven't any medical treatises about. I'm sure I need read but a paragraph or two, and you will become ravenous with lust and begin tearing off my clothes."

All he had to do was stand there—sit there—to make her ravenous with lust, she thought. She drew back. "Would you like that?"

"Your tearing off my clothes? Of course I'd like it." He bent his head and whispered in her ear, "I am mentally unbalanced, recollect."

She glanced toward the door. "What if Hoskins comes in?"

Dorian slid her hand into the opening of his shirt. "We'll tell him it's a medical treatment," he said.

She turned back to him. Behind the laughter glinting in his eyes, desire smoldered, fierce and hot.

One day, too soon, the fierceness and heat would turn dangerous—deadly, perhaps.

But she would deal with that day when it came, Gwendolyn told herself. In the meantime, she was happy to burn in his strong arms.

She lifted his hand to her breast. "Touch me," she whispered. "Make me mad, too, Dorian."

He had an attack the next day.

They had just finished breakfast when she saw him blink impatiently and brush at the air near his face.

He caught himself doing it and laughed. "I know it does no good," he said. "A reflex, I suppose."

Gwendolyn left her chair and went to him. "If you go to bed now and I give you a dose of laudanum, you'll scarcely notice when the headache starts."

He rose, and went upstairs with her, his expression preoccupied. She helped him undress, and noticed that his vision was not so impaired that he couldn't find her breasts. He fondled them while she wrestled with his neckcloth.

"You are remarkably good-humored," she said when she'd finally got him under the bedclothes. "If I didn't know better, I'd suspect my lord only wished to lure me into his bedchamber."

"I wish it were a trick," he said, blinking up at her. "But there the damned things are, winking and blinking at me.

And you were right, Gwen. They are not like ghosts, after all. You described it better. 'Like colliding with a lamppost,' you said. 'First you see stars, then the pain hits.' I should like to know what it was that persuaded my brain I'd suffered a blow to the head."

She knew, all too well.

I told you he must be insulated from all sources of nervous agitation, Kneebones had said.

He was a real doctor, with decades of experience. He understood the malady, had studied Dorian's mother for months.

You saw what the news about his family did to him: three attacks in one week.

She recalled yesterday's conversation, and her conscience stabbed.

"I can see what it was," she said tightly. "Yesterday, I obliged you to relive the most painful experiences of your life. And I was not content with the general picture, was I? I pressed you for details, even about the post-mortem report on your mother. I should have realized this was too much strain for you to bear all at once. I cannot believe I did not think of that. I do wonder where I misplaced my wits."

She started to move away, to fetch the laudanum bottle, but he grabbed her hand. "I wonder where you've put them now," he said. "You've got it all backwards, Gwen. Our talk yesterday did me nothing but good. You eased my mind on a hundred different counts."

He tugged her hand. "Sit."

"I need to get your laudanum," she said.

"I don't want it," he said. "Not unless I become unmanageable. That's the only reason I took it before. I wasn't sure I could trust myself. But I can trust you. I'm not your first lunatic. You'll know when I need to be stupefied."

"I also know the pain is dreadful," she said. "I cannot let you lie there and endure it. I must do something, Dorian."

He shut his eyes then, and his face set.

"It's started, hasn't it?" It was a struggle to keep her voice low and even.

"I don't want to be stupefied," he said levelly. "I want my mind clear. If I must be incapacitated physically, I should like to use the opportunity to think, while I still can."

Gwendolyn firmly stifled her screaming conscience. Her guilt would not help him.

She had come with low expectations, she reminded herself. She had hoped to learn while ameliorating, insofar as possible, his suffering. She had never had any illusions about curing what medical science scarcely understood, let alone knew how to treat.

She had not expected to fall in love with him, almost instantly. Still, that changed only her emotions, and she would simply have to live with them. She would not, however, let them rule, and be tempted to pray for a miracle, when what she ought to be doing was listening to him and ascertaining what he needed and how best to provide it.

"You want to think," she said, frowning.

"Yes. About my mother and what you said about her. About my grandfather. The experts. The asylum." He pressed a thumb to his temple. "I do not believe I've burst a blood vessel, but I distinctly see my life passing before me." Smiling crookedly, he added, "And it is beginning to make sense."

She felt a surge of alarm, which she ruthlessly suppressed. "Very well," she said calmly. "No soporifics. We shall try a stimulant instead."

Gwendolyn gave him coffee. Very strong coffee and a good deal of it.

Two hours and countless cups later, Dorian was fully recovered and his wife was staring at him as though he'd just risen from the dead. She stood by the fire, her hands folded in front of her, her expression a comical mixture of worry and bewilderment while she watched him yank on his clothes.

"I begin to suspect you believed I *had* burst a blood vessel," he said as he fastened his trouser buttons. "Or was about to."

The comical expression vanished, succeeded by the familiar steady green regard. "I do not know what to think," she said. "Frankly, I am confounded. Two hours, from start to finish. This makes no medical sense at all."

"I told you I distinctly felt the pressure ease after the fourth cup," he said. "As though my head were being released from a vise. Perhaps the coffee washed the pressure through my system and"—he grinned—"into the chamber-pot."

"It does have diuretic qualities," she said.

"Obviously."

"But you should not respond in this way." Her brow furrowed. "Perhaps I misinterpreted your account of the autopsy report, though I do not see how. Your mother's was hardly an unusual case."

"I should like to know what's troubling you," he said. "Have I been babbling incoherently without realizing it? Am I manifesting signs of mania? Is the extraordinary sense of well-being a danger signal? Because if I am at death's door, Gwendolyn, I should appreciate being informed."

She let out a shaky breath. "I don't know. I had thought the dilating blood vessels and increased blood supply—possibly augmented by leakage—triggered the aura and pain. But for the pain to stop, the vessels must contract again and diminish blood flow—and your cells and tissue are supposed to be too weak and damaged to do it so quickly and thoroughly."

He recalled what she'd told him yesterday about brain

function. "I see," he said. "You fear that something has cut off blood supply too abruptly, perhaps in a dangerous and abnormal fashion—and this is a temporary and illusory surcease."

"I cannot say." Her voice was the slightest bit unsteady.

Perhaps he'd fall down dead in the next minute, Dorian thought. That did not seem possible. He had never felt more alive. Nonetheless, he wasn't going to take any chances.

He went to her and gathered her in his arms and kissed her, long and thoroughly, until she melted against him. He went on kissing her, then caressing her, and soon, carrying her to the bed.

That wasn't what he'd intended. He'd only wanted to make sure she understood how he felt about her.

But there was no stopping, once they'd begun. In a little while, the garments he'd so recently donned lay strewn about the floor, along with hers, and he was lost, drowning inside her, in the hot sea of desire.

And later, when they lay together, limbs tangled, he found his heart was still beating and his brain was still working, and so he told her what she'd done for him.

Yesterday, he'd told her of his debauched past, expecting shock and disgust. Instead, she'd impatiently dismissed his whoring and drinking as normal male behavior.

He'd told her about his mother, the pitiable and monstrous creature she'd become, and Gwendolyn had not turned a hair. "It's like consumption," she'd said, after reducing the horrors to a logical series of physiological events. "There is no saying that her infidelities and secrets made it worse or triggered the breakdown. Her marriage was unsatisfactory. For all we know, the romantic intrigues may have reduced the emotional strain and delayed the inevitable, instead of hastening it."

If Dorian had stayed with his mother, he might have

added to her agitation, Gwendolyn had theorized, because Aminta had a stronger emotional bond with him than with his father.

Moreover, the conditions at the madhouse must be put into perspective, Gwendolyn had told him. The moral faculties were often destroyed in such cases. Patients might appear calm and rational without having any more awareness or control over their thoughts and behavior than if they had been marionettes, with the damaged brain cells pulling the strings. And aware or not, patients often forgot what they were angry or sad about, just as they forgot basic hygiene, and even who they were or who they'd imagined they were minutes before.

Then he'd realized that his mother might not have endured continuous humiliation and pain, because she'd been living for the most part in a world of her own, where little could reach her.

"You have truly eased my mind," Dorian told his wife now. "Even my grandfather does not seem so monstrous. Pitiable, actually, in his ignorance, his fear of what he didn't understand, and his dependence on 'experts.' But you are not like him or his precious experts. You have a knack for making the incomprehensible make sense. You've reduced it to manageable proportions. Even this last attack seemed like little more than a damned nuisance."

She lifted herself onto one elbow and studied his face. "Perhaps, because you became less agitated, your brain did not have to work so hard," she said. "You said you needed to think, and it appears your reflections were positive. It's possible that stimulating such thought, rather than stupefying it, was the more beneficial approach."

"Lovemaking instills in me any number of positive feelings," he said. "Perhaps we must regard that as a beneficial treatment as well."

She arched one eyebrow. "I recall nothing in the medical literature recommending coitus as a course of treatment."

He slid his fingers into her wayward hair and drew her down to him. "Maybe you haven't read enough books."

Six

Three weeks later, Dorian stood in the doorway of his wife's sitting room, watching her frown over a pamphlet.

Her books had arrived a fortnight ago, and he and Hoskins had helped her convert the sitting room into a study. The medical tomes stood in neat rows in a bookcase.

Her desk was not so neat. Pamphlets, notebooks, and sheets of foolscap lay in haphazard heaps.

Dorian leaned against the door frame and folded his arms and studied his preoccupied wife.

He knew what she was looking for. Not a cure, because there wasn't any, but clues to his "positive response to treatment." Though she would never admit it, Dorian knew she had hopes of prolonging his sanity, if not his life.

He had every reason to cooperate. He would be glad of an extra month, even an extra day. Yet her dogged search made his heart ache for her. She was not "practical and selfish," as she'd claimed. She cared, deeply, about her patients. She had even cared about Mr. Bowes, whose dementia made Dorian's mother's fits seem like mere sulks.

But at present it was not simply a matter of caring. Dorian

feared Gwendolyn's dedication was crossing the line, from a quest for intellectual enlightenment to obsession. Last night she'd muttered in her sleep about "idiopathic inconstancy" and "lesions" and "prodromal symptoms."

He was strongly tempted to send the books back and order her to cease and desist before she developed a brain fever. Yet he couldn't deprive her of what he knew was the learning opportunity of a lifetime, or show a lack of respect for her maturity, intellect, and competence.

Fortunately, he'd been able to devise something like a solution because his mind was still functioning adequately, despite two more attacks. The last, a week ago, had continued for twenty-four hours, until he'd made her dose him with ipecac, to make him vomit. After that, he'd slept like the dead for another half a day.

Yet he'd recovered with the same sense of well-being and clarity of mind he'd experienced the two previous times. He was sure it was because she'd exorcised the demons of fear, shame, and ignorance, thus reducing emotional pressure on his damaged brain. He knew the reprieve was temporary, and he wasn't going to waste it. He had no future, but she did, and he'd spent the last week looking into hers.

"Is this a bad time to interrupt?" he asked.

Her head went up and her preoccupied gloom vanished, and the sun came out in the endless smile that could still make his heart turn over in his breast.

"There is never a bad time for you," she said. "You are the most welcome interruption in the world."

Dorian came away from the door frame, crossed to her desk, and perched on the edge. His gaze settled upon the pamphlet she'd put down when he approached: *"An Account of Acute Idiopathic Mania as Manifested . . . "*

"It is one of Mr. Eversham's studies," she said. "But your behavior does not fit his model."

He took it up and scanned the pages. "I wonder how you

make anything of this gibberish." He set down the pamphlet and took up a narrow volume. "This is still worse. I should go howling mad trying to read the first sentence—and it's only three-quarters of a page long."

"They are doctors, not writers," said Gwendolyn. "You ought to see their penmanship. It is a wonder the printers are not all in Bedlam by now."

"Yours is nothing to boast of," he said with a meaningful glance at the untidy pile of foolscap covered with her even more untidy scrawl.

She wrinkled her nose. "Yes, my handwriting is horrid. Not at all like yours. I'm sure you were the finest copyist those London solicitors ever had."

"I should be happy to copy your notes legibly," he said. "In fact, I . . ." He trailed off, his mind snagging on a recollection. Something she'd said weeks ago. Something "misinterpreted."

Catching her worried look, he shrugged. "I'm all right. My mind wandered, that's all. I had interrupted for a specific reason, and the medical jargon and your ghastly handwriting distracted me." He ruffled her hair. "I came to ask if you'd like to visit Athcourt with me."

"Athcourt?" she said blankly.

"I wrote to Dain a few days ago," he explained. "I need advice on some business matters. He's now a member of the family, his place is but a few miles southeast of here, and he's an excellent manager, from all one has heard."

"Athcourt is reputed to be one of the most prosperous, well-run properties in the kingdom," Gwendolyn said, nodding. "I'm sure his business judgment is sound."

"At any rate, he's made me feel welcome." Dorian withdrew a letter from his pocket and gave it to her.

As she perused it, her mouth began to twitch. "The man is incorrigibly wicked. And what is this?" She read aloud, " 'If that nitwit Trent is still loitering about, you might as well bring him, too, since mayhem can only result if he's left to his own devices. Still, you know what will be expected of you in that case.'" She looked up. "It would appear you are better acquainted than I had guessed."

Dorian laughed. "Dain was still at Eton when Bertie first came," he explained. "About once a fortnight, Bertie would fall down the stairs or trip over something or otherwise contrive to stumble into His Lordship's path. Fortunately, I was on the spot the first time and hustled Bertie away before Dain could dispose of him by more violent means. After that, whenever your cousin strayed into the Satanic presence, His Lordship would summon me. 'Camoys,' he would say, as cool as you please. 'It's back. Make it go away.' And so I would make Bertie disappear."

"I can see Dain doing it. And you, too." She patted his arm. "It is your protective streak."

"It was my instinct for *self-preservation*," Dorian indignantly informed her. "I was scarcely twelve, and Dain, even at sixteen, was as big as a house. He had but to set one huge hand on my head to squash me like a bug." He grinned. "Still, I admired him tremendously. I should have given anything to get away with what he did."

She laughed, a delicious sound. "So should I," she said. "It was not hard to understand why Jessica was captivated with him. Or why she was so vexed about it."

"I thought you'd enjoy visiting with her while Dain and I talk business," he said.

"I should, very much." She gave the letter back. "I am glad you thought of Dain as a business advisor. A better choice than Abonville. The duc is a foreigner and of another generation."

"I knew you had reservations about him."

"He's a wonderful man, but he can be *too* paternal."

Dorian hesitated. He did not want to upset her; on the

other hand, they could not spend the remaining time avoiding all mention of what lay ahead. "I trust you won't mind, then, if I end by making Dain my guardian instead," he said quietly.

There was only the briefest pause before she spoke. "If I encountered difficulties, and you were unable to assist me, there's no one I'd rather have on my side," she said. She met his gaze, her own clear and steady.

He could guess what the composure and steadiness cost her, and it distressed him. Nevertheless, they couldn't pretend they would have forever when they didn't.

He bent and lightly kissed her. "That's how I feel," he said. He drew back and grinned. "If we must choose an ally, it makes sense to pick the biggest one we can find."

A few days later, they went to Athcourt, intending to stay for two days. They wound up staying for a week.

Dain turned out to be knowledgeable—and obstinately opinionated—about a vast array of topics, and the two men were soon quarreling happily, like old friends or brothers. They raced each other over Athcourt's vast park and into the surrounding moorland. They fenced and practiced pistol shooting. One day, Dain undertook to teach Dorian some of the finer points of pugilism, and they knocked each other about in a corner of the stable yard, while their wives cheered them on.

Dain's bastard son lived at Athcourt as well. He was a wicked piece of mischief, eight years old, whom Dain proudly referred to as the Demon Seed.

Little Dominick was wary of Dorian at first, but within two days, he was inviting the Earl of Rawnsley to visit his treehouse. This, Dorian learned, was a signal honor. Until now, only the boy's adored papa had been privy to the refuge's location and initiated into its mysteries.

And so, Dorian came away from Athcourt with scraped knees and elbows, Dain's assurances that Gwendolyn's affairs would be properly looked after . . . and a mad yearning for a child.

Dorian told himself it was ridiculous to long for a child he would never see born and ruthlessly focused his energies on realizing Gwendolyn's hospital dream.

Dain had agreed with him that her influential title and wealth would not fully compensate for her being a female, and a young one at that. She would be contending with scores of men, few of whom held an enlightened view of feminine capabilities.

"I can deal with the men," Dain had said, "but I should want precise instructions. I know nothing about hospitals, even the everyday variety, and it seems that your lady has something novel in mind."

"I'm not sure she'll be as precise as one would wish, when the time comes," Dorian had answered. "Already I detect signs of emotional strain. I had thought that if I started the project now, it would make a healthy distraction. Moreover, if I am directly involved in its founding, others will take it more seriously. If the Earl of Rawnsley says the building must be a perfect hexagon, for instance, another fellow won't pipe up that it must be a perfect cube and start a row with someone who says it must be an octagon, according to the best authorities. Instead, they will all murmur, 'Yes, my lord. A hexagon. Certainly,' and write down my every word with the greatest care, as though it came direct from the throne of Heaven."

Dain had chuckled, but something in his dark gaze made Dorian edgy. "Am I overly optimistic?" he'd asked. "If you have doubts of my capabilities, Dain, I wish you—"

"I was only wondering why the devil you don't cut your hair," Dain had said. "While I doubt your coiffure would affect your credibility—you're a Camoys, after all—I should think it was a damned nuisance to look after—as though there won't be enough in organizing this project."

Dorian had smiled sheepishly. "My wife likes it."

"And you are besotted, poor fool." Dain had given him a commiserating look, then laughed. "Well, then, I collect this is as rational as you're ever going to be. Make the most of it, I say."

Dorian was determined to make the most of it.

Accordingly, on the second night of their return home, he explained to Gwendolyn his idea about getting an early start on her hospital.

She told him it was an excellent idea and she seemed very enthusiastic, but Dorian could not shake off the feeling that her mind was elsewhere: on his accursed ailment and its provoking mysteries. He was strongly tempted to lecture her. He suppressed the urge and made love to her instead.

The following afternoon, they settled down in the library to discuss the matter in detail, and she was the same. She talked enthusiastically of her ideas, and obligingly sketched out a rough plan for the building itself, and described the functions of different areas. All the same, Dorian sensed that her mind was not fully engaged.

In the following days, she went on working cheerfully with him, transforming her dreams into orderly facts and specifications, but the note of abstraction remained.

Dorian bore it patiently. He had learned from her that it was often possible to combine several treatments to combat an ailment's array of symptoms. One remedy for sick headaches, for instance, combined laudanum with ipecac—the former to dull the pain and the latter to relieve the nausea by inducing vomiting.

He had, likewise, devised a combination treatment for her. One of the "medications" arrived a week after their return from Athcourt.

Dorian slipped into her study and left the packet on her

desk while she was consulting with the cook about the following day's menu. Then he left the house, to work on the next part of the remedy.

An hour later, Gwendolyn stood in the study doorway, gazing blankly at Hoskins.

"He's gone to Okehampton," the manservant said for the second time. "He had an appointment. Something to do with the hospital, he said."

"Oh. Oh, yes. With Mr. Dobbin." Gwendolyn turned away. "He reminded me at breakfast. So silly of me to forget. My wits must be wandering. Thank you, Hoskins."

She stood in the doorway, staring at the thick letter on her desk while Hoskins's footsteps faded away.

Then she shut the door and returned to her desk and took up the letter again with trembling hands.

It was from Mr. Borson, the physician in whose care Aminta Camoys had been placed. It was in response to an inquiry from Dorian. He had written to Borson a fortnight ago, it turned out, without telling her.

Dorian had attached a note to Borson's letter: "Here it is, Doctor Gwendolyn—with all the deliciously grisly details. I shall expect to find you writhing with uncontrollable lust by the time I return."

Gwendolyn read the note again, for the tenth time, and this time she could not control herself. She covered her face with her hands and wept, not because of Borson's reply, but because of what it had cost her husband to obtain it, to write and seek a favor from the man he viewed as his mother's torturer, if not her murderer.

Dorian had done it for Gwendolyn's sake, and that was what made her heart ache, unbearably, so that she wept, like the wife she was instead of the doctor she wanted to be.

Or had thought she wanted to be.

Or imagined she was capable of being.

She was not behaving very capably now, she scolded herself.

She wiped away her tears and told herself there would be plenty of time to cry later. A lifetime, if she chose to devote it to grief, and throw away the gifts God had given her, and all that her husband was trying to give her. He knew she was trying to learn, and he was trying to help her in every way he could.

She had no business weeping about it. She knew it made Dorian happy to help her. Furthermore, Borson's letter contained exceedingly valuable information. She had seen that in the first quick perusal. He had even enclosed a copy of the post-mortem report, which would solve several nagging riddles . . . once she could get her mind to focus properly. And stay focused, which was not easy lately.

She kept forgetting things and missing things. She had spent a full week with Jessica before realizing her cousin was breeding. Gwendolyn had not been able to put the simplest symptoms together: physical evidence any medical student would have discerned, not to mention the uncharacteristic moodiness. Twice, while Gwendolyn had been there, Jessica—who never wept—had burst into tears for no apparent reason, and several times she had lost her temper over the most trivial matters.

Jessica had said nothing about it, and Gwendolyn had tactfully refrained from questioning her. After all, it was early days yet, and the first trimester was a notoriously uncertain . . . period.

Trimester . . . twelve weeks . . . symptoms . . .

Gwendolyn stared blindly at the autopsy report.

She had been wed for more than six weeks.

Her last menses had been two weeks before the wedding.

The report dropped from her nerveless fingers, and her gaze dropped to her belly.

"Oh, my goodness," she whispered.

*   *   *

Dorian sat in a private parlor of Okehampton's Golden Hart Inn, not with the fictional Mr. Dobbin, but with Bertie Trent, whose square face was twisted into a painful grimace.

This was because Bertie was trying to think.

"Well, Eversham do need money," Bertie said finally. "But he ain't the sort that gets on with other fellows so well, which if he was, he wouldn't be stuck in Chippenham, which even Gwen said, but he got on fine with her, and Aunt Claire liked him well enough, seeing as how he was the only one knew what to make of her spells."

"He doesn't need to get on with the other fellows," Dorian said. "He only needs to tell us what to do. Dain and I agree that we need an experienced physician on the hospital planning committee."

He also needed someone who could talk to Gwendolyn in her own language and make her listen and face facts. And take better care of herself.

But all that was explained in Dorian's letter. The thick packet lay on the table between him and Bertie, who was eyeing it dubiously, still reluctant for some reason to take it up.

"It's hospital information," Dorian said. This was partly true, although the bulk of the contents consisted of his copies of Borson's materials—so that Eversham would arrive armed with facts for his intellectual joust with Gwendolyn. "I hope he finds the proposal irresistible. If he doesn't, I am counting on you to use your unique powers of persuasion. As you did with Borson."

As soon as Dorian had realized he must write to Borson, he'd realized he'd need more than a letter. Physicians could be balky, and they did like to keep secrets, Gwendolyn had said. Also, they were often too busy with patients to attend to correspondence. Unwilling to risk a wait that could extend to months, Dorian had decided to send for Bertie.

What Trent lacked in intelligence he made up for in loyalty and stubbornness. He was loyal to Dorian, and Bertie would stubbornly persist until Borson gave him what he came for. Which Borson had done, when he realized there was no other way to get rid of him.

Dorian trusted that Bertie's loyalty and obstinacy would serve equally well with Eversham. Gwendolyn's hero had not sounded like the sort of man who would come running at the snap of a nobleman's fingers.

"Still, if it doesn't work, we can try something else," Dorian added, because Bertie was still frowning. "I realize this will be more difficult than dealing with Borson. We're asking Eversham to give up his practice and pick up and leave, which is no small matter. Even if he agrees, I realize it will take some time to settle his affairs. But you will make sure he understands I'll cover all expenses and use my influence as needed. Make sure he realizes I'm a man of my word, Bertie—that this is no madman's whim. If he has doubts, he can write to Dain."

Bertie blinked very hard. "You ain't mad, Cat. No more 'n I am—and looking well, too, better than before. She's done you good, hasn't she?"

"Of course I'm not mad," Dorian said. "And it's all thanks to Gwendolyn. She is wonderful and I am . . . exceedingly happy," he added with a smile. *I want her to be happy, too*, he added silently.

The clouds vanished from Bertie's expression and a light shone in his pale blue eyes. "I knew you'd like her, Cat. I knew she'd do you good."

Dorian understood what the light signified and had no trouble guessing what Bertie wanted to believe.

But Bertie had not read Borson's account or the post-mortem report, and even if he had, he wouldn't have grasped even the fraction Dorian had comprehended. And that was far more than he'd done the first time, seven years ago, long before Gwendolyn had explained about the brain's unique self-sufficiency, which made it so susceptible to self-destruction.

Bertie wouldn't understand that the destruction couldn't be repaired or halted, even by Gwendolyn. He didn't know that, once begun, the decay continued relentlessly . . . the way it had at Rawnsley Hall, quietly moldering under the surface until the roof caved in.

Bertie believed that "good" equaled "cured," and Dorian hadn't the heart to explain the difference.

"I like her immensely, Bertie," he said. "And she has done me a world of good."

Gwendolyn wanted to build the hospital in Dartmoor.

Which meant she intended to stay here, permanently.

She stood at the library window, looking out, and Dorian gazed at her in despair.

He stood at the table, where he'd laid out several rough architectural sketches of the hospital, moments before pressing her for an answer to the question he'd asked every day for the past five days.

He had not wanted to press her.

Two weeks had passed since his clandestine meeting with Bertie, and Dorian had received no word from him. Meanwhile Gwendolyn was becoming ill. Her countenance alternated between weary pallor and a hectic flush, and she was becoming short-tempered, doubtless because she was sleeping poorly. Last night she'd bolted up from the pillows babbling about "extravavasation" of something or other.

"Gwendolyn, you can't live here," he said, his voice calm, his mind churning with troubling images of her future.

"I like it here," she said. "From the moment I came, it felt like homecoming."

"This is not a healthy climate," he said. "Even in the valleys, the damp settles in and—"

"Poor people cannot afford to transport sick relatives to

coastal resorts or travel back and forth to visit them." She turned around. "The moor folk need a modern hospital. And damp is scarcely an issue. Bath is damp and cold, and people in all stages of illness and decrepitude live there while taking the waters."

"This is not a healthy place for you," he said tightly. "You've been here only two months and—" He thrust his hand through his hair. *Say it*, he commanded himself. It was time to stop pretending. She was ill, and he was making her so, and it was time to confront that, with or without Eversham.

The fellow should have been here by now, curse him, Dorian thought. Eversham would know what to do, what to say. He was an experienced, allegedly brilliant physician. He would solve the exasperating riddle for her, and make her face facts.

"You are not well," Dorian said. "You don't eat properly or sleep properly and you are tired and—and unreasonable. You sulked for two hours last night because dinner was 'boring,' you said."

"She was supposed to use the spices," Gwendolyn said stiffly. Her hands fisted at her sides. "I sent to London for them, and explained to Cook—about phlegm and congestion and reducing the pressure from excess fluid—and she went ahead and made . . . *pap*."

Dorian sighed. He had talked to Hoskins, who'd talked to Cook, who'd said the pungent spices would give Her Ladyship indigestion, which was what kept her awake nights. Everyone knew they "raised the blood," Cook had said.

"Cook is worried about you," he said. "We are all worried about you."

She rolled her eyes. "Oh, this is lovely. I am on my way to a medical breakthrough, and no one will cooperate—because they have taken it into their heads to *worry*." She marched to the table. "If I were a man—accepted as a *scientist*—I would merely be 'preoccupied' with my work. But because I am a woman, I am taking a fit of the vapors, and my blood must be lowered. *Lowered*." She struck the table with her fist. "Of all the antiquated, *medieval* notions. It's a wonder I can think at all, with so much nonsense and anxiety clouding the atmosphere about me. As though it were not enough trouble concentrating, in this cond—" She broke off, scowled at the drawings, and moved away from the table toward the door.

"I need some fresh air," she said.

But Dorian got there before she did, and blocked the way. "Gwen, it's raining," he said. "And you . . ." The rest of the sentence faded as he took in her appearance. Her face was flushed and her bosom was rising and falling rapidly, as though she'd been running for miles, and . . . He frowned. "Your frock has shrunk."

She looked down at herself.

"It's a wonder you can breathe," he said. "It's a wonder the seams of your bodice haven't split."

She retreated a pace. "It is not a wonder," she said, her gaze averted. "This happens to all the women in my family. We are so obvious." She drew a long, shaky breath. "I'm . . . breeding."

"Oh." He sagged back against the door. "I see. Yes. Of course."

The room was dark, reeling about him, while within, another darkness settled like a vast weight. His eyes ached, and his throat, too, and his heart was a wedge of solid pain in his chest.

"Don't!" she cried. "Don't you dare give way, Dorian. Don't even *think* about sickening now." She flung herself against him and his arms closed, reflexively, round her.

Her head pressed against his aching chest. "I am happy," she said shakily. "I want our baby. And I want you to be there."

"Oh, Gwen."

"It isn't *impossible*," she said. "Another seven months or so, that's all we need." She drew back and gave him a smile as wobbly as her voice. "If I were an elephant, it would be different. The gestation period is twenty and a half months."

He managed a shaky laugh. "Yes, let's look on the bright side. At least you are not an elephant."

"I shall look like one at the end," she said. "You wouldn't want to miss that, would you?"

He wove his fingers through her wild hair. "No, I wouldn't, sweet. You present me with an irresistible temptation."

"I hope so." She patted his chest. "The patient's motivation can have a pronounced effect on treatment, Mr. Eversham says." Her voice was nearly returned to its normal cool efficiency. "I should have told you about the baby sooner, but this is an uncertain period, and I did not want to get your hopes up for nothing. Still, perhaps I was overcautious. It is rare for the women of my family to miscarry."

Seven more months, Dorian thought. He'd been given less than that before she came, and she'd been here for two months now.

Yet he was doing better than his mother had at this stage. The visual chimera had not worsened, blossomed into demons. His temper remained relatively even. No sudden black melancholy or inexplicable fits of gaiety or rage.

Instead, there was the fierce rapture of their lovemaking, and the moments of quiet contentment, and the joy of working with her, planning something worthwhile.

According to Borson's account, Mother had continued articulate to the last. Mad, and living in a perverse world of her own, but articulate . . . and cunning, even devious at times. Perhaps she would not have sunk into a demon-plagued world of her own if the real world had offered understanding and joy and a sense of being useful and valued and worthy of affection. Perhaps she might have lived a little longer and died more peacefully.

It was not impossible.

A few extra months, he told himself. Long enough to see their baby. That would be wonderful. And if it did turn out to be impossible, at least he would have given Gwendolyn a child, which would surely gladden her heart and banish any sentimental inclination to mourn for him.

Nevertheless, her wishing to remain here was not a good sign. She needed to start a new life, in a new place, away from sad memories. But Eversham would arrive eventually, Dorian assured himself. Her mentor would set her right.

Dorian drew his wife tightly against him. "I shall try to maintain a positive attitude," he promised softly.

"And you must speak to Cook," Gwendolyn muttered into his shirt front. "Remind her who is the doctor in this house. I ordered a curry for dinner—and it must be *hot*."

He chuckled. "Yes, crosspatch." He kissed the top of her head. "But first, let us see what Doctor Dorian can do to sweeten your temper."

Seven

*Ten days later, Gwendolyn was recalling that con-*versation and the methods Dorian had employed to sweeten her temper. He had used the same techniques every day since, kissing and caressing the irritation away, drawing her out of her annoying moods and into his strong arms, to take her to heaven and back, and leave her dazed with bliss.

Now, sitting in Mr. Kneebones's surgery, she focused on those blissful sensations in order to keep her temper from taking over and leading her to do the physician a severe, possibly fatal, bodily injury.

It was hardly the first time she'd humbled herself with doctors, she told herself, and Dorian was far more important than her pride.

She treated Kneebones to an apologetic smile. "I only want to know whether those materials prove absolutely what made Mrs. Camoys's brain start breaking down."

Kneebones scowled at her, then at the autopsy report in his hand. "One cannot prove anything *absolutely* in such cases. One makes logical inferences based on observable facts and the patient's history. Mrs. Camoys did not drink to

239

excess or indulge in opium eating, which rules out toxic insanity. She had not sustained a high fever prior to or during the decline. And if she had suffered a blow to the head, as you surmise, do you not think Mr. Budge, the family physician, would have mentioned that little detail in his account of her medical history?"

"What if he didn't know?" Gwendolyn persisted.

"Budge is a competent man. I reckon he knows a concussion when he sees one."

"But one can't, precisely, *see* them," Gwendolyn said. "She had lovers. What if one of her lovers did it? If he did as great an injury as we're talking about, she might not have even remembered." She tipped her head to one side. "Did you question her maid, by any chance? Servants often know more family secrets than the family does."

Kneebones took off his spectacles and rubbed his eyes. "I do wonder how it is that Lord Rawnsley is not in a strait-waistcoat by now," he muttered.

"That is what I am wondering, too," she said. "Otherwise I should not have come to pester you. I know there must be a logical explanation, but I cannot find it."

Kneebones set his spectacles back on his nose. "That may be due to an overactive—and highly *melodramatic*— imagination and underactive attention to observable facts."

"Tell me where I'm wrong," she said.

He pushed the autopsy report toward her. "Let us suppose your little theory is correct, Lady Rawnsley. Let us suppose Mrs. Camoys's condition arose from a blow to the head, sustained many months before the early symptoms of traumatic insanity appeared, as often happens. What difference does it make? Her son's history easily allows for physical violence, fever, alcoholism, not to mention a host of morbid conditions of the system, all of which produce similar consequences. Perhaps this has not occurred to you. Nor do you seem aware that a man may inherit character, and with it a predisposition toward an irrational, self-destructive mode of life. You fail to take into account the patient's degenerate morals, irrational behavior, and savage appearance. No matter how the initial damage began, these symptoms clearly indicate progressive deterioration."

At this, Gwendolyn's fraying patience snapped. She stood up. "My husband is not and never has been degenerate, irrational, or self-destructive," she said stiffly. "He has a powerful instinct for self-preservation—else he would never have survived a month in the London slums, let alone years." She took up the autopsy report and stuffed it into her purse. "I cannot believe you overlooked that," she said, "and I cannot believe that you, a man of science, would diagnose him as insane, simply on account of his *hair*."

She stalked out.

Lord Rawnsley did not know that his wife had been quarreling with Mr. Kneebones in Okehampton. She was supposed to be making a tour of possible hospital sites with Hoskins and quarreling with him, because his orders were to (*a*) find fault with all sites and (*b*) keep her busy until teatime.

Unaware that she was racing home at this very minute, obstinately immune to all Hoskins's delaying tactics, Dorian stood by the library fireplace. His hands were clasped tightly at his back and his gaze was fixed on a disconcertingly young and gentlemanly physician.

Eversham stood at the library table. Having finished perusing Gwendolyn's latest notes, he was now thoughtfully perusing Dorian.

"She's very near the mark with your mother's case," Eversham said. "The same theory occurred to me when I read your letter and your copies of Borson's materials." He smiled faintly. "Very handsomely written they were, my lord."

"Never mind my penmanship," Dorian said. "You were about to tell me what you learned in Gloucestershire."

Eversham's arrival had been delayed, it turned out, on account of a detour to the Rawnsley Hall estate in pursuit of information about Aminta Camoys. He had made the detour partly because Dorian's letter had aroused his medical curiosity and partly because of Bertie Trent's tear-filled litany of Dorian's noble and heroic qualities. It had taken them several days to locate Mother's former maid.

"Shall I be delicate or brutally direct?" Eversham asked.

Dorian's heart pounded. "Brutal, if you please."

"Your mother had been having an affair with your Uncle Hugo," Eversham said dispassionately. "They were meeting secretly, in the estate's laundry house, when her maid came to warn them that your grandfather had returned unexpectedly. Your mother panicked, tripped, and hit her head on a stone sink. Since she seemed to recover almost instantly, there seemed no reason to summon the doctor—and risk discovery of the accident's circumstances."

Eversham went on to explain concussions, which could be insidiously deceptive: internal injury with no external evidence, sometimes no discernible symptoms for weeks, months, even years—by which time it would be difficult to connect the symptoms with an apparently minor accident of long before. Thus she had been misdiagnosed initially as suffering a "decline," or constitutional breakdown.

"As you may not be aware," Eversham said, "the brain functions—"

"I know how it works," Dorian cut in. "Gwendolyn explained that—and how it breaks down as well."

Eversham nodded. "It seems to break down in more or less the same way following a trauma—a blow, for instance—as it does in a number of other, quite different maladies. The point is, my lord, your mother evidently suffered a severe concussion, which it is impossible to inherit."

He took up one of the sheets containing Gwendolyn's notes. "Furthermore, Her Ladyship has detected in you none of the usual symptoms of brain degeneration. That is not surprising, since there are none to detect."

Eversham eyed Dorian assessingly. "You are remarkably fit," he added, "especially for a member of the upper classes. Your brain is in excellent working order. Both your penmanship—evidencing superior motor control—and the logical and orderly presentation of highly personal and emotionally laden information leave that in no doubt." He returned his attention to the sheet in his hand. "She reports no lethargy or fatigue. No restlessness or sleeplessness. No difficulties with attention to detail and concentration—as your proposal for the hospital clearly demonstrates." He cleared his throat. "And it would appear that the reproductive functions are—er—functioning." He looked up, smiling. "I congratulate you, my lord. That is a pleasant event to look forward to, is it not?"

His Lordship had only just managed to digest the matter of a concussion he could not possibly have inherited. It took him a moment to catch up with the rest, during which he stared stupidly at Eversham.

It took another moment to force the words out. "What are you saying?" he asked, dazed. "Look forward to—? I have— You have—" He thrust his hair back. "Haven't you overlooked something? The things. The—the 'visual chimera'—'first you see stars, then the pain hits.' Physiological phenomena, common to a host of neurological ailments, my wife said."

Eversham nodded. "Indeed, quite common. Among others, these are classic symptoms of migraine headache. That, I collect, is what's ailing you."

"Migraine?" Dorian repeated. "As in . . . 'megrims'?"

"Not merely headache—which is what most people mean by 'megrims'—but severe, debilitating headaches. Still, they're not fatal, for all that."

"You are telling me," Dorian ground out, "that all this time . . ." His face heated. "All these months, I have been playing bloody tragic hero—and all I've got is a bleeding, damned *headache*?"

Eversham frowned and returned the paper to the pile with the rest and straightened them, while Dorian listened to the silence stretch on and wondered what would come to fill it. Eversham had just said they were headaches. Not fatal. Why then, was he hesitating?

Gwendolyn had thought she heard Dorian's voice, but when she reached the library door, all was quiet within. She opened it for a quick peep to be sure.

At that moment, another, equally familiar masculine voice broke the silence.

"I wish I could say otherwise, my lord, but the ailment is incurable. Though it has been studied for centuries, it remains a medical enigma. I have never yet encountered two cases precisely alike. I am not sure I can even promise you relief, which I deeply regret, for I know it is murderously painful. And I cannot promise that it will not be passed on to your offspring, for there is strong evidence that it is an inherited predisposition."

A choked sob escaped her.

Two masculine heads swiveled sharply, and two gazes— one blue, one golden—shot to her before she could retreat.

"Oh," she said. "I do beg your pardon. I did not mean to interrupt." She hastily shut the door . . . and fled.

Gwendolyn ran blindly down the hall, yanked the front door open, hurtled through it and down the steps—and ran straight into Bertie.

"I say, Gwen, where are you—"

She pushed past him and hurried to his gelding, which one of the stablemen was leading away.

She snatched the reins from the groom.

Bertie hurried up to her. "I say, Gwen, what's happened?"

"Give me a lift up," she said tightly.

He bent and clasped his hands together. "Don't tell me Cat's gone and bolted again," he said as he hoisted her up. "I thought he'd get on well enough with Eversham, and I was just setting out to let Dain know, when I seen you turn into the drive and never was so astonished in all my life. You were supposed to be in—

"Gwendolyn!"

Bertie swung round. "There he is, Gwen. Ain't gone after all. What was you—"

"Let go of my foot, Bertie."

He let go, but Dorian reached them in the same moment and caught hold of the bridle. "My dear, I don't know what you—"

"I am a trifle . . . out of sorts," she choked out. "I need . . . a ride. To clear my head."

"What you need is a cup of tea," he said soothingly. "I know it was a shock to see Eversham, but I—"

"Oh, I wish he'd never come!" she cried. Her voice shook, and her eyes filled. "But that is silly, I know. It is always better to know . . . the facts. And you have made me . . . so happy—and I love you—and I shall love you always, no—no matter what h-happens." Her voice broke then, and with it the last shred of her control. She wept, helplessly, and when he reached up and grasped her waist and lifted her down, all she could do was cling to him, sobbing.

"I love you, too, sweet, with all my heart," he said gently. "But I do believe you've got this backwards."

"No, I heard," she sobbed. "I heard what Eversham said— and he knows. He's a p-proper doctor. Incurable, he said. Kneebones was right and I was wrong, and I should have known b-better."

"Backwards, indeed," Dorian said as he threaded his fingers through her hair. "The London experts, Borson, and Kneebones all got it wrong. So did I. You knew better than any of us. I feel like an utter dolt. But your Mr. Eversham says my brain is functioning and one cannot inherit concussion, and so I collect you are stuck with me—and my confounded megrims—indefinitely."

She lifted her head, and through her tears, she saw the truth glimmering in his golden eyes. "M-m-megrims?"

"Migraine, he calls it," Dorian said. "Providence has played you another joke, I'm afraid. You came all this way to nurse and comfort a dying madman in his last wretched months, and advance the cause of medical science by studying his fascinating case . . ." He smiled. "And you wound up with a perfectly healthy fellow with a boring old headache."

She reached up and stroked her husband's hair back, blinking at him through the tears that continued to fall though she no longer had anything to cry about. "Well, I love you anyway," she said.

She heard the gelding snort, and looked round to see the groom leading the horse to the stables and a worried-looking Bertie hurrying back to her and Dorian.

"By Jupiter's thunderbolts—I say—Good gad, Cat, what's happened? What's she bawling about? I never seen Gwen do that before."

"It is perfectly normal, Bertie," Dorian answered while he gently stroked her back. "Your cousin is going to have a baby. It makes her emotional."

"Oh. Well. Oh, that is—I mean to say—Oh, yes. Jolly good. Indeed." Gingerly, Bertie patted her head. "Well done, cuz."

"And you may be godfather." Dorian drew back to peer into her face. "That's right, isn't it, sweet?"

Gwendolyn gave a watery laugh. "Oh, yes. Of course Bertie will be godfather." She let go of Dorian's lapels and wiped her eyes.

"And you shall have a lovely hospital, with a lovely new physician with modern ideas," her husband told her as he gave her his handkerchief. "And we shall make tiresome old Kneebones go away, so that he can't interfere or make obstacles or quarrel with sensible people. We shall send him as private physician to the dithering old Camoys ladies at Rawnsley Hall. If their own quacks and patent medicines haven't killed them by now, it's unlikely Kneebones can do them any harm."

She laughed again and wiped her nose—which was probably as red as her hair at present, she thought. And her hair must be a sight as well, judging by Bertie's expression.

"There, you see?" Dorian told him. "She is practically herself again."

Bertie was still eyeing her dubiously. "She's all red and splotchy."

"She simply needs time to . . . adjust," Dorian said. "It turns out, you see, that Gwen will be stuck with me for—oh, heaven only knows how long. Poor girl. She came all this way to comfort a dying madman during his last tragic days—and now—"

"And now it turns out that all Cat's got is a headache," Gwendolyn said. Her voice was still wobbly. She steadied it. "It's only megrims, Bertie."

Her cousin blinked. "Megrims?"

"Yes, dear."

"Like Aunt Claire's spells?"

"Yes, quite like my mama."

"And Uncle Frederick? And Great Uncle Mortimer?"

"Yes, dear."

"Well, then." Bertie's eyes grew very bright. He rubbed them. "But I knew it would be all right, all along, like I told you. Mean to say, Cat, it ain't all right, exactly. Very sick-making. Great Uncle Mortimer bangs his head against the wall. But megrims ain't killed any of our lot yet." He clapped Dorian on the shoulder. Then he took Dorian's hand and pumped it vigorously. Then he hugged Gwendolyn. Then, red-faced, he broke away. "By Jupiter. A baby, by gad. God-father. Megrims. Well. I'm thirsty."

Then, frantically rubbing his eyes, Bertie hurried on to the house.

An hour later, while Bertie was recovering his emotional equilibrium in the bathing chamber, Dorian stood with his wife, watching Mr. Eversham's battered carriage lumber down the drive.

"We must get him a better carriage," Dorian said. "People judge by appearances, and young doctors have a difficult time inspiring confidence. But a handsome equipage will indicate a profitable practice. If people believe he's greatly sought after, they'll be less likely to doubt his competence."

"You think of everything," Gwendolyn said. "But it is your protective streak—which I am beginning to suspect is a throwback to the Camoys's feudal origins and the lord of the manor looking after all his people."

"Don't be silly," he said. "I'm only being practical. The man will have enough to do between doctoring and supervising the hospital construction, without having to prove himself as well and get involved with local rivalries and politics."

"Yes, dear," she said dutifully. "Practical."

"And you will have enough to do, without having to leap to his defense a dozen times a day—or bothering me about it. Pregnancy makes you cross enough as it is. Can't have you antagonizing all of Dartmoor."

They watched the carriage round a turning behind a hill and descend out of view. "The sun is setting," he said. "The pixies and phantoms and witches will be at their toilette, preparing for the night's revelries."

His gaze returned to her. "Will you walk with me?"

She tucked her hand into the crook of his elbow and walked with him into the garden. He took her to the stone bench where he'd found her quietly waiting weeks earlier. He sat, taking her onto his lap.

The sun hovered over a distant hill. Its glow set fire to the clouds scattered about like goose down pillows on a celestial bed of blue and green and violet.

"Do you still want to build in Dartmoor?" he asked.

She nodded. "I like it here, and so do you. And Dain and Jessica are near."

"We'll need a larger house if we're going to raise a family," he said. He glanced behind him at the modest manor house. "I suppose we could add a wing. It would not be very grand. But Rawnsley Hall was grand and it felt like an immense tomb. Couldn't wait to get out of there. At present, in fact, I am strongly tempted to forget about repairs and raze the whole confounded pile."

"You don't like it, but your heir might," she said. "If you rebuild, you might give it to him as a wedding gift."

He lightly caressed her belly. "Are you sure you've a boy in there?"

"No, but we are bound to have one eventually."

"Even before I realized there would be an 'eventually,' I knew I should be just as happy if it were a girl," he said.

"Ah, well, you have a soft spot in your heart for females," she said. "But you also seem to have a way with little boys, and so I am not anxious either way. You will make a doting, devoted papa. Which is a good thing," she added with a little frown, "because the women of my family are rather negligent mothers. But then, they are always breeding, you see, which is distracting."

"Then I shall look after the children," he said. "Because I should like a great many, and you will have the additional distraction of hospital matters."

She stroked his hair back. "You have a gift for thinking ahead."

"I've been blessed with a great deal to look forward to," he said. "Watching the hospital rise from the ground, for instance. Discovering what modern medical ideas and principles can and cannot achieve. The possibilities. The limitations." He shook his head. "It amazes me how much I've learned about medicine in these last weeks, and how interesting it turns out to be. It even has a sort of poetry to it, and its own logic and riddles, like any intellectual pursuit. And there is the same wonderful feeling of discovery as mysteries are solved. I felt that today, when Eversham explained where your notes had led you." He kissed her forehead. "I'm so proud of you."

"You should be proud of yourself," she said. "You did not put obstacles in my way, though you wanted to—to protect me from myself. Instead, you tried every possible way to help me solve my riddle—by writing to Borson and sending for Eversham."

"Eversham is not like any other doctor I've encountered," he said. "He certainly does have his own ideas. While you were washing your face, I asked him why he had accepted you as a colleague. He told me that in olden times, women were the healers in many communities. But their arts, to ignorant folk, seemed like magic, which was associated with the Devil. And so they were reviled and persecuted as witches." He chuckled. "And so I realized I had been right from the first. I had wed a witch. And he was right, too, for you are a healer. You've healed my heart. That was the part that was ailing."

She curled her fingers round his neck. "You've healed me, too, Cat. You made the doctor part and the woman part fit together."

"Because I love both parts," he said softly. "All your parts. All of you."

She smiled, the sweet everlasting smile, and weaving her fingers into his hair, drew him down and kissed him, slowly, deeply, lingeringly.

While he lingered with her in the warm forever of that moment, the narrow red arc of the sun sank behind the glowing hill. A faint thread of light glimmered on the horizon. The night mists stole into the hollows and crevices of the moors, and the shadows swelled and lengthened, shrouding the winding byways in darkness.

The sharpening breeze made him lift his head. "A beautiful Dartmoor night," he murmured. "At moments like this, it is easy to believe in magic." He met her soft gaze. "You're magic to me, Gwen."

"Because I'm your witch, and you are my devoted familiar."

"So I am." He smiled down at her. "Let's make a spell, sorceress."

She frowned her endearing medical frown. "Very well. But first you must help me find some eye of newt."

He laughed. Then, cradling his bride in his arms, the Earl of Rawnsley rose, and carried her into the house.

LORETTA CHASE holds a B.A. from Clark University, where she majored in English and minored unofficially in visual art. Her past lives include clerical, administrative, and part-time teaching at Clark and a Dickensian six-month experience as a meter maid. In the course of moonlighting as a corporate video scriptwriter, she fell under the spell of a producer who lured her into writing novels . . . and marrying him. The union has resulted in more than a dozen books and a number of awards, including the Romance Writers of America's Rita® Award. You can talk to Loretta via her email address Author@LorettaChase.com, visit her website at www.LorettaChase.com, and blog with her and six other authors at WordWenches.com.

Scandal's Bride

Samantha James

One

London, 1820

Had she known what fate awaited her, she'd never have kissed him.

But Lady Victoria Carlton, only daughter of the marquess of Norcastle, did not act out of a mere frivolity of nature. Oh, no. In all truth, she was desperate to seek an end to her predicament.

She was convinced her only hope lay in scandal.

Unfortunately, there was precious little time. Papa had informed her this very morn that she must choose a husband by midnight tonight.

Or else *he* would.

It was not an idle threat—of this, Victoria was very certain. Much to Papa's vexation, she had passed through several Seasons, turning down each and every one of the marriage proposals that had come her way. But now Papa's patience had come to an end. He'd received three proposals during the last fortnight. He was usually not a tyrant, but when in one of his testiest moods, he was an imposing figure—there was simply no crossing him. And since she had no engagements other than the Remingtons' ball that evening, it must be soon. *Very soon . . .*

The ball was a typical gala affair. A din of voices rose in the air. Dozens of couples swirled across the floor in time to a lively waltz. The ballroom and adjoining salon had been decorated with huge clusters of pink and red roses.

With a deep curtsy, Victoria laughingly retreated from the arms of her latest dance partner. Her steps carried her to the edge of the salon, near the terrace doors. It wasn't so crowded there, and she needed time to think. Good heavens, time to *act,* for only a few hours remained before midnight.

There was a touch on her arm. Victoria turned to her good friend Sophie Mayfield. Two years her junior, Sophie had just come out this Season. Sophie gazed at her, her brown eyes softly beseeching. "Victoria, I beg of you, please do not do this. Perhaps your father is right. Perhaps you should have chosen a husband long ago. Certainly it's not from a lack of suitors—"

"Pompous and selfish young bucks dazzled by the size of my dowry, and none of whom I cared to spend the rest of my life with." A finely arched blond brow rose high as she spoke. Though her tone was light, the strength of her resolve was not.

She had entered her first Season with stars in her eyes and romance in her heart—with the dream of catching a dashingly handsome young man, of having him fall madly in love with her. Vivid in her mind was the certainty that marriage would follow, and they would live out the rest of their lives in blissful enchantment.

Another dear friend, Phoebe Tattinger, had shared that very same dream.

It was Phoebe who found her prince first. She'd tumbled head over heels in love with Viscount Colin Paxton the instant they met. Victoria did not envy Phoebe her good fortune—no, not in the least! How could she, for never had she seen Phoebe so happy! She discounted the rumors that Colin's proposal stemmed from his desire to marry an heiress, though Phoebe was indeed an heiress. Colin loved Phoebe—she was as certain of it as her friend.

Phoebe's joy had not lasted even three months after the wedding.

A pang swept through Victoria. She tried not to remember, yet she couldn't help it.

She and Phoebe had been out walking in Hyde Park one day; Phoebe had only recently learned she was with child. For that very reason they'd stopped to rest, sitting on a secluded bench with a view of the pathway, where they could watch the members of the *ton* strut and parade their fine feathers on this sunny spring morn.

A man and woman passed by. 'Twas very clear both gentleman and lady were of an amorous inclination. One lace-gloved hand lay tucked into the gentleman's elbow. The other was snugly enfolded within his. Even as they watched, the couple stopped, touching their lips together in a sweet, binding kiss.

Phoebe had laughingly commented. "It must be the air in London, Victoria. *Everyone* is in love these days—"

But all at once her voice choked off. Victoria's regard snapped back to the pair in question.

The man was Colin, Phoebe's husband.

Never in her life would Victoria forget her friend's expression. She had watched as Phoebe's heart shattered into a million pieces. She'd held her while Phoebe cried throughout the day. And she had waved good-bye when Phoebe departed for the country two days later.

Colin remained in town, where he continued his association with his ladybird, the Lady Marian Winter, a widow.

Since that day, Victoria had lost count of the women who had been associated with him. For the most part, Phoebe remained in the country. Victoria had seen her only a few times since that horrible day, but the change in Phoebe was sobering indeed. She was no longer lively and vivacious. There was no light in her eyes, no dazzle in her smile, where before there had been sunlight bursting in her heart and soul.

Slowly, her attention was drawn back to Sophie. "Oh, come now," Sophie was saying. "Victoria, when I think of your suitors—why, none have been so terrible! And this very moment, your father has offers from three prospects. What about Viscount Newton—"

Victoria's generous mouth had turned down. "A man whose arrogance I cannot abide," she finished succinctly.

"Well, then, what about Robert Sherwood?"

"A cad, Sophie, and you know it as well as I."

"But there's still Lord Dunmire's youngest son Phillip—"

"Boorish and dull, Sophie. I should grow weary of my own voice were I to marry him. And I'm told he gambles to excess."

"Victoria, I beg you reconsider."

"There's nothing you can say to change my mind, Sophie."

"But your reputation will be ruined—"

"Quite," Victoria pronounced grimly.

Sophie sighed. "'Tis because of your friend Phoebe, isn't it, that you refuse to marry? But I would remind you, Victoria, not all men are scoundrels such as her husband."

"I'm quite aware of that, Sophie. Indeed, there are times I enjoy their company very much." It was true. Oh, she laughed. She danced, but she was no longer the innocent she'd been when she entered her first Season.

Her chin came up. "But I would remind *you* that you are only in your first Season, and I am not so naive as I once was. I have borne witness to countless infidelities—husbands with mistresses, wives with lovers. I've seen fortunes lost and amassed with the turn of a card. The *ton* is filled with despicable men whose vices are exceeded only by their monstrous ego."

"And so you will *never* marry?" Sophie remained unconvinced.

Victoria's gaze turned cloudy. "I would never bury myself in the country as Phoebe does," she said slowly. "But long ago I abandoned my foolish notions about love and marriage. I've learned that marriages are made to gain money, power, position, or land—perhaps to breed an heir—perhaps any and all of these."

Sophie fluttered her fan in utter distress. "But you will spend your life alone, Victoria, with no husband, no children. Why, I find the thought simply unbearable!"

Victoria said nothing. She couldn't deny that Phoebe's painful experience had left its mark, for she had no wish to suffer a betrayal such as Phoebe had done. She would not allow any man to use her as a pawn, for his own gain . . .

Her heart twisted, for there was a part of her that was torn in two—a part of her that could not disdain love entirely. Her parents had loved each other, something she never doubted for an instant. Though it had been nearly ten years since Mama died, Victoria still remembered shared, subtle glances between them, a lingering touch on the shoulder that spoke with such eloquence . . .

If she were ever to wed, it must be to a man she could love enough to trust . . . ah, but could she trust enough to love?

She had no answer.

She knew only that she could not spend her life as Phoebe did, in melancholy despair, hopelessly in love with a man who shared nothing of her feelings . . . never being loved in return . . .

She *would* not.

She would far rather spend her life alone.

But now Papa was insisting she marry . . . oh, she truly did not wish to defy him!

And so she turned her attention back to her mission, which was simple. Were she embroiled in scandal, her suitors would want no part of her—neither those present nor prospective. As for Papa, surely he would consider her totally beyond redemption and would at last cease his efforts to see her wed.

Twisting her white lace handkerchief between slender gloved fingers, Victoria directed a fervent prayer heavenward. *Forgive me, Mama.* Her poor dead mama would be horrified at what she proposed to do, yet Victoria could see no other way. All she needed was a gentleman to help her carry out her plan, such as it was.

The only problem was *who.* In all truth, she couldn't quite summon the nerve to approach a gentleman with whom she was already acquainted. It must be a stranger then, for she knew she'd never have the courage to face him again. With that singular thought high aloft, she scanned the sea of bodies. Faith, but there must be *someone . . .*

A figure brushed by, elegantly clad in black. The man was tall, long of limb and broad of shoulder, a study of lean, masculine grace. Victoria caught her breath, for it was as if he'd been lifted from the very essence of her mind—from those dreams she'd cast aside long ago. Her gaze followed him as he passed through the terrace doors and out into the shadows of the gardens.

Something leaped in her breast. There would be no better time. There would be no better *man.* Anticipation sparked within her. If all went as planned, by midnight her fate would at last be her own.

She turned to Sophie and saw that Sophie had again gleaned her intent. Her friend looked ready to cry.

Victoria lightly squeezed her shoulder. "Don't look like that," she scolded gently. "I shall be fine, you'll see. You have only to come to the terrace in a few minutes' time, but make sure someone is with you as well. And don't forget, you must pretend to be horrified at finding us—"

"I *will* be horrified!" Sophie's eyes were huge. "Victoria, when I think of what you are about to do . . . throwing yourself at a gentleman . . ."

"Shhh," Victoria cautioned, then summoned a smile and pinched poor Sophie's cheek. "Wish me luck, love." With that Victoria turned and fairly flew through the terrace doors.

It was a moment before her eyes adjusted to the dimness. The man stood perhaps ten paces distant. His hands were locked behind his back, his dark head slightly inclined as he stared out into the night. Victoria had to force her feet to do her bidding. But a rustle of skirts warned of her presence. Before she could say a word, the stranger spun around just as she came to a halt.

Wide sapphire eyes met those of steely gray. Victoria's eyes flew wide, and she clutched at her skirts. It was all she could do to stand her ground. Her heart knocked wildly, both in fear and anticipation. All sense of reason fled her mind. The moment was upon her, yet she knew not what to say. She knew not what to *do*.

It was he who spoke first. "If you're looking for someone, I fear you're destined for disappointment. I'm the only one here."

"Oh, but I'm hardly disappointed. You're the very one I sought." The words tumbled forth before she could stop them. Victoria colored as she realized how rash—and how audacious—she must surely sound. But she couldn't tear her gaze from his face. She was tall for a woman, yet he was half a head taller than she. And he really was stunningly hand-some, with winged brows as black as his hair, and a square, masculine jaw. His eyes were most unusual, like clear crystal with a glimmer of silver. She found herself thinking that he would be quite irresistible if only he smiled . . .

But now it seemed she was the one who merited a closer look. The stranger proceeded to inspect her from the shining blond coronet atop her head to her narrow, slippered feet. Though Victoria had always prided herself on her ability to remain unruffled no matter the circumstances, there was a sharpness to this man's gaze that rendered her distinctly ill at ease.

A dark brow hiked upward. "Indeed," he responded coolly. "To my knowledge, we've never met."

"No," she agreed. "We have not." Her mind was turning frantically. However was she to accomplish her mission without sounding like a brazen hussy?

"You sought me out, yet you don't know who I am?"

"Yes. You see, I have a favor to ask of you."

"A favor. Of a man you do not know."

"Precisely. You see, I find myself in a situation only you can help me with."

His eyes narrowed. "How so?"

Victoria forced a light, buoyant laugh, even as she battled the urge to turn and flee. "Men are very fond of gambling, are they not? Well, you see, my friend Sophie proposed a rather outrageous dare, a dare I simply could not refuse. She dared me to kiss the first stranger I met tonight. And so, kind sir, I wonder if you are willing to oblige me."

The moment was tortuous. Victoria held her breath and waited.

Nor did she have long to wait.

"Oblige you? Ah, but we have not *met,* have we? You have no idea who I am. I haven't the faintest idea who you are, and I do believe it's best we keep it that way." His smile was cutting. "In short, my lady, I think it best if I remove myself from your silly, schoolgirl schemes."

Victoria understood; truly she did, for already she had recognized that this man was not a carefree, frivolous young buck like so many others in the *ton*. He was older, for one, and his bearing was that of a man who knew what he wanted and knew it well.

Panic flared high and bright as he stepped past her. It appeared he had every intention of returning inside.

"Wait!" she cried. "I beseech you, please do not leave!"

He swung back to face her. Victoria cringed inside, for his expression was no less than forbidding.

"Young woman," he said sternly, "please do not make this more difficult than . . ."

Victoria never heard the rest. A medley of voices came from behind him, near the terrace door.

She had been polite. She had *asked*. And now it seemed she must take the matter into her own hands. Quickly, before she lost her courage, she flung her arms around him and pressed herself against him.

Strong hands clamped down on her waist. Victoria felt him stiffen, but she didn't give him the chance to do more. She tangled her fingers in the hair that grew low on his nape, pulled his head down and levered herself upward in one fluid move.

Her lips met his. Her eyes squeezed shut.

The world seemed to tilt and spin. A hundred different sensations bombarded her. His mouth was soft, while his body was hard. She battled the strangest urge to clutch at him wildly, to press herself against him and feel even more of him against her . . . In her heart she was appalled at such a wickedly unladylike thought, yet she could not deny the hungry surge within her.

In some distant corner of her mind, she heard his swiftly indrawn breath; she sensed that he was as startled as she. Though his fingers bit into the soft skin of her hips, he didn't thrust her away. An odd little quiver shot through her, for she'd never thought to find pleasure in this moment—yet pleasure there was, a world of it, intoxicating and sweet. Her lips parted, a silent invitation . . .

Behind her there was a gasp . . . That would be Sophie, she thought hazily.

Aware they were no longer alone, Victoria reluctantly broke off the kiss. She levered her heels to the floor and prepared herself for the sight of Sophie standing there, pretending to be horrified. With a breathy little sigh, she opened her eyes . . .

Only to confront her father's blistering regard.

"Oh, dear," she whispered. Sophie was behind Papa, her eyes huge. Their host, Lord Remington, was there as well.

The stranger, too, had turned toward the door. Oddly enough, one lean hand remained anchored on her waist, the gesture almost protective. "Good heavens," he said irritably. "Who the devil are you?"

Papa straightened himself to his full height. "I am the marquess of Norcastle," her father said grimly. "And I'll thank you to unhand my daughter."

Two

An hour later the three of them filed into her father's study. Though his features were stoic and tight-lipped, Victoria knew he'd never been angrier. It wasn't his way to rage and shout. Indeed, she thought half-hysterically, she almost wished he would!

The dark stranger sat stiffly beside her—only now she knew his identity. He was Miles Grayson, earl of Stonehurst. Clasping her fingers in her lap, Victoria dared to steal a glance at him . . . oh, and how she wished she had not! His shoulders were as rigid as a soldier's, his profile as cold as the sea.

Yet she couldn't deny that Miles Grayson had been remarkably civil, and very decent, thus far. Nor was it Papa's way to make a scene. Papa had quietly requested that the earl accompany him to his town house that they might discuss the matter further.

But a man could only be pushed so far . . .

The proof was in her father.

Victoria's stomach was churning. She felt very much like a child about to be punished for some misdeed. But this was no childish prank. She'd been caught kissing a gentleman—scandalous behavior in polite society! She reminded herself that sullying her reputation was what she had intended . . . yet somehow it had gone terribly awry . . . she'd never dreamed that Papa would actually *see* it . . .

And she had the awful sensation it wasn't over yet.

"Now." Papa's voice rang out. "I will not ask either of you to explain yourselves, since 'tis very obvious what the two of you were about." He turned his formidable gaze to the earl. "The *ton* is filled with foolish young wastrels who dally whenever and wherever they please and care not a whit about the consequences. 'Twas my belief that you, sir, were above such outlandish behavior—an honorable, respectable man whom I have held in the highest regard. Frankly, my lord, I am appalled at your behavior."

Beside her, the earl said nothing. But Victoria did not miss the way one hand clenched into a fist.

Then it was her turn to bear her father's displeasure as he turned baleful eyes toward her. His tone was stern. "As for you, Victoria, there are no words to express my disappointment."

Victoria could not bear to look at him. In all her life, she had never been so ashamed. "I-I'm sorry, Papa." Swallowing, she slowly raised her chin. "But indeed, you are right. The *ton* is filled with wastrels who dally where they may. Well, I have no wish to marry such a man—"

Her father cut her off with a sound of disgust. "And I would never allow you to marry a scoundrel, Victoria. But you should not spend your life alone and—"

"I would rather spend my life alone than marry a man who would further his own interests by marrying the daughter of a marquess, for that is what happened to my dear friend Phoebe—her husband chose her for her fortune." She spoke with heartfelt candor. "I simply have no desire to marry—not Viscount Newton, not Robert Sherwood, not

Philip Dunmire. And that is why I-I did what I did. I thought they would each withdraw their suit when they heard what had happened. And I thought you would consider me beyond redemption and cease your efforts to see me wed."

"Hmmmph!" Her father's mouth compressed. He directed his attention to the earl. "Have you anything to say, my lord?"

Victoria interrupted before Miles could say a word. "I assure you, Papa, the earl had no idea what I was about!"

From the corner of her eye, she saw the earl stiffen. "I am quite capable of speaking for myself," he said curtly. One elegantly shod foot tapped on the carpet. "You have my sincerest apologies, my lord. My behavior with your daughter was most reprehensible. Beyond that, I fear I can offer no more."

"Now that's where you're wrong, my lord." The marquess drummed his fingers on the desktop. "Because I am not prepared to let the matter end here."

An ominous foreboding descended over the room. Victoria's eyes darted between the two men, who beheld each other in rigid silence. Why didn't Miles Grayson speak up and agree with her? Why didn't he tell Papa that he hadn't kissed her—'twas *she* who kissed him! For in truth, the blame was not his at all.

"Papa," she said in desperation, "did you not hear? It was I who kissed him!"

"Either way, Victoria"—her father's tone was biting—"the earl appeared ever so willing. Or am I wrong, my lord?"

Miles Grayson's jaw might have been hewn of iron. He spoke not a word, neither agreement nor denial.

"Very well then," Papa went on. "My daughter's reputation has been compromised, and I will not permit this scandal to go further. The only question that remains is how to rectify the damage."

He fixed his gaze on his daughter. "Since your mother

died, I have provided for you the best I knew how, Victoria. I am proud to say, you have disappointed me in only one thing—your reluctance to take a husband. I have been patient. Through three Seasons I have waited for you to do what is expected of you, I have bided my time whilst you turned up your nose at first one suitor, then another, for I could not bear to see you unhappy. But you are a woman now, Victoria. And you must live with the consequences of your actions."

He transferred his attention to the earl. "Now then. I believe it's best if we speak privately, my lord. Victoria, a moment alone with the earl, if you please . . ."

Victoria needed no further urging. She leaped to her feet and fled.

Miles was furious—with himself, the marquess, and his troublesome daughter. He'd only accepted Lord and Lady Remington's invitation because Lord Remington had stood as godfather to him. But going to the ball had been a monumental mistake.

His trips to London were rare, usually confined to business only, for he'd grown tired of society long ago—the parties, the false gaiety, the endless gossip, the never-ending pretense of manners and goodwill. He much preferred the solitude of Lyndermere Park, his estate in Lancashire; he enjoyed far more the company of farmers and shepherds . . . and of course, Heather.

He'd very nearly departed London for Lyndermere Park that very morning. He hated the noise and grime of London— and he missed Heather. His mouth twisted. God, but he should have listened to his instinct. Then this would never have happened . . .

The marquess's voice cut into his thoughts like the prick of a needle. "I have a proposition for you, my lord. Would you care to hear it?"

Miles's smile was a travesty. "Not really," he drawled.

"Nonetheless," the marquess stated with icy precision, "you will."

Miles shrugged.

"Now. What I propose is very simple. I want you to marry my daughter."

Miles's smile was wiped clean, his reply heated and instantaneous. "You're mad."

"I assure you, my lord, I am not."

Miles forced a calm he was far from feeling. "What!" he said scathingly. "I heard you say quite distinctly, my lord, that your daughter is in her third Season. I cannot help but wonder what's wrong with the chit that she's been unable to find a man willing to marry her."

The marquess only barely managed to restrain his temper. "I would be careful were I you, my lord. When you insult my daughter, you insult me as well, and that is not wise. And surely you have eyes. Victoria is a beauty, as comely as any. She has had numerous suitors, more than I can recall. And I've had in my hand this past fortnight three offers for her hand."

"Then let one of them marry her!"

Leather creaked as the marquess leaned back in his chair. "Ah, but they did not dishonor her, sir. *You* did."

Miles very nearly retorted that the chit had no one to blame but herself. But just as he opened his mouth, a voice tolled through his mind. *Papa, did you not hear? It was I who kissed him!*

The girl had been remarkably forward—and incredibly fetching. And that kiss . . . An unguarded taste of innocence, sweeter than ripe summer berries, a hint of heaven . . .

At first he'd been too startled to move. And then—God above but he couldn't lie—he hadn't wanted to. Desire struck the very instant their lips met—strange, for he was not a man to yearn for a woman so quickly—and so intensely. He'd wanted to snatch her against him. Plumb the depths of her mouth with his tongue while his hands explored the lithe ripeness of her body . . . But something had stopped him. Perhaps the innocence he'd sensed in her . . .

No, he thought soberly. He hadn't expected to like it so much. He hadn't expected to want her sweet, stolen kiss to go on. And on . . .

He could have stopped it. He could have ended it at any given moment . . .

His lips tightened. "I accept my part in this. But do you really expect me to *marry* her?"

"I will make myself very clear, Lord Stonehurst. If you don't, you will live to regret it."

Miles clenched his jaw so hard his teeth hurt. "A threat, my lord?"

The marquess shrugged. "Call it whatever you like." Shaggy brows drew together over his nose. "I understand you have a daughter."

Miles had been about to tell him to go straight to hell. But at the mention of Heather, he froze. "My ward," he said curtly. "Heather Duval. She's been with me since she was a very young child. Her parents were killed in a carriage accident." His tone was level, as level as his gaze. But his heart had leaped high in his chest. The marquess couldn't possibly know . . .

The marquess frowned. "Ah, now it comes to me!" he explained. "You were once betrothed to the former Lady Margaret Sutherland, were you not?"

"What of it?" His voice was clipped and abrupt. Miles couldn't help it.

"But you broke off the engagement only days before the wedding, as I recall."

"Marriage between Margaret and I would have been a mistake." Miles felt compelled to defend himself.

"Ah, but Margaret's mother was most distressed. I remember her telling me that Margaret had gone to Lancashire to visit you. Did she and your ward not get on well, my lord?"

Miles's tone was tight. "That, my lord, is none of your affair."

The marquess paid no heed. He tipped his head to the side. "Who did you say the little girl's parents were, my lord?"

"I didn't," Miles said from between his teeth.

"Hmmm. Odd, but I suddenly find myself most curious, my lord. Most curious, indeed."

Miles's eyes glinted. "You bastard," he accused baldly. "I'll tolerate no one prying into her past."

"And there'll be no need if you marry my daughter." The elder man's tone was as smooth as oil. He didn't take his eyes from Grayson's face. "Well, my lord? Do we have a bargain?"

Miles was up and on his feet in a surge of restless anger. Damn him. He couldn't possibly know . . . Yet he couldn't take the chance the marquess might find out the truth. Oh, it wouldn't hurt him. But Heather's life would never be the same—and he wanted only the best for her. She would *have* only the best.

"Let it be done," he muttered.

"Excellent!" proclaimed the marquess. "Now, I think the wedding should take place posthaste . . ." He rose and opened a massive oak door and called for his daughter.

Victoria walked slowly into the study, feeling for all the world as if she were entering a dungeon of darkest doom. The earl stood near the window, arms crossed over his chest; he made no acknowledgement of her presence. As for her father, Papa's expression told the tale only too well—he was pleased with the outcome of his discussion with the earl. His words bore out her suspicion.

"The earl has some news for you, my dear."

Miles Grayson turned and gave her a stiff bow. "It seems

we are to marry, my lady. I trust you'll understand that I am less than overjoyed."

Victoria's face drained of all color. "Marry," she echoed, her tone half-strangled. "No, it cannot be. You—you cannot want this."

"No." His mouth twisted. "But your father is a persuasive man."

Stricken, Victoria looked at her father. "Papa. Papa, *please* do not make me do this."

She didn't acknowledge the spasm of pain that passed over his face. The marquess shook his head. "I warned you, Victoria. I warned you but you would not heed me. And so I have no choice."

A horrible knot of dread coiled in her belly. He was right. She'd been caught. Caught in a trap of her own design.

Nor had Papa lied. He'd said if she did not choose a husband this very night, then he would. And as she soon discovered, Papa was determined to see the deed well and truly done . . .

This very night.

A vicar was summoned to the town house. He took his place in front of the massive marble fireplace, his Bible in hand. Smiling and sleepy-eyed, he glanced between the two men. "Shall we proceed, my lords?"

Papa gave a curt nod. Stoic and silent, the earl stepped before the vicar. His posture was wooden.

He spared no glance for his bride-to-be, standing in the shadows at the back of the room.

Victoria stifled the urge to shrink away into the darkness of the night. But then Papa was there, offering his arm. Her steps heavy, Victoria crossed the carpet, feeling as if she were being led to an early grave. As she took her place beside the earl, a feeling of sick dread tightened her middle. Her mind screamed silently. How could this have happened? She was about to marry this man—Miles Grayson, earl of

Stonehurst. Sweet heaven, she was to *marry* him, a man she'd not set eyes on before this very night . . .

She stole a glance at him, only to regret it. His profile was as rigid as his spine, his expression grim and angry. There was scant comfort in knowing he wanted this marriage no more than she . . .

She hadn't wanted to marry, most certainly not this night. And she would never have wanted it like this, in this sterile, lonely room at midnight . . . Despair pierced her breast. If it had to be, she'd have wanted it differently . . . Four prancing steeds would have delivered her to the steps of the church. She'd have walked down the aisle in a long, flowing gown of satin and lace. Friends and acquaintances would have filled every pew. Sophie would have been there, beaming at her shyly, and Phoebe, too . . .

The ceremony passed in a haze. She roused only when her hand was laid within the earl of Stonehurst's. She nearly snatched it back—his skin was like fire.

Then all at once it was time for the vows. The earl spoke his in clipped, staccato tones.

She whispered hers.

In the corner, the clock began to toll the hour of midnight.

Victoria watched numbly as the earl pulled a gold, crested ring from his smallest finger and slid it onto hers. The ring was heavy . . . as heavy as her heart.

At the very last stroke, the vicar raised his head and cleared his throat. "I now pronounce you man and wife," he intoned. "My lord, you may kiss the bride."

Three

Victoria's numbness receded. Aware of Miles Gray-
son's burning gaze on her profile, a flurry of panic took hold,
swift and merciless. She sought to withdraw her hand but he
wouldn't allow it. His grip tightened. An unpleasantly strong
arm slid about her waist and caught her up against him.

His head swooped down.

His mouth crushed hers, fierce and devouring; it was a
kiss far beyond Victoria's limited experience. Oh, she'd allowed a few of her gentleman callers a chaste peck on the
lips now and again—and thought herself quite daring!

But this was different. Her husband's possession of her
mouth was far from worshipful. She could feel the rampant,
seething fire of his emotions in the hot brand of his mouth
on hers, filled with stark, relentless purpose. He meant to
defile her—to dishonor her.

Gasping, she tore her mouth free. She knew it for certain
then. He raised her head, and both triumph and challenge glit-
tered in his eyes. Victoria's spine went rigid. She would have
slapped him were it not for the sharp rap of Papa's voice.

"A word of warning, my lord. Although Victoria is now

your wife, do not forget she is my daughter. Misuse her and you'll feel my wrath—and I promise, you'll wish you had not!"

The earl was undaunted. Instead his mouth curled in what could only be called dry mockery. "My lord, I could hardly forget," he drawled. "I trust you'll forgive our hasty departure." He turned to his bride. "Countess, I suggest you hurry and have a maid pack a bag for you. Our wedding night awaits."

Victoria's eyes flew wide, then slid back to her father. This couldn't be happening! she thought wildly. Miles Grayson had no right to take over her life like this! *Ah, but he does,* whispered a niggling little voice.

And they all knew it.

Her bag was packed and ready all too soon. The earl's carriage clattered around to the front of the house. With a steely-fingered hold about her elbow, the earl proceeded to lead her outside. But as he would have handed her up and into the carriage, she broke away.

She rushed back to where Papa stood on the steps. Throwing her arms around him, she clung to him unashamedly. "Papa," she choked out. "I cannot do this. I cannot bear it!"

The hand that smoothed her hair was not entirely steady. "Shhh," he whispered. "It will be all right, Victoria. I know it."

"He is so hard. So cold!"

"I know what he seems at this moment, child. But he is not. Dear God, do you think I'd give my only daughter to such a man?"

An ache rent her breast. In her heart, Victoria knew her father wanted only what was best for her. Yet she couldn't see what good could possibly come of this marriage.

"Victoria!" From the shadows behind her, the sound of her name sliced through the night.

Victoria paid no heed.

Papa kissed her cheek, then squeezed her shoulder. "Go now, Victoria, and remember. You now have a husband, but I will always be your father—and I will always love you."

Though her throat was hot with the burning threat of tears, somehow those words gave her the strength she needed to turn and retrace her steps. This time when the earl handed her into the coach, her head was high, the set of her shoulders proudly erect.

The interior of the coach was thick with an oppressive silence. Victoria felt the earl's gaze on her—dark and angry— like the man himself, she thought with a shiver. Despite her resolve, she was sorely tempted to fling open the door and flee.

Soon the carriage rolled to a halt before a fashionable red-brick mansion in Grosvenor Square.

"Our humble abode, countess."

Victoria gritted her teeth. The wretch was baiting her—and enjoying it immensely. She disdained his hand and alighted without his assistance. The door was opened by a stoop-shouldered butler and they were ushered inside a wide, flag-stoned entrance hall.

Miles wasted no time imparting the news. "Nelson, meet my wife, the former Lady Victoria Carlton. Would you please show her to the gold bedchamber?"

Nelson was all agog but recovered quickly. "Certainly, sir." He picked up her bag and inclined his head toward his new mistress. "Please come with me, my lady."

Victoria brushed past the earl without a word. The bed-chamber she was shown into was lovely. The carpet was of pale cream. Deep yellow brocade draperies framed the win-dows. A matching counterpane covered the bed. Under other circumstances Victoria might have exclaimed her delight aloud, but not now.

What was it the earl had said? Her mind flew like wind across the fields. *Our wedding night awaits.* She shivered. He hadn't meant anything by that, had he? No. Of course not. After all, their marriage had hardly been planned. Surely he would not expect her to—to behave like a bride. Or—God forbid—to share his bed . . .

"I trust this room suits you?"

The voice startled her. Victoria whirled around to see her husband standing in the doorway. He leaned with careless ease against the doorjamb, one lean hand curled around a glass of wine. Despite the lateness of the hour, he looked as elegantly handsome as he had hours earlier.

The room does, she longed to shout. *It's you who does not.*

She nodded.

"Good." There was a small pause. "Will you join me for a drink in the drawing room?"

She politely declined. "I think not. It's been a tiring night."

"A tiring night! But you saw the fruition of your plans, didn't you? I should imagine you'd want to celebrate." His tone was falsely hearty.

Victoria stiffened. "Celebrate? I fail to see what there is to celebrate," she informed him archly.

"Oh, come now, countess. This was your plan all along, wasn't it? To trap me into marriage."

Her jaw closed with a snap. It was all she could do to maintain a civil air. "It's just as I told my father, my lord. I wished to marry no one—least of all you," she said cuttingly. "Indeed, it was the very thing I sought to avoid."

"Ah, and you went about it quite admirably, didn't you?" Mockery lay heavy and biting in his voice.

Victoria's face burned painfully. "A mistake, my lord. A costly one for both of us, I admit, for I misjudged my father grievously. But perhaps you may draw comfort from the fact that you stand to gain far more than I. My father is a wealthy man. My dowry is a fortune unto its own. I should imagine *you* would be celebrating." Her gaze lowered to the glass of wine in his hand. She smiled with acid sweetness. "But you are already, I see."

Her barb struck home. His mouth hardened. His grip on the fragile stem of the glass tightened so that the skin of his knuckles shown taut and white; Victoria was certain the stem would snap at any moment.

He straightened. "This seems as good a time as any to tell you of my plan. I suggest we dwell under the same roof for as long as it takes to appease your father. In time, I have no doubt you'll be able to charm him into seeing this marriage was a mistake. When that happens, the marriage can be annulled and we'll go our separate ways. Is that agreeable?"

"Quite," she snapped.

"So be it," he said. He started to turn away, only to pause.

"A word of advice for you, countess. I shouldn't force my attentions on a gentleman—let alone kiss him—the way you did me in the Rutherfords' garden. A man"—his smile was but a travesty—"I fear there is no polite way to put this . . . a man finds such boldness distasteful." With that he left her.

Victoria was speechless with rage. She glared at the door through which he'd just passed. Miles Grayson, earl of Stonehurst, was the most odious, hateful man alive!

This was war.

Her pride had been stung, the gauntlet cast. Her husband had insulted her, cutting her down with naught but the lash of his tongue.

Oh, she would do as he said. They would reside beneath the same roof, for the sake of her father. But they would share nothing else—not a single meal. Not a room.

But if he thought to make her cower, he would be sorely disappointed, for Victoria was determined not to wilt away, to hide in the corner.

So it was that the next morning, she summoned the earl's staff and introduced herself . . . and promptly rang for the carriage. While she waited in the entrance hall, she stopped before a gilt-framed mirror and retied the satin strings of her bonnet, humming a merry little tune.

"Going out so soon, my dear?"

Victoria very nearly choked herself.

Thank heaven her recovery was mercifully quick, even though her heart pounded and her mind turned wildly. He thought her bold and audacious, so that was what she would give him. Giving a final tug on her bonnet strings, she turned and bestowed on him a smile that would surely melt the hardest of hearts.

But not her husband's.

"Well, Victoria?" He stood before her, an imposing figure garbed wholly in black. Her stomach fluttered strangely. He seemed taller than ever, lean and muscular. Seen in the full light of the day, she could detect no flaws in his countenance, save the almost wicked slant of his brows. Indeed, he was so very handsome he nearly took her breath away. But there was no mistaking the disapproval inherent in his regard, and that fired more than a twinge of resentment.

She gave a trilling little laugh. "What!" she said breezily. "Did you think I'd be given to vapors? If so, I'm sorry to disappoint you."

His eyes seemed to sizzle. "On the contrary, Victoria"—he spoke with precise deliberation—"you are exactly what I expected."

She paid him no further heed as she swept out the front door. Minutes later the carriage drew up before Sophie's house. When the butler announced her, Sophie thrust aside her embroidery and leaped up.

"Victoria! Oh, I'm so sorry . . . I-I don't know how it happened . . . your father followed me onto the terrace and asked your whereabouts. And suddenly there you were . . . ! Oh, I've been so worried. Mama rushed home from shopping this morning with the news you'd wed the earl of Stonehurst!

Is that who you were with in the garden? The earl of Stone-hurst? I told Mama she must surely be mistaken . . . she is, isn't she?"

There was no need to answer. Victoria practically fell into Sophie's arms and collapsed into tears.

Within the day, their marriage was the talk of the *ton*.

Within the week, the talk of London.

Victoria had feared she would be ostracized, for the *ton* was notorious for turning a condescending eye to those who committed the slightest *faux pas*. Yet the ladies sighed with envy, for they thought marriage between Victoria and Miles Grayson grandly romantic—and quite a catch! As for the gentlemen, they merely smiled quietly to themselves, for they were well aware the earl of Stonehurst had captured a covet-ous prize—a wife who possessed both beauty *and* money.

All in all, her social calender changed little, for invitations continued to arrive daily. But Victoria felt very much the in-truder in her husband's house; oh, not because of the servants, for they were only too anxious to please. No, it was Miles. She couldn't forget he disdained her very presence in his home, her so-called role as wife. And so she stayed away as often as she could. On those rare occasions she encountered her hus-band, he was unfailingly polite, yet chillingly so.

One morning, she accompanied Sophie to a seamstress on Bond Street. While Sophie and the seamstress went back to the dressing room, Victoria idly sifted through a handful of hair ribbons in the far corner of the shop. The doorchime sounded, and she glanced up. Two matrons stepped within; one was Lady Carmichael, the other Lady Brentwood.

Her greeting died on her lips.

"Why, I've never met such a gentleman as Lord Stone-hurst in all my days," Lady Carmichael was saying.

Curious, Victoria ducked her head low and listened in-tently.

"I find him utterly fascinating," Lady Carmichael went on, "and *most* charming."

"Yes, indeed." This came from Lady Brentwood. "Charles has had numerous business dealings with him. Why, only last evening I distinctly recall he told an acquaintance there's no man he respects or admires more than Lord Stonehurst—and Charles is not a man to give his praise lightly."

But Lady Brentwood had not finished. "As for his marriage to Lady Victoria Carlton, why, many a man would have left her to her own devices, no matter the harm to her reputation. The haste with which they married simply proves that he is a noble fellow indeed." She gave a trilling laugh. "To say nothing of handsome!"

Victoria's lips tightened. Handsome, oh, exceedingly. That she couldn't deny. But charming? Noble? *They* did not have to live with the subject in question. Little did they know—why, the man was a veritable fencepost!

"I do hope Victoria appreciates how lucky she is to have landed such a catch!" said Lady Carmichael. "I find it rather odd that she continues to go about as if she'd never married! Why, my Theodora sobbed the night through when she heard Stonehurst had wed."

Victoria's head snapped up. She was sorely tempted to tell Lady Carmichael that her Theodora was welcome to Miles Grayson, earl of Stonehurst!

But she was unwilling to fuel gossip any further, and so she maintained her silence, keeping her presence hidden until the two ladies had left the shop.

But the conversation nagged at her throughout the next few days. Was Miles truly so respected among the *ton*?

For the first time she began to see her husband in a different light . . . and reluctantly admitted that to her knowledge, Miles was neither a cad nor a bounder. He didn't overly frequent the gaming tables. She heard no tales of wild or reckless behavior, nor did he drink to excess. If he had a mistress, he was so discreet she never even suspected. Indeed, it seemed her husband possessed none of the vices she might have despised in a husband . . .

Soon she began to feel guilty, for neither malice nor spite was in her nature. What need was there to live together as enemies? One morning as she prepared to go downstairs, she decided perhaps it was time to make the best of their situation. On impulse, she tapped on the door of his room. When he bid her enter, she stepped inside . . .

Only to stop short at the threshold.

Apparently he'd just come in from riding. His riding jacket lay in a heap upon the bed; a rumpled white shirt lay next to it.

All at once her mouth was dry as dust, her gaze riveted to his form. Victoria had never seen a man in a state of dishabille, not her father or any other.

His hips were incredibly narrow, his boots spattered with mud. His fawn-colored breeches were like a second skin; they clung to his thighs, cleanly outlining every muscle. But it was what lay nestled between those iron-hewn thighs that drew her gaze in a manner most unseemly . . . the swelling there hinted at a masculinity that—were it unfettered and released from constraint—promised a sight to behold indeed . . .

Egad, whatever was wrong with her! Stunned by such audacious thoughts, she tore her gaze upward, only to realize that his naked torso was no less disconcerting.

His shoulders were strong and wide, the muscles of his arms smooth and tight and sleek. A mat of dark curly hair covered his chest and belly, disappearing beneath the waistband of his breeches. Her mind ran wild. Oh, but there was beauty in the male form, of a kind she'd not thought to find . . . most certainly not in her husband!

"Was there something you wanted, Victoria?"

His regard was cool and unsmiling. Victoria swallowed,

praying he hadn't noticed her staring. Quickly she gathered her courage—and her senses. Yet still her voice was a trifle breathless.

"There is a garden fete at the Covingtons this afternoon. I-I wondered if you would care to attend with me?"

His reply was most emphatic. "I am not one of your London peacocks to strut at your side for all to admire you, countess. If you wish to attend, then go. But do not trouble me about such trivial matters again."

Victoria felt as if she'd been slapped. Stupid, foolish tears stung her eyes. She blinked them back, and somehow managed to salvage her pride. Raising her chin, she matched his disdain with dignified aplomb.

"As you wish, my lord," she stated levelly. With a swish of her skirts she turned and was gone.

By the time she reached the dining room, a seething resentment had replaced the hurt. So much for her peace efforts, she reflected bitterly. She had tried, and she could do no more.

The next step—unlikely though it was—was up to Miles.

So it was that in the days that followed, Victoria went riding in Hyde Park. She attended birthday parties and routs. She waltzed until the wee hours of the morning at Almack's. The Lady Carmichaels and Lady Brentwoods of the *ton* could gossip all they pleased about the state of her marriage. When queried about the whereabouts of her husband, she would simply shrug and say lightly, "It's hardly the thing to be in each other's pockets. Besides, what marriage these days is a love match?"

Never had she been so miserable.

One man in particular, Count Antony DeFazio from Italy, was frequently at her side. No matter where she was, more often than not he was there as well. Eventually—unfailingly—he would make his way over to her. Sophie thought he was to-swoon-for handsome. In all honesty, Victoria supposed he was. Yet somehow when she looked into eyes as dark as midnight, she was reminded of eyes the color of storm clouds . . .

It was most distracting—and highly vexing.

In any case, Antony was charming and warmly attentive. He complimented the rich gold of her hair, the creaminess of her skin, the remarkable blue of her eyes. He was an outrageous flirt, but when it seemed her husband wanted nothing to do with her, his praise was balm to her wounded pride.

But her husband was not as heedless of her activities as she thought.

Miles remained in the background, watching all unfold with mounting displeasure. Even before that disastrous night at the Rutherfords, he'd heard rumors of his new wife; in his estimation, she was a lady of fashion who thrived on attention. He couldn't help but think of Margaret Sutherland, the woman he had very nearly married. Once the toast of London, he'd fallen victim to Margaret's sultry beauty, her vivacious charm.

He'd not be so foolish again.

His mouth turned down. No, Victoria was no different than Margaret. Indeed, how could she be anything but shallow and vain? In the end, Victoria would prove herself selfish and hurtful, and Miles would not expose Heather to such a woman.

You judge without evidence, whispered an irascible little voice.

Hah! What more did he need? Why, they'd been wed nearly a fortnight and the chit had not spent one evening home!

Still, he was reminded how Victoria had stood up to her father and announced that *she* had kissed him. Odd, how she'd tried to protect him. Rather honorable, really, to say nothing of noble and courageous . . .

But Miles was a man who didn't need the glitter of London

to be happy. He'd chosen a more simple life in the country, an infinitely more satisfying life. Margaret would never have been happy anywhere but London. Neither would Victoria, which was yet another reason he was convinced they had no future together.

That very thought was high in his mind as he strolled inside his home that evening. Nelson hurried to greet him.

"Good evening, my lord."

"Good evening, Nelson." He handed the butler his gloves and cane.

Now came the inevitable question . . . "Is the countess home?"

. . . and the inevitable answer. "No, my lord." The butler's eyes flitted away.

"I see. And where is she this fine night?"

"My lord, she mentioned something about a ball at Lord and Lady Raleigh's. I believe the invitation arrived last week."

It was then Miles saw it—a calling card on a silver tray. He picked it up and read the name—COUNT ANTONY DE-FAZIO. Sheer red misted his vision, for Miles had also heard the count's name bandied about—in conjunction with his wife's!

"The count was here?"

"This afternoon, my lord. He and the countess took tea together. Then he returned to escort my lady to the ball."

So now the chit was entertaining her admirers in his very house! A stark, blinding fury came over him. He damned himself for giving in to it, even as he damned his errant wife for her part in it.

He jutted out his jaw. "Nelson, have the carriage brought round."

In all her days, Victoria didn't know when she'd been so bored. The lilting music all sounded the same. The crush of faces around her had blurred to indistinction, and she found the scent of fresh flowers almost cloying. If she had to attend one more wretched affair like this, she would surely scream.

Whirling around the dance floor with Antony, she prayed he would unhand her. Her head ached and her feet hurt. All she wanted at this moment was to go home . . .

Home, she thought with a pang. There was a painful catch in her breast. She no longer knew where she belonged. Papa had foisted her off upon the earl, and the earl would just as soon be rid of her . . .

The dance ended. One hand possessively at her waist, Antony would have led her from the floor. But Victoria gently broke away. "Oh, there's Sophie!" she exclaimed. "Please excuse me, count, but I must have a word with her." She gave him no chance to protest, but breezed away in a swirl of skirts.

Across the room, she kissed Sophie's cheek. "Thank heaven you appeared when you did, Sophie. Antony is sweet, but he can be a bit much at times."

"Oh, Victoria, but he is so dashing and handsome! And just think, he is quite entranced with you."

Victoria smiled slightly. She found two seats at the edge of the dance floor and sank into one of them, wriggling her toes gratefully. "Granted, he is quite pleasant to look at, but there are times when he's really quite full of himself, Sophie."

Sophie gave a wistful sigh. "Still, that I could be in your slippers tonight . . ." She had yet to sit, and her gaze drifted out to the dance floor once more. All at once she gasped.

"Victoria, look! He—he's here!"

Victoria accepted a glass of champagne from a tray. "Who, love?"

"Your husband!"

Your husband. Victoria's heart lurched. She very nearly dropped her glass of champagne.

"Victoria, what if he saw you dancing with Antony? Do you think he'll be angry? Do you think he'll be jealous?" Sophie gasped. "He's coming this way and . . . oh, dear . . . I don't think I wish to be in your slippers after all! Victoria, I could almost swear . . . he *does* look rather jealous."

Her gaze tracked Sophie's. Sure enough, Sophie was right. Miles was there, already bearing down on them. But judging from the expression on his face, she guessed he wasn't jealous at all . . .

He was positively livid.

Four

Yet no trace of it showed in his demeanor as he stepped up before them. He bowed low, a gesture of graceful elegance. "Victoria, I had no idea you were here." He turned to Sophie, chiseled lips drawn into a devastating smile. "Who is your companion, my dear?" Victoria saw a dreamy appreciation enter Sophie's eyes and nearly groaned.

She hastened to her feet, and lay her hand on Sophie's arm. Her stomach twisted in dread but she was determined not to show it. Lifting her chin, she matched his smile. "My lord, this is my dearest friend in all the world, Miss Sophie Mayfair. Sophie, my husband, Miles Grayson, earl of Stonehurst."

"Miss Mayfair, I do hope you don't mind if I steal my wife away. Can you imagine, married nearly a fortnight and we've yet to dance together."

He allowed no protest, but set aside her champagne, captured her hand, and pulled her onto the dance floor. Victoria glared her outrage. "'Married nearly a fortnight and we've yet to dance together,'" she quoted. "I wonder, my lord, whose fault that is."

"The opportunity could hardly present itself when you were not present, countess."

"My lord," she said sweetly, "I could say the very same of you."

He chose to be silent for several moments. His arm was hard about her back. He held her close—far closer than was proper!—so close she fancied she could feel the muscled breadth of his chest. She felt suddenly giddy . . . from the way he whirled her around, she told herself.

It was then she noticed they had attracted more than an idle number of glances. "We're being watched," she murmured. Her gaze caught his. "Should we give them something to talk about?"

"My dear, I do believe you already have." He sounded almost angry.

Shuttered behind his oh-so-pleasant facade was an anger even deeper than she'd realized. Her heart bounded clear to her throat.

"In fact," he went on, "I do believe we should continue this discussion at home." He whisked her off the dance floor.

Victoria was suddenly not at all eager to leave. She tried to twist away without making it appear she did so. "But I came with—"

The arm about her waist tightened like a band of steel. "I know who escorted you. Nonetheless, you're leaving with me."

There was a tap on Miles's shoulder. "Excuse me," said a thickly accented voice, "but Victoria promised this next dance to me."

Victoria held her breath while Miles squared off to face the count. But he only shook his head and said easily, "Then I'm afraid you're out of luck, old man. Because my lovely wife has promised the night to me—along with every other night."

A very red-faced count fell back, murmuring his apologies.

Victoria clamped her mouth shut. When they were alone in the carriage, she vented the full force of her wrath. "I do not recall promising the night to you, my lord. Not this night or any other."

"Ah, but I beg to differ with you, countess. Or do you forget our wedding vows so soon?"

Victoria lapsed into silence. Drat the man and his facile tongue, she decided furiously. Why must he always have his words so ready at hand?

Once they were inside his home, he ushered her into the salon and closed the doors. Ignoring her, he removed his coat and unwound his cravat, dropping them onto the back of a chair. Her stomach dropped clear to the floor when he proceeded to undo the top buttons of his shirt. She balked. Surely he would not . . . But no. Why, the thought was ridiculous. He'd made no secret of his distaste for her. Of course he had no intention of asserting his husbandly rights . . .

Stifling a pinprick of hurt, she seated herself in a velvet wing chair while he poured two glasses of wine. He turned to face her.

Silence mounted, thick and heavy. Victoria's heart lurched, for he stared at her most oddly. Why, she could almost believe that he *was* jealous . . . But no. She was mistaken. That familiar glacial coolness was very much in evidence as he presented himself before her. He wordlessly extended a glass of wine.

Victoria opened her mouth to decline but he cut her off abruptly.

"I suggest you take it, countess. You didn't get to finish your champagne, remember?"

She would rather not, she decided uneasily. Indeed, she would far rather put this entire night behind her and pretend it hadn't happened, for there was an air of danger about her husband that sent warning bells ringing all through her.

He wasted no time. "You had a caller this afternoon, did you not?"

Her chin lifted a notch. "What, my lord? Am I not allowed to have callers?"

"Of course you may. It's this particular caller I have a problem with, countess. So tell me, who was he?"

Lying was not an option. He already knew. "Count Antony DeFazio," she ventured calmly.

"It's my understanding you've been seen with the count on numerous other occasions. Are you aware of his reputation?"

Her smile was as false as his had been earlier. "Why, yes, indeed I am. Antony is a wonderful dancer. An engaging conversationalist, to say nothing of being an immensely charming escort—"

"That's not what I mean and you know it."

Victoria shrugged. "Men have mistresses and ladies have lovers," she stated daringly. "'Tis the way of the world."

"Well, it's not my way." Suddenly he was there before her. For the second time in just a few short minutes, her glass was set aside. Without further ado, she was hauled up and out of her chair. Strong hands imprisoned the fragile span of her shoulders.

"You've had free rein these past few weeks, Victoria, but no more. I will not have you behaving in a way that will cause embarrassment or dishonor to my name—to *your* name," he emphasized.

Temper flared but she held it in check. "And what behavior might that be?"

"Dancing with Count Antony DeFazio. Receiving him in our home when I am not present."

"Our home?" she retorted archly. "This is *your* home, my lord."

"It is also yours," he countered, "at least until such time as your father ceases to peer over our shoulder."

The soft line of Victoria's mouth thinned with suppressed fury. "Is there more, my lord?"

"Indeed there is. You will not cavort with the count—nor any man—for all to see."

"Why, my lord," she stated with acid sweetness. "I could almost believe you're jealous." She mocked him. She knew it, and was secretly appalled at her daring. But another part of her, deep in the recesses of her being, yearned to hear him say it was true—that he *was* jealous of DeFazio. And—God help her—that very same part of her desperately wanted the strength of his arms hard around her back—the brand of his mouth upon hers, hot and searing, banishing these angry words so that nothing else mattered.

Oh, it made no sense! She wanted to be rid of him—and he of her . . .

"Well, my lord. *Are* you jealous?" She was aching inside. Quivering. Praying as never before . . .

"Of course not. Why, the very idea is nonsense."

He denounced her baldly—heaven help her, a knife in the heart. But she wouldn't let him know it, not in a thousand years.

"Nonetheless," he went on, "I mean what I say, Victoria. I won't allow you to meet DeFazio again."

Her eyes narrowed. "You forbid me?" she said pleasantly.

"Call it anything you like. Either way, you won't be seeing him again. Nor will you stay out till dawn."

Anger flared at his imperious tone. "Till dawn," she sputtered. "Why, I did no such thing!"

"Nor will you."

"You can't stop me!"

"Oh, but I think I can."

"What will you do? Lock me in my room like a child?"

"If that's what it takes, yes." He was deadly serious. "You need a firm hand, Victoria. You are wild and reckless and I'll have no more of it."

Victoria gasped. "You presume to know me quite well when you know me not at all." She wrenched herself free. Her eyes smoldered, twin flames of pure fire. "Why do you even care what I do—and with whom I do it?"

He stood before her, a pillar of stone. "A ridiculous question, countess. I care because you are my wife."

"The wife you didn't want." Victoria spoke bitterly. Odd, but it burned inside to hear the words aloud.

"Regardless of the circumstances, we *are* wed. And you will mind your manners and your tongue—"

"I need no lessons in manners, my lord earl. Certainly not from you—a man who's been too long in the country!"

"I mean what I say, Victoria. I'll not have you making a spectacle of yourself, running wildly about town with a man like DeFazio—"

Victoria cried out indignantly. "Why, I do believe if it were up to you, I'd stay here in this house and—and mold!"

His smile was utterly maddening. "A vast improvement, I daresay."

Tears stung her eyes, tears she blinked back furiously. "I'm going home to Papa," she announced. She sought to step past him, only to find herself snared by the elbow and whirled around to face him.

She flung up her hands between them. "Let me go!"

He caught her up against him. His smile had vanished; his expression would surely have curdled cream. "You are not leaving this house, Victoria."

"Oh, yes, I am. I'm going home! Papa did not dictate to me like this."

"Well, perhaps he should have. Perhaps then we would not be in this wholly untenable predicament."

It was the wrong thing to say. Miles knew it the instant the words left his mouth, for Victoria's face whitened. For an instant, she looked as if she'd been struck. And then she did the one thing he never expected.

She burst into tears.

For the space of a heartbeat, Miles could only stare. He'd been prepared for a fiery rage. A spiteful defiance—anything but this.

She sobbed as if her heart were broken.

He wrapped one arm around her slowly. Her body was pliant and limp as he directed her to the small divan just to his left. He sat, cradling her against his side, her head nestled against his shoulder. He spoke not a word, but stroked the shining cap of her hair, holding her as he might have held Heather.

In time, the sobs eased to deep, jagged breaths. He stilled the movement of his hand, resting it between the narrow plane of her shoulder blades. "Now," he said quietly. "Would you like to tell me what distresses you so?"

Oddly, she made no move to distance her person from him. "It's . . . everything."

He studied her as she glanced up at him. It struck him how exquisite she was, even with her features ravaged by tears. "Everything?"

She expelled a sigh, her breath misting warmly across the line of his jaw. "I hate knowing how I displeased Papa. And I—I regret that I chose to involve you in my foolish scheme. But I did and—and now you're utterly miserable."

Miles wiped the pad of his thumb across her cheek, then held it up for her inspection. "I beg to differ with you, Victoria. I do believe you're far more miserable than I."

She smiled. Oh, a shaky smile, at best, but a smile nonetheless.

But all at once her breath caught audibly. She withdrew from his arms and sat up. She didn't meet his regard; it was as if she couldn't bear to look at him. "It's just that I . . . I feel like I don't belong here." A tear traced a lonely pathway down her cheek as at last she lifted her head. She spoke, her tone very low. "I-I know you hate me for ruining your life—"

"Stop right there. I don't hate you, Victoria."

Her eyes clung to his. "Truly?" she whispered.

"Truly."

And indeed, Miles had never been more certain of anything in his life. His eyes darkened, roving over her face. Her skin was flushed, her eyes still damp and bluer than ever, her lashes deeply spiked and glistening. God, she was sweet. Yet this was not a disobedient child he'd held in his arms. He could still feel the soft, womanly imprint of her curves against his. He wanted to kiss her again, he realized suddenly. But a kiss was what had got them into this mess . . .

And indeed, he wanted far more than just a kiss.

These last weeks had been hell; knowing she slept beneath his very roof sheer torment. He had only to walk into a room and the lingering scent of her perfume sent him into a tailspin. He lay awake long into the night, his manhood rock-hard and nearly bursting. His dreams were as wantonly erotic as a youth's; he indulged his every fantasy.

Ah, yes. In his dreams he knew her body as well as he knew his own. He felt her come alive beneath his hands; with lips and tongue he teased the tips of her breasts to quivering erectness. The soft down between her legs hid flesh that was damp and sweetly wet. And when at last he came inside her, she moaned into his mouth. God! but she was like warm silk around his turgid shaft.

But it wasn't only the pleasure of the flesh that Miles envisioned. He imagined what it would be like to hold her through the night while she slept, their passion in check. He longed to wake with her sleep-flushed and warm, her sweet curves tucked against his own.

But he'd not force himself on any woman, let alone his *wife*.

And so he held himself very still, uncertain of himself in a way he liked not at all. He watched as her fingers plucked at her skirts. "We haven't tried to make this situation more palatable, either of us," she said.

She was right, he realized. He was not an ogre, though he'd behaved like one thus far. A sliver of guilt stabbed at him, for he disliked knowing he was responsible for her unhappiness.

"It's true we don't know each other very well," he said slowly. "I admit, I've behaved rather abominably these past weeks."

"And I rather shrewishly."

"No." They looked at one another, for they spoke at the very same time.

Victoria had caught her lip between her teeth. All at once the tension was no longer quite so evident.

"Nor have we chosen to rectify the situation, either of us," Miles went on. "But . . . perhaps we should."

This was crazy. Dangerous. She was no different than Margaret, a voice in his head warned. They simply did not suit. And God knew, he wasn't the only one who would end up hurt. There was Heather to think of . . .

"I-I would like that, my lord."

"So would I," he heard himself say . . . and knew it for the truth. "Your social calendar, countess. I suspect it's quite full?" His tone was deliberately offhand, yet his heart was suddenly thudding.

"Indeed it is. For the next week, in fact." Her reply was rather breathless.

"Then I fear we have a slight problem, for I am at a distinct loss as to how I might persuade you into crying off for just one evening—to have supper with your husband." As he spoke, he reached for her hand where it lay atop her silk-covered thigh. He felt her start of surprise. Slowly, giving her time to withdraw if she wanted, he laced his fingers through hers.

But she didn't pull away, as he thought she might. Instead, she stared at their hands, at his fingers entwined with her own. Then she raised her head and smiled, a smile that held him spellbound.

"My lord," she said softly, "you have only to ask."

Five

Odd, that such a simple thing as supper with her husband could bring about such excitement.

By seven o'clock the next evening, Victoria was happier than she'd been in days—why, weeks! She labored over her toilette in a way that she hadn't even done for her come-out ball. Indeed, she could scarcely sit still as her maid dressed her hair, twisting it into a smooth gold coil atop her crown. Her gown was of pale blue silk, long and flowing; beneath the high-waisted, low-cut bodice it fell in dozens of tiny pleats.

At last she was ready. As she descended the stairs, Miles was just exiting the library. When he saw her, he stopped short at the foot of the stairs. Victoria held her breath, for his gaze was riveted upward. She was half-afraid to glance at his face yet neither could she stop herself.

But then she could have pinched herself in sheer delight, for though he spoke not a word, it appeared he very much approved of what he saw.

She was suddenly very glad she had taken such pains with her appearance.

When she reached the last step, silently he extended his arm. Lightly she placed her fingers on his sleeve.

In the dining room, Nelson had seated them opposite the other, at each end of the long table. Miles frowned and said something to the footman. Plate, silver, and glass were hurriedly swept up and placed directly to the left of his.

Victoria could never quite remember exactly what she ate. Dishes were set before her, then removed. It might have been straw, for all that she knew.

It was over dessert when she finally tipped her head to the side and regarded him.

"Why have you never wed?"

"My dear, correct me if I'm wrong, but I do believe I *am* wed."

She wrinkled her nose. "You know what I mean. Why did you never wed before now?"

A dark brow arose. "Why do you ask?"

"Well"—her tone was earnest—"you're a bit old to have never married."

She had shocked him. It was only then she realized she must have reached for her wine glass just a bit too often. Her fingers stole to her lips. "Oh, dear me, I can't believe I dared to say such a thing. I-I did not mean to be so rude, truly."

Miles shook his head. "It's quite all right." There was a brief pause. "It was several years ago, but I was, in fact, engaged to be married."

"Then why didn't you?" This, too, emerged before she thought better of it.

"It simply wasn't to be." Though his tone was light, his features had turned rather solemn. "And since that time, well, I never found a woman I wished to wed."

And he still hadn't, she acknowledged with a pang. He would never have married her if his hand had not been forced. The realization caused a sharp, knifelike twinge in her chest.

Why it should hurt so—why it even mattered—she didn't know.

But she didn't allow it to show when supper ended and they arose. She was surprised but pleased when he invited her to play chess, and then all was forgotten. Victoria had always prided herself on her skill at the game—Papa had taught her when she was barely out of short-coats. But like Papa, Miles was a clever opponent, and it took all her concentration to pose a substantial challenge.

Miles won, but Victoria didn't mind. This was the most enjoyable evening she'd passed in weeks.

A short time later, he escorted her upstairs to her room. At her door, they stopped. He stood close, so close were she to draw a deep breath her breasts would have brushed the lapels of his coat. There was an odd tightening in her chest. The evening had passed in such accord, she wondered almost frantically if tonight would be the night he would make her truly his wife. And if it were, how would she feel . . . ? She was afraid—oh, not of him, but of what he would do—to be sure. And yet, a shiver of excitement coursed along her veins.

"Victoria."

The sound of her name startled her. Eyes like silver dwelled on her upturned face. She glanced up, swallowing a gasp.

"Yes?" The word was but a breath. All the world seemed to totter on this one moment.

A half-smile curled his lips. "I merely wished you goodnight, countess. And—sleep well."

With that he was gone. Her hopes plunged. She gazed into the shadows after him, her spirits forlorn.

It seemed she had her answer after all.

A week passed in much the same fashion. Supper, then chess. Sometimes a glass of wine in the salon. Victoria gladly put aside other engagements to sup with her husband.

Just being near him made her stomach clench—not that

he was unsightly. Lord, no! The sweep of his neck was long and corded, his jaw taut and strong. His brow was broad and regal, his lips beautifully chiseled. No longer was his mouth so sternly set as it was during those first days of their marriage. He didn't smile often, but when he did . . .

But it wasn't enough to be with him. She wanted him to touch her. She ached for him to hold her as he had the night she'd cried, to feel his arms snug and tight about her once more.

She couldn't deny what her heart was telling her.

Something was happening. Something strange. Something wonderful.

Something . . . impossible.

Oh, there was no doubt that Miles's reserve had thawed. He was unfailingly polite, occasionally teasing, no longer coolly remote. With every day that passed, he treated her with an ever-increasing familiarity. But Victoria wanted more. She longed to be treated like a woman.

She longed to be treated like a wife . . . *his* wife.

It was a point that caused her no end of frustration. Other gentlemen had been drawn to her. Other gentlemen had found her face and form attractive. Why not Miles? And perhaps most difficult of all, what was she to do?

Painful though it was, she couldn't forget what he'd said the night they wed.

A word of advice for you, countess. I shouldn't force my attentions on a gentleman—let alone kiss him . . . a man finds such boldness distasteful.

Perhaps it was time she did something she'd never dreamed she would do. Something she'd never thought she would *have* to do.

Seduce her husband.

She'd indulged in mild flirtations now and again. But to go about seducing a gentleman was something she'd not dared to consider.

So how did one go about seducing one's husband?

Miles was different than the men she knew. It was apparent almost from the start that he was not a man to spend his evenings dining and gambling at the various gentleman's clubs. No, he was not a bold and strutting London peacock.

So, Victoria determined, she must be industrious in her efforts, without being obvious. Persistent, without throwing herself at his feet. Sophisticated, like a *femme du monde*, for perhaps that was the sort of woman he wanted.

With that in mind, she knocked lightly on the door to his study one afternoon. Without waiting for him to bid her enter, she strolled within, as if she'd done so a hundred times before. Miles sat behind a huge mahogany desk, his quill poised over the open pages of a thick ledger. His head came up at her entrance.

His eyes flickered. Clearly he was startled to see her.

"Victoria. What brings you here?"

She positioned herself directly before him. "I'm here to take you away from such drudgery as this." She nodded at his ledger. Her tone was airy and gay, or so she hoped. Inside she was a quivering mass of nerves.

Leather creaked as he leaned back in his chair. "Oh?"

"I thought we might take the curricle, you and I. I know a lovely spot just outside the city, and I thought we might have luncheon there."

"This afternoon?"

"Yes."

"Why?" There was no bite in his tone, just blunt curiosity.

Her face felt stiff from smiling. "Because it's a lovely day outside."

He hardly looked convinced.

"And because I-I'd like to share it with you." So much for sophistication, she thought dryly. But at least it was out, though all in a rush.

But she had captured his undivided attention. He looked

at her then, and in a way that had never happened before. Something kindled in his eyes, something she dared not name for fear it was otherwise. She thought surely her heart would burst the bounds of her body when he put aside his quill, arose, and came to stand before her.

Time hung suspended, a never-ending moment. A lean, dark hand lifted toward her face. His lips parted, as if to speak.

But whatever he was about to say was not to be. The doors were swept wide and Nelson stepped in.

"Your lordship, we've just received a note from your tailor asking if he may stop by this afternoon, if at all possible."

"It will have to wait." Victoria's heart skipped a beat, for his gaze never wavered from hers. "I'm spending the afternoon with my wife."

Several hours later they lounged beneath the shade of a stout oak tree, replete from the meal Cook had packed. Victoria sat upon a soft down blanket, her skirts spread out around her.

There was a farmhouse nearby. A low stone fence traversed the fields. Errant shafts of sunlight winked through the branches, bathing them in warmth and sunshine. As she had just told Miles, this place was one she knew well. When Mama was still alive, she and Papa had brought her here often. Even when Mama was gone, she and Papa had continued to visit.

Miles lay stretched out beside her, leaning back on an elbow. He'd removed his neckcloth and discarded his jacket. In polished boots, skin-tight breeches and shirt, an aura of undeniable masculinity clung to him. Conversation was like the stream that flowed nearby, lazy and idle and meandering.

"There's a place much like this near Lyndermere Park," he murmured.

"Lyndermere Park?"

"My estate in Lancashire."

"Lancashire! What a long way from London. I didn't know you had an estate there."

There was a brief pause. "Actually, I live there most of the year. I usually stay in London only a month or so while attending business matters."

"Well, I can certainly see why. London becomes quite tiresome at times." She pulled a face. "Hot and smelly in summer. So dreary and cold in winter."

Miles made no comment.

"So," she went on lightly, "if you were in Lyndermere Park this very moment, what might you be doing?"

The makings of a smile tugged at his lips. "I might well be mucking through a field in search of a lost sheep."

Victoria chuckled. "You? I can't imagine you chasing after lost sheep."

"And I can't imagine you in anything but silk and ribbons, the toast of the Season."

His voice was so quiet, almost somber, that she glanced at him sharply.

"Miles?" She probed very gently. "What is it?"

His lips continued to carry the slightest trace of a smile. "Nothing, Victoria. You needn't concern yourself."

Something was wrong. She couldn't see it in his features. But she could *feel* it.

Unthinkingly she placed her fingertips on his sleeve. "Miles," she pleaded softly, "if something is troubling you, I wish you would tell me."

His gaze dropped to her hand, then returned to her face. "Do you, Victoria?" Slowly he sat up. His tone was almost whimsical. "And what would you say if I told you I lusted after my wife—now. This very moment."

A smile grazed her lips. "I would say . . . you need lust no more."

In one swift move she was caught up hard against him.

For the space of a heartbeat, his eyes blazed down on her. "Do you have any idea what you're saying? Do you?"

Her fingertips splayed wide across his chest. Beneath she could feel the strength of muscle and bone. "Yes," she whispered recklessly. Dangerously. Uncaring that all she felt lay vivid in her eyes. "*Yes.*"

That one word was like a trigger being pulled. His arms locked tight around her back. Then his mouth came down on hers, and it was just as she'd imagined it. His kiss was fierce, yet wondrously so. She could taste passion, heady and sweet, and a driving need that matched her own.

Her heart rejoiced, for nothing had ever felt so right—nothing.

Blindly she clung to him, caught in the tempest of emotions gone wild and rampant. She felt herself seized by a strange, inner trembling. Her breasts seemed to ache, for what she didn't know. Lean male fingers traced the deep rounded neckline of her bodice. Victoria's heart slammed to a halt, but she didn't pull away.

The pad of his thumb just barely grazed the peak of her breast.

Fire seemed to blaze from the place he touched so fleetingly, but now she knew what she so longed for. Time stood still while those devil fingers circled and teased first one nipple, then the other, until those soft pink crests stood thrusting and erect. Her breath was but a ragged tremor. *Miles,* she thought yearningly. *Oh, Miles . . .*

But there was more. No protest found voice as he tugged loose the drawstring of her bodice. The neckline of her gown was swept from her shoulders, exposing the rounded softness of her breasts. He stared down at her, at pink swelling flesh that no man had ever seen before.

Victoria's eyes locked helplessly on his face. She prayed that she would find favor in the eyes of her husband. But all at once his features might have been carved in stone.

"No," he muttered, as if to himself. And then again, with a fierce bite in his tone: "This isn't right. Dammit, this isn't right." He nearly flung himself from her.

She felt his withdrawal like a blow. Stunned and confused, Victoria sat up slowly. "Of course it is," she said faintly. "We—we're married!"

His jaw clenched hard. His gaze veered away from her. "It's time we left," he said curtly. His profile was stark and unyielding.

Her fingers were shaking as she tried to retie the strings of her bodice. He didn't want her, she thought numbly. She'd made a fool of herself for nothing. She had *thrown* herself at him for nothing.

At last she was ready. Through eyes that were painfully dry, she stared at him. At a loss for words, for understanding, she struggled for both. "Miles," she said, very low. "Miles, please tell me—"

"We're leaving, Victoria. *We're leaving.*"

His voice sliced through her as cleanly as a knife. Despair clamped tight around her breast, raw and bleeding. Choking back tears, Victoria picked up her skirts and ran toward the curricle, her heart in shreds.

Not one word passed between them the entire way home.

Once there, Victoria fled to her room. Only then did the tears come, slow and scalding.

Six

At first Victoria was devastated . . . little wonder
that she avoided Miles over the next few days—or did he
avoid her? It was only later, when she could react to the
incident with her mind and not her heart, that she realized . . .

His kiss had not lied. He had felt something for her. She
hadn't imagined the fire in his kiss, the longing in his arms.

Something was holding him back. That was the only answer. Yet what could it be? *What*? Another woman? She
didn't believe it. She *couldn't*.

Her husband was a quiet, private man, a man who would
not reveal his every side for all to see; she had concluded
that Miles was not one to trust lightly. Yet neither would she
have deemed him a man of secrets. So why was it only now
that he had spoken of his home in Lancashire?

It was odd . . . or was it? Perhaps it was only that the days
had swept aside the boundaries between them.

Only now the barriers were back, as staunchly formidable
as ever.

Still, she was determined not to sit home and wilt away.

When an invitation to a ball given by Lord and Lady Devon arrived one morning, she decided she would attend the event, to be held the next week.

Supper that night was a dismal affair. Yet Victoria took quiet note of Miles's attention upon her, his regard unsmiling— and enigmatic. Yet once—once—she caught the flare of some unknown emotion on his face . . . He stared at her with eyes that seemed to burn her very soul.

Hope burgeoned within her. As a footman removed the roast hare she'd hardly touched, she managed a bright smile.

"We received an invitation today from Lord and Lady Devon. They are giving a ball the Thursday after next. I should very much like to attend."

His reply was brief and to the point. "Then do so."

A pang swept through her. Gone was the man who had held her fast against him, whose mouth had covered hers with a passion unbridled and uncontrolled, a hunger fierce and un-checked. Everything within her cried out the injustice—she hated the cold, indifferent stranger he had become.

Her smile slipped. Icy-cold fingers linked together in her lap, for she was not prepared to let the matter rest so easily. "Miles," she said softly. "Will you attend with me?"

"I think not, Victoria. You are fond of such affairs. I am not."

They spent the rest of the meal in strained silence. Victoria pleaded tiredness soon thereafter. She excused herself and fled to the sanctuary of her bedchamber, blinking back tears.

She did not sleep. In anguished turmoil, she paced the length of her room, back and forth. But one thing was clear . . . This could not go on. *They* could not go on like this.

It seemed she had but one choice.

Miles had come upstairs some time ago; she could still

hear him stirring in the room next to hers. Quickly, before she lost her nerve, she tapped on his door.

He opened it. A winged black brow arched. "What is it, Victoria?" His tone was gruff, his manner impatient.

Her eyes were riveted to his face. His expression was remote and scarcely encouraging.

"May I come in?" she ventured.

He wanted to refuse. She could see it in the flicker of his eyes, yet he opened the door so she could step within. She advanced several paces, then turned to face him, thankful he couldn't see her knees trembling.

"I don't mean to intrude," she said quickly, "but I thought we might . . . talk."

"Oh? And what is on your mind, Victoria?"

Her eye ran over him nervously. She was still fully dressed, while Miles wore only a maroon velvet dressing gown. Loosely belted at the waist, there was a generous slice of bare chest exposed. Her stomach fluttered, for she had the oddest sensation he wore not a single stitch beneath. Her mind balked. Did he *sleep* naked? Victoria couldn't help it; her imagination ran away with her. His body would be like his chest, all long, hair-roughened limbs. And all she could think was that he would be as breathtaking *without* benefit of clothes as he was in his most elegant attire . . .

She gestured vaguely. "I know our marriage did not start off well," she said, her voice very low. "But I'd begun to think it was not such a mistake after all—and not so very long ago." She paused, but Miles said nothing. He merely remained where he was, his hands at his side, his expression impassive.

Victoria swallowed, forcing herself to go on. Faith, but this was the hardest thing she'd ever done! "Indeed, Miles, I-I thought things were progressing quite well. I-I thought everything had changed between us. That day in the country, when you—you kissed me. Or"—her voice fell, no more than a wisp breath of sound—"have you forgotten?"

His tone was harsh. "It *should* be forgotten."

In but an instant her wistful longing was shattered. Her control grew perilous. It was all she could do not to run crying from the room. "Why should it be forgotten? You—you act as if you are ashamed of what happened."

The cast of his jaw was rigid. "It shouldn't have happened, Victoria. Need I say more?"

Pain was like molten fire in her lungs. "Yes," she said raggedly. Recklessly. "Yes! Why is it wrong to—to desire me? To kiss me? To hold me? Miles, I-I don't understand."

Her voice caught as she struggled for words, for composure. Then suddenly it was all coming out in a rush. "I-I wanted you to kiss me, Miles. I wanted you to touch me and—and never stop. I wanted to be your wife in . . . in every way. Oh, Miles, I-I thought you wanted me, too!"

His features were cast in stone. "I think you forget, Victoria. If I had not stopped, there could be no annulment. Did you consider that?"

Victoria stared at him unblinkingly. Her lips were trembling so that she could hardly speak. "Is that it?" she whispered. "You still wish an annulment?"

Miles said nothing. He merely stood there, his posture wooden, his eyes downcast.

She persisted. "Do you want an annulment, Miles? Do you?"

Time slipped by. And in that deepening silence, she could almost hear her heart breaking . . .

Her throat clogged painfully. "You do. You do, but you don't have the courage to tell me to my face. Look at me, damn you." Her chin climbed high. Tears shimmered in her eyes, tears that betrayed the cost of her jagged cry. "Look at me and *tell* me!"

He looked at her. For one heart-stopping, frozen moment,

their eyes collided . . . and what she saw there—what she *didn't* see there—shredded the last of her control.

He didn't need to tell her. It was over, she thought brokenly. She meant nothing to him. She never had . . .

She never would.

She rushed forward with a low, choked sob. Escape was her only thought. But in her headlong flight, her fingers were clumsy. She twisted the doorknob frantically, but it refused to open . . .

Then suddenly *he* was there, a looming presence at her side, a hand on her arm.

"Victoria—"

"Don't!" she cried. She tore herself away and whirled on him. Suddenly her eyes were blazing. "Just leave me be," she whispered fiercely. "Do you hear, Miles Grayson? Just leave me be!"

The latch finally lifted. The door opened. Victoria fled blindly down the hall to her chamber. She flung herself on the bed, her heart bleeding.

In the morning her pillow was still wet with tears.

But she was dry-eyed and determined. She was a woman scorned, a woman who would not offer herself again. No, she would not beg or plead . . .

She, too, had her pride.

Nor would she wile away in misery.

She saw little of her husband, and soon the day of Lord and Lady Devon's ball arrived. In an attempt to boost her spirits, she had indulged herself with a new ball gown. Though she was not given to pettiness, it had proved immensely satisfying when she'd informed the seamstress the bill was to be sent to her husband.

She was waiting in the entrance hall for the carriage to be brought around when Miles suddenly appeared.

Eyes the color of storm clouds flickered over her. Only moments earlier her maid had commented that she'd never seen her mistress appear more entrancing. The gown was of white satin shot through with shimmering silver threads that brought out the highlights in her hair. The style was off-the-shoulder and daringly low cut; it emphasized the pale fragility of her neck and shoulders.

Her heart quavered, for despite the odds, she had prayed nightly that he would tear down the barriers he'd erected between them; that he would choose to alter their stalemate.

But all he said was, "Going out for the evening, countess?"

Summoning an icy strength, Victoria met his regard head-on. "Yes. If you recall, we were invited to Lord and Lady Devon's ball. You told me you didn't wish to attend."

Miles made no reply, but he did not appear pleased.

She took a deep breath and prayed she wasn't about to make a horrendous mistake. "Do you disapprove of me going alone, Miles?"

"It's hardly the first time you've done so. Why should I disapprove?"

But his expression revealed otherwise.

Some devil seized hold of her. "Oh, and by the way"—she smiled sweetly—"please inform the staff there's no need to wait up for me. I shall undoubtedly be quite late."

She experienced a certain grim pleasure at seeing the lightning change in his expression. She could almost hear the crack of thunder in the air. Relishing her brief moment of triumph, she picked up her skirts and swept outside to where the carriage now awaited her.

"Damn!" With an exclamation of disgust, Miles pushed himself away from his desk. He'd just spent the last few hours tending to his correspondence—or trying to. His efforts had proved quite futile.

He strode to the side table where he poured himself a

generous glass of port. He grimaced as the brew slid down his throat.

No doubt Victoria was having the time of her life. He had no trouble picturing the scene that was surely even now taking place at Lord and Lady Devon's ball. No doubt she was surrounded by half a dozen young pups, eagerly fawning over her. Or perhaps she was with that cad, Count DeFazio!

The thought that DeFazio might be helping himself to his wife made him clench his teeth. Not that Miles could blame the oily-tongued Italian rake. When Victoria had come down the stairs tonight, he'd felt as if he'd been punched in the gut. Her gown set off to perfect advantage the gleaming slope of bare, slender shoulders. She'd looked particularly delectable, and he'd felt a stab of pure possessiveness—along with no little amount of male pride—that this woman was his.

That's right, you pompous ass, sneered a voice in his head. *She's yours. So why aren't you with her?*

His lips twisted. "Why indeed?" he said aloud.

He had no one else to blame but himself. He could be with her now, this very moment. He *should* be with her. Moreover, he *wanted* to be with her.

But it wasn't so easy, he argued silently, for he was still struggling with his dilemma.

Do you want an annulment, Miles? Do you?

His insides twisted in dread remembrance. Dear God, he couldn't say yes. He couldn't say the words. Yet how could he say no . . .

I-I wanted you to kiss me, Miles. I wanted you to touch me and—and never stop. I wanted to be your wife in . . . in every way. Oh, Miles, I-I thought you wanted me, too!

The memory of that night still haunted him. He could still hear her, her voice raw. And he could still see Victoria, her face so pale, fighting back the tears she thought he didn't see.

His heart squeezed. He'd never meant to hurt her. God, if only he could, he'd make it up to her . . .

You were so convinced she was shallow and vain, jabbed a voice in his brain. *But you were wrong. You know it and still you refuse to see it!*

Long fingers tensed around the glass. He *was* a fool, he admitted at long last, for these last few weeks had been a revelation. Victoria was strong-willed and spirited, even a bit headstrong, but not wild. A bit reckless perhaps, but most assuredly not rebellious. The admission provoked a slight upward curl of his lips. She had a bit of a temper, but no less than his own.

His smile withered. She wasn't like Margaret. She wasn't!

But experience had left him wary, and it was that which held him back. There was so much at stake—too much to allow for another mistake.

A pang of guilt shot through him as he thought of Heather. He'd been gone from Lyndermere Park too long already. It was time he returned home to Lancashire. To Heather. Oh, he'd sent letters and gifts he knew would entertain and cheer her, but he knew how terribly she missed him when he was away . . .

Which only brought him full circle. What was he to do with Victoria?

Take her with him to Lyndermere? Or leave her here in London? Everything within him rebelled at leaving her behind. But it wasn't just her reaction to country life that he feared. What about Heather? What would Victoria think of Heather? That was his foremost concern—he could not allow Heather to be hurt as Margaret had hurt her.

He should have told her, he thought heavily. Perhaps he should have told her long ago and let fate take its course.

His gaze sought the clock on the wall. Just after eleven. The ball was in full swing. Victoria wouldn't be home for hours . . . What was it she'd said?

*Please inform the staff there's no need to wait up for me.
I shall undoubtedly be quite late.*

Lord, but she'd been so cold . . . but no colder than he had
been to her.

It was then that an awful thought crowded his mind—and
his heart.

Had he lost her? Had he? *You fool*, the voice inside him
chided. *You've no doubt driven her straight into the arms of
that scoundrel DeFazio. And you have no one to blame but
yourself.*

No. *No.* He couldn't lose her. He *wouldn't.*

His glass slammed down on his desk. He strode to the
corridor and threw open the door. "Nelson!"

The servant hurried out from the kitchen. "Yes, my lord?"

"Please see that my evening jacket is laid out. I shall be
joining the countess at Lord and Lady Devon's ball."

"Very good, my lord." Nelson smothered a smile and
trotted away. There was a considerable amount of wagering
going on belowstairs regarding the outcome of lord and
lady's current state of affairs. He had the sudden feeling
a rather tidy sum would soon line his pockets . . .

Victoria didn't care if she had provoked Miles—all the better if she had! Yet several hours later, her defiance had given
way to something else entirely. Oh, she danced and laughed,
chatted and smiled. But all in all, it was the most tiresome
affair of her life. As she confided to Sophie, were it not for
her friend's company, she'd have quit the affair long since
and gone home. Indeed, as she stood on the edge of the ballroom with Sophie, she was just about to voice that very intention.

There was a tap on her shoulder. It was Count Antony
DeFazio.

"Dance with me," was all he said. His arm snug about her
waist, he whisked her onto the dance floor.

Dark eyes roamed her face. "I've missed you, *cara*."

"Have you?" Her tone was polite but detached. Manners alone dictated a reply.

"Oh, yes, *cara*. Never have I been so lonely!" he proclaimed grandly. "Did you not hear my heart call out to you?"

Lonely? How Victoria stopped herself from rolling her eyes, she never knew. Why, he must believe her a dimwit to fall for such drivel!

"But enough of me. Where have you been these past days?"

"Actually"—she spoke very demurely—"I've spent many a delightful evening at home with my husband."

He laughed. "Oh, but I can make you happy as he cannot." The arm about her waist tightened. His voice deepened to intimacy. "I can make you forget any man but me. Shall I show you, *cara*?"

Victoria was speechless. How had she ever thought this man charming? Apparently he was convinced she was joking, the cad! Such ego deserved a dressing-down.

"Rubbish," she said forcefully.

He blinked. "I beg your pardon?"

"Rubbish," she stated baldly. "You see, Count, there is only one man who can make me happy. Of a certainty that man is not you."

Her partner was left standing in the middle of the ballroom. He gaped at her, stunned and open-mouthed.

Amidst gasps and whispers, Victoria strolled across the floor. Oh, she was fully aware her conduct was scarcely commendable. No doubt her name would be on every tongue the rest of the night and well into the next day. Still, it was worth it, she decided rebelliously, and she didn't regret that she'd given Antony the dressing-down he deserved. Perhaps he wouldn't be so arrogant in future.

The thought kindled a smile, a smile she maintained as she breezed her way across the ballroom, intent on fetching a breath of air in the garden.

There was a touch on her elbow. Thinking it was Antony, she spun around, prepared to loose on him the full force of her disdain.

"I thought I made myself quite cl—" she began.

The rest died unuttered in her throat. Because it wasn't Antony at all . . .

It was Miles.

In an instant she was whirled back onto the dance floor. "You mustn't look so shocked, countess." Miles's eyes were somber, but his voice held a trace of mirth. "Lord knows you've just given the gossipmongers a juicy little tidbit. I should hate to give them another."

"My very thought, my lord," Victoria echoed faintly. Her heart pounded a bone-jarring rhythm. Her mind was all agog. What on earth was he doing here?

Miles glanced toward Count DeFazio, who glared at the pair, then pointedly turned his back. "Your tongue is rapier-sharp tonight, I take it. I pray you'll not turn it against me tonight."

He bent his head low. Warm breath rushed across her skin . . .

He kissed the side of her neck.

Victoria's pulse was clamoring, her emotions a mad jumble. "To-tonight?" she stammered.

"Yes, sweet," he said softly. "Tonight."

And then he said the words she'd never thought to hear. "You were right, Victoria. I *was* jealous, jealous of every moment you spent with DeFazio. But I have the feeling you made another assumption—only a quite erroneous assumption, I fear." His gaze pierced hers. "I don't want an annulment, Victoria. Not now. Not ever."

Her heart stopped—along with her feet. Was she in heaven? Surely it was so, for this couldn't be happening . . .

He kissed the tiny hollow before her ear. "Did you hear me, sweet?"

Her eyes clung to his. His regard was so tender, his words so sweet. She nodded, for she could do no more.

"Good," he said gently. "Now dance again, love."

Hope flowered in her breast, hope that warmed her like the heat of summer sunshine.

"Are you . . . certain?" She ventured the question cautiously, then held her breath.

"Very." Quiet as his tone was, beneath was a gravity that left no doubt he meant what he said.

Yet even while hope burgeoned still further, a pang rent her breast. Never had she been so afraid!

Her eyes slid away. "Why," she said, her voice very low. "Why not?"

"The reason is simple, Victoria. I am your husband."

"A reluctant husband," she said unsteadily. "And as I recall, you made your feelings for me quite clear. You—you found me distasteful." She fought to keep the hurt from her voice and wasn't entirely successful.

The arm about her back tightened. His gaze was unerringly direct. "No, Victoria. Never distasteful. Never that."

But Victoria could not forget so easily. A rending ache seared her breast. "What then if not distasteful? You wanted nothing to do with me," she said haltingly. "You said it . . . it wasn't right."

"And what if I was wrong? What if I was a fool? What if I told you that I wanted you then? That I want you now. That I will *always* want you."

The music and voices around them faded into oblivion. There was a note in his voice she'd never before heard; it might have been just the two of them. She was half-afraid to speak, lest it be a dream.

"Then you must show me," she whispered.

And God above, he did.

She scarcely noticed they had glided to a halt. She had one paralyzing glimpse of glowing silver eyes before his dark head descended.

He kissed her then, there before all the *ton* to see. Slowly. Leisurely tasting, as if they had all the time in the world. Victoria couldn't have moved if she'd wanted to. It was as if he had some strange power over her. The pressure of his mouth on hers was magic. Bliss beyond reason.

By the time it was over her head was spinning. Her hands had come up to clutch at the powerful lines of his shoulders. As he raised his head—reluctantly, it seemed to her—she realized the room had gone utterly quiet.

And every eye in the ballroom was turned to the two of them.

She didn't know whether to laugh or cry. "Oh, dear," she murmured, catching her lip between her teeth. "I do believe we've caused yet another scandal."

Miles hiked a brow in sardonic amusement. "Scandal be damned," he said baldly, "for I should very much like to escape this crowd and take my wife home—if that meets with her approval, of course."

Victoria wanted to weep with relief and happiness. She raised shining eyes to his. "It does indeed, my lord. It does indeed."

He pressed her hand into the crook of his elbow. "Then let us be off, countess."

Together they strolled from the dance floor. But it seemed Miles was not yet ready to leave, for he snared two glasses of champagne from a passing footman.

Heedless of the gazes which had yet to leave their figures, he touched the edge of his glass to hers.

"To my beautiful wife," he stated for all to hear, "and to a long and happy marriage."

His head came down. He rested his forehead against hers. As his gaze captured hers, heat shimmered between them, as hot and blazing as a fire. Only now his words were a velvet whisper, for her ears alone . . .

"And to the night ahead . . ."

Seven

Miles's bedroom door clicked quietly shut. Victoria had stopped in the middle of the room. She was quick to flash a beaming smile at him, but he knew she was nervous. Nor had he missed the way her eyes flitted to and from the four-poster on the opposite wall. His own dropped to where the creamy skin of her breasts swelled above the lace of her bodice. Blood rushed to his head and loins, firing his desire into a raging need, swelling his manhood to an almost painful fullness.

He tightened his shoulders, fighting to hold himself in check. Slowly he expelled a long, pent-up breath. He could wait, he cautioned himself. He *must* wait, for he knew full well Victoria was a virgin, well born and gently bred. He didn't want to shock her, nor did he want to frighten her.

He extended his hand. "Come here," he said softly.

There was a rustle of skirts as she breached the distance between them. Shyly she placed her hand within his. Her fingers were ice-cold.

Raising his free hand, he curled his knuckles beneath her chin and tipped her face to his. His tone was very quiet.

"You know where this will end, don't you? There will be no annulment after this night."

Her eyes clung to his. "I-I know."

"And this is what you want?" He searched her face intently.

She didn't retreat from either his gaze or his question. "Yes," she said breathlessly. "Yet still I wonder, my lord, if you are certain that is what *you* want."

In bringing her here, Miles realized he had made not one, but two choices. The first was to make her truly his wife. He wanted that, he realized. He wanted it so much he could taste it. As for the other . . .

He could no longer hide the truth from her. But there was time enough to tell her about Heather. For now, Miles wanted the moment to stay just the way it was—the two of them alone, secluded from the world, with no one to think of but each other.

"Do not doubt me, Victoria. My choice was made when I came after you tonight." He spoke very quietly. "I have no regrets and it's my hope you will have none either."

The wispiest of smiles touched her lips. "I've known for quite some time what I want, my lord. I am here . . . and I am yours."

Miles needed no further encouragement. He caught her up in his arms and carried her to the side of the bed. Lowering her to the floor, he let her body slide against the hardness of his, then turned her mouth up to his. He fed on it endlessly, like a feast before a starving man. His fingers slid into her hair. It tumbled about his hands, thick and heavy and silken.

It was he who dragged his mouth away. Holding her gaze, he shrugged off his jacket, waistcoat, and shirt.

He saw the way her eyes widened at the sight of his naked chest. Two spots of color bloomed on her cheeks. He sensed her uncertainty, but her fingers fluttered to the neckline of her bodice.

His hand engulfed hers. At her questioning glance, he shook his head. "No," he said. "Let me."

He undressed her down to her shift, so sheer the outline of her body was clearly visible beneath. He pulled her close, suppressing a groan, letting her grow used to the feel of him. His mouth sought hers, at first slow and exploring, then with mounting urgency.

But suddenly she drew back, burying her face against his shoulder.

He smoothed the tumbled gold of her hair. "What, Victoria? What is it?"

The breath she drew was deep and uneven. "Oh, I know 'tis silly, but . . . we have been a long time coming to this moment. What if I should do something foolish? What if I should do something wrong?"

He caught her hand and brought it to his lips. "You need not worry, Victoria. You are perfect. In every way. In all ways." There was a small pause. "And now, countess"—it was his turn to tease as he tugged slender arms up and around his neck—"I would very much like for you to kiss me."

Her head came up, only now there was a faintly teasing light in her beautiful blue eyes. "What is this, my lord? Why, I do believe you told me once I should not force my attentions on a gentleman—let alone kiss him!—for a man finds such boldness distasteful." It was her turn to arch a slender brow. "Your exact words, if I recall."

He smiled, his expression tender. "I think I will go quite mad if you do *not* kiss me. Besides, I am not just a gentleman. I am your husband." His smile faded. "And your husband would very much like to make love to his wife."

Tears sprang to her eyes, yet she was smiling, a smile he knew he would carry in his heart forever. Her arms tightened around him. The dewy softness of her mouth hovered just beneath his, a provocative invitation. "And your wife wishes you would wait no longer, my lord."

And indeed, Victoria knew beyond any doubt that this was all she wanted—*he* was all she wanted. With infinite gentleness, he kissed her, then lifted her in his arms and laid her on the bed. When he stretched out beside her, she pressed herself against his length, eager for all he would teach her.

Her shift was soon but a flimsy pile on the carpet. With her palms she skimmed the sleek outline of his shoulders. She could feel the knotted tension in his muscles, yet he did not hurry her. The touch of his hands on her breasts was a divine torment. With his thumbs he teased the sensitive peaks until they throbbed and stood up hard and erect. His head lowered. His tongue touched her nipple, leaving it shiny and wet and aching. She gasped as he took one deep coral circle into his mouth, sucking and circling, sweeping across that turgid peak with the wild lash of his tongue.

His hand drifted lower, down across the hollow of her belly, sliding through dark gold curls. Victoria's heart began to hammer, for there was a strange questing there in the secret cleft between her thighs. Surely he would not touch her there, she thought in half-panic, half-excitement. Surely she did not *want* him to, for such a thing was scandalous . . .

It was heaven. A jolt of sheer pleasure shot through her. The gliding stroke of his fingertips was boldly undaunting, skimming damp folds, dipping and swirling against the pearly button of sensation centered within.

Her eyes widened. Her nails dug into his shoulders. "Oh, dear," she whispered faintly. "Miles, I do not think—"

"It's all right, sweet." He stared down at her, his features were strained, his voice thick. "All I want is to please you." Sweat beaded his upper lip. His blood pounded almost violently. As she gave a muted little whimper, his shaft swelled still further, straining his breeches until he felt he would surely burst the bonds of his skin.

Her lashes fluttered closed. One long, strong finger slipped clear inside her, a blatantly erotic caress. Blistering flames leaped deep in her belly, for his thumb now worshiped that sensitive kernel of flesh. Her hips began to move. Seeking. Searching for something maddeningly elusive. And then it happened. Her body seemed to tighten, then explode in a blinding flash of ecstasy.

Her eyes opened, smoky and dazed. Miles had pulled away, but it was only to strip away his breeches. Lamplight flickered over his body, turning his skin to burnished gold. He looked like a god, she thought wonderingly, strong and proud and irresistibly masculine.

Tentatively, she touched the hair-matted plane of his chest. He sucked in a harsh breath. Emboldened, she dared to explore still further, brushing the grid of his abdomen with the backs of her knuckles. His eyes half-closed.

"Touch me, Victoria." His voice was taut. With his own hand, he dragged hers where he wanted it most.

Her cool fingers curled about his shaft. He was enormous, hot and thick. A fingertip traced the velvet-tipped crown. Even as she marveled that something so steely hard could be so soft, she swallowed, for she could not imagine how she could accommodate something so immense . . .

His breath rushed out. "God, Victoria. Oh, God . . ."

Then he was there between her thighs, kneeling between them. He levered himself over her, his features heated and searing. His belly was hard as stone against her—as was his manhood. One swift, stretching stroke of fire and virginity was no more; his shaft pierced hard and deep inside her, to the very gates of her womb.

A ragged sound broke from her lips. Above her, Miles went utterly still. Victoria blinked, for he lay buried to the hilt within her. Her velvet heat clamped tight around his swollen member, the pressure of his shaft stunningly thorough.

"Oh, my," she said shakily.

He braced himself above her. His lips grazed hers. His voice was but a breath of air. "Do I hurt you, love?"

She was stunned to find her body had yielded. Already the stinging pain was but a memory. She shook her head, wordlessly offering her lips . . . her body . . .

Her very soul.

He kissed her then, a lingering, binding caress. His shaft withdrew, only to return with a deft, sure plunge that stole her very breath. Pleasure, dark and heady, swirled all around her. The flame was back in her belly, burning higher and higher as their hips met again and again. His hands slid beneath her buttocks. Guiding even as she blindly sought . . . Lifting as she arched to meet each downward plunge . . .

The rhythm of their love dance was hot and driving, frenzied and urgent. She felt herself swept high and away, deep into a white-hot vortex of sheer rapture. She was only half-aware of crying out. Above her, Miles gave one final, piercing lunge. She could only cling to him while his climax erupted inside her, a fiery rush of molten heat.

The tension eased gradually from his body. His lips nuzzled the baby-soft skin behind her ear. "Sweet," he whispered. "So sweet."

Without warning she began to cry.

Warm fingers brushed the dampness from her cheeks, a touch of infinite tenderness. "Victoria. Victoria, love, what is this?" He froze, propping himself on an elbow and staring down at her. "Never say I hurt you!"

"It isn't that." She buried her face against his chest. "It's just that—I thought you did not want me," she sobbed. "I thought you didn't want me—I thought you would never want me!"

In some strange way, she knew he understood. A possessive arm locked around her, drawing her close and tight against him. A hand beneath her chin, he brought her gaze to his. "Never doubt that I *do* want you, sweet. Never doubt *me*."

And in that moment, she didn't.

Eight

A soft rapping on the door woke the pair the next morning. Miles rose and reached for his breeches, then walked barefoot to the door. From the depths of the bed, Victoria stirred, vaguely aware of a low-voiced exchange.

The door shut. As he retraced his steps, she peered at him sleepily. "Miles? Who was it?" Her voice was still blurred from sleep. "Is something wrong?"

His features grave, he sat on the edge of the mattress. With his fingers he smoothed the tumbled hair from her shoulders, leaning forward to kiss her before he spoke. "I'm afraid so, sweet. I've an estate and holdings in Cornwall, and it seems a vicious storm has just swept through the area. It destroyed a number of tenants' homes and also damaged the manor house."

Victoria sat up, tucking the counterpane over her bare breasts. Despite the night just past, she was still a bit shy about Miles seeing her naked. Gently she touched his forearm. "Oh, no. I do hope no one was hurt."

"Luckily, there were no serious injuries." His gaze snared hers. "But I'm afraid I must be off as soon as I can to assess the damage."

She spoke quickly. "Would you like me to go with you?"

He considered but a moment. "I think not. It's a long, arduous journey in the best of times, and frankly, I'm not sure what I'll encounter when I arrive. If the manor house is damaged extensively, it might well be a hardship for you." He paused. "Will you wait for me here?"

"Of course," she said promptly.

His lips quirked. He patted a rumpled portion of the coverlet. "I mean here, love"—his gaze warmed—"in this very spot." The pitch of his voice grew seductive. "Preferably, dressed as you are, though perhaps I should say *un*dressed as you are."

Victoria blushed furiously. Miles chuckled, then rose to hurriedly bathe and pack. She remained where she was, content to watch him lazily.

At last he was ready. He looked dashing and handsome, and as he returned to the bedside, a tiny little thrill went through her. She slipped her arms around his neck. "Hurry back," she whispered.

He rested his forehead against hers. "Oh, I will, sweet," he murmured huskily. "Of that you may rest assured."

The kiss they shared was long and passionate.

Victoria spent the next few days quietly. Though she longed for Miles's return, her heart was filled with burgeoning hope. Their marriage was not the disaster she had feared. Miles had made her feel cherished and special in a way she'd never dreamed possible. Indeed, she was suddenly quite certain marriage could be all her heart had ever wanted . . .

Late one afternoon she returned from tea with Sophie. Nelson greeted her at the front door. "My lady, while you were out, a messenger arrived from Lyndermere Park."

Victoria frowned. Lyndermere was Miles's estate in Lancashire. "A messenger?"

"I didn't have the opportunity to speak with him myself, my lady. But he brought with him this note for his lordship."

Nelson picked up a small missive from a silver tray, extending it toward her. Victoria hesitated before picking it up.

"The maid who took it said the messenger was directed to deliver it in all due haste, my lady. Unfortunately, she neglected to tell him his lordship was in Cornwall at the moment." Nelson cleared his throat. "That's why I thought it best to direct it to your attention, my lady. If it should be a matter of importance . . ."

"Yes. Yes, of course. And thank you, Nelson." Victoria dismissed him with a smile.

Upstairs in her room, she laid the letter on the bureau, then stripped off her gloves and untied her bonnet. Laying the bonnet aside, she bit her lip.

Her gaze was drawn to the letter.

Should she open it? Despite Nelson's concern, she was reluctant to do so. She couldn't help but feel she would be trespassing where she should not. Yet that was silly, wasn't it? After all, she was Miles's countess. And if the contents should indeed be urgent . . .

With a sigh she went to retrieve it. Uncomfortable as she was, she decided it was best to open it after all. Before she could change her mind, she broke the seal.

The letter was short. It contained but a few sentences. Quickly she scanned it.

You've been gone a very long time. I miss you dreadfully. Please, please come home . . .

Love,
Heather

A faint, choked sound escaped her throat.

It was written in a precise, flowing . . . and unmistakably feminine hand.

Love, Heather.

There was a crushing pain in her chest.

Love, Heather.

How could he do this? she screamed silently. The memory of their night together rose swift and high in her mind. He had been so sweet. So tender. God! she thought brokenly. She had been almost certain that he cared—and cared deeply—for her. That perhaps he'd even begun to love her . . .

What was it he'd said? *Never doubt that I* do *want you, sweet. Never doubt* me.

It was all a lie. A *lie.*

Only one thing could have made it worse—oh, how great her humiliation would have been if she'd told him she loved him.

Because she did.

She just hadn't known how much . . . until now.

But his betrayal was too much for her wounded heart to bear. So Victoria did the only thing she could think to do. She ordered her bags packed and went home to Papa.

The marquess of Norcastle was quite astonished when his daughter appeared in the entrance hall, bags and baggage in tow.

"Victoria! Good heavens, girl, what is this?"

Victoria took one look at Papa and burst into tears.

Enfolded snugly in his ample arms, Victoria cried her heart out against his shoulder. Little by little, the story came out. How, against all odds—against all reason!—she had fallen in love with her husband. How she had only just discovered there was another woman in his life . . .

Her lips were tremulous. "'Twould have been silly for me to expect to be the first, nor did I expect it. But he gave me every reason to believe that"—her voice caught—"that he truly cared. Papa, I believed him! And now I feel so—so foolish!"

The marquess sighed and touched her hair. "Victoria," he

said slowly, "I have always taught you to judge fairly and without bias, have I not?"

Victoria nodded, her face still ravaged by tears.

"Then I ask you now to be fair, child. Give him the chance to explain."

Slowly she drew back. "Papa, no! You—you would defend him? Against your own daughter?"

He gestured vaguely. "No, of course not. But remember the night you were wed? I told you that he was not so cold as you believed. I was right, wasn't I?"

He detected a faint layer of bitterness in her tone. "Only yesterday I would have agreed wholeheartedly, Papa. Now I am not so sure. Indeed, I think he is cruel beyond words! He held me in his arms, knowing all the while that this woman named Heather awaited him in Lancashire! Perhaps she is his mistress. Or perhaps she is the one he meant to marry, for it was his intention that in time our marriage should be dissolved. He was only biding his time and awaiting the right moment." Her eyes blazed as she announced, "Either way I-I do not care. I shall consider myself well rid of him!"

The marquess cocked a shaggy brow. "You deceive no one, daughter, least of all yourself. You love him. You love him or none of this would matter." He studied her for a moment. "And it may not be as it seems, Victoria. Have you even considered this?"

"What need is there to—" she began, then stopped abruptly. Her eyes narrowed. "You confuse me, Papa. Why, I could almost believe that you know something you refuse to tell me—"

"No." He quelled her swiftly. "I know very little, except that I would never entrust my daughter to a man I thought to be a scoundrel."

"And you believe Miles is *not* a scoundrel?"

"I do."

"Papa, you are a traitor!"

The marquess winced. "No, daughter, I am not, and I can say no more, for it is not my place." He sighed. "These doubts must be laid to rest, Victoria, and only Miles can do that. Go home. Go home and await your husband's return."

"I don't want to go to Miles," she cried. "I don't want to see him ever again. I-I am home and I want to stay here!"

The glaze of tears in her eyes was almost his undoing. The marquess spoke softly, yet there was no doubting his conviction. "No, Victoria. This is no longer your home. You are the countess of Stonehurst and for now, your home is with your earl. Look to him for answers. But know this, child. If all is as you believe, I will do everything in my power to see this marriage ended, for I could not bear to see you unhappy. But first you must find out the truth—and that must come from your husband."

Her shoulders drooped. Her anger fled as suddenly as it had erupted. Papa was right. Deep inside, Victoria knew it. But that didn't make it any easier to bear. Battling a feeling of helplessness, she kissed him good-bye and returned to Grosvenor Square. For the second time that day, a parade of servants traipsed through the house carrying an array of trunks and baggage.

Sleep eluded her that night. But by the next morning a righteous resolve had fired her blood—as well as an unfaltering purpose.

Papa had advised her to wait for Miles. Well, that was all well and good. But Victoria remained convinced that she fully understood why Miles had been so reluctant to speak of Lyndermere. Perhaps it was folly. Perhaps it was sheer foolishness . . .

But she would see for herself this woman named Heather— the woman she'd come to consider her rival.

She set out for Lyndermere the next day. By the following morning, she was rolling along the hills of Lancashire. It was a part of England she'd never before visited. Had her mood been more lively, she'd have exclaimed with delight over the brilliant green valleys and flower-strewn fields. Before long, the coach turned down a long lane bowered with dozens of gracefully arched trees. Soon the coach rolled to a halt before an E-shaped stone building.

Her stomach knotted and tight, Victoria peered through the carriage window.

Naturally the coach was emblazoned with the Stonehurst crest. Apparently it had already been spotted, for a dozen or more servants had filed out the front doors and down the wide stone steps. They stood in a scraggly line, beaming nonetheless.

Those smiles froze when Victoria descended from the carriage. Daniel, the driver, quickly introduced her.

"His Lordship's wife, the new countess of Stonehurst. She and the earl were married last month."

This was news, indeed, judging from the openmouthed expressions. But the servants quickly surrounded her, bowing and bobbing curtsies, their manner all warm friendliness. To Victoria, there was just a blur of faces and names.

"I'm delighted to meet all of you," she said crisply. She seized on the one name she could recall, that of the housekeeper. "Mrs. Addison, I would very much like to meet someone I believe is in residence here, someone named Heather. Could you please direct me to her?"

"Of course, ma'am. If you'll just follow me." Victoria was right behind her as the housekeeper trekked up a grand staircase and turned to the right.

She stopped at the first door and tapped lightly upon it. "Miss Heather? Someone to see you," she called. She stepped back toward Victoria, lowering her voice to a whisper. "You'll have to forgive her, my lady. I'm afraid she's very disappointed that it wasn't His Lordship in the coach."

Victoria's spine had gone stiff. *I should imagine,* she thought blackly. When the housekeeper withdrew, she reached for the door. Pushing it open, she braced herself. No doubt Heather was a beauty, for she couldn't imagine Miles with anything less.

Boldly she stepped within the room.

The room's sole occupant was perched on a window seat across the room. Indeed, she *was* a beauty, with hair like the darkest night tumbling down her back. And those huge, thick-lashed eyes . . . somewhere between blue and purple, like the flower for which she was named.

But in that mind-splitting instant, Victoria also received the shock of her life . . .

Heather was just a child.

Nine

Shame coursed through her, for she had harbored such venomous thoughts! Fast on the heels of that was a relief which left her weak in the knees, yet a dozen questions flooded her mind. Who was this child? And why had Miles never mentioned her?

Gathering herself in hand, Victoria ventured a smile. "Hello, Heather," she said softly. "May I come in?"

The child hesitated, then nodded. As Victoria moved forward, something caught in her chest, for only now did she glimpse the unshed tears in the little girl's eyes.

She stopped several feet away, not wanting to upset the child any more than she was already. "Heather"—she tipped her head to the side—"is it all right if I call you Heather?"

Again that silent nod.

Carefully she felt her way. "Well, Heather, I understand you were expecting the earl. It was you who sent the note to London, wasn't it?"

The girl seemed to hesitate, then nodded. "Actually, I-I asked Mrs. Addison to write it for me. Her writing is so much better than mine."

"And I arrived instead of the earl," she said with a nod. "Well, Heather, I'm very sorry I disappointed you."

The girl dashed a hand across her cheek. "It's all right. It's just that I—I thought you were Papa."

Papa.

Victoria's mind reeled. So Heather was Miles's daughter? This was news, indeed. He'd never been married, or had he? Or was the child illegitimate? Yet none of that seemed to really matter in that moment, for Heather sounded so woeful that Victoria knew a sudden urge to gather her close against her breast and turn those tears to laughter.

"Well, Heather, your papa would be here if he could. But I'm afraid he's gone to Cornwall, where a storm damaged one of his estates there. But I am certain that as soon as he is able, he'll return here to Lyndermere."

"Soon, do you think?"

She sounded so hopeful that Victoria very nearly laughed. Yet she knew that to do so might well be a mistake. "Very soon, I daresay. And I daresay you don't have the foggiest notion who I am."

For the first time the merest glimmer of a smile tugged at the girl's rosebud mouth. "To be perfectly honest, my lady, I don't."

"That's what I thought." Victoria held her breath and moved closer. She eased down to her knees so that her eyes were on the same level as the little girl's. "Heather, your papa and I were married in London last month. I am Victoria, his wife." She spoke very gently, hoping she wasn't making a terrible mess of this. "I have the feeling I'm going to like Lyndermere very much, Heather. And I should like to stay on here because I'd very much like for you and I to get to know each other."

Heather gazed at her unsmilingly. "Are you quite certain you wish to?"

Victoria found the question quite baffling. "Of course I am."

"But why? Why would you wish to?"

"Because I suspect we're going to be spending a great deal of time together."

"Lady Sutherland didn't want to be with me. She wanted to send me away."

Victoria's smile froze. "Lady Sutherland?"

"Yes. Papa was going to marry her—oh, a long time ago!"

Lady Sutherland . . . So this was the woman he'd told her of, the woman he'd intended to marry.

"Oh, but surely you must be mistaken, Heather." Victoria strived for a light tone. "Lady Sutherland couldn't possibly have wanted to send you away."

"She did, my lady. She did. She hated me." Heather's tone was notably fierce.

Such strong words . . . from one so young. Gazing across into that somber little face, Victoria was struck by the fleeting sensation that Heather was old beyond her years. But before she could say a word, Heather's gaze slid away. Her voice very small, she added, "I heard Lady Sutherland with Papa one day. She called me a cripple."

"A cripple. Good heavens, why on earth—"

And in that moment Victoria discovered precisely why. Heather slid from the window seat and started across the room.

This bright and beautiful, charming little girl . . . walked with a limp.

Halfway to the door, she stopped and turned. She stood silently—waiting, Victoria knew, for her reaction. The child's expression was half-defeated, half-defiant.

Something caught in Victoria's chest, something that hurt as surely as Heather had hurt in that moment. But she didn't allow herself to pity Heather; she suspected Heather would never accept pity. And so she didn't flinch from those wide-set violet eyes. Instead she swallowed her anger at Lady Sutherland . . . and swallowed her heartache.

She held out her hand. "Heather, please come here."

The little girl returned to stand before her.

"Heather, I want you to understand something. Normally I do not presume to judge someone I do not know—and I confess I do not know Lady Sutherland. But 'tis my opinion that Lady Sutherland was quite addle-brained—and should have been taken out and whipped for daring to say such a thing!"

It was Heather's turn to blink. "That's what Papa told me," she said slowly.

"Good for him. Heather, Lady Sutherland had no right to judge you so harshly, especially without knowing you." Victoria's regard was steady, her tone firm. "Heather, I will not make that mistake, for I am nothing like Lady Sutherland. It doesn't bother me in the least that you have a limp. I shouldn't care if the entire world should limp! And now, I would ask something of you, Heather."

"Yes, my lady?"

Was it her imagination—or was Heather standing a bit taller? Yes, she most definitely was!

"Please, do me the honor of not lumping me in with the likes of Lady Sutherland!" A faint twinkle in her eye, Victoria smoothed the muslin shoulder of Heather's gown. "Do you think you can do that for me, love?"

Heather's head bobbed up and down.

Victoria wanted very much to reach out and hug the little girl close, but she sensed it was too soon.

"Now," she said crisply, "on to the business of getting to know one another. I suddenly find I'm quite thirsty. Why don't we go downstairs and have a spot of tea and biscuits in the salon, just you and I?"

For an instant Heather seemed uncertain. Then she leaned forward. "Can we ask Mrs. Addison to use the best silver?" she asked in a whisper.

"An excellent idea, Heather. I'm glad you thought of it!"

Heather's face had begun to glow. "Papa says Cook makes

the best plum cake in all of England, and I know she baked some just this morning. Do you think we could have plum cake, too?"

Victoria rose to her feet. "Do you know, I'm really quite famished! Plum cake sounds quite the thing. Why, we'll have a tea party!"

Heather's eyes had grown huge. "A tea party?" she breathed. "Like a grand lady in London?"

"Like the two grand ladies of Lyndermere Park," Victoria chuckled. Holding her breath, she held out her hand.

When Heather took it with no hesitation whatsoever, Victoria felt her heart turn over.

"It was quite odd, my lord. A messenger arrived from Lyndermere Park with a letter for you. He said it was quite important, so I gave it to my lady. Then my lady packed her bags and left for her father's, only to return that very evening! Then not two days later she set out for Lyndermere. It was really quite odd," Nelson repeated.

Miles had set a breakneck pace back to London in the pouring rain. He was exhausted, drenched, and ached from head to toe. All that had sustained him was the certainty of a warm, loving welcome from Victoria.

But now an awful tightness gripped his heart. "Where is this letter?" he demanded.

Nelson coughed. "I believe my lady took it with her."

"Damn!" Miles tore up the stairs, but Nelson was right. There was no letter in either his bedroom or Victoria's.

He stood in the middle of the floor, his mind racing. He could only guess at the contents of the letter, but he had the terrible feeling Victoria had found out about Heather. God, but he should have told her the truth long ago!

For now the truth might very well mean his downfall.

He set out for Lyndermere within the hour.

*   *   *

For the most part, Victoria spent the next few days quietly, coming to know Heather . . . but it was also a time of deep reflection.

She came to realize that she was no longer the desperate young woman who sought to avoid marriage at all cost; for in truth, marriage had changed her. Or perhaps more precisely, *love* had changed her.

It was odd, how she had come to want all she had dismissed with such disdain, all that she'd been so convinced was not important . . .

And it was here at Lyndermere Park that Victoria made a great discovery indeed.

She didn't want to spend her life alone, as she had proclaimed to Papa—and Sophie. She wanted a home—a home such as this!—that echoed with the sounds of laughter and love and life. She wanted children to cherish and nurture and protect . . .

And she wanted it with Miles.

She had thought he cared. She'd even thought he loved her just a little . . . She was furious with him. She felt betrayed—and so very confused as well! But it pained her unbearably knowing that Miles had chosen not to tell her of Heather's existence. It was as if he had some—some secret part of him that he would keep forever hidden from her.

Why? *Why* hadn't he told her? It was a question that caused her no end of torment. Miles loved Heather deeply; the way Heather spoke of him—and his behavior toward the child—left Victoria in no doubt that it was so. At first she'd thought Heather was his by-blow. But she'd learned from Mrs. Addison that Heather was Miles's ward; how and why it came to be, Victoria had yet to learn. Yet few men would have taken in another's child, and in Victoria's estimation, it was an act of tremendous generosity. So it was that she couldn't imagine that Miles was ashamed of Heather because of her limp; it was not in his character to be so petty.

Victoria was left with just one conclusion. He hadn't wanted her to know about Heather.

Did he trust her so little? Did he think she wouldn't care about this sweet, young child who waited so anxiously for her papa to come home?

It hurt to realize he thought so little of her—that he chose to share so little with her. But Victoria stifled her hurt and hid her troubled state of mind whenever Heather was near.

On this particular day, Victoria sat with Heather in the drawing room, one arm around the child's narrow shoulders. Heather's dark head was nestled against her shoulder, her expression quiet and tranquil, her eyes ever alert. The pose was reflective of all the pair had shared these past days. For both it was a time of discovery. At eight years of age, Heather was an extremely thoughtful, intelligent child. She also had quite a talent for watercolors. But she also possessed a maturity—and sensitivity—far beyond her tender years.

For Heather, it was a time of learning as well—learning to trust someone other than her papa—the *way* she trusted her dear Papa.

Though she was quite capable of doing so herself, she loved it when Victoria read to her. And she listened raptly when Victoria told her stories.

"Tell me the story about the scandalous bride," Heather pleaded on this particular evening.

Victoria smothered a grin. The story about the scandalous bride was one which Heather never tired of hearing—one which Victoria was altogether familiar with . . . and for good reason.

"There once was a young woman whose father was a marquess. Like all fathers, the marquess was anxious for his daughter to make a suitable marriage. The young lady, however, had a mind of her own, you see, and had no wish to marry the boorish and foppish young men who offered for her. If she were to marry, she wanted to marry a man she could love, and who loved her in return. But after several Seasons in London, she'd begun to give up hope that such a man existed.

"But by now the marquess had grown ever so impatient with his daughter. The young lady knew this, but she'd decided it was better to live her life alone than to marry a man she didn't love. And so she concocted an outrageous scheme, a scheme she thought would put her beyond the pale."

Heather snuggled against her. "What did the young lady do?"

"She followed a man into a garden and kissed him—can you imagine, she dared to kiss him! But you see, Heather, the young lady was not quite so clever as she'd thought, for her father demanded she marry the fellow, a man who happened to be of good family—an earl, in fact. So it was that she ended up a bride, though as you can imagine, a rather scandalous bride."

Heather peered up at her. "Was her husband handsome?"

"Oh, yes, this lord was so handsome he made her heart flutter madly and she tingled clear to her very toes just looking at him! But you see, they both were a stubborn pair, and rather resentful of each other for being forced to wed."

"They didn't like each other, did they?"

"No, love, not at first." The corners of Victoria's lips lifted. Though she didn't realize it, her voice had gone all soft and dreamy. "But do you know, strange as it may seem, the young lady ended up falling hopelessly in love with her handsome young lord."

"And what about him? Did he love her?"

Victoria's heart twisted. *If only I knew,* a voice inside cried. *If only I knew . . .*

"Yes, pet, he loved her quite madly." Though she still smiled, her eyes were full of wistfulness. "He loved her, and they were happier than either dreamed possible."

Usually Heather was content to move on to the next story.

But today, she was silent for a moment. Her dark head dipped low. It spun through Victoria's mind that she seemed troubled. Then all at once she spoke.

"I will never marry," she said.

Quiet as the child's voice was, there was a ring of finality that stunned Victoria. She frowned. "Heather, sweet, why on earth would you—"

"Lady Sutherland said I would forever be an encumbrance around Papa's neck. She said no man would want me for a wife. I-I heard her."

Victoria gritted her teeth. Lady Sutherland again. Anger simmered within her. She could cheerfully strangle the woman!

"Heather," she stated firmly. "I thought we'd established that Lady Sutherland hasn't a brain in her head."

Heather still had yet to look at her. "I think she is right. I think I will never marry. The boys in the village. They stare at me. They stare because I'm different than other girls."

Victoria's throat grew thick with tears. She wrapped her arms around Heather and pulled her close. "Oh, darling, I know it may seem impossible now, but nothing could be further from the truth! You're a beautiful little girl and you'll grow into a beautiful young woman. It may take some time, but someday there will be a man who loves you very much and you will be happy, I promise you."

Slowly Heather raised her head. Victoria nearly cried out when she saw that the little girl's eyes shimmered with tears. "As happy as the lord and lady in the story?" she asked in a tiny voice.

Something broke inside Victoria then. She ducked her head and rested her cheek against Heather's dark, shining cloud of hair. "Yes," she choked out, only barely able to speak. The ache in her breast was nearly unbearable.

Not wanting to distress Heather further, she gathered herself in hand and gave Heather a quick hug. Raising her head, she offered the little girl a shaky smile.

Heather regarded her curiously, tipping her head to the side. "Do you know," she said after a moment, "I'm still not certain what to call you. 'My lady' is so formal."

"I agree," Victoria said promptly. "What would you like to call me?"

Heather pondered a moment. "Well," she murmured, "Papa isn't really my papa. I'm his ward, you know."

Victoria nodded. "Yes, I know, dear. Mrs. Addison told me."

"Still," Heather went on thoughtfully, "I call him Papa." A tiny frown furrowed her brow. "My mother died when I was very young. Mrs. Addison and my nanny are very nice, but . . ." Her voice trailed off. She bit her lip, opened her mouth as if to speak, then abruptly closed it.

Victoria encouraged her gently. "Yes, love, what is it?"

A small hand stole into hers. "May I call you Mama?" she whispered.

"Heather. Oh, Heather, of course you may." Touched beyond words, Victoria pulled the little girl onto her lap and hugged her fiercely. She was laughing; she was crying, tears she couldn't withhold and didn't try to.

It was the faint click of a door that alerted her . . . They weren't alone. Someone else was in the room . . .

And that someone was her husband.

Ten

*Conscious thought was but a blur. Despite every-*thing, all she could do was stare, as if he were a veritable feast for the eyes.

Heather had spied him as well. "Papa!" she exclaimed. She slipped off Victoria's lap. But before she could take more than a few steps, Miles was there. He caught her high in his arms.

"My black-haired little poppet. I missed you, love."

Heather giggled. "Did you bring me a present?"

Miles's mouth quirked dryly. "I brought you a whole trunkload of presents, poppet."

"Can I see?" She fidgeted eagerly.

Miles kissed her cheek, his eyes tender. "In just a bit, love." He paused. "I see you've met my wife."

Heather glanced shyly back at Victoria. She curled her fingers around Miles's collar and bent her forehead to his. "She said I could call her Mama."

Miles's gaze rested on his wife. "So I heard," he said softly.

Victoria's eyes flitted away. She linked trembling hands together in her lap. Her heart lurched. What else had he heard?

When she finally found the courage to glance back at him, she was disconcerted to find herself the object of his attention.

"I'd like to spend a few minutes with Heather and get her settled for the night." His eyes cleaved the distance between them. "Will you wait for me here?"

Victoria's nod was jerky; she could manage no more. To Heather, she called a wobbly goodnight.

The time passed all too quickly. Victoria sat and then paced. She paced and then sat. Then suddenly Miles was there before her, and it was just as she'd said in her story—he was so handsome her heart fluttered madly. The very sight of him made her tingle all the way to her toes.

He moved to stand directly before her. One corner of his mouth curled up in a half-smile. "I must say, Victoria, this is the last place I expected to find you."

Her head came up. "No doubt," she snapped. She was up and on her feet, her eyes blazing. She'd suddenly remembered how angry she was with him—and she was, so furious she was shaking with it.

"You're aware a letter came for you from Lyndermere?"

"Yes. Though I've yet to discover the contents."

"I opened it only because Nelson thought it might be urgent." She defended herself fiercely. "It was very brief, my lord. Something on the order of . . . 'I miss you terribly. Love, Heather,'" she quoted.

"And you thought Heather was a woman, didn't you? A woman I kept here in the country? A mistress perhaps?" When she glared at him, his lips quirked. "And that was what sent you packing to your father's?"

"Oh, I can see you find it vastly amusing," she flared hotly. "And I had every intention of never seeing you again, Miles Grayson! But Papa had the audacity to tell me you might not be such a scoundrel after all. He knew about Heather, didn't he?"

Miles's grin had faded. "Yes—and no. He was aware of her existence—that she was my ward—but I had no way of knowing if he knew the truth . . ." He sighed wearily, running his fingers through his hair. "Victoria, it's a long story. And I know you're angry that I didn't tell you about Heather—"

Tears burned her throat. "Yes, I'm angry. Angry because in all the weeks we've been married, not once did you see fit to tell me about your ward! Why, when I came here, I had no idea Heather even existed—I've never felt so foolish! And I'm angry because all the time you were in London, this poor, neglected child was here alone—"

"Neglected? Come now, Victoria, you exaggerate. I have never neglected Heather, nor will I. And she was hardly alone, for there is a house full of servants who love her and care for her every need—"

"But it was *you* she needed, Miles. She wanted her papa, and you should have been here with her! For that matter, she—she needs a mother, too, though apparently it's never occurred to you that your *wife* could be the mother she needs."

Guilt flickered across his face. "Did you think it was easy for me? I stayed because of you, Victoria." His tone was intense. "Because I wanted to be with *you*. That's the truth."

"The truth!" The breath she drew was deep and shuddering. "How am I to believe you when you hid the truth from me—you didn't tell me about Heather! How am I to trust you when you refused to trust me? Because you didn't, did you, Miles? You didn't trust me with the truth about Heather, did you?"

Miles's face had gone pale. "No," he said very quietly.

Victoria began to cry openly. "Why?" she cried. "Why didn't you trust me? Did you think I'd fly into a rage? Did you think I wouldn't understand? Did you think I'd want to send her away like—like that witch Lady Sutherland?"

She saw him flinch, as if he'd been struck. And she knew then . . .

"That's it, isn't it?" Pain slashed through her, like a rapier through the heart. Her words were a trembling, broken whisper. "You—you thought I was like her . . ."

Miles's body had gone stiff.

"You're right," he said, his tone wooden. "I *did* think you were like Margaret. You see, I'd heard of you, even before that night at the Rutherfords, the beautiful—and much sought-after—daughter of the marquess of Norcastle who refused to choose a husband. Victoria, how can I explain . . . ? The next thing I knew we were wed. I knew you didn't want to be a wife . . . why would you want to be a mother, and to a little girl who wasn't even your own . . .

"I never loved Margaret, not really. I want you to know that, Victoria. I admit, I was swept away by her beauty and charm. I proposed to her because I thought Heather needed a mother—because I thought she could make us happy. I-I thought I was doing the right thing. Margaret came from an impeccable family. She loved the glitter of London, the parties, the gossip.

"But as the wedding date drew near, I'd begun to have doubts—to think her shallow and vain—but I kept them to myself. I brought Margaret to Lyndermere to meet Heather. Victoria, she was . . . horrified when she saw Heather. She looked at Heather as if she were a—a monster."

Tears coursed down her cheeks. Everything he said was like a knife turning inside her. "I know that, Miles. But you must have known later that I wasn't like her. I-I could never be so cruel! Yet still you didn't tell me. You refused to believe in me. God, and I"—a jagged cry tore from her lips—"I thought you cared for me."

He seized her hands. She tried to snatch them back but he wouldn't let her.

"I do. Victoria, I *do*." His tone was low and fervent. "But I was still afraid, sweet, and you must admit, you were scarcely at home those first weeks of our marriage. It seemed you thrived on the parties, the crowds, the adoration from those silly young bucks in London. I-I didn't think you could be happy with a simple life in the country. I didn't think you could be happy with *me*!"

His voice grew raw. "But above all, I had to protect Heather. I've remained here at Lyndermere in order to spare Heather the pain of gossip and whispers among the London highbrows. I couldn't let her be scorned or disdained by anyone. I couldn't let her be hurt again the way Margaret hurt her! Victoria, the night we made love . . . I knew you were different or I wouldn't have let it happen. My God, I wouldn't have *wanted* it to happen. But I did, Victoria. I wanted you so much it hurt inside. And then the next morning I intended to tell you about Heather, but the news from Cornwall came and I had to leave . . ."

He pulled her shaking body into his embrace. "I'm sorry, sweet," he said achingly. "I'm so sorry. I knew how wrong I'd been when I saw you with Heather. I was so relieved and yet so ashamed!"

Victoria searched his face. The depth of emotion reflected in his eyes nearly took her breath away. It was going to be all right after all . . . With a tiny little cry she wrapped her arms around his waist and clung.

"I want you to know everything, sweet, how Heather came to live here . . . everything. There was a carriage accident nearby some years ago. The coach carried three passengers—a man, a woman, and a child of about three."

Victoria's tears had begun to slow. She turned her tear-stained face up to his. "Heather?" she whispered.

Miles nodded. "The driver and the man were killed immediately. The woman lingered for several days."

"Heather's parents?"

"I believe so. I know for certain the woman was her mother. I brought her here to Lyndermere." An odd note entered his voice. "Victoria, never in my life have I heard such vileness! Her mother knew she was dying. She heaped curses on her daughter and spewed the crudest of obscenities—because Heather would live and not her!"

Victoria went cold inside. "The accident. Is that how she came to be lame?"

"No. Her injuries were serious, but her knee was already scarred and malformed. The physician said it was likely some other accident. She was too ill to be moved—and she was so small—that I kept her here with me to recuperate. By the time she was well—oh, I know it sounds strange—but I loved her too much to let her go."

Victoria rubbed her cheek against the soft wool of his jacket. "It's not strange at all," she whispered. "I feel the same already."

His arms tightened. "There's more, Victoria. Heather was an orphan. I do not condemn them, but her parents' clothing was ragged and unkempt. Had I let her go, she would have been called a guttersnipe. I couldn't let that happen. Nor could I let her go to an orphan house—my God, the conditions in those places are deplorable!"

Victoria felt him swallow.

"I lied, Victoria. I asked the courts to declare her my ward. I told the magistrate her parents were very dear friends of mine; that her father was an impoverished lord from France—Heather's mother told me her name was Duval—who'd married an English lady. I said they were on their way to see me, to resettle here in England, when the accident occurred."

His palm was warm upon her nape. With his thumb he urged her face to his. "Heather believes herself to be the daughter of a French aristocrat and an English lady. Until this moment, no one knew the truth but me." His eyes darkened. "It's a secret I will guard with my life."

For an instant Victoria couldn't speak. Her throat was too tight. "Why? Why do you tell me this? Why now?"

"Because I trust you with my heart, sweet. I love you, Victoria. *I love you*."

To her utter shame, she began to cry all over again. Miles swept her close, so close their hearts beat together as one. "Shhh," he soothed. "I didn't mean to make you cry again, sweet. I'll make it up to you, I swear."

Her smile was tremulous. "It's all right. It's just that I—I never thought to hear you say that."

His gaze had fallen to her lips. "No? What about the story you told Heather?" he teased. "The lord loved his lady quite madly, did he not?"

"That was just a-a fanciful dream," she confessed.

His expression was incredibly tender. "It's no dream, sweet. I *do* love you. But I fear I must know—did the lady truly fall hopelessly in love with her lord?"

Victoria pressed her hand into his cheek, her smile misty. "Oh, yes," she whispered. "Quite hopelessly indeed . . ."

Epilogue

Nearly a year had come full circle, and fragrant spring breezes rippled across the broad fields of Lancashire. It was late May, and on this warm spring eve, twilight cast a purple haze across the western sky.

Victoria and Miles had remained at Lyndermere Park for much of the year. She had come to love Lyndermere as much as her husband. Trips to London were few—a necessary nuisance, Miles called them. But while Victoria occasionally found herself missing a night at the opera or an evening of waltzing at Almack's, it was here at Lyndermere—with Miles—that her heart and hopes and dreams resided . . .

She could imagine no other life . . . nor a life more perfect.

But there had been an addition to the family. They were no longer three, but four . . .

Beatrice Louise Grayson had made her entrance into the world on a wild, stormy night in late February, much to her father's delight . . . and her mother's relief.

Beatrice had now reached the ripe old age of three months. Her belly had grown round and firm, her cheeks pink and plump. A cap of pale gold curls covered her head, and her eyes were as blue as sapphires; her grandpapa proudly proclaimed Beatrice the very image of her mother.

Now, having finished nursing the babe, Victoria smoothed a tender hand over the fine gold fuzz covering her daughter's scalp, then handed the babe into the waiting arms of her husband so that she could adjust her gown.

Miles pressed a warm kiss on that tiny brow. He chuckled when Beatrice flashed a sunny little grin, for such was her nature. He laid her in the cradle, his hold on her immeasurably gentle.

Heather looked up eagerly from where she sat reading in the window seat. "May I rock her, Mama?" she pleaded. "And tell her a story, too?"

Victoria's eyes softened. "Of course you may, love." Smiling, Victoria pulled a small chair next to the cradle so Heather could sit.

When Heather flashed her a beaming smile as she took her place, Victoria felt her heart squeeze. It was her most fervent wish that Beatrice would someday come to be like Heather, for there was no sweeter child on the face of this earth; and indeed, for Victoria there was no greater privilege than hearing this beautiful, dark-haired child call her "Mama" . . .

Heather extended a finger toward the babe. Beatrice curled a tiny pink fist around it and held on fast. "Now then, Beatrice. Here is the story I will tell you. There once was a young lady who was all the rage in London. But this young lady . . . I think we shall call her Lavinia, yes, Lavinia!"

Beatrice stared at Heather raptly, as if she understood every word.

Victoria's lips quirked, for Miles was shaking his head, an indulgent smile on his lips. When he held out his hand, she accepted it wordlessly.

Heather continued. "Well, Beatrice, Lavinia was very

opposed to marriage, but she came up with a most unusual idea in order to lay to rest her papa's insistence that she marry. Can you imagine, Beatrice, Lavinia followed a man—an earl—into a garden and kissed him! But her plan failed, you see, for her papa demanded she marry this man!"

Hand in hand, Miles and Victoria quietly retreated. At the threshold, they paused to listen once more.

"Oh, but this scandalous bride was at wit's end, being forced to marry this earl, for though he was quite handsome, he was a wicked one indeed!"

Miles was taken aback. "Handsome, yes," he concurred in a whisper. "But wicked?" He shook his head in mild affront. "I think not!"

Victoria's eyes were dancing. "A woman's perspective," she informed him gravely. She pressed a finger to her lips, for Beatrice was yawning, and her eyes had begun to droop.

Heather hastened to finish. "And so, Beatrice, the scandalous bride Lavinia set about taming her wicked earl and making him fall quite madly in love with her . . ."

Miles pulled his wife into his arms. "She did indeed," he murmured against the smooth skin of her temple. He drew her into the hallway where he claimed her lips in a long, ardent kiss that sent their senses soaring.

When at last he released her, a teasing smile curled her lips. "Ah," she said playfully, "but the scandalous bride does have one regret."

One dark brow arched roguishly. "And what might that be, countess?"

Victoria twined her arms about his neck. "Had she known what fate awaited her that long-ago night, she'd have kissed her wicked earl much, much sooner . . ."

It was SAMANTHA JAMES's love of reading as a child that steered her toward a writing career. Among her favorites in those days were the Trixie Belden and Cherry Ames series of books. She still loves a blend of mystery and romance, and, of course, a happily-ever-after ending. The award-wining, bestselling author of eighteen romances and one novella, her books have ranged from medieval to Regency to the American West. Please visit her on the web at www.samanthajames.com.

Turn the page for a sneak peek at

IN PURSUIT OF A SCANDALOUS LADY

The first in a new series from *USA Today* bestselling author Gayle Callen

The biggest secret in London is about to be . . . revealed.

Every gentleman is wondering: Who is the beauty in the scandalous nude portrait hanging in one of London's most fashionable clubs? Is it true that she's a member of the ton? *Who would be so daring? So reckless?*

Julian Delane, Earl of Parkhurst, has a good idea. So good, in fact, that he's willing to make a wager on it. If only the bet were all that's at stake . . .

Determined to clear the family name from a scandal that claimed his father's life, Julian believes the ravishing model will lead him to answers. Rebecca Leland—spirited, adventurous, with a bit of a wild streak—is just as determined to evade his questions. But when Julian finally corners his quarry, he may find Rebecca well worth the pursuit.

Rebecca felt a secret little thrill. She saw the way both women and men stepped out of Lord Parkhurst's way. He ignored them all, his every focus on her. Awareness was a prickling flush that started at the nape of her neck and spread along her body. She barely felt Susanna's fingers clasping hard on her arm, as she had to look up and up as the earl came closer and closer. Good lord, he made her feel positively dainty.

She'd been longing for something different to happen to her—and now here he was, large and bold and threatening beneath a veil of civility.

Lady Rosa beamed at her daughters. She had the same shade of dark brown hair as Rebecca, with only a little gray to betray her age. Susanna had inherited her warm brown eyes. She was a striking woman, displaying the easy elegance of her birth, yet at the same time showing her compassion and strength. She'd endured the fear of losing Rebecca to count-less childhood illnesses and suffered through a year believing her son dead. Her marriage had almost floundered under the weight of a lifetime of scandal, but Lady Rosa had emerged victorious. Now the only triumph she seemed to truly want was to see her daughters well—and happily—married. And Rebecca almost regretted that she could not appease her mother in such a way.

"My dear girls, how pleased I am to find you together," Lady Rosa said, beaming. "Lord Parkhurst, allow me to introduce my daughters, Miss Leland and Miss Rebecca Leland. Oh dear, I've already gone on so long about them, you probably feel as if you know everything there is to know!"

Rebecca's smile stiffened. Everything there was to know, indeed. Lord Parkhurst probably *did* think such a thing, especially after the way he'd studied the painting for what seemed like forever.

And then it was as if she were in the dark, candlelit saloon again, standing too close to this giant of a man, meeting his intelligent, assessing gaze. He should seem out of place in this false garden, where people talked with little substance. Instead, she could imagine him one with the forest, hunting a beast of prey.

And she realized that she was the prey.

A flush of heat had her wondering if he could see her blush.

"It is a pleasure to meet you, ladies," the earl said, bowing his head politely. His voice was mild rather than challenging, though still deep and rumbling.

She and her sister curtsied. Rebecca could feel some of Susanna's tension subside. Up close and by the light of day, he seemed a bit . . . different. There were lines of strain across his forehead, as if he regularly frowned. His eyes were hooded, almost tired.

Had he spent much of the night thinking about her, as she'd thought about him?

No, she wasn't worth that to him. He was a bored aristocrat who'd found something to amuse himself for a few days—a month at most, she reminded herself. Though he might *look* different, he was surely the same as every other man of her acquaintance.

"Is this truly the first time we've spoken, Lord Parkhurst?" Rebecca asked politely. "I feel like I've seen you at several events."

"And I have seen *you,* Miss Leland."

He spoke with all politeness, but she heard another meaning in his words, and barely withheld a shiver.

"I wish to congratulate you all on the miraculous return of Captain Leland," he continued.

"Thank you, my lord," Lady Rosa said with a happy sigh. "I was . . . quite devastated by the loss of my son. With his return, my husband and I are restored in spirit and in our hearts. The captain is spending time with his cousins this month."

"Ah, so I heard," he said, glancing at the Leland sisters. "The captain himself told me. We have had several shared investments recently."

Why hadn't he said that he knew her brother last night? Rebecca wondered with annoyance. She was feeling more and more deflated. The earl was not so removed from Society. She only wanted him to be.

"Did you meet my son at university?" Lady Rosa asked.

Lord Parkhurst linked his hands behind his back, his appearance casual—far too casual. Rebecca sensed . . . something beneath the surface.

"No, I did not, my lady."

"Ah, then you must have gone to Oxford. My husband lectures at Cambridge."

"I came into my title at eighteen," Lord Parkhurst said. "I did not have time for much else."

Lady Rosa's expression turned momentarily pained. "Do forgive me, my lord. I had forgotten that your father died so many years ago."

Rebecca looked between them, curious at what wasn't

being said. But if she asked her mother for details later, Lady Rosa would think her interested, and never let her hear the end of it.

To cover the vague unease she sensed in her mother, Rebecca said, "Our cousin, Madingley, did not attend university either, for exactly the same reason."

He nodded. "I remember that."

"Even though you are without an advanced education, my lord," Lady Rosa said, "I hear men talking with much admiration of your knowledge and skill."

"Admiration is it now?" His wide mouth quirked in a faint smile. "That is putting it kindly. But yes, there is education to be had, even if it is self-motivated. Yet formal education is something that should be taken advantage of—as I keep telling my brothers."

"How many brothers do you have, my lord?" Rebecca asked.

He glanced at her, those gray eyes impassive. "Two, Miss Rebecca, eighteen-year-old twins."

"Young then," Susanna said, nodding. "I feel like my eighteenth birthday was so long ago."

Lady Rosa flashed her a mortified frown, as if Susanna should never allude to her advanced, unmarried age of twenty-seven.

"Youth does not excuse common sense," Lord Parkhurst said.

"Perhaps they see that you do not have a university education, my lord," Rebecca said, "and yet you seem to have survived."

They looked at each for a moment—a moment too long, for Lady Rosa's brows rose.

"Susanna, do escort me to the dessert table," Lady Rosa said. "I am suddenly quite famished. Enjoy your afternoon, my lord."

Wearing an apologetic look, Susanna was led away.

Julian watched the gaze exchanged between the two sisters and withheld his amusement. Susanna thought she was leaving Rebecca with the devil himself—and who could blame her, after their evening together?

But Rebecca . . . he did not quite understand her mood. Last night, she'd been bold, in command, even fearless, though three men held her and her relatives practically captive. Today she was a subdued lady of the *ton*, patiently allowing her mother the lead, as any daughter who expected to be led to the altar would.

"Lady Rosa did that quite neatly," Julian remarked.

"She has had much practice," Rebecca said dryly.

"Then I suggest we reward her." He held out his arm. "Would you care to walk?"

She eyed him, her eyes faintly devilish, her lips curved in a lovely smile. Then she placed her hand lightly on his arm. "I imagine I cannot come to harm in a conservatory."

"You could always scream," he countered.

"And find myself married before the week is out? I think not."

"Ah, you are crushing my self-esteem. Would not many young ladies wish to be married to an earl?"

"Perhaps not many, for you are not married."

"By choice. And neither are you."

"Stating the obvious, my lord."

They walked quietly for several minutes, weaving their way out of sight of the other guests, although the murmur of voices never quite went away. At the rear of the conservatory, the glass separated them from the walled garden outside. They paused as if to admire it, but Julian knew she must not be thinking of the view.

He was thinking of *his* view . . . of her. Her lovely rose-colored gown hugged her torso, revealing herself to be shaped much as she'd been painted. She was slender but not fragile, small, yet rounded. Her hair was styled artfully, curled, with carefully placed ribbons. Her bodice was high enough that he found himself wondering if she hid the Scandalous Lady beneath her garments.

Patience, he reminded himself. He'd spent the morning speaking with people about her family. Though he'd heard of several of the family scandals, the Lelands and the Cabots certainly did not seem like thieves. And Rebecca was far too young to have stolen the diamond herself almost ten years before. So how had she come by it?

He'd realized during the long night that the best way to discover answers to his questions was to earn her trust. He had diligently tried to be unassuming at the luncheon, wanting her to believe that his intensity of the previous evening was more about his overindulgence. And to some degree, that was true. He shouldn't have intimidated her, standing too close, looking so menacing, which was always rather easy for him to do.

She didn't seem intimidated. She inhaled the scents of the flowers all around them, then exhaled almost on a sigh—but not a sigh of resignation. There was something very . . . unusual about her nonplussed reaction to the wager.

But then again, only an unusual woman would pose for a nude portrait. He wondered how unfettered her morals truly were.

And that aroused him far too much, he realized. He could not let himself dwell on her nudity, her lack of inhibitions. He had to focus on the Scandalous Lady, and bringing it back to its rightful owner—him.

He began the hunt for information. "You and Miss Leland seem close to your cousin Lady Elizabeth."

She eyed him, a smile touching her full lips. "We are of an age, and we were raised together at Madingley Court."

"Your families all lived together?"

"Have you seen Madingley Court?" she asked, amused.

He nodded. "Ah, I see. The palace of a duke, of course. So you were not too crowded living together."

"Not at all," she answered, searching his face with the faintest confusion.

He knew she wondered at his motives, why he didn't bring up the wager. And his talk of crowded living conditions revealed too much of his own childhood issues.

"So the three of you were like sisters," he said.

"We still are," she answered, her voice firm. "We support each other through anything."

"Obviously," he said. "They risked much for you with their declaration last night."

"We would risk anything for each other."

"You'd risk exposure and humiliation?"

He thought she'd drop her hand from his arm, but she didn't, only looked up at him coolly.

"Are you threatening such a thing?" she asked. "I would have thought you a gentleman."

"I am a gentleman, Miss Leland. But that painting does not make a gentleman remember the civilized part of his brain."

He felt her stiffen.

"But then you knew that would happen when you posed," he continued mildly. "Or did you not think beyond a momentary thrill? Why would you do such a thing?"

"Are you *lecturing* me, my lord? A true gentleman would protect a lady's sensibilities, would forget the things he'd seen."

"You have not displayed a lady's sensibilities, have you?"

She dropped her hand and faced him now, speaking in a low voice, her hazel eyes flashing. "Now you're offending me. You know nothing about me."

"I would like to."

"No, you wouldn't. You want to win a wager with your silly friends."

"Which you and your silly female relatives made possible by your behavior last night."

"How disapproving you sound, my lord."

"No, I am simply stating a fact. Your guilt makes you believe that everyone is censorious."

"Guilt?" she cried, then looked down the path and lowered her voice. "I feel no guilt whatsoever."

"Then why else would you attempt to steal the painting?"

"For the simple reason that it was supposed to be in France, not here where people who know me will see it."

"Then why pose, Miss Leland? Why risk it?"

She paused, and in her mercurial eyes, he could see her weighing what to reveal. He waited almost impatiently—and he was never an impatient man. Then to his surprise, she stepped closer. He could feel the heat from her body, imagined how it would feel with just another step, as she pressed against him. His logical brain threatened to shut down, and that had never happened to him.

"Did you ever just want to be adventurous, my lord?" she asked softly.

IN PURSUIT OF A SCANDALOUS LADY
by Gayle Callen

On sale now from Avon Books